The River of No Return

The River of No Return

BEE RIDGWAY

MICHAEL JOSEPH
an imprint of
PENGUIN BOOKS

MICHAEL JOSEPH

Published by the Penguin Group

Penguin Books Ltd, 80 Strand, London WC2R ORL, England

Penguin Group (USA) Inc., 375 Hudson Street, New York, New York 10014, USA

Penguin Group (Canada), 90 Eglinton Avenue East, Suite 700, Toronto, Ontario, Canada M4P 2YR
(a division of Pearson Penguin Canada Inc.)

Penguin Ireland, 25 St Stephen's Green, Dublin 2, Ireland (a division of Penguin Books Ltd)

Penguin Group (Australia), 707 Collins Street, Melbourne, Victoria 3008, Australia
(a division of Pearson Australia Group Pty Ltd)

Penguin Books India Pvt Ltd, 11 Community Centre, Panchsheel Park, New Delhi – 110 017, India

Penguin Group (NZ), 67 Apollo Drive, Rosedale, Auckland 0632, New Zealand
(a division of Pearson New Zealand Ltd)

Penguin Books (South Africa) (Pty) Ltd, Block D, Rosebank Office Park, 181 Jan Smuts Avenue,
Parktown North, Gauteng 2193, South Africa

Penguin Books Ltd, Registered Offices: 80 Strand, London WC2R ORL, England

www.penguin.com

First published 2013

001

Copyright © Bee Ridgway, 2013

Set in 13.5/16pt Garamond MT Std
Typeset by Palimpsest Book Production Ltd, Falkirk, Stirlingshire
Printed in Great Britain by Clays Ltd, St Ives plc

A CIP catalogue record for this book is available from the British Library

Hardback ISBN: 978–0–718–17698–3
Paperback ISBN: 978–0–718–19981–4

www.greenpenguin.co.uk

MIX
Paper from
responsible sources
FSC
www.fsc.org FSC® C018179

Penguin Books is committed to a sustainable
future for our business, our readers and our planet.
This book is made from Forest Stewardship
Council™ certified paper.

ALWAYS LEARNING   **PEARSON**

For Paul

Prologue

Castle Dar, Devon, 1815

Julia sat beside her grandfather's bed, holding his hand. The fifth Earl of Darchester was dying.

Heavy velvet curtains were drawn across the tall windows, but the late-afternoon sun found a thin opening and as the day grew older a narrow ribbon of light moved slowly across the floor and over the bed. Lord Percy's breath was shallow. Julia felt life guttering in his fingers, saw death written on his beloved face. Motes of dust moved slowly in the shaft of light. Once Grandfather was dead, Cousin Eamon would be the new earl and would live here, at Castle Dar. Julia sighed, making the dust dance with her breath, then squeezed her eyes shut, willing herself to be calm. Time enough to worry about tomorrow's problems.

The house was almost completely silent, except for Grandfather's painful gasps. The sun inched up the counterpane, touching their fingers now.

The sound of hooves and jangling harness broke the spell. Julia went to the window and pushed aside a swathe of curtain with the back of her hand. Far away across the lawn, where the long drive disappeared into the wood, she saw a tired old travelling coach, piled high with luggage and drawn by a team of broken-down job horses, lurching towards the house.

'Is it Eamon?' The voice from the bed was little more than a whisper.

Julia turned back, letting the curtain fall. 'Yes.'

Lord Percy closed his eyes. 'I will be dead before the sun goes down. Why couldn't he wait until morning?'

'Because he is cruel.' Julia walked back to the bed.

Only a few weeks ago Grandfather had been as hearty as an oak. But the disease that was wasting his flesh had progressed with terrifying speed. And now here was Eamon, rushing to gloat over a dying man.

Lord Percy's hand moved anxiously on the counterpane, as if searching for something.

Julia caught it. His fingers were terribly cold. 'What do you need?'

He swallowed, then whispered. What he said clearly pained him. 'I can no longer protect you.'

Julia sat on the bed, raising the hand she held and kissing the knuckle above the emerald ring that once looked right on a strong hand but now seemed too big. 'It is you he has tormented all these years. I mean nothing to him.'

His fingers tightened around hers. 'It isn't only Eamon. There may be others. Julia . . .' He raised his head, and his whispering grew harsh. 'Tell no one anything. No one at all. You must pretend —'

'Hush.' Julia pressed his palm to the counterpane, and his head fell back against the pillows. She bent and stroked his high forehead. 'I have nothing to tell. I have no secrets.'

'You have no secrets, because you don't *know.*' His fierce gaze softened; he let out a long, shuddering sigh and closed his eyes. 'I am a fool,' he said. 'A blind fool.'

'Hush now.' The sound of the approaching carriage was getting louder. 'You must remain calm. He is coming.'

His eyes fluttered open. 'If only I had time.'

'You have had your share of time, old man.' Julia smiled.

His lip twitched, the shadow of a grin. 'I am greedy.'

'It's not a nice trait.' She smoothed one of his eyebrows with her thumb.

'I have never been nice. I have taken what I wanted. Time, money, women.' His voice took on some of the volume it used to have when he would thunder through the house, and he raised himself to one elbow. 'I have lived my life! But I have never snivelled and whined. Always I have taken what was given willingly, or I have paid with money or passion or blood . . .' He collapsed back against his pillows. 'I hate this blasted dying!'

Julia let her fingers rest against his sunken cheek. 'So do I.'

Together they listened to the carriage drawing close, a growing percussion beneath the old man's laboured breathing. They heard the wheels hit the bump just before the driveway split to curve in front of the house. Julia's stomach clenched; soon Eamon would be in this very room.

'Julia?'

'Yes?'

His cheekbones and his nose were sharp; it was the look of death. 'Let's speed the time. Let's outwit him. Just once more.'

'Do you have the strength?'

'Yes, yes. I shall twist time to my own ends and then . . .' He paused and tremblingly tucked a strand of hair behind her ear. 'Then you shall be orphaned after all.'

Julia bit the inside of her cheek, tamping down the tears. He would never do that again, that little motherly gesture.

He let his hand fall from her face. 'I had hoped . . .' He sighed. 'Well. The angels must watch over you now.'

'Religion, Grandfather? At the eleventh hour?'

'Ha!' He flashed her a real grin then, the irrepressible, scapegrace expression that she loved. 'It is not the eleventh hour, my dear. It is a minute or two before the twelfth. And

3

those minutes crawl. We must bid them gallop. Come. Let us play, my little foundling. My darling one.'

Julia's tears spilled over then, and she didn't care. 'One last time.'

'Good girl.' His hands fluttered, and she took them both in hers. The sliver of light streamed between them, illuminating their fingers.

'Watch the dust, there in the light. Watch as I make it dance, my poppet.'

Together they focused on the dust. Julia felt her grandfather's great power, felt how he willed the dust to dance. At first it only shivered, then it began to move faster and faster until it seemed to blow like snow in a blizzard. In the light on either side of them, the dust moved as slowly as it ever had. Lord Percy's eyes blazed, then broke focus. His fingers clasped hers strongly, then released. He fell back with a choked cry.

The dust slowed immediately, and Julia was left gripping hands that responded not at all to her kisses and tears.

Eamon Percy, now the sixth Earl of Darchester, threw open the door to find Julia pressing her grandfather's palm to her wet cheek. The old man's head was thrown back, his dead face grinning defiance.

Hartland, Vermont, 2013

Nick was on his way into town when the text came through from Tom Feely: 'get here now cheese inspector'.

Nick pulled a youie, then made a sharp right onto Densmore Hill Road. It was a cold December and the hill would be hard going, but Nick had chains on his tyres. He'd get to the farm in time to charm the inspector.

4

The pickup crested the hill with a groan and Nick patted the dashboard. The sky was a thin blue and the bare trees shivered resentfully in the wind. Still, the view out over the snowy valley struck Nick much as it had the first time he'd seen it on a glorious autumn day four years ago: This corner of Vermont was a place he could learn to call home. He let the good feeling in and burst into a loud rendition of 'The King Shall Enjoy His Own Again'.

Down below him, Thruppenny Farm hugged the base of the hill like a child trying to hide in its mother's skirts. Nick could see the red barns with their thick caps of snow, and the barnyards, tramped to mud by the forty Guernsey cows that Tom Feely kept for his artisan cheese business. Nick bellowed as the truck picked up speed: '"Then let us rejoice, with heart and voice! There doth one Stuart still remain!"'

Nick shifted down a gear and eased around the last curve. He was happy to play lord of the manor for the elderly cheese inspector, who was a dyed-in-the-wool Anglophile. The visits were always the same. The old man would greet him with shy deference, they would chat for a few minutes about the queen or crumpets, and then they would go into the cheese-making room, and from there into the smaller cheese cave. Immediately on the left were the shelves dedicated to raw-milk Bries and Camemberts, cheeses yielding enough to melt a heart of stone – and entirely against the law. The inspector would pass them right by, saying something like, 'English cheese! People go on and on about French-style cheeses but they don't even exist for me. No, I don't even see them. Give me a good, firm English cheese every time. Isn't that right, Mr Davenant?' His eyes would twinkle at Nick, and Nick would murmur his agreement. Then the inspector would linger over the shelves of stolid Cheddars, aged enough to be lawful – the prize-winning truckles for which Thruppenny Farm was becoming famous.

Nick didn't mind indulging the old man with a touch of Merrie Olde. It had been so very long now since Nick had been home that he took a guilty pleasure in following the cheese inspector to his green and pleasant fairyland. And Tom had nothing to complain of. For nigh on four years the inspector had given Thruppenny Farm top marks in every category, signing off on his list of checkboxes even as the seductive funk of bloomy rinds filled his nostrils.

Nick parked nose to nose with Tom's Methuselah of an old Farmall tractor, its pigeon-toed front wheels capped with snow. Downgrading his song to a whistle, Nick swung out of his pickup, shoved his hands into the pockets of his coat and walked into the barn. The sweet smell of well-tended animals and hay hit his nose. He stood for a moment breathing it in while his eyes adjusted to the dim light. Tom usually waited for him here, but aside from the cows shifting in their stalls and an insinuating cat making free with his ankles, there was no one around.

Then he heard the distant clank of metal against metal and realized Tom must already be in the cheese room. He went out the barn's back entrance and across to the small, new building with the stainless-steel door. It opened into a vestibule where Nick took off his boots, fished a pair of Crocs out of the tub of disinfectant, shook them vigorously and pushed his thick-socked feet into them. He opened another stainless-steel door into the brightly lit cheese-making room, the heart of this farm and Tom Feely's pride and joy.

Tom was there, heaving the illegal cheeses out of the cheese cave and into a big plastic trash can that he'd clearly dragged in from the barn; it was far from clean.

'What the hell?' Nick stared as Tom hurled a particularly

gorgeous wheel of Brie down into the mess. It burst open like a smashed melon.

'New cheese inspector,' Tom said over his shoulder, already reaching for another wheel.

'Shit.' Nick pitched in. This was serious. Only last summer a dairyman in the next county had been led away from his farm in leg manacles by machine-gun-toting FDA officials for the crime of making unpasteurized cheese. Jailed for months. Nick put some effort into it, scooping up two wheels at a time. A new cheese inspector would want to flex his muscles. Make a name for himself.

In a minute more the shelves in the cave were bare of the beautiful, tender wheels that Tom Feely – a hatchet-faced man who wore his Purple Heart pinned to his Red Sox cap – could not and would not stop making. 'I was born to make Brie,' he said of himself. 'And I was born to make it right.'

Together Tom and Nick dragged the heavy trash can out and behind the barn, and Tom covered the voluptuous ruination of a month's hard work with a hay bale. The scent of hay and cheese together was so good that Nick actually felt tears behind his eyes. 'By God, Tom, that's the saddest thing I've ever seen.'

'There's always more milk and more time.' The farmer crossed his arms over his chest and stared up the driveway, waiting for the inspector.

The two men had met on the day that Nick had first seen the view from the top of the hill, a mere ten minutes after he had first fallen in love with Vermont. Thruppenny Farm had been on the market, and Nick had pulled in when he'd seen the 'For Sale' sign in the yard. Tom gave him a tour. The farm had been in Feely hands since the Revolution, but Tom told Nick that day with a shrug, 'Nothing lasts for ever.'

7

Nick knew a good soldier when he met one. He assumed that selling the farm felt quite a lot like dying to Tom Feely, and he also assumed that Tom would rather die than show those emotions. But Tom was an American, and sometimes Nick thought he would never really understand Americans. They were deceptively simple. Tom might have been feeling nothing at all under that baseball cap.

The tour had ended in the state-of-the-art cheese-making room and cheese cave. Nick had watched as Tom bent and looked closely at a broad-shouldered, cloth-wrapped Cheddar, his hand resting on its mottled surface. Tom straightened again and closed his eyes, the better to sense through his fingers. He was figuring out if time had done its work. It was as if Nick wasn't there at all.

Nick made his proposition without thinking, before Tom had lifted his hand away from his cheese. And so Nick became the owner of a small Vermont dairy farm. The Feelys paid him a nominal rent and kept him in legal and illegal milk products. For himself, Nick had ended up buying a house a few miles away. Since then he had bought up a few more struggling farms, and he had four families under his guardianship. Nick spent most of his time in Vermont and was considering abandoning New York altogether.

But now there was a new cheese inspector, one almost certainly less susceptible than his predecessor to the charms of a plummy British accent.

'Here we go.' Tom straightened his blue and red baseball cap on his head, and Nick noticed how his fingers lingered for a split second on the Purple Heart.

Owner and tenant stood side by side, watching as an old white BMW E21, streaked and spotted and marbled with rust, turned into the farmyard.

*

8

It was the feeling of it – as if Nick's sabre were an extension of his own body. As if it were his own hand he was thrusting into the young man's neck, as if it were his nails ripping through the soft flesh, catching on the tendons, pulling, then slicing through. The man's eyes, staring with a sort of blank surprise as red blood spilled richly over his blue uniform. Black eyes and red blood. The sabre withdrawing, as if it were Nick's own arm he was pulling back, pulling away – and now he was flying away, backwards, into a tunnel of smoke . . . he was being sucked away at hideous speed, and at the distant end of the tunnel the splash of red and the young man's face fixing in death . . .

Nick's eyes flew open, but it was a while before he fully realized that he had been dreaming. In the dream, it had been a smoky dusk, punctuated by the flash of cannon. But as always the dream had altered his senses. The cannon, the men and horses, the gunfire and shouting had gone silent. He heard only the sound of his own breathing and the slow, funereal drumbeat of his heart.

He took a deep breath. He was miles and years away from that battlefield. 'Miles and years,' he whispered, and then started playing with rhyme, as he did sometimes to calm himself down. 'Tiles and beers. Piles and jeers. Niles and tears.' *Niles and tears* was a good one, he thought. It captured the weariness of the distances he'd marched and the sorrow of the years he'd lost. 'Niles and tears,' he whispered again, and yet again, letting the sound of his own voice drown out the sound of his heart. The woman next to him was curled into an S, sleeping quietly. 'Niles and tears,' Nick said more loudly, perfectly aware that he wanted her to wake up and keep him company.

But she slept on and now he was wide awake. He sat up, letting the feather duvet fall away from his bare chest. The cold against his skin reassured him; he never turned up the heat, even on the bitterest nights. He kept the thermostat just high enough to stop the pipes from freezing. Just high enough for it to feel like an English wintertime of long ago.

The night was dark; there was no moon. He could see the showy splash of the Milky Way through the wrinkled old window glass. He savoured the feeling of the cold air in his lungs and the sweet smell of the wood fire they had enjoyed after a first frenzied tumble on the couch, their thick winter pullovers still on.

The pond on the other side of the driveway was frozen over. The frogs of summertime were sleeping under the ice, the crickets gone to wherever they went. Cricket Valhalla? He seemed to remember from some nature programme that crickets hibernate. He wished they'd wake up. There was no sound except his shallow breathing, and his heartbeat, beginning to boom again. 'Niles and tears . . .' He squeezed his eyes shut. The panic was winning. Nick gave up the rhyming game. It clearly wasn't going to work tonight.

So he reached, in his mind, for her. And she was there. As she always was. She stepped into his consciousness with a certain lightness of tread, as if she were walking over wet ground. The dark-eyed girl. Nick's thoughts cleared; his breathing slowed. She was standing at the shadowy edge of a summer wood. Her eyes were candid, friendly. She watched him until he felt his heart begin to mend. Then she faded.

His bedfellow shifted in her sleep, uncurling towards him, her face turning into the starlight. 'Get over here,' she said in a bossy, sleepy tone. She reached for him and, realizing that he was sitting up, murmured grumpily and flounced over onto her other side, soon to be lost deep in sleep again.

He liked her better asleep than awake. She was the kind of person who took life by the scruff of the neck and made it dance to her tune. It was an admirable trait, but experience had taught Nick that such people were best admired from a safe distance. And he was right. But now here he was.

In bed with the new cheese inspector.

Yesterday she had scrutinized every corner of the farm's operations. When she'd passed the bin full of cheese and hay she had stopped and snuffed the air like a bloodhound. Then she'd turned and fixed Nick with a long stare. 'You own this farm?' He'd seen her take in his pristine wax jacket. 'Like to come up on the weekends from New York and play with the cows?'

He'd been surprised at how much that had stung. 'I live in New York, yes,' he'd said. Then added defensively, 'But I was raised in England.'

'Well now, England,' she'd said, lingering over the -*gland* with contempt. She had a southern accent of some sort or another. 'I'm guessing you have some rather fine raw-milk Camembert in your fridge on . . .' She looked at her copy of the form where Nick's info was printed. 'Jenneville Road. I'll follow you home and give it a try. Then I'll report on this farm.'

Now, Nick looked at the curve of the cheese inspector's shoulder, barely visible in this light. Thruppenny Farm would be getting its good report, and the cheese inspector would be off after breakfast, in that jalopy of hers. Back to her usual Burlington beat. The old cheese inspector would return to duty next month.

He sighed, and stared out of the window.

The stars seemed close. It was hard to believe that they were, in fact, very far away, in time as well as space. How many light years into the past was he looking? Long before his own birth, surely. Each one of those stars was an inferno, a terrible burning hell, spilling its light from endless raging fires out into time and space. But from this distance they were beautiful. Watchful. Like the eyes of animals in a midnight barn, shining in the swinging light of the farmer's lantern.

The stars reminded Nick of bivouacking on frosty winter nights in Spain, a rabbit stew warming his belly, the sound of the slumbering army soothing him to sleep. The stars had been bright and close then, too. Now the war was far away and long ago, very long ago. The world had become a different place. Yet the war still shed the light of its conflagration down through his dreams. Nick pressed his palms against his face. The girl with the dark eyes. She was also from that time long ago. Only the thought of her could ever beat the dream back into the past.

The past.

Nick Davenant had far too much past.

He had jumped forward in time. Two hundred years.

Two hundred years. It had been unbelievable when it happened and it was still unbelievable ten years later. Nick laughed out loud, and without humour.

'Put a sock in it, England.'

His hard laugh softened into a real smile. He had to hand it to the cheese inspector: she was sure of herself in every way. He was glad she was leaving and never coming back. 'Sorry,' he said.

'Hmpf.' She buried her nose into her pillow and veered sharply back into sleep.

Two hundred years were hard to hide, even in casual relationships. He realized now that when his lovers accused him of being 'uptight' or 'emotionally distant', what they meant was that he was weirder than even an eccentric Englishman should be. American women would overlook a great deal in a passably good-looking British boyfriend. But eventually they began to pry, wanting explanations.

His terrible scars? A car accident, he said. He *had* been in a car accident, but the scars were obviously war wounds. Hence his avoidance of women who were doctors or nurses. The scar that cut across one eyebrow was dashing and ambiguous enough, but the jagged sabre cut up his left thigh was heavily punctuated where the wound had been tied up with thick catgut. Roping his left shoulder, a scar from a gunshot wound. It was the ugliest scar of all, because of the infection that had set in.

There were other, more subtle oddities. The flourishes of his signature were neither manly nor timely. Then there were his antiquated tastes in food. This very evening, as she ate the glorious Camembert, the cheese inspector had reminisced about Oreos and milk and then she had gone on to sing a TV jingle about them. Nick had no favourite childhood commercials, and he craved boiled mutton, beef jelly, blancmange and bits of pig, pickled.

Sleep was clearly not going to come again tonight. Nick got quietly out of bed and went downstairs, enjoying the bracing cold of the floorboards against the soles of his feet. He loved these floors. The boards were as old as he was. The trees from which the boards had been painstakingly hewn were much older even than that – they must have stood in these hills for hundreds of years before they were felled. This house had been built in the year of his birth – 1790 – and Nick took comfort from its sturdy construction, the way it had hunkered down through all the years like a bear in its den. He imagined it being raised, enormous beam by enormous beam, even as he had quickened in his mother's womb. It was as if the house had been built for him and had simply been waiting across so many winters for him to come home.

The embers were still glowing in the fireplace, and he scrunched up some newspaper, made a pyramid of kindling around it, crouched, and blew the fire back to life. As the kindling crackled into flame, he added two apple logs from the old tree that had fallen in a spring storm. Tending a fire made him feel eternal. It made him feel that he could have been born at any time, in any place. It made him feel that there was nothing so very strange about skipping almost two centuries in one's twenty-third year, then living out the rest of one's life in a previously unimaginable future. He wrapped his scarred, naked body in a cashmere throw and watched the flames dance.

But as he followed a spark flying upwards into the chimney, his eye was distracted by a white envelope propped up on the mantelpiece.

Shit.

The letter from the Guild.

Nick had successfully avoided thinking about it for several days.

He had run into the postman at the bottom of the long driveway a few mornings ago. 'Looks like an old-fashioned love letter,' the postman had said, admiring the thick wax seal on the back of the envelope. The wax was stamped with the Guild's symbol: a blooming tulip, bulb and roots and all. He handed the letter to Nick, along with the L. L. Bean catalogue that seemed to come every week. 'Romantic.'

It was anything but. As soon as he'd glimpsed the seal, Nick had guessed. And when he had turned the letter over in his hand and seen that it was addressed in Alderwoman Gacoki's spidery hand, he had known. The letter was a summons. Not just any summons, but a Summons Direct. A tulip in wax. A tulip, when they were coming for their pound of flesh.

He had propped the letter there on the mantelpiece and then he had forgotten about it, wilfully. He was good at that.

It was another skill he'd learned during the war. Don't want to think about it? No problem. Don't think about it. Think about the girl with the dark eyes instead.

Now, in the flickering firelight, the Alderwoman's writing seemed to scuttle across the envelope. Nick wanted to rush the letter like it was a living thing and sweep it into the fire. But he couldn't. He had to read it.

If he didn't answer the summons, they would come for him.

I

It had happened ten years ago. It had also happened two centuries ago, in the hills south of Salamanca. As the Most Honourable Nicholas Falcott – Lord Nick to his men – led his cavalry division in yet another charge, his horse was shot out from under him. He freed his feet as the horse fell and he rolled away unharmed, looking up and to his left. There was Jem Jemison, locked in combat with a big French foot soldier. Jemison caught Nick's eye, and Nick saw that he was in trouble; alarm flickered in those black eyes. As Nick began to raise himself he saw the horse rearing directly over him, the French dragoon on its back, sabre lifted high. Jem wasn't the one in trouble, Nick thought, as the hooves descended.

One moment he was staring at his death, the next he was in the path of an impossibly bright light bearing down on him with equally impossible speed. Then he was screaming into the roar of a thousand furnaces as the light crashed over him.

When he opened his eyes, that horrible white light still blinded him. But instead of charging towards him it was glaring from three big rectangles that seemed to be affixed to the ceiling of a blank, white room. The light hurt his eyes – hurt his entire head. He groaned.

So this was death.

'Nicholas Falcott?'

Nick turned his head slowly. There was an old man sitting by his bed.

'Where the devil am I?'

'You are in London.' The man had a faint accent and wore an outlandishly oversized yet strangely delicate species of spectacles. 'You are in the care of the Guild. The year is 2003.'

Nick laughed, then winced. Laughing was a bad idea. 'That's a fine jest,' he whispered. 'Almost literally side-splitting.'

'I'm afraid it's not a joke.'

Nick closed his eyes. The light was too brutal. 'If it's really 2003, then what has happened to my mother? My sisters?'

'As you would imagine.'

Nick kept his eyes closed. He was surely dead, but his pain was real enough. Perhaps he *was* alive, trapped in some blanched and fevered nightmare. How cruel of his dreams to mock him like this, when the war was grim enough.

When he opened his eyes, the old man was still there, watching him with soft-eyed compassion. Nick had to pull himself together. Even in a dream he wanted no mawkish tenderness. He would play his part. 'So.' He tried to sound like a gentleman and a soldier, assured and calm in the face of crisis. 'They are dead in 2003. But they are not dead in 1812. They need me. You must send me back.'

The old man sucked in his cheeks and regarded Nick over the top of his peculiar eyewear. 'There is no going back.'

'Surely if I came to this time, I can return.'

'There is no returning, I'm afraid. Progress is only forward. No one has ever gone back.'

'Then I shall be the first.'

'You cannot.' The old man spread his hands, like an inn-keeper apologizing for having run out of roast beef. 'I'm sorry, but no one ever returns. It is impossible.'

'I am not no one.' Nick made a motion to straighten his

cuffs, a gesture that never failed to intimidate, only to discover that he was dressed in almost nothing.

'I'm very much afraid that, in this regard, you are. Even if
it were physically possible to go back, which it is not, the
Guild has rules and you must abide by them.'

'Guild? What control can a guild have over me? I am
Nicholas Falcott, Marquess of Blackdown. I am no artisan.'

'Please, listen to me.' The man leaned forward and propped
his elbows on his thighs, his hands clasped down between his
knees. Behind his freakish spectacles, his hazel eyes were
huge and earnest, like the eyes of an old plough horse. 'I
know it is hard to understand, but please be attentive.'

'Which monarch now reigns? I must speak to the king
immediately –'

'Young man!' The hazel eyes flared, their fire stirred. 'You
will listen to me!'

Nick raised his eyebrows but shut his mouth.

The old man subsided into his seat. 'Thank you.' He took
a deep breath. 'Now. You are in the year 2003. It has been
almost two centuries since you are believed to have perished
in Spain. You left no heir. The marquessate of Blackdown
died with you.'

The marquessate – extinct. It had passed from father to
son since Lord Clancy Falcott had routed the nuns and razed
the convent that had stood by the River Culm; for his pains
he had been made the first Marquess of Blackdown by Henry
VIII. Nicholas had never seen a nun until he went to Spain,
and then, at Badajoz . . . He shut his eyes. This deathly dream
was bad enough. He did not wish to add to its horrors by
thinking of Badajoz. Yet how fitting it would have been for
the marquessate, born from the destruction of a convent, to
expire at Badajoz, in defence of those pitiful women.

But that hadn't happened. Instead, Lord Blackdown and

his title had marched away from Badajoz with the rest of Wellington's infamous army. He and his title had stumbled together across Spain for a few more hot and desolate weeks, only to die together for no cause at all, scrabbling in the dust, watched by the flat black eyes of Jem Jemison . . .

The old man cleared his throat, and Nick opened his eyes. 'I'm dead.'

'You are not dead,' the man said. 'Nor do you dream. The marquessate is extinct. Falcott House is now owned by the National Trust. And the king is a queen.'

'The National Trust? What in blazes is that?'

'It means, essentially, that your former estate is well cared for. By a charity.'

'My former estate.' Nick blew his breath out between pursed lips.

'Yes. I know it is a shock, but I'm afraid I have news you might find even harder to stomach. It is a harsh rule, but the Guild insists that you must leave the country of your birth. Leave and never return. Not ever. Not for as long as you live.'

The dream became truly terrible then. Nick's head seemed to crack open with pain, and his sight darkened and the room filled with people. Nick heard his own voice but wasn't sure if he was speaking words. Then something sharp pinched his arm, and the dream was washed away into blissful nothingness.

When Nick woke again, he was without pain. But he was still in the too-white, too-bright room, and the old man was still beside his bed, though he was wearing a different shirt, a bright orange one which had the word *GAP* printed across it in bold, black letters. Nick puzzled over that, then looked up into the man's face. 'You again? Lord grant me a different dream!'

'Good morning.'

'I suppose it is still the future?'

'I'm afraid so.'

Ten minutes later Nick had stormed about, rattled and banged upon the frustratingly locked door, stared mesmerized out of the window at the horseless traffic in the street fifteen (fifteen!) storeys beneath him and at the unrecognizable sprawl that was, apparently, London, the river nearly devoid of boats and laced across with bridges. He was, he guessed from the position of a shockingly white St Paul's and a few – a very few – steeples, somewhere in Southwark, of all the godforsaken places.

'Is the abbey gone?'

'Westminster Abbey still stands. You can't see it for the new buildings.'

Nick turned from the window. 'I'm in London, though. London of the future.'

'Yes.'

'Why? Why am I here?'

'I am glad to finally hear a rational question from you. You are in London because this is the Guild's European hospital. You will stay here until your concussion is healed. But then you must leave. For ever.' He looked at Nick a little warily.

'So when I am healed you will put me on a ship and send me off? Wherever the winds take me? An exile?'

'Oh, no.' The old man smiled. 'The Guild will choose your new country for you, and prepare you in every way to live in it. The Guild will care for you. First you will spend a year at one of our compounds, getting ready to enter modern life. Most people remember their year in the compound as one of the happiest they have known.'

Nick wondered if that was the light of fanaticism behind the old man's eyes. 'And then?'

'At the end of the year you will move to your new home. The Guild will provide you with wealth, property, whatever you need to start anew. The rest is up to you. You can take a job if you like. Many of us end up working for the Guild. Like me.' He straightened his shoulders. 'I am a greeter.'

Nick leaned back against the window ledge and looked the man up and down. His mysteriously declarative shirt had short, cuffless sleeves. His hairy forearms were on show, like a labourer's. GAP. Was that some sort of code? Or was he branded, like a criminal?

'It's a shock, isn't it?' the old man said gently. 'This city, my clothes, everything. I assure you, you'd think I was exactly as funny looking if you saw me in the clothes I wore in my old life.'

'Who were you?'

'I am – was . . .' He hesitated. 'I still have trouble keeping my tenses straight, and it has been so many years since I jumped. I was a Frank. A butcher by trade. I jumped from Aachen in 810 and landed in 1965. An unusually long leap.' There was a note of pride in his voice. 'I was sent to London and I have never returned to Austrasia. Or even to what is now known as Germany. It is forbidden.'

'And you abide by these rules?'

'Yes. You will, too.'

Nick thought he would keep his own counsel on that. 'How did you know who I am?'

'We keep a log of people who vanish, and of people who appear.'

'Surely people get lost every day.' Nick turned and looked down again at the teeming city. His eyes followed a tiny person as he – she! The person was wearing trousers, but Nick saw now that it was a woman – strode to a street corner. She stepped with confidence into the path of an enormously tall, perfectly rectangular red carriage that was bearing down on her without any visible means of locomotion. Nick gasped, but somehow the ghastly machine came to a stop mere inches from her. She seemed not to notice it at all, but sauntered boyishly on her way and disappeared behind the blank glass wall of another building. Nick turned slowly to face the white room and the little man who was his only anchor in this strange dream world. 'Please tell me that I am dreaming, or dead. And this is either heaven or hell.'

'No.' The butcher shook his head. 'I will not tell you that, for it isn't true. This is the same world you left, only it is a little bit older, and a little bit greyer.'

Nick looked at the rectangles on the ceiling emanating light. They were miraculous, but they were neither beautiful nor comforting. Was he in hell? 'That dragoon was about to skewer me.'

'You could see you were about to die, and so you jumped. It is the most common prompt. I jumped right before a burning beam crushed me; I was trying to save my donkey from a fire.' The butcher sighed. 'I am sure she burned, poor Albia.'

'Do you mean to tell me that what happened to me is commonplace?'

'No. Not at all. But it does happen, and when it does, the Guild tries to be ready. We have a global network of researchers who document such cases. There is an enormous library in Milton Keynes and another in Chongqing. Our records go back many hundreds of years. Your disappearance was witnessed on the battlefield and one of your comrades gained a reputation for being insane by telling everyone about it for years afterwards. Your mother was informed that you were dead, but the Guild listened to the rumour that you had vanished into thin air. Sure enough, you appeared again, last week. Quite dramatically – you were mown down by a car.'

Nick frowned. He had been in the maelstrom of battle. Nothing could be more all-consuming, more purely sensual, than the experience of fighting for your life and against the lives of others in a mass of men and horses, choked and blinded by smoke, deafened by gunfire and screaming . . . there was no disappearing in that moment, none whatsoever . . . except into death.

After a moment the butcher spoke again, softly. 'You jumped from the Battle of Salamanca. It was the twenty-second of July, 1812.'

'The Battle of Salamanca.' Nick repeated the words slowly. So it had a name. It had already happened. It was over. 'Did we . . . ?' Nick stopped. It felt gauche to ask how the day went. The battle had only just begun when he was unhorsed. Many men were still to fight and die or survive.

'It was a glorious triumph. And in 1815, your armies won not only the battle, but the war.'

The whole war. Over. Folded away into history books like bridal linens into an attic trunk. Salamanca a glorious triumph . . . but what did they say of the siege of Badajoz and its aftermath? Everything? Nothing? Nick shook his head. 'This is madness,' he said.

'I'm sorry.'

'Sorry?' Nick scrubbed at his face with the palms of his hands, then ran his fingers up into his hair. Rage boiled up in him. 'What am I meant to say to that? "No matter, my dear Sir Butcher"? "That's quite all right"? Good God, man, you have told me how my mother came to learn of my own death. Except that I am not dead and my mother is. Two centuries dead.'

The butcher leaned back in his chair and appraised Nick for a moment, much as he might have assessed a leg of pork before chining it. Then he turned to the bedside table and picked up a large, pale envelope filled with papers. He reached in and found a smaller envelope. 'The Guild wishes you to have this,' he said. 'The location of your jump and your uniform strongly supported the thesis that you were the long-lost Lord Blackdown, but we knew for certain when we saw this.' He dipped his fingers into the envelope and extracted Nick's signet ring.

Seeing it there in the butcher's hand made Nick feel for it, irrationally, on his own finger. His finger was bare. Bare of the ring he had worn since the day his father died. Nick looked and saw that his hand was sun-bronzed except where the ring had been.

His finger was real. His ring was real. Why wasn't his ring on his finger? How had the butcher come to have it? Nick groped his way back to the bed and sat down. 'You are . . . telling me the truth,' he whispered. As he said it, he knew, for the first time he really knew, that it was true.

'Yes.'

'This is the year 2003.'

'Yes.'

Nick closed his eyes for a long moment, then opened them again. 'May I have my ring?' he said quietly.

The butcher handed it to him, and Nick held it in his palm for a moment. It felt heavy, just as it had the day his mother removed it from his dead father's hand. She had turned from the body where it lay, broken by a fall from a horse, and looked into Nick's eyes for a moment. She wore a riding habit, and the train was swept over her arm. She curtseyed almost to the ground, the train rising to her wrist like a wing. Then she held out the ring for him to take. Nick, fifteen years old, had pushed the still-warm metal down over his knuckle as he stared at the top of his mother's bent head.

Now he slipped the ring onto his finger again. This was

the sign of his privilege, his belonging. And yet no one living had ever known him.

'I'm afraid that is the only trinket you will be able to keep from your former life,' the butcher said. 'Most of us aren't lucky enough to have anything at all, but instructions from the Guild headquarters here in London are clear – you will be allowed to keep the ring.'

The butcher sounded faintly jealous, and a ripple of pride washed over Nick. 'I'd like to see them try to take it from me,' he said, and was mortified to hear how childish he sounded.

Those hazel eyes regarded him levelly for a moment, then dropped to his hand. 'You must be careful with that. No one must guess its meaning. Or perhaps I should say, its former meaning.'

Nick rubbed his ring with the thumb of his other hand and vowed that no one would ever take it off him again. 'What is your name, butcher?'

The man gave him a wan smile. 'Thank you for your interest,' he said. 'But it is rude to ask a Guild member his or her real name. Never do it; no one would tell you anyway. My Guild name, and the name I go by now, is Ricchar Hartmut. Your Guild name is up to you. It can contain only one of your original names. I chose to give them all up. It was easier that way.'

Nick's thumb stilled on the broad, flat surface of his ring. The man before him had jumped more than a thousand years forward in time. His face was patient, but his eyes were bleak. 'Gracious God,' Nick muttered under his breath.

'Yes.' Ricchar nodded. 'Now you begin to have the feelings. It is a hard road.' He stood, suddenly all business. 'But you have no worries. The Guild will take care of you, educate you, give you all the money you need to build a comfortable new life. We want you to be happy.'

Happiness was a feeling Nick couldn't imagine experiencing ever again. Already he could tell he was trembling on the edge of an abyss of grief so deep he might never reach its bottom. He said nothing.

Ricchar continued. 'Once you choose your Guild name, which you must do before you leave this room, no one will ever call you by the name you were born to, or by your title, again.' He paused, then said, as if the words left a bad taste in his mouth, 'My lord.'

So he was to be nameless and nationless. He considered for a few seconds, then chose. 'Nicholas Davenant.' His own first name and his paternal grandmother's maiden name.

'Pleased to meet you, Mr Davenant,' Ricchar said, and held out his hand.

'Call me Nick,' Nick said, shaking the hand, and he felt the change begin to happen. I am shaking hands with a Frankish butcher, he thought. I have just told him to call me Nick. And then: By rights we should both be dust.

2

Nick awoke in a luxurious bed made up with red sheets and blankets. The walls of his room were of golden polished wood, and although the lighting was the electric kind he had learned about during his two weeks in the hospital, it was mellow, and seemed to emanate from around corners or behind panels. Nick stretched, remembering the long flight to Chile, which had terrified and then thrilled him; the late-night arrival in Santiago; the warm welcome to the Guild compound from many happy strangers. He had fallen into bed exhausted, without exploring his new home, and had slept the whole day.

Now Nick swung his legs out of bed and stood. A fire burned in a copper stove that was built directly into the wall. Dark-blue curtains were pulled across the far wall. He crossed an intricate oriental carpet to the curtains and pulled them aside.

The entire wall was one impossibly large, smooth pane of glass. Outside, a square sheet of water the size of the room he stood in reflected mountains that eclipsed any he had ever seen. They climbed the sky, their razor-sharp peaks capped with snow that was pink with sunset. He put his hands against the glass, then noticed that there was a handle on the far edge. Fiddling with it, he established that the wall of glass could slide aside.

He stepped forward, out into the cool air. Now he could see that the square of water was a pool. He dipped a toe in, expecting it to be icy, but it was as warm as a bath. Its edge seemed to disappear into nothingness, meeting the more distant mountains. How did that work? Nick walked along the protruding edge of the pool and learned that the little house in which he had woken up was built into a hillside. The false horizon was produced by a small waterfall that spilled over the edge and back again into a replenishing reservoir. It was a clever design, functioning much like a ha-ha. Standing now at the edge of the pool, which was also the edge of the hill, Nick looked down into a broad green valley that stretched for a mile until it reached the uncompromising cliff face of the nearest mountain. A series of curving glass and wooden buildings, stark to his eye, but strangely beautiful, stood among tall trees. Nick let his gaze climb the mountains, then descend. He took a deep breath and pulled his loose cotton shirt over his head. He would inaugurate his new life with a swim.

In the months that followed, Nick's depression began slowly to lift. There were thirty others like him at the compound, all at different stages of their year of initiation. In addition to the students, a good fifty Guild members lived there full-time, serving as instructors, doctors, guides, cooks, gardeners, architects, researchers. Some practised new professions that Nick had never heard of. Psychologists, personal trainers, computer techs, masseurs, yogis, ski instructors. The curving structures he had noticed on his first day were parliament buildings of sorts, and Guild officials were always coming and going, including Alice Gacoki, the Alderwoman herself, whom Nick had met for the first time during his third week in Chile.

The architect had included a spa and a vacation resort in his design, with ski slopes in the mountains, extensive bridle paths and even an amusement park. Families – Guild members who had met and married in their shared futures – could come for a week or a month of relaxation. Their children, born into this time, could not be told the truth about their parents' origins. Nick was the sort of man children liked, perhaps because he treated them like he did everyone else, politely, even distantly – until suddenly the little ones were climbing all over him and asking him what happened to his eyebrow and would he please be a Tyrannosaurus rex? He liked being a Tyrannosaurus rex, a beast that astounded and fascinated him as much as it did the children. But he didn't like lying to his small friends. So he learned to avoid the resort area of the compound.

Nick was expected to change himself from what he had been into what he had to become, and the lessons were administered constantly. First, he learned the Rules of the Guild. He had to recite them, with the rest of the students, every day before classes began. There were only four:

There is No Return.
There is No Return.
Tell No One.
Uphold the Rules.

The first two rules sounded the same, but one was for time and one was for space – though the more he thought about it, the more Nick felt that he couldn't tell time and space apart.

'Uphold the Rules.' The last rule struck Nick as ridiculous; the Guild made following the rules supremely comfortable. Each and every member received two million British pounds a year, every year. Nick's first two million was already waiting in an account set up in his new name when he woke that first evening in the compound. A man calling himself a 'financial adviser' had told him all about it on his second day. The money, he said, was a token. An annual gift from the Guild to its members. 'No strings attached', whatever that meant.

Language was the huge hurdle for most new Guild members. Three were required. First, twenty-first-century English, which Nick already spoke after a fashion. Second, the language of the country to which they were reassigned – but Nick got a pass on that one, too, since he'd been assigned to the United States. The third was medieval Finnish, the official language of the Guild bureaucracy. Nick hated Finnish. After months of instruction the only phrase he had mastered was '*Mÿnna tachton gernast spuho somen gelen Emÿna daÿdä*': 'I willingly want to speak Finnish, but I can't.' This got a laugh – the first time he said it. But Nick could survive Finnish: there were only two classes a week, on Tuesdays and Thursdays after dinner. Apart from this, his time was more or less his own.

There was another lucky English-speaker in the group, who had arrived only a fortnight before Nick. She was a sixty-five-year-old Irishwoman named Meg O'Reilly, assigned to Australia. One day in County Mayo in 1848 she had found an apple sitting in the road, red and unblemished: a miracle. She had picked it up and was turning it round, trying to decide where to take her first, ecstatic bite when two starving women attacked her with clubs. She and the apple had jumped forward one hundred and fifty-five years. 'Do you know,' she said to Nick, 'I was so hungry that it didn't even bother me. I stood by the side of the road, eating the apple and watching the cars go by, as calm as you please.' Now her ambition was to become fat before her year was out.

Meg and Nick were told to study together during their free hours. Their task was to cram as much popular culture into their heads as possible. Books, movies, TV – anything published or filmed since 1960. Commandeering a comfortable room in the library, which was fitted out with a huge TV and big squishy chairs, they divided their mornings between watching, reading and discussing. And eating. Meg always turned up with food.

They had to start with picture books, since Meg didn't know how to read. Nick surprised himself by how invested he became in her progress, and how much he came to like the peppery old woman as the days passed. He spent hours with her, poring over the brightly coloured pages, until one afternoon the letters aligned themselves and she hooted like an owl and the two of them danced round the room together, shouting, '"Do you like green eggs and ham? I do not like them, Sam-I-Am!"'

Over the course of a few weeks Meg went from stammering her sentences out loud, her finger pressed to the page and pulling along under the words, to reading everything about Ireland that she could get her hands on. When he turned up one morning to find her tucked up in an easy chair reading a tome entitled *Making Ireland British, 1580–1650*, Nick tried to intervene. 'We're meant to concentrate on this thing they call contemporary pop culture,' he said. 'I don't think that's it.'

Meg looked up over the top of her book, her eyes bright beneath her white hair. 'Do as you like,' she said. 'I'm not in your road.' Down she dived again, her hand groping blindly for an enormous sandwich that sat just out of reach on the table beside her. Nick sighed and pushed the plate closer to her. It had been so companionable while she was learning to read: They had taken breaks from Dr Seuss by watching their way through *The Sopranos* and *The X-Files*, with breaks from that for episodes of *Father Ted* and *Leave It to Beaver*. Now Meg was annoyed when Nick watched TV without a headset: 'I can't read with that noise in my ears!'

The star student in every subject was a twenty-year-old Pocumtuk man named Leo Quonquont, who had arrived at the compound six weeks after Nick. The Guild had assigned him to Bangalore, so he had to learn Finnish, English, and Kannada. By the end of his second month, Leo was cracking jokes in English. By the end of his sixth month, he outgrew the English class and joined Meg and Nick in their study group. They made an odd threesome. An English aristocrat, an American Indian genius and an elderly, ravenous Irish-woman, all watching soccer on a Saturday afternoon, eating popcorn and hollering advice and recriminations at the screen. It shouldn't have been possible. Yet they could joke together, argue together and learn together: they were friends.

Nick discovered that he loved 'future school', just as the butcher had said he would. But nothing lasts for ever. In retro-spect, Nick believed that his friendship with Leo and Meg began to unravel the day he saw Leo talking to Mr Mibbs.

It was a beautiful late afternoon. Nick had just spent an hour with a coach, practising modern American manners, slang, facial expressions, hand gestures. He was exhausted. Then he caught sight of Leo walking under one of the huge screens that were everywhere in the education quad, project-ing a constant, silent stream of visual information about the present. Nick struck out across the grass, hoping to divert his friend into the bar for a beer. It wasn't until he was several yards from Leo that he realized that the man walking near his friend – in front of him and a few feet to the left – was actu-ally conversing with him. It was strange. They were not to-gether, and yet they were.

Nick slowed down, and Leo turned as if he had eyes in the back of his head. His face was still and serious. He shook his head once, with intent: Don't come near.

Nick nodded. It had been a soldierly communication, and all Nick's battle senses were awakened. He put his hand in his pocket and fished out his phone, flipped it open and tucked it against his ear. Then he changed the angle of his walk to move parallel with the pair. He strolled along pretending to be talking on the phone, his eyes on Leo's companion.

At first he could only see the man's back. His hair was thick and brown, blow-dried. He wore a wide-shouldered business suit as blue as the summer sky, which he filled with meaty precision. The tailoring was immaculate and expensive, but the suit was absurd.

Nick, who tended to dress for the future in jeans and soft cotton shirts, smiled to himself. Maybe that terrible suit was why Leo was keeping his distance.

Then the man turned, as Leo had – as if he knew Nick was watching him. He had a square chin and a thin mouth, and that blow-dried hair was styled up and off his forehead. He looked like the handsome, anodyne white men who predicted the weather on American TV.

But there was something wrong with the way the man looked at Nick.

Even from several yards away, Nick could feel the flat, frozen emptiness of that gaze. He lowered his phone and stared back unblinkingly, no longer pretending disinterest. Time seemed to stop . . . thought fell away . . .

Then Leo turned, too, and his expression recalled Nick to himself. Leo was communicating something. A more urgent warning. Nick blinked, pivoted on his heel and walked in the other direction.

When Nick asked Leo about it the next day, Leo said the man had asked the way to the amusement park, and Leo had led him there. Leo wasn't telling the truth – or at least not the whole truth – but Nick didn't push it. He'd learned in Spain. A soldier will tell you what you need to know when you need to know it.

*

34

Two weeks later, Nick, Leo and Meg were floating in the pool outside Nick's house, watching a custard-coloured full moon rise over the mountains. Something akin to joy filled Nick's heart. He was bobbing like a cork in a heated infinity pool in the Andes, his formerly stiff rump tucked into a plastic flotation device made to look like a spotted frog. His two friends were bobbing, too, one in a dragon and one in a panda bear. He was happy – like the Frankish butcher had said he would be. He found himself employing a phrase he'd gleaned from TV: 'You guys are the best.'

They laughed at him, and Meg used her own new slang: 'Sucker,' she said.

'I'm not a sucker,' Nick said.

'You are so.' She sipped at her cocktail – Sex on the Beach – through a straw and paddled her feet in the water. 'You love the Guild.'

'In that case we're all suckers,' Nick said. 'All we have to do is be happy and uphold the rules.'

Leo, rotating gently in his panda bear, snorted. 'That's a pretty tall order,' he said. His slang was better than both of theirs, and he loved to show off.

'What does that mean?'

'A tall order?' Leo put his head back and let his three braids dangle in the water. His head was plucked bald except for a square patch of hair at the back, which was long and braided into three thin plaits. He had been told this hairstyle would not be acceptable in Bangalore, but he still had a few months in Chile, and Leo wasn't going to reach for the razor until the plane was waiting for him. 'A tall order is something that is nearly impossible. So you say that all we have to do is be happy and uphold the rules. I say, "That's a tall order." It means that I'm not sure I can do it.'

'Why not?'

35

Leo rolled his head to the side and looked at Nick. 'I'm disenchanted with the Guild.'

'Why?'

'Remember that guy, a couple of weeks ago? I was walking with him across the quad.'

'Yes,' Nick said. 'The man in the baby-blue suit.'

'The Man in the Baby-blue Suit,' Meg said. 'It sounds like a song.'

'He wasn't anything like a song,' Leo said. 'Unless it was a song about ominous government types.'

'What was his name?'

'He never told me.'

'All right, so.' Meg thought about it. 'We'll call him Mibbs.'

'They call me *Mister* Mibbs!' Nick was pleased with his joke.

Leo didn't laugh. 'You saw him, Nick. He wasn't funny.'

'No,' Nick agreed. 'Even in that suit he wasn't funny.'

'He walked at a distance from me,' Leo said. 'As if he were afraid to come too close. He asked me about my experiences on what he kept calling the "warpath".'

'That's nothing new. Everyone's always asking you crazy questions about being an Indian,' Nick said. 'Like that thirteenth-century Japanese guy who keeps challenging you to an archery contest.'

'And that German woman,' Meg piped up. 'Astride von What-have-you.'

Leo put his hands over his ears. 'Oh God, Astride! I was so glad when she finally left.'

Nick laughed, but Leo dropped his hands from his ears and his eyes were serious. 'He asked me all sorts of intense questions. Very specific. About certain practices of, shall we say, revenge? *Revenge* isn't quite the right word. It's about compensation, completion . . . but to an outsider, it can look . . .'

'Vicious?' Nick supplied the word, thinking of Badajoz.

'Perhaps. In any case, Mr Mibbs had very broad questions about what "Indians" do with white captives.'

'Like, torture?'

Leo shrugged. 'He had all this crazy mixed-up information about the Mohawks and the Mixtecs, most of it complete bullshit. He seemed to think that Mohawks sacrifice babies on top of pyramids and eat their livers, which is absurd because . . . well, never mind. The point is, he was obsessed with how to find out if a stolen baby had been killed or adopted. I told him that I'm Pocumtuk, not Mixhawk . . .' Leo laughed, then frowned when Nick and Meg just stared at him. 'Well, anyway, he told me to shut up and answer his questions. So I said I could only speak for my nation, but that it was important to understand that when it is deemed appropriate for our captives to die, they die in a manner that we feel mirrors the agonies of our own hearts. If it is deemed appropriate that they be adopted, they are ceremonially incorporated into the nation –'

'It would be great if you would use shorter sentences,' Meg said.

Leo rolled his eyes and carried on. 'At which point he interrupted me too, and said he didn't care about the particulars; was there some sort of computer database recording what happened to white babies stolen by – and I am using his words here – bloodthirsty savages like myself? I just started laughing because what else was I supposed to do?'

'Scalp him and eat his liver on a pyramid, I guess,' Nick said, swishing his hands through the warm water.

'Well, yes. I should have thought of that, of course. And he does have a great head of hair, but who would want to touch it?'

Nick smiled, and so did Leo, but Nick knew they were

37

both pretending to make light of Mr Mibbs. Just the thought of touching that man gave Nick the creeps, like hearing a door close in an empty house.

'So I laughed,' Leo said, 'and I asked him which part of the past he was from. He said it was an official question: Was there such a database? I said he could take his official question and stuff it up his ass. He said that if I didn't answer his question I would be sorry.'

'You think he was Guild brass or something?' Meg's voice was high with excitement.

'Yes,' Leo said. 'I think he was.'

'What happened then? He said he'd make you sorry, and then what?'

'Then he . . . well, he looked at me,' Leo said. 'He'd avoided looking at me up until that point, and then suddenly he just lifted his head and stared. You must have felt it, Nick. That thing he did with his eyes. When he looked at you. That feeling, that desolation.'

'Felt what?' Meg asked.

Nick recalled the emotion that had flooded him when that gaze had been turned on him. 'Despair,' he said.

'Yes. It was like he was pushing into my head. Pushing out my emotions and replacing them with his.'

'Mind control,' Meg said. 'The Guild uses mind control.'

'Surely not,' Nick said. 'It's easy enough to read people's emotions when they look at you. He was just a weird, unhappy man with a disturbing imagination. He wasn't a Guild official. Think about all the Guild officials we know here at the compound. Think about the Alderwoman, Alice Gacoki. She's nice and normal. This guy wasn't representing Guild policy. They would have called you in to the parliament buildings if they'd wanted to know something about . . .' he tried to remember the tribes Leo had mentioned, and couldn't. 'Your culture.'

38

Leo sucked in his cheeks.

'But that's not the point,' Nick said. 'The point is that that guy was just weird. Weird people must jump, too.'

'You are a happy camper, aren't you, Nick?' Meg held the tiny paper umbrella from her drink over her head, and imitated Nick's accent. 'Is it raining fire and brimstone? Goodness gracious, I hadn't noticed!'

'If I'm a happy camper, you're a conspiracy theorist,' Nick muttered.

Meg shrugged. 'Mind control doesn't seem unreasonable to me. Everything about the Guild is too comfortable, too nice. Like the fact that there actually aren't any weirdos here, and as you say, weirdos must jump. So where are they?' Meg sucked the last of the Sex on the Beach from her glass with an obnoxious slurp. 'Something's wrong. There has to be a catch.'

'She's right.' Leo twirled his panda so he was facing Nick. 'The Guild is too perfect, and that guy was way too creepy for your average asocial modern guy. I could feel it. There was something very wrong about him, and about what he was asking.'

'Feelings!' Nick scowled. 'Can we stop talking about feelings? God!'

'Have it your way.' Leo sounded tired. 'I'm sorry I brought it up.'

'I think you – both of you – are jumping to conclusions. The Guild has been perfectly open, and more than generous with us.'

'The Guild is rich and powerful,' Leo said, 'and it tells us what it wants us to believe.'

Nick, in his frog, felt chilly. He wasn't used to arguing. In his world, one either gave opinions or received them. For a long time now, as Marquess of Blackdown and then as the leader of a company of soldiers, he had been at or near the top of every

39

hierarchy. He took a deep breath. 'Okay, let's assume you are right. What are your options? Abandon the Guild?'

'Why not?'

'Oh, please. Do you really think you could make it out there alone?'

Leo closed his eyes and swished his fingers in the water. 'The Guild can't possibly catch every single person who jumps. There must be people out there who don't belong.'

Nick laughed scornfully, but neither Meg nor Leo responded. So he put his head back and stared up and out into the night sky.

They had one more good day, the three of them. Two weeks after the unpleasantness in the infinity pool – unpleasantness to which they never referred but which hung around them like a cold fog – Meg, Leo and Nick drove down to Santiago for a couple of days' break from the compound. They roared around the city in one of the Guild's fleet of BMWs, a yellow convertible. They shopped and ate in restaurants and wore their modern clothes without a hitch. In the evening they celebrated by going dancing.

Nick and Leo were both propositioned by the same girl in the club, though neither accepted her offer. Leo had left a woman behind him and wasn't, as he'd told Astride and several other interested Guild women, 'ready'. But Nick? Looking into the girl's slightly smudged, pretty face, he found that he simply didn't want to. It was as if the rakish young marquess who had rutted his way across the early 1800s was still back at the terrible white hospital, asleep. Or dead in the dirt of Salamanca.

Only Meg actually took someone back to her hotel room that night, a fact that kept Nick and Leo up, laughing over a bottle of wine in the hotel bar, until the dawn.

The next day the adventurers stumbled out into the afternoon sun, looking for something to eat before getting back on the road. They ended up at the Mercado Central, eating shellfish and admiring the 1872 cast-iron market building.

'Each one of us is older than this place,' Meg said, quaffing her champagne. She was on her third glass.

Nick shrugged. 'We aren't older than those mountains.'

'How do you know?' Leo cracked a crab claw, scowling as he tried to dig out the tender flesh with a yellow plastic devil's fork. 'Maybe they were put up last year as a tourist attraction.'

'Look,' Nick said. He pointed through the crowd that pressed its noisy way past their table. 'It's Alice Gacoki.'

Meg and Leo swivelled in their seats. The Alderwoman was standing alone, absorbed by the spectacle of a mountainous pile of fish cakes. Then she glanced at her watch and moved along to the next stall.

Leo pushed back his chair. 'Let's follow her.'

Meg was on her feet in a second. 'Quickly, Nick. She's short. We'll lose her in the crowd.'

'Just why are we doing this?' Nick shoved a last bite of lobster into his mouth, threw a careless wad of pesos onto the table and caught up with his friends.

They followed the Alderwoman through the crowd, ducking behind slender pillars that couldn't actually hide them and laughing out loud when it seemed certain that she would notice them. But she didn't, and they successfully trailed her all the way to the women's toilets. She disappeared inside.

'I'm going in,' Meg said.

'Don't. It's ridiculous. Let's get back.' Leo jangled the car keys in his pocket. 'I want to get some of the driving done in daylight.'

But Meg was already pushing the door open, turning as she did so and putting a finger over her lips.

The two men waited outside for ten minutes. Women entered and left again, but there was no sign of either Meg or the Alderwoman.

'Do you think one of us should go in after her?'

Nick frowned. 'They must be talking in there.'

A minute later Alice Gacoki emerged. She saw them immediately. 'Hello,' she said, coming forward. Her business suit was perfectly tailored to her slight form. She was Kikuyu, with close-cut white hair. She wore a ring with a pale yellow stone on one of her long, elegant hands, which moved balletically as she talked. She had jumped forward three centuries in her thirteenth year and had been the Alderwoman for decades now. 'It's Nick, isn't it? Nick Davenant.'

'It's good to see you again,' Nick said, and bowed.

'Be careful with that bow,' she said, and held out her hand. Nick flushed and shook it. Her skin was cool, but the ring on her finger was warm.

She turned to Leo. 'And you're . . .' She paused, looking up into his face. He waited for her to remember him. And she did. 'Leo Quonquont.'

Nick was impressed. How many thousands of names and faces did she have logged in her mind? The Alderwoman stood back now and crossed her arms over her chest. 'What are you fellows doing here?'

Leo pointed with his chin at the bathroom door. 'We're waiting for our friend Meg.'

'Ah. The hungry one. I'm in a rush to get up to the compound, so please say hello to her for me. See you back at the ranch.' She nodded to them both and walked away into the crowd.

Meg popped out a moment later. Her mouth was a tiny, tight line, her eyes wide and frightened.

'What happened?' Leo touched her shoulder.

She looked from one to the other of them. 'Did you see her?'

'Yes.' Nick had never seen his friend so perturbed. 'She said to say hi. She was in a rush. What the hell happened in there?'

'I'll tell you in the car.'

But when they reached the convertible Meg had second thoughts about getting in. 'I shouldn't tell you in there. It's probably rigged with some sort of recording device.'

'Bugged,' Leo said. 'That's the word for it.'

'I doubt very much whether –' Nick reached for the door handle.

'Whatever.' Meg was looking up and down the street. 'Just come on.'

With her arms tucked into theirs, the two men had to bend over Meg to hear her whisper as she trotted them along at a furious pace. 'I slipped into the cubicle next to her,' she said. 'I popped right up on the toilet and looked over the top.'

'You didn't!' Nick laughed, horrified.

'Sure and I did. Why not? Well. There she stood, holding her phone. I thought for certain she'd look up and see me. Then the phone vibrated, and she answered it.' Meg looked up at her companions, first Leo, then Nick. 'I could barely hear her. But she said, "She has disappeared. Ignatz has fled. The Brazilian resistance is fractured for the moment. Whenever they regroup, we have to be ready."'

The two men stopped and stared down at her.

'I'm not telling you a lie. God strike me dead if I tell a lie.'

Whether the car was bugged or not, they argued about it all the way home. Meg fought loudly, Leo calmly, Nick with a disbelieving contempt for his friends' opinions. Meg and Leo said this proved what they had suspected. The Guild

43

was corrupt. They were killing people. Somewhere out there – in Brazil – there was a resistance movement.

'I don't believe it.' Nick folded his arms and stared at his reflection in the car window. The sun had set; they had been around this argument three or four times already. 'Every member of the Guild is made a millionaire, no strings attached. Why would anyone resist that?'

'No strings? No strings?' Meg's voice filled the car. 'You don't have the sense that God gave a billy goat!'

'It's good that you're content, Nick,' Leo said, calmly glancing over his shoulder, then turning the wheel to change lanes. 'But you cannot force us to . . .' He paused, clearly searching his prodigious memory for a phrase. 'You cannot make us drink the Kool-Aid. The evidence is incontrovertible. Someone has disappeared, and someone else – this Ignatz person – is in hiding. Gacoki said "the Brazilian resistance". Meg heard her say it.'

'No,' Nick said. He heard the way his voice was shifting registers, moving to the front of his mouth, taking on the clipped precision of an affronted aristocrat – but he was too frustrated to temper his condescension. 'This is paranoia – a delusion of Meg's.'

'Are you calling me a liar?' Meg was, technically, sitting in the back, but she was so angry she had thrust her skinny shoulders up between the front seats.

Nick turned his head and looked her in the eye. 'I'm not calling you a liar, Meg. I'm calling you a drunken left-footer.'

After that there was complete silence between them.

The next day, Meg and Leo were gone. Disappeared from the compound.

For a couple of days everyone gossiped about it. The general consensus was that they'd been cherry-picked for jobs in

44

the Guild, airlifted out of the compound to glorious new lives in London, at the Guild headquarters.

Nick knew better.

Either his friends were on their way to Brazil, seeking their fantasy of a resistance movement, or they were dead. In Wellington's army the smallest infraction had been a capital crime. Theft. Insubordination. What Meg and Leo had voiced last night was bigger than that: tantamount to treason. They had broken the fourth rule: Uphold the rules. No questions. No unhappiness. No disloyalty. Perhaps the car *had* been bugged. Maybe the cost of dissent was death. Maybe the Guild had taken them away and killed them.

Nick stopped going to classes, stopped socializing. He was thrown into grief – for Meg and Leo, and back into all his original grief for what he had lost when he jumped. For everyone he had ever known. His entire world.

He would have been completely alone if not for the girl with the dark eyes. At least she hadn't deserted him. Her eyes, her smile – they absolved him. As they had that first time, and every single time afterwards. He floated around his pool in Leo's panda and dreamed of that warm, comforting gaze.

Exactly a year after his arrival Nick had left the compound outside Santiago and begun his life in the United States. Nine years later he was still here. He told people he was thirty-three years old. But when he counted to himself, he counted in centuries.

He divided his time between a loft in SoHo and his house in Vermont. He managed, for the most part, to forget about the Guild. He followed the four rules, and he attended the Guild convention, held biannually in either Santiago or Mumbai. It was basically a mandatory week-long cocktail party, and Nick hated it. Every kind of human from down the timeline, and all they could think to do was stand around and brag about how they spent their money. Most were collectors. Antique dowry chests. Antique guns. Antique musical instruments. Always it was antiques – or if it wasn't antiques it was BMWs and Apple gadgets. The Guild patronized both brands with equal fervour.

Nick didn't collect antiques and he drove an old Chevy LUV pickup. It pretty much expressed the state of his emotions: misspelled, and a little cramped for space. But he knew that in spite of his small resistances, he was like any other Guild member, skimming the fat off the top. It was a good enough life, tinged at the edges with loneliness, but padded, too, with luxury. Of course, he might have had another story, if he'd survived the war and not jumped. He might have gone home and settled down. Fallen in love. Found the girl with the dark eyes grown up and waiting for him. Married her. Set up his nursery. Lived out his life surrounded by the hustle and bustle of servants and children and a wife, dogs and horses and tenants and seasons. Never leaving Devon. Eating beef and drinking claret and bouncing fat babies on his knee.

But that other life existed only in cloud cuckoo land. He was here in Vermont in 2013 and that was all there was to it.

Nick stretched his feet out to the fire and put his hands behind his head. He stared at the letter on the mantel. Instead of the girl with the dark eyes he had the Guild. The generous foster mother of time's little orphans. Generous and controlling. He thought of Meg and Leo. Controlling and maybe even murderous.

The envelope seemed to stare back at him. What the hell did they want? All his skills were obsolete. Slaughtering Frenchmen; ignoring the stench of open sewers; dressing in absurdly tight clothing; seducing the buxom, sleepy-eyed daughters of innkeepers. Useless talents in this slick and modern present. These days Frenchmen were unavailable for slaughter. Pretty women were skinny and looked at a single man like Nick with starving intensity, as if he were a piece of low-fat cheese.

Nick stood up, letting the throw fall away from his body. The fire was burning well now, and he could feel the heat increase as he stepped forward. He plucked the envelope from the mantel.

With the letter heavy in his hand, he remembered the dream that had awoken him. His terrible intention to kill, and then the will to follow through. The boy dying. Perhaps the dream had been prophetic. Maybe the Guild needed a hit man. Well, they could look elsewhere. He was done with killing.

He slipped his finger under the flap of the envelope and slowly ripped it open along its crease. The bright sound of tearing paper set his teeth on edge. He drew the single sheet out and unfolded it.

The words were printed in big black letters across the top of the page, with the tulip seal of the Guild embossed over them: 'SUMMONS DIRECT'. Then below it, dashed off at a casual angle in Alice Gacoki's hand: 'Never mind the rules. Catch a flight. See you at Heathrow.'

Julia wandered aimlessly through Castle Dar, waiting for the men to return from the funeral. It was half castle, half house, and it had piled up over the centuries around a square Norman tower. The tower's broken-toothed crenellations still crowned the rest, poking up in the midst of sloping roofs and mismatched gables. Julia knew every inch of the place, and before Grandfather's death she would have said she loved it. But now she walked through the rooms as if she were a stranger and the house a ruin. It felt like a ruin without Grandfather's voice filling it, without his long strides eating up the hallways as he charged from one end of the castle to the other. There used to be a thrumming energy here, a thrill in the air. But with every day that passed since Grandfather's death, it grew less. Castle Dar was Eamon's now, silent and unwelcoming.

Julia hugged her arms around her ribs, noticing how dark the house was, how it was crumbling. The portraits that lined the hallways seemed to have receded further into black, greasy obscurity since last she looked at them, with Grandfather by her side. They didn't recognize her, these painted ancestors. Even the one of her young father, Grandfather's son. She stood and looked up at him now. The portrait had been completed the month before he went to Scotland, where he had met and married Julia's mother in a whirlwind romance. He'd stayed there with his bride until she was brought to bed of a daughter, and then the three of them had set out for the south. A carriage accident in the borderlands had taken her parents' lives; little Julia had survived. Grandfather had never even met his daughter-in-law, and suddenly he was rushing north to bury her and to take her baby girl back south. Julia had no image of her mother, only a couple of trinkets that had been hers. But she used to love this portrait of her father. Now his eyes seemed as distant and cold as any of the others'. They all stared over her head, looking past her . . . they were looking for the earl. Looking for Eamon.

The house wasn't entirely Eamon's yet, however. Grandfather's collection of stones still cluttered every available surface. Julia picked one up from a windowsill as she passed. It had been his habit to return from journeys with his greatcoat pockets full of them. Stones with things in them. A fern. A fish. Or stones that were things. This one, for instance, was an enormous tooth, like a giant's molar.

'The world is old, Julia,' Grandfather had said once, when she was fifteen. 'Older than old. Older than anyone guesses. Time is long. It stretches back and back and back . . .'

'Older than Eden?'

'Much older than Eden.'

'But God made the world in seven days.'

'Perhaps. If each day was an aeon of aeons.'

'How do you know?'

At that he had patted her cheek, as if she were still little. 'Questions, questions. Time enough for answers when you are older.'

'I am fifteen. How old must I be before you tell me?'

He had frowned at her words. But then he had winked, again as if she were a child. And he recited the nursery rhyme that used to freeze her blood when she was little: '"Whither old woman, oh whither so high?"' He used a creaky voice and opened his eyes wide, so that white showed all around the brown iris. '"To brush the cobwebs off the sky! Shall I go with thee? Aye, by and by!"'

She had smiled to please him, but she wasn't pleased.

After that she stopped asking anything about the stones he continued to bring back and leave in piles around the house.

Aye, by and by. Julia squeezed the tooth in her hand until she could feel it almost bite into her skin. He was gone, like that old woman they had tossed up in a basket, seventeen times as high as the moon. He had never taken her with him, on any of his journeys. Now he was brushing the cobwebs off the sky all by himself, and she was here in his lonely house, a house that no longer loved her.

Once, just once, when she was nine, he had brought back something that wasn't a stone. It was a brightly coloured, tiled, lacquered box, and he had tossed it to her as he climbed down out of the carriage. 'See what you make of that,' he'd said. She'd caught it in her hand. It was much lighter than it looked.

She examined the pretty thing. She knew there must be a trick to opening it. She had heard about such puzzles. Oriental boxes with secret hinges and buttons. She found that this one could be twisted, but it never seemed to want to open. The lacquer was very fine. 'Is it a Chinese box, Grandfather?'

'Yes, it was made in China. See if you can discover its trick.'

She quickly twisted it, matching colours until each side was fully one shade, thinking that then it might open. But it remained closed. 'I can't do it. Show me.' She glanced up to find him looking at his pocket watch, and then at her, a gleam in his eye. She held the box out to him, and he took it, tucking it away in his pocket. 'Another time,' he'd said. But he never brought it out again. He just piled up more and more stones, with their strange captive bones and insects and bits of leaf.

Julia came back to herself and realized she was staring blindly from an upstairs window, down over the fields towards the village, the enormous tooth still clutched in her hand. The men were returning from the funeral. She could see them coming from a long way off, picking their way back across the fields in a straggly line. Eamon was the last. He wore his hat crammed down over his ears and he strutted along with a curiously rolling yet elbowy gait that made him look much like a pompous crow. Julia set the tooth on the sill, took a deep breath, and went back down to the hallway to meet them.

The men came in quietly, bobbing their heads to her. Mr Pringle, the butler, stopped and said a few words to her. The sermon was affecting, though not necessarily suited to Grandfather's personality. There was a great deal of talk about lambs and meekness. But all the village men had turned out, dressed very neatly, and there were quite a few fine London and even foreign gentlemen in attendance as well, whom Pringle hadn't recognized. Pringle dropped his voice. And one lady. Yes, a woman had attended. She arrived at the last minute in a shiny, black coach drawn by a team of matched blacks. Travel-stained, mind you; she had come from afar. Her gown was magnificent – sewn all over with jet beads – and she wore a matching veil that shielded her face and hair entirely. She didn't stay to see the coffin put into the vault; they all heard her coach pull away soon after the end of the sermon.

Eamon came up while Pringle was talking. 'Move along, man,' he said, and shoved his way in. Mr Pringle stood aside, and took Eamon's disreputable hat and threadbare coat with obvious distaste. The poor butler was an admirer of fine tailoring, and Grandfather had been, among many other things, a dandy. Pringle felt the loss acutely. 'Will that be all, my lord?'

'Brandy in my study,' Eamon said, and set off for that room.

'Cousin?' Julia walked after him. 'Will you tell me about the funeral?'

Eamon turned and fixed her with his fishy eyes. 'A dead man lay at the front of the church, and some forty living men muttered over his corpse. Then he was bundled into a hole beneath the floor.'

Julia stared and he stared back, his nostrils wide and trembling. Was that rage he was suppressing? Or laughter?

In any case he was clearly finished speaking to her. Julia sank into an absurdly deep curtsey. 'Thank you, Cousin. That was illuminating.'

He inclined his head. 'I am always pleased to enlighten you, Julia.'

She watched as he strutted into the study and slammed the door shut behind him. Grandfather had died three days ago. This was the longest conversation she had yet had with the new earl.

Julia knew that life in Castle Dar would be unbearable after Grandfather died and Eamon acceded to the title. And it was – but differently than she had imagined. Before Grandfather's death, when Eamon had visited from time to time, he had always taken a cruel delight in teasing her, pestering her relentlessly until she lost her temper. Now that he was living here, he barely spoke to her. Not only that, but he had shut her off from the outside world. Her days were silent, enclosed, stifling.

After breakfast that first morning following Grandfather's death, Eamon had given orders to the servants that no one was to be admitted to the house until further notice. When Julia protested that the neighbourhood would be coming by to offer their condolences, Eamon turned his pale eyes on her. 'Pray, do not speak unless spoken to, Julia,' he had said. Then he had talked over her head to Pringle. 'Castle Dar is not accepting visitors. I will not receive them, and neither will Miss Percy. See that it is so.' He stood, brushed the crumbs from his jacket and disappeared into the study.

This became the pattern of his days. A morning spent eating breakfast with – but not talking to – Julia, then a long day in the study, then a dinner as silent as breakfast had been. Mrs Cooper, the housekeeper, told Julia that Eamon spent hour after hour going through every drawer, every paper, every book in the study, sometimes cursing out loud. When he emerged each evening his mood was worse than it had been than the night before.

The silent meals were excruciating. And not silent enough. Julia could hear each noise Eamon made, clinking his cutlery against the china, chewing, swallowing. As the days went by she grew attuned to more sounds. His sleeves shushing against his jacket as he reached for the salt. His stubble – he was a man who shaved only once a week – scratching against his badly tied cravat. The night after the funeral he managed to extract a truly swampy squelch from the blancmange as he dug his spoon into it. Julia had to stifle the urge to scream. For the two nights following, she claimed a headache and kept to her room.

Dinners with Grandfather had always been wonderfully loud. He had talked with his mouth full, exhorting her to argue with him about everything and nothing. He had waved his food around as he talked, and once he had even inadvertently launched a duck leg down the table. It was Julia's moment of greatest triumph. She reached up and caught the drumstick mid-flight, then she ate it with ladylike dignity. The servants cheered, and Grandfather leapt to his feet and made her a toast right then and there.

Well, those days were over, and Julia would have to learn to be deaf to Eamon's vile table manners. But she suspected that his campaign of slobbering silence had some purpose. It wasn't that she didn't interest him. She interested him enormously. She could sense him watching her, and when she glanced up his eyes were always just sliding away from her. She felt sure that all his energies were directed towards her, even as he affected boredom. When, after her two-night desertion of the dinner table, she received word through Mrs Cooper that she was not to miss dinner ever again, she was certain.

Eamon was trying to drive her mad.

Finally, a full week after Grandfather's death, Eamon looked up from his breakfast and spoke. 'Julia.'

She froze, her cup half lifted to her lips. 'Yes, Cousin?'

'When you have finished eating you will attend me in my study.'

'Very well.'

He stood, sketched her a mocking bow, then stalked past her and out of the room.

Julia set her teacup down, her hand shaking so badly that the cup clattered in the saucer.

'Miss?'

Julia looked up. It was Rob, the footman. 'Yes?'

He came forward quickly. 'Miss, I know it is not my place to speak to you, but I wish you to know – we all wish you to know – that we are in your corner, should you need us.'

Julia twisted her napkin in her lap. 'Thank you. I am sure all will be well.'

'I don't like him,' Rob said. 'Neither does anyone else below stairs.'

'Change is difficult, I know, Rob.'

'It's more than that, miss. He's searching for something, and he isn't finding it. Last night I heard him as he was going to bed, and he was muttering your name, over and over again. It gave me a chill, and I said to myself, "There's no harm that will come to Miss Percy while I'm here," and I said so to everyone at our morning gathering, and Mr Pringle and Mrs Cooper agreed with me. We consider you our mistress, miss, despite him being the man who holds the purse strings. We want you to know that.'

Julia had known Rob for years, and liked him, but she had never really thought about who he might be, besides a perfectly amenable footman. Now she saw that he was the earnest sort, the kind of man whose heart shone out of his eyes. 'Thank you, Rob,' she said. 'I'm sure there will be no need for you to act on your feelings, and you really must keep them to yourselves. Eamon – Lord Percy – is not someone to cross.'

Rob was short and very thin, but he straightened his shoulders and managed to convey a sense of strength. 'I know that, miss, and you may be sure we will all be as subtle as snakes, but I thought you should know how we feel. When the time comes that you need our help, you need do nothing more than ask.'

'Thank you, Rob.'

'It is my pleasure, miss.' He bowed. 'May I serve you some more coffee?'

'No, thank you. I shall go and beard the lion in his den now.'

'That's the way, miss.'

Julia stood and smoothed her skirts. She wasn't sure whether to be comforted by Rob's promise of support or troubled that the servants had noticed that Eamon's behaviour was strange. Now she couldn't pretend that everything was as it should be, that Eamon was simply taking his place as earl and they must all adapt. If the servants were disturbed, well, then things were disturbing.

Eamon was writing. He motioned her to a straight-backed chair placed squarely before Grandfather's desk. The desk was still cluttered with Grandfather's favourite objects – stones, bits of sculpture, pots of various coloured inks – and a few books remained splayed open to the place where Grandfather had stopped reading them when he took to his bed, his big, bold handwriting in the margins still black and fresh. Julia could read one word upside down, scrawled half across the print of a book of sermons: 'Hogwash!' She allowed her lips to quirk upwards: Grandfather had raged against the inanities of the world until the very end.

The parasite who now sat in Grandfather's chair could not have been more different from that fiery old man. Eamon was big and bald like Grandfather, but he was tight. He even held his quill tightly, and his handwriting was choppy. He kept writing, line after line, making her wait. She sat and listened to the scratch of his quill. It needed trimming, and had it been Grandfather sitting there writing, she would have simply taken it from him, wiped it clean and trimmed it. He would have snapped his fingers as she worked, trying to hurry her along, even as he talked to her about what he was reading, what he was writing. Now Julia rejoiced in the quill's irritating noise and in the way it split the line of ink, making Eamon's ugly writing even uglier.

Finally, Eamon laid the quill down, sprinkled sand over his page, dusted it off and set it aside. Only then did he look up at her. She met his eyes for a fraction of a second. 'You must pretend,' Grandfather had said. Julia dropped her gaze.

'Julia, Julia, Julia.' Eamon steepled his fingers and leaned forward, propping his pointy elbows on the desktop. 'How old are you now?'

'Twenty-two.'

'Twenty-two, twenty-two. And not yet married.'

Disgust traced its way up her spine, like a cold finger. She would not answer a question that was no question at all.

'No offers?' Eamon's voice was unctuous.

Julia snapped her eyes at him for a moment.

'You haven't lost that temper, I see. You try to hide it but . . .' He paused, and she saw the long, white fingers descend to the desktop in fists. 'Look at me, Julia.'

She fought to keep her expression bland.

'You try to hide it, but I see everything. Do you understand? I see everything. You can have no secrets from me.'

'I have no secrets.' Julia heard the quaver in her voice and hated herself for it.

Eamon leaned back in his chair. 'Have you never been in love, Julia? At your advanced age?'

Julia said nothing. There was nothing to say.

'Oh, come now, Julia. Surely you know if you have been in love. Such a dusty, dried-up old maid you are becoming. Surely you must have longed to go to London to catch a handsome, rich husband. Surely you begged and pleaded.' He raised his voice into a sickly falsetto. '"Please, Grand-papa. Please let me go."'

Julia had to fight to keep her temper even. Eamon was so much nastier and more repellent than she remembered. Over the years she had met him five or six times. He would turn up at Castle Dar belligerent and in need of money. He would stay a night or two, and Julia remembered his needling her, teasing . . . she would get angrier and angrier until she was about to burst, and she would stare at Eamon until she seemed to see him at the end of a long, dark tunnel, fixed in her gaze like an insect on a pin.

Always at that moment, just when she had Eamon in her sights, Grandfather would say her name, catch her angry glance, and wink. Then he would stop time. Eamon would be caught, frozen, and Grandfather would walk over to him and make him stand in ludicrous positions or stick a twist of paper up his nose. Julia and Grandfather would laugh at him, and then Grandfather would put everything to rights and make time speed up again. Eamon would awaken, entirely unaware that any time had passed.

Now Grandfather was dead and couldn't use his time tricks to control Eamon any more. Grandfather was dead, and Eamon had inherited his wealth, his land and his title.

'Speechless, kitten? Do not think I'll take you to London to find you a husband, because I will not. Your grandfather ruined you for marriage, anyway. You, Julia, are abrupt and rude. Half unpolished girl, half uncouth boy. Already twenty-two years old, with only a thousand a year upon marriage or when you turn twenty-five.' Eamon shook his head. 'It's a pity. You ain't a very good prospect, Cousin. You will have to stay and be a comfort to me in my bachelorhood. And when I find a wife, I'm sure she won't mind having a spinster cousin to help her tend the babes.'

Julia was losing the battle to stay calm. When she was twenty-five she would be free . . . but that was three years away. Grandfather should have thought about this. But he had considered himself invincible, a lion. 'Time for that tomorrow!' She could almost hear him say it. He was a dead lion now. A tear coursed down her cheek, and she dashed it away angrily with her fist. She took a deep breath and tried to steady her nerves, but her hands were shaking in her lap.

'Fascinating,' Eamon said. 'Are you crying because you

don't want to give up your place in the household to another woman? Or because Grandpapa didn't give you more money? Neither reason is very flattering, kitten. You are either selfish or greedy or both.'

Julia grew cold and then fiery hot. 'You disgust me. If Grandfather were here, he would – he would –'

Eamon raised his eyebrows in mock surprise. 'You stammer when you are angry. It is almost charming.' Eamon got up from the desk and stalked past her until he stood behind her chair. 'But I am interested in that hopeless threat you were about to make. If Grandfather were here he would what?'

Julia could smell Eamon's acrid eagerness. Her stomach clenched.

'What would Grandfather do, Julia?'

'I don't know.'

'But you do know, don't you?'

'No, I don't.'

'It had to do with time, didn't it?'

Julia's breath caught in her throat. He knew! 'I don't know,' she said again.

'Yes, you do, kitten.' Eamon's voice surrounded her. 'Let me save you the trouble of telling me. The old rogue could pervert the flow of time. He could make it stop. He could do whatever he wanted then. He could quietly rearrange some accounts or some records or some wills to suit himself. Isn't that so?'

Julia stared straight ahead, her heart pounding. He knew. It was impossible, yet he knew.

Eamon's breath tickled her hair; he must be bending over her, like a vulture. 'Your grandfather could play with time like a child plays with mud, isn't that right? He was a dirty thief.'

Julia raised her voice before she could stop herself: 'Grandfather was not a thief! He only did it when –'

'Aha!' Eamon gripped Julia's shoulders, pinning her to the chair and pulling it up hard against his legs. The breath left her body and fear stilled her blood. He bent down to breathe in her ear. 'He only did it when what?'

Julia held perfectly still for a moment, then burst into frenzied struggle. Eamon held her firmly, pulling her shoulders cruelly back. She kicked and twisted, and his bruising grip on her shoulders released. The chair fell back and Julia leapt to her feet, whirling to face him. 'Do you really want to know, Eamon? Because I will relish the telling of it. He did it when you visited; I saw him do it. He froze you. You couldn't move, and he tied a housemaid's apron around your middle. We laughed at you. We laughed in your horrible, gaping fish face! We laughed at you for ten minutes at a stretch before he started time up again. Oh!' She pressed her hands to her mouth.

Eamon's jaw clenched and unclenched. His face changed colour, from white to red to white again. Then, with visible effort, he smiled. 'So it is true.' He dusted his hands together, then gestured for her to sit again. 'Please,' he said. 'Please be seated. I am sorry if I scared you. But you see, my tactics take me far in a short span of time. And *time* is what we are discussing, yes?'

Julia's heart was pounding. He had tricked her, playing on her temper, which had always been her weakness. She forced herself to calm down. 'I will discuss nothing with you.'

'Sit down, Julia. We have begun our discussion and you cannot choose to stop now.'

'I have nothing to say.'

'Sit down.' There was an edge to his voice, and she saw his white hands clench.

'I prefer to stand.'

'As you wish. But I shall sit.' Eamon made a show of walking back around his desk and arranging himself in his chair, enjoying every second of his rudeness in sitting while she remained on her feet. Now Julia stood before him as a servant stands before her master, and she felt the insult in her bones. But if Eamon expected to cow her this way . . . She straightened her back.

'Now,' Eamon said, examining his fingernails. 'To our discussion. I have named your grandfather's little hobby, and you have agreed that he had what you might call a "gift", yes?' He looked up at her.

Julia said nothing.

'I take your silence for assent. He had a gift, and that gift was nothing more nor less than the ability to manipulate time; to wit, he could stop it for considerable periods, and while it was stopped, he could move about, doing what he wished with aprons and the like, was that not so?'

Julia cursed herself. It had taken Eamon one week of silence and a few insults to break her. He had known it already, but still. She had admitted knowledge of Grandfather's secret. The deepest, darkest secret in the world. Julia's earliest memories were of her grandfather drilling her with the necessity to keep quiet about what he could do. On his deathbed Grandfather had told her to pretend. Instead she had given in to her temper and blabbed like a magpie.

Eamon picked up the carved marble head of Mercury that Grandfather had used as a paperweight. 'Your grandfather knew how to stop time. A remarkable gift indeed. You and I may disagree on how he used it; you say he larked about humiliating his relatives, and I say he was a thief. He wanted to steal my inheritance from me, and he tried to use time itself to do it.'

'He was not a thief, and you are a blackguard.'

Eamon looked up, hefting the marble head. 'Careful, kitten. Claws.' He passed the head from hand to hand. 'He wasn't a thief, you say. Then why did he spend years trying to disinherit me? Me, his last living male relative?'

'Perhaps because he was a good man and you are an excrescence!'

Eamon slammed the two-thousand-year-old marble head down on the table, and its blank eyes glared accusingly at Julia. 'Your grandfather a good man? You clearly know nothing of men. He never once brought you to London, my dear. You should have seen him there. No respect for his own rank. Always to be seen in the most disreputable parts of town with his gang of foreign friends. Thieves and drunkards and revolutionaries. And his mistress. Opening her house and her legs to any passing riff-raff. Your precious grandfather threw his money away on her, and on his ridiculous coterie. Meanwhile I, his own flesh and blood, was left to suffer in penury.'

'I hear nothing in that to diminish him in my eyes,' Julia said.

'You don't? Then why did you blush when I spoke of his mistress?'

'If my face is flushed, Cousin, it is because I am angry.'

Eamon leaned over the desk. 'Are you so hardened that talk of mistresses – of the women with whom men lie for pleasure alone – falls on your ears as easily as talk of the weather? I wonder why that is? Perhaps you are already fallen, kitten. Tell me, was it that little footman who ran off with the prize? Or old Pringle?'

Julia was not to be tricked twice in the same way. She sneered down her nose, her temper perfectly under control. 'If it amuses you to ride roughshod over my reputation, think again before dragging the servants into it. They are hardworking, honourable men.'

Eamon's fishy eyes glimmered and he leaned back. 'Ah,

self-righteousness. The spinster's weapon. How well you wield it already, kitten.'

Julia went cold all over. Spinsters' weapons were no weapons at all. She was defenceless. She and Grandfather had been living in a fools' paradise. Julia could see that now. Grandfather thought they could always go on just the same, a little girl and her hearty grandfather, with no more need to think about tomorrow than a pair of pigeons. Teaching her to be a lady, finding her a husband . . . those were problems he had always put off. His life had been an endless stream of todays, until, suddenly, it was over.

'Poor little kitten.' Eamon's voice sounded almost tender. 'You were a pretty child, you know. Whoever would have thought you'd end up a spinster?' He put his hands behind his head and leaned the chair back onto its hind legs. 'Nothing to play with but bits of old rock. Do you know, I never once saw you with a doll?' He bumped the chair back down and picked up a rock from the desk. It had been the greatest prize in Grandfather's collection. On one flat surface was the skeleton of a small bird, as if in flight, the faint impress of its wing feathers still to be seen. Grandfather had taken a magnifying glass and shown her the incredible detail in the impression, how each feather was composed of smaller feathers – and yet the beautiful, delicate things were gone, leaving only their perfect trace in the hard rock. Eamon held the stone up and looked from it to Julia and back again. 'You had a queer childhood, Julia, and it's made you into a strange woman. Unmarketable. But I am glad of it, for if you were married and gone, I would not be able to learn from you. I must know everything about your grandfather's talent, and you will be the one to tell me.'

'I know nothing more.'

Eamon smirked and set the stone down. 'It is ironic, these

noble efforts you are making to protect him. Do you know how I first discovered that your grandfather could stop time, Julia? It was you. You were the one who revealed his secret.'

'I never would have!'

'Yet you did. When you were four years old. You were a stormy little thing, all curls and eyes. You ran everywhere, at top speed, and your nurse could hardly keep up with you. One day I was driving my team up the lane behind the stables, the narrow one with tall hedges on either side. I rounded a corner, and there you were in the lane, all alone, turning in a circle with your head up, playing at making yourself dizzy. I thought it would be good sport to drive you before my team. I drove the horses right up to you and you started to run. Your skirts caught up in your little fists, running for your life.' Eamon chuckled. 'Oh, it amuses me even now.'

Julia searched her memory but found nothing. How could she forget being driven before a team of horses? Perhaps it was simply too awful to remember. But it must have been the origin of her lifelong hatred of Eamon. Now, watching him laugh, she realized with calm certitude that he was more than simply cruel and selfish; he was a madman, and must have been back then, to be so vicious to a four-year-old child.

Eamon sobered. 'Then, suddenly, in an instant, everything was different. You turned your head as you ran. You caught my eye, and a split second later I was on the ground in the lane, some distance back, along the way that I had come. Your grandfather was standing over me with my whip in his hand. I'm telling you, one minute I was driving along having a bit of fun, and the very next second I was on the ground being whipped like some dog.' He pushed his cuff back and held out his wrist, white as a bone and sprinkled with black hairs. It was laced across with an ugly, ropy scar. 'I bear this scar to show for that day, and he would have cut my face if I hadn't buried it in the dust. He branded me, like a damned convict. And you, you stood beside him, and when it was all over you said, clear as a bell, "You be good, Cousin Eamon, or Grandfather will freeze you in time again." The old man tried to hush you but it was too late. The secret was out, and I could see in his face, even as I grovelled there in the dust, that you had spoken an incredible truth.'

Julia closed her eyes. It was her fault. No wonder Grandfather had drilled her in secrecy after that. She sighed and opened her eyes again. 'Be that as it may, Cousin, Grandfather is dead now. His talent died with him.'

Eamon traced his finger along the edge of the desk. 'Ah, but did it?'

'Of course it did.'

Eamon traced his finger back. 'I'm not so sure, kitten. After that interesting afternoon I demanded that he tell me how he stopped time. He must have felt shame at his treatment of me, I think, for he revealed it was a power he gained from an instrument of some kind. He called it a talisman.' Eamon spoke dreamily, watching his finger as it stroked the desk. He looked up at Julia. 'What is the talisman, Julia?'

'I have no idea,' she said. Nor had she. She had never heard Grandfather mention a talisman, not once.

Eamon narrowed his eyes and searched her face. 'It must be an ancient or a strange object, one of these stones of his perhaps. Something that carries a spell locked up inside. I spent years trying to get it out of him. Again and again I pressed him for the information. But he never told me, damn him. I even thought that maybe he had lost it since that day he whipped me. But you have just told me differently, with your tale of that housemaid's apron.'

So she *had* already told Eamon more than he had known. She had to gather her wits, and fast. Eamon believed there was more to the secret, and perhaps there was. But a talisman? Julia didn't believe it. Grandfather's talent had been vital, a part of his body, his spirit. It didn't rely on some trinket. He must have spun Eamon a yarn about a talisman in order to lay a false trail. Keep him from the truth. Whatever that was. If only Grandfather had trusted her with more information – or told her nothing at all. Other people played spillikins or fox and geese with their granddaughters. Would that he had amused her that way and kept his time games to himself.

She looked up to find Eamon watching her. 'You have been informative this morning,' he said. 'I told you that you could keep no secrets from me. Now.' He leaned forward over the desk. 'Sit down, Julia. No more baulking. You started to tell me the secret when you were four years old. Now you are going to finish what you began. You are going to tell me what your grandfather's talisman is, where he has it hidden and how to use it.'

'And if I cannot?'

'Oh, but you can and you will, kitten, I'm sure of it.'

4

The huge jet plane overflew London, banked through 180 degrees and followed the Thames back towards Heathrow. In the early-morning light Nick could see the Isle of Dogs sparkling with tall glass buildings, the New Globe, St Paul's scrubbed clean and white, the London Eye, the Houses of Parliament, Battersea Power Station. He traced out the river's ancient, familiar shape through all the new developments: Kensington, Wimbledon, the gargantuan sprawl of the City. He was returning to England, breaking a cardinal rule of the Guild at the express command of Alderwoman Gacoki herself. He had with him a few changes of clothes, a blue US passport and, tucked into the inside pocket of his jacket, his Summons Direct. He didn't intend to stay long.

The Alderwoman was waiting in Arrivals with Arkady Altukhov, her enigmatic and seldom-seen husband.

'This is an honour, Alderwoman Gacoki,' Nick said as he took Alice's cool fingers in his own. He had last shaken her hand at the fish market in Santiago. Leo had been beside him. He felt a brief sensation of falling backwards. It had been almost ten years. Where was his brilliant, uncompromising Pocumtuk friend now? What would he look like at thirty? Or was he dead? Nick let himself remember that last night, fighting in the car. He had been a stubborn fool – but still. Leo surely would have forgiven him by now; found a way to make contact if he were alive. And what was Nick doing, shaking hands with the woman who may well have ordered Leo killed?

'Thank you for coming,' Alice said, as if the Summons

Direct had been a party invitation. 'And please, call me Alice. You know Arkady . . .' She gestured to the man beside her.

The Alderwoman's husband shook hands as if handshaking were a contest of strength. He was a tall, white-haired Russian of few words. Nick had seen him at conventions but had never spoken to him before and knew almost nothing about him. Altukhov's accent was thick: 'Welcome back to England, Mr Davenant.'

Alice looked at the canvas and leather bag slung across Nick's shoulder, then let her gaze skim down his body and up again. 'Is that all you've brought?'

Nick patted the bag and looked lightly around him at the shifting crowds of travellers. 'I don't plan on staying.'

Arkady snorted, but Alice took Nick's arm and began steering him towards the escalators. 'We have much to discuss. Come. Have you ever ridden in a helicopter before?' She flashed Nick a white smile, as if he were a child and she were taking him on his first pony ride.

He had to admit that it was exhilarating, buzzing like a wasp over the city, headphones clapped to his ears. Nick stared down at the streets, at the people hurrying along, the traffic. It all looked normal to him now. The cars and buses, women in trousers, electric lights and tall buildings. The helicopter dropped and landed on top of a building on the South Bank, and soon enough he and Alice were zipping up the skyscraper known as 'The Shard'. Arkady had disappeared.

The lift doors opened onto an elegant reception area of stark white marble walls and a black marble floor. A beautiful young man sat behind a huge black reception desk.

'Hello, Badr,' Alice said. 'Water for me, please, and a pint of bitter for Nick.'

'It's not even noon,' Nick protested.

'Ah, but I want to see you taste English beer again. We

keep traditionally brewed ale on tap here, always perfectly cellared. I believe today we're pulling Theakston's Old Peculier, isn't that right, Badr?'

The beautiful youth flashed an even more beautiful smile of assent, but Nick shook his head. 'No, thank you.'

'Have it to please me. It's been ten years, hasn't it, since you tasted the real thing?'

'Thirteen. I was in Spain for three years before I jumped, you may recall.'

'Ah yes. Spain. Thirteen years. Surely the small matter of the time of day won't hold you back.'

Nick couldn't help but smile at her absurd manipulations, all to get him to drink a beer. 'A half then, please.'

Badr nodded and disappeared. Alice led Nick down a long hallway and into a vast boardroom. A long table set about with chairs filled the room. In the centre of it, a crystal vase holding at least fifty white tulips was clearly intended to relieve the corporate severity of the space but served only to heighten it. One entire wall of the room was glass. Nick went to look out at the city.

Badr reappeared with a glass of water for the Alderwoman and what was, truly, a beautiful beer for Nick. He took a sip. It tasted marvellous. In fact, nothing had tasted so good in his entire life. 'Has ale improved across the last two centuries?'

'Many things have improved. Please. Take a seat, Nick. And thank you, Badr, that will be all.' The young man left them alone.

Nick sat, and the Alderwoman took the first chair along the table's side. 'There is more to the Guild than you know.'

'Ah.' Nick allowed some sarcasm into his voice. 'You mean that it's more than what we tell the kids? More than a swanky social club?'

The corners of Alice's mouth twitched. 'Much more.'

Nick sipped his beer and regarded the Alderwoman. She seemed to be waiting for him to speak. He decided to try to take control of this extremely strange situation. 'Why am I here? In London, where I'm not allowed to be?'

'Give me your hand,' Alice said, reaching for it. She wore that same ring he remembered from Chile, the one set with a large, yellow jewel. She turned his hand over and contemplated his palm.

'Are you going to read my fortune?'

Alice smiled and traced his lifeline with a short, perfectly manicured fingernail. A tremor extended up his arm to the base of his skull. 'Time,' she said. 'It is like a river. It always flows in one direction.' She placed her finger at the intersection of Nick's heart line and his fate line. 'Or does it?'

'I'm losing respect for you, Alice. Next you'll be pulling out a crystal ball.' It felt like her finger was resting at the crossroads of him.

'This hand has done many things.'

'Do you see my past deeds written in the creases?'

'No.' She tapped her finger twice at the centre of his palm. 'I know very little about palmistry. But I do know about you.' She leaned back, releasing his hand. 'I know because, as the Alderwoman of the Guild, I have more information at my fingertips than you can possibly imagine. I also know because I am a good reader of men and women. You wear your past in your body and your face. We all do.'

'When you say I've done many things with my hands, do you mean killing?'

'You have killed, haven't you? In Spain.'

'Yes.'

'But you've done many other things as well.'

Nick lifted his glass. 'Drinking,' he said.

Alice nodded. 'And loving women.'

Nick took a sip. He wasn't going to respond to that one.

'Writing letters and sealing them with that ring.'

Nick glanced at his ring. Its crest gleamed in the morning sun. 'What are we talking about, Alice? Why am I here? Am I to become one of your hit men?'

'You think the Guild has hit men?'

'Of course it does.' He thought of Meg and Leo. 'Don't treat me like a child.'

Alice let her breath out slowly, looking over Nick's shoulder at something. Her dark eyes seemed curiously blank for a moment. Then they snapped back to his. 'Look outside, Nick,' she said.

He raised his eyes and gasped. The sky had changed. The sun was well risen now, and there were a few clouds where, before, there had been none. As much as an hour might have passed. He scanned the room. On the table under the tulips there was a fallen petal that had not been there before. He leapt to his feet. 'What did you do to me?' He looked down at his beer, picked it up, sniffed it. It had the flat, unappetizing smell of a drink left sitting too long. 'Damn it! I was enjoying that.'

Alice leaned back in her chair and favoured Nick with a smile. 'I stop time, and you worry about your beer.'

'You stopped time? What do you mean? What the bloody hell do you mean by that?'

'Sit down, Nick.'

He sank back down into his chair. He felt like throwing up. But he clenched his jaw and stared at the Alderwoman, waiting for an explanation.

She reached over and pushed his flat beer away, down the table. 'I stopped time,' she said, and her voice was crisp and businesslike. 'Though only in this room, and only for you. For almost an hour, I did various things. Wrote a few e-mails.

Made a phone call. Then I started time up again and you started up too. It is much like pressing pause and then play on an iPod.'

'But . . . I thought –' Nick stopped. He could tell before he even finished his sentence that much of what he had believed a few moments ago – an hour ago, apparently – was about to be revealed as infantile nonsense.

'You thought what the Guild wanted you to think,' Alice said. 'You thought that you'd jumped in time ten years ago and that was the end of that. But now, Nick, the Guild has cleared you for Level One security. We need you, and we need you to know a little more.'

He swallowed. 'Why me?'

Alice waved her hand as if shooing away a mosquito. 'Don't worry about that. We need you for reasons that have to do with your past. But to be of use, you will have to learn more about the Guild, about yourself and of what you are capable. Some of what you learn might disturb you, or make you angry.'

'I can handle it,' Nick said gruffly. 'For God's sake, I've jumped two bloody centuries and remade my life from the bottom up.'

The Alderwoman touched a drop of water that was running down her glass and drew a wet, undulating line on the tabletop. 'Indeed you have. Admirably.' She looked up. 'Do you remember the first rule of the Guild? And the second?'

'There is no return.'

'That is, indeed, the first and also the second rule of the Guild. But rules . . .' She paused. 'I believe they say that rules are made to be broken.' She smiled at him, waiting for him to understand.

Nick stared back, not wanting to know what he suddenly did know. When he spoke, he spoke slowly and softly, to keep from screaming. 'You have brought me here to London, thus breaking the second rule of the Guild, in order to tell me that the first rule is also a load of bollocks.'

'In a nutshell, yes.' Alice smiled at her own witticism. 'Unless it is the other way round. I always considered the first rule to be about place and the second about time. But I suppose the order really doesn't matter.'

Nick stared at her, not hearing her words. 'So it is possible to go back in time,' he said, when her voice died away.

'Yes.'

Nick lost it then, and said a great deal that, later, he wasn't proud of. There was a lot of cursing, and the vase of tulips ended up smashed against the window.

After a few minutes, Nick stood looking out at the city, struggling to regain his composure. Finally he turned back, to find Alice quietly texting someone on her iPhone.

'What are you going to do to me?'

Alice finished tapping at the screen, waited until the soft shush told her the message had been sent, then looked up. 'We're not going to *do* anything to you. We're extending an invitation. Wouldn't you like to see your mother again? Your sisters?'

'They are dead.' Nick heard the gravel in his voice. This woman, twice his age, was calmly skewering him with a red-hot poker, right through the heart. Ten years he had lived here on the edge of time, ten years of mourning his family, of berating himself, of blaming himself, of hating himself.

'They are dead now,' Alice said, 'but they aren't dead then. Are you telling me you don't want to see them?'

'Damn you.' Nick squeezed his eyes shut, balled his fists.

'This is a happy thing,' Alice said gently. 'I'm telling you that you can go back.'

5

Two days had passed since Eamon had confronted Julia in the study. He had spent the time running the full gamut of threats. Without result, of course, for Julia had no idea what Grandfather's talisman was or where it might be hidden. Indeed, she didn't even believe in it. She thanked God she didn't know, didn't believe. It was easy enough to keep a secret she didn't know.

'You are a damned witch, Julia,' he growled over breakfast on the third morning. 'The servants are all wrapped round your finger. My meals have been inedible, my bed was short-sheeted and my fire smoked all night. They have made it perfectly clear that they disapprove of me and favour you. But mark me, Julia, your friends below stairs cannot protect you. You are going to help me find that talisman.'

'I assure you, Cousin, I never saw any talisman, nor did Grandfather mention one. The occasions when I saw him play with time were purely for fun. He used it as a trick to make me happy when I was sad or angry.'

Eamon looked down his nose at her. 'But still you knew. You saw. What did he do exactly? Tell me again how it worked.'

Julia sighed and went through her story. 'Nothing that I could see. He would simply catch my attention, wink, and then the fun started.'

'But what did he *do*? Did he do anything different with his hands or his eyes?'

'No. Nothing like that.' Julia's spine tingled when Eamon

mentioned eyes, for of course it had seemed to be something Grandfather did with his eyes, concentrating on a small thing, ignoring the larger space, and focusing his intent onto a meaningless object. Then there would be that telltale rush behind her ears as the moments slowed or sped. There was no visible talisman. It was simply something Grandfather could do.

Eamon stalked back and forth. 'He must have been staring at something, or perhaps holding something. Did he say any words? Any incantations?'

'No. He just . . . did it.'

'Blast it all to hell!' Eamon pushed his chair away from the table, stormed past Julia and slammed the door of the breakfast room behind him, but immediately opened it again and stuck his head in. 'You, Julia, are not to leave the house for any reason. No rides, no pottering about the estate. You will stay indoors until the talisman is found.'

'Yes, Cousin.'

Eamon slammed the door again. Julia made a sharp, very rude gesture at its blank, unresponsive face.

Arkady and Nick were sitting in matching leather armchairs before a roaring fire in the Mayfair mansion Arkady shared with Alice. Back in the day, this had been the city home of the Duke of Kirklaw. Nick had smoked cigars and quaffed illegal French brandy with the young duke in this very room the night before he left for Spain. The room and its décor were only slightly different now, and it gave Nick a decidedly vertiginous feeling to be sitting here again, another well-aged brandy in his hand and another well-cured cigar sitting half smoked in another ashtray. But he shoved that distraction out of his mind and tried once more to concentrate. 'Describe the feeling to me again,' he said.

Arkady twirled his cigar between his thumb and fore-finger. 'Time slows down around you. It stops. Unless you can feel it happening, you will slow down and stop, too. That is bad. That is what happens to Naturals. You are not one of them. You must learn to *feel* it. You must learn to *know* when time is slowing down. If you feel it, if you know, you will never be caught. You will stay awake and not be frozen.'

'But how can I know how to feel it if I don't already know how to feel it?'

'You English! You have no imagination. I describe it to you so you understand. Do you recall the first time you desired a woman?'

Nick sighed, half amused. He had learned across the course of the afternoon that the older man was very fond of sexual metaphors. 'Yes,' he said. 'Of course I do.'

'Describe it to me.'

Nick cast his mind back. 'I was ten,' he said.

'Such a big boy.' Arkady pulled on his cigar.

Nick resisted the urge to roll his eyes, and continued. 'I was hiding in the creamery, crouched down behind a mess of pails that needed mending. My sister Clare and I were playing hide-and-seek. It was a hot day, but the creamery was cool and dark. The door opened, and I peeked out, expecting to see my sister. But it was a dairymaid, coming in with two pails of milk hanging from a wooden yoke she wore over her shoulders. She wore a tight-fitting bodice . . .'

'Yes, yes,' Arkady said, leaning forward. 'It was so in Russia at that time, with the dairymaids and their tight bodices.'

'Are you of my time, then?'

'Yes.' Arkady sharpened his focus on Nick. 'And of your class as well, Lord Blackdown.'

Nick started. No one had used that title or that name since the butcher, in the Guild hospital. Now Arkady used them with, if not exactly respect, then some sort of acknowledgement. Nick coughed. 'What . . . what am I to call you, then?'

'Are you asking me my name? The name to which I was born?'

Impatience pricked him. 'I know that's against Guild etiquette. But for God's sake, Arkady, I'm sitting here in London waiting for the Guild to send me back to my time. I'm breaking cardinal rules every way I turn. I'm simply asking you to tell me whatever it is that I need to survive this escapade. Perhaps your blessed birth name is one of those things.'

Arkady blew a smoke ring. Nick watched it rise tremblingly and then dissipate. He puffed on his own cigar but performed no smoky tricks. He was in no mood for them. Arkady took another puff, then spoke, the smoke boiling out with his words. 'You were allowed to keep your signet ring when you jumped.'

'Yes.' Nick glanced at his hand.

'I too. I kept my ring.' Arkady held his hand out to display his ruby ring. The jewel was huge and looked like a wound on his bony hand. 'The Guild chose us early on.'

'But how could they know?'

'We are aristocrats. Power likes power. The Guild is always happy to welcome a leader.'

'But I lost my title. My land. My name.'

'Yes, yes.' Arkady waved his hand and the ruby glinted like an eye. 'In your mind, yes, you became the simple man of the people, the commoner Nick Davenant. But the Guild has always known. You are *Blackdown*. The Guild let you believe it was forgotten. But the Guild did not forget.'

Nick had been happy to be allowed to keep his ring. Was he still? 'And you? What manner of aristocrat are you? How noble, Arkady? Are you a prince? A czar?'

'I am Count Lebedev.'

Nick nodded his head in the old gesture of respect between equals. 'Lebedev.'

Arkady smiled thinly. 'Nice to meet you, too, Blackdown. But do you think I believe in this thing, this aristocracy? I know the future. I am not the fool. I am merely happy to be the count when it is good for the Guild. And you will be happy to be the marquess.'

'If you say so.' These old titles, these old gestures – Nick felt a little dizzy.

'I say so. I know it. You will have to struggle against how much you are happy to be the marquess. In fact, he will try to eat you up, this marquess who waits for you in the past. You will have to fight him. I will help you in that struggle.' Arkady spread his hands. 'I am coming with you. Back to 1815.'

'You're coming too?'

'Yes.' Arkady leaned back in his chair and steepled his fingers. 'Does that please you?'

'I'm not exactly pleased with anything having to do with this mess.'

'Such friendliness. But you will be glad, I assure you. In the meantime, Nicholas Falcott, Marquess of Blackdown, we must accustom you again to your old names and your old personality.'

Arkady had said those names – names that had once been his – three times in a minute. In this room, no less; the same room where Nick had spent his last night in London before leaving for Spain. Before breaking his mother's heart. Before destroying his patrimony. Before ruining his sisters' lives. Before damning his own sorry soul to hell at Badajoz.

Arkady's voice was tender when he spoke again. 'Shall we return to the more pleasant topic of the lovely dairymaid?'

'The dairymaid. Yes.' Nick took a deep breath, let it out and packed his bad feelings away for another day. 'She was lovely. Buxom. She came in, set the pails down and drew the scarf from her bosom. Her bodice was low-cut, but the scarf hid everything, you understand.'

'Yes, I do understand.'

'She took it off, and her breasts rose up plump. One nipple peeked over the edge of her bodice. She used her scarf to wipe her face and stood fanning herself with her hand for a moment in the cool of the creamery. Her cheeks were flushed, and then as she bent to scratch her ankle, her breasts simply seemed to spill out. I was only about a foot away, crouched at that level. The world turned upside down. I was flooded with sensation. It seemed mostly to be in my head, a rushing of blood, or something like that.'

'Did you do anything?' Arkady puffed his cigar.

'No. Of course not. I was ten.'

'But I, I would have taken the opportunity. I would have said, "Now is my chance to become more educated."'

Nick took a sip of his brandy and eyed the lanky Russian. His head was thrown back and he was blowing smoke rings again, clearly lost in his own fantasy. 'Remind me why we are even discussing this?'

Arkady rolled his head to one side to look dreamily at Nick. 'I am trying to describe to you the feeling. You do not know what it is. Like a little boy who does not know what it is to desire a woman. Then, suddenly, you do know what it is. Forever afterwards you know. At first you cannot control this feeling; it is – how do you say it nowadays – the boss of you. It arrives when it arrives. But soon you learn how to control it. You can make the feeling come and you can make it go. You are the boss of it. Do you see?'

'So it feels like desire? Someone near me is shifting time and I think, "That's lovely. I want to have sex."'

'No. Deliberately you misunderstand me. It feels like . . .

79

like you almost trip and think, "Oh! I am falling." But then you do not fall. Or you are drinking and you think, "Oh! If I drink more the room will spin." But you do not drink more and then it does not spin. Do you see?'

Nick drew on his cigar and didn't answer. Sex, drinking, falling. He was beginning to suspect that this old Russian had led a far more interesting life than he had.

Arkady tried again. 'Do you remember the feeling the moment you jumped in time?'

'Yes.' Nick recalled Jem Jemison fighting near him. Catching his glance. The bloody gravel under his fingers as he scrabbled for purchase. He recalled the cold intent in the Frenchman's eyes, and then the terrifying, blind sensation of being yanked forward, as if by a team of wild horses. 'It was like I was being pulled forward uncontrollably, and at great speed.'

'Yes. This is the feeling I describe, only much, much smaller. Softer, this feeling. Someone near you is playing with time. You feel it; it is like a little pull in your belly. A little rushing in your ears. That time you jumped, it was a big pull, a big rush. You were saving your own life. You think it was an accident, a strange trick that takes you from the battlefield to the future. No, it was you. It was your gift, something inside you that was saving you. But you had no control over this thing, this gift. You were unaware. Much like a boy when he dreams of a woman, and when he wakes he finds that –'

Nick held up a hand. 'Please, Arkady. Is it possible to continue this conversation without constantly referring to sex?'

'But why? Sex is related to everything. It is the most powerful human drive.'

Nick sighed.

Arkady pointed at Nick with his cigar. 'Your years in America have ruined you. You are prudish, like a priest. Remember your old self, Blackdown. Would he have said to me, "I will not talk with you about women"? "I am embarrassed to talk with you about women"? No. He would have said, "Arkady, we are friends. Let us drink brandy and smoke cigars and talk about women.""

'But we aren't talking about women. We are talking about freezing time. I am still not entirely sure what dairymaids have got to do with it.'

Arkady unfolded himself from his armchair and stood glaring at Nick from his beanpole height. 'Our skill – it is sensuous. It is warm. Making time stop at your will, it is like caressing a beautiful woman. Caressing her and feeling her surrender.'

Nick slumped back in his chair. 'Fine,' he said. 'I am merely the student here.' He could not believe this man was Alice Gacoki's husband. But, across the few days that he had lived with them, he had learned that, in private, Alice was a very different woman from the cool and collected Alderwoman he knew. They wouldn't let Nick out into London – 'You must still abide by Guild rules as far as possible' – and so they ate at home together. Alice was an inspired cook, reciting English poetry or singing in Kikuyu as she moved around the kitchen, unless – and Nick couldn't bear to be in the kitchen at these times – she was listening to *The Archers* on the old-fashioned radio that sat like a cat, humpbacked and purring, on a sunny windowsill. She was a mean poker player and she liked her drink. She flirted constantly with her randy husband, while he, for his part, worshipped his beautiful, powerful wife. But Nick now also understood why Arkady was so seldom to be seen at official events and was silent and mysterious when he did attend. The man was incorrigible.

Arkady stood beside Nick's chair. 'Close your eyes this time, Blackdown,' he said. 'I am going to stop time. Try again to feel it.'

Nick closed his eyes. The room was silent except for the crackle of the fire. They had been through this again and again already this afternoon. Each time Nick missed it, and between one second and the next Arkady would seem, as if by magic, to have flown across the room, or moved Nick's cigar, or built up the fire to a roar. Now Nick didn't even try. He let his mind drift back to that voluptuous dairymaid, and the thing he hadn't told Arkady. When she bent down, she had seen Nick gawping at her. Instead of screeching, or hiding her breasts, she had simply smiled. 'Hello,' she said. Then she straightened again and carefully rearranged her fichu, taking her time. Whether she knew that she was tormenting him with her exquisite beauty, or whether she thought of him as an innocent child, Nick could not tell. But the replacement of the scarf became the fuel for years of dreams. She had taken her sweet, sweet time tucking the fabric in, arranging it, making it perfect. The process was infinitely more erotic even than when she had taken it off, for now Nick knew she knew he was watching. Then, with a twitch of her skirts, she was gone, and Nick was left alone, a very different boy than he had been when he had scampered in to find a good hiding place.

'Nick?'

Nick opened his eyes with a heavy sigh. 'What's different?' He looked around the room.

'Look at the fire.'

He looked. It was as still as a photograph.

'Stand up, Nick. You are in a moment of stopped time with me.'

Nick slowly got to his feet. All around him, the room was entirely motionless. The clock wasn't ticking. The curtains, which had been moving in a slight breeze, were frozen. Outside the window the traffic went by as usual, but in this space, time was not only stopped, it didn't seem even to exist. Arkady was beaming at Nick with triumph and something like teacherly pride. 'How did it feel? Tell me.'

Then Nick was laughing, so hard he had to sit down again. 'Arkady, you devil. I was thinking about sex.'

6

For three days Julia had stayed inside, as Eamon had ordered, although at almost any time she could have simply walked out of the front door and down to the stables. She could have saddled a horse and ridden away, if only she had had the funds to support herself. But she had no funds – and wouldn't have for three long years – so until she could come up with a viable plan, she was opting for a show of obedience. She schooled herself to show Eamon no temper. Whenever he asked where the talisman was, as he did ten times a day, she looked up from whatever she was doing and quietly informed him that she did not know. Meanwhile, he had the servants turn Castle Dar inside out. They went through every chest in the attics, pulled every wine bottle from the cellar racks, searched the scullery, the empty bedrooms, the gunroom, the kennels. Their orders were to bring him anything unusual, or beautiful, or old, or foreign. After two days the study was piled with bizarre objects. In one corner, all of Grandfather's rocks, sorted by size. Another corner housed a pile of especially old and mysterious-looking books. The rest was a miscellany, culled from all over the house and grounds. An embroidered reticule three generations old. A badger skull. A lock of grey hair tied with a rotting black ribbon. A scarab. An armoured glove. An angel farthing. A shoe buckle made of enormous black-spot paste jewels. Eamon sat in the midst of it all like Job on his dung heap, growing progressively more enraged and bellowing now and then for Julia. When she appeared, he demanded that she look over any new additions to the collection. Had she ever seen Grandfather with this object? This ivory needle case, for instance. Surely that was a magical symbol carved into it? Some sort of mystical rune?

'No,' she had said in the quiet voice she had learned to use with him. 'I'm sorry, but I don't recognize that.'

'Blast it all. This could be it. This could well be it, and yet how am I to know it or access its powers?' He'd held the cylinder of needles up and perused it from all sides, then hurled it in a rage across the room. Then he'd looked at her and screamed, 'Get out!'

Julia had risen quietly and walked regally out of the study, but once the door had closed behind her she stormed up to her room. She slammed the door and, barely pausing to pull the chair out and sit down at her writing desk, she scrawled a letter to her childhood friend Lady Arabella Falcott. Bella had grown up on the neighbouring estate and was now in London for the Season. Julia's letter was impassioned, almost every sentence underlined, and it ended with a blotted plea for help.

Minutes after finishing it, Julia burned it. She could not foist herself on the Falcotts. The dowager marchioness, once a leading light in London society, had become a recluse since the young marquess had been killed in Spain. Clare, the elder sister, was firmly on the shelf. But Bella had always wanted to escape Falcott House. The minute she put off her mourning for her brother she began to pester her mother for a Season. Finally, the dowager marchioness gave in. But Bella was twenty-one now, long in the tooth for a debutante, and if she was only to have one Season she needed to make the most of it. Having a penniless friend in deep mourning descend on her would cause her nothing but trouble.

Now it was dinner time. Eamon was scowling at his plate

and pushing his food around with his fork, making a paste of his meal. Julia eyed him analytically. He was revolting, but she was fairly certain that he wasn't actually dangerous. The real danger was to her reputation. The country society round about would forgive a week or two of domestic irregularity as the new earl settled in. But it had already been ten days since Grandfather's death, and Eamon had shut the house to visitors. Before long the gossip would begin.

Eamon looked up and caught her eye. 'Penny for your thoughts, kitten,' he said. 'Are you thinking of the talisman?'

'No, Cousin. I am thinking of my reputation.'

He waved his fork airily. 'A thing of rags and patches.'

'It pleases you to make fun of it, Cousin, but you should be worried, as I am.'

Eamon snapped his fingers in the air. 'That is what I think of your precious reputation, Cousin. It can hang from a gibbet for all I care.' He pushed his plate away.

It was then that Julia felt something break. It was the taut thread of her patience. 'You,' she said in a low voice, 'are no better than a bastard.'

He raised his glass to her. 'A thrust! But alas, my dear, so easily parried. My parents were married a sure three years before my birth. If any claim to legitimacy is fragile, it is yours. Your runt of a father, marrying a commoner in Scotland? Over the anvil?' He shrugged. 'She is seen by no one. And then they simultaneously perish in a carriage accident?'

Julia gaped at him. 'How dare you question my parents' virtue? Their deaths were tragic. Grandfather had given them his blessing! What you suggest is ludicrous.'

'I did not suggest it, Julia.' Eamon drank and set his glass down carefully. 'You did. I am merely agreeing with you. Your reputation is fragile. Indeed, it is more fragile even than you know. Probably it is already destroyed.'

'You cannot keep me here a prisoner, Cousin. You must appoint a chaperone. And you – we – must accept visitors and invitations and be seen to be sociable, or we shall both become pariahs.'

Eamon rolled his eyes. 'The pariahs of Devon. My dear kitten, who cares? Soon I will find the talisman and be richer than Croesus. I shall marry a diamond, and society will beg me for my very fingernail clippings. And you?' Eamon opened his eyes wide in a look of false concern. 'What will happen to you then?' He stuffed a hunk of bread into his mouth.

Julia didn't answer. But she allowed all her contempt to show in her face as she watched him.

'I shall tell you.' He spoke with his mouth full, spraying masticated crumbs. 'I shall drive you from the gate like a whore, be you one or nay.'

Julia took a sip of wine, impressed that her hand was steady enough to do so. 'You wish to find an aristocratic wife? Who will have you, Cousin? Everyone will say that you have been living in sin with your own young cousin. Furthermore, they will say that you abandoned her when you set out to find a rich wife. I think you will find that most eligible young ladies have better options than that.'

Eamon slammed his fork and knife down on the table. 'I am the Earl of Darchester,' he bellowed. 'The Earl of Darchester! Any woman would be glad to have me. Once I find the talisman I shall make my pick.'

Julia twirled her wine glass recklessly in her fingers. 'But if you don't find it? Which you will not, for it does not exist. What will you do then?' She considered the sparkle of candle-light on the cut crystal. 'After all,' she said, 'who is the Earl of Darchester? Is he well regarded in London? Is he a man of political influence? Is he a man of dashing good looks? Is he such a paragon that he can survive the scandal of a rumoured liaison with the old earl's twenty-two-year-old granddaughter?' Julia took a sip of wine and eyed him over the rim of her glass. Then she spoke again, in a soft voice. 'I believe the answer to all those questions is a firm no, Cousin. I believe that in fact the Earl of Darchester is an ugly man of late middle age, without dash or influence enough to charm a pig.'

She had gone too far. She could see it in his eyes. They were almost popping from his head. Then suddenly everything flew into motion. Eamon was charging down the table, gripping the carving knife, his teeth bared. She scrambled to her feet, but he was upon her, throwing her across the table, sending the china shattering to the floor. She looked wildly around, but the room was empty of servants. She screamed, but his hand was over her mouth and the knife was at her throat. She could feel it pressing into her flesh. His face was inches from hers, his mouth wet and floppy. 'I should have killed you that day in the study,' he hissed, his breath smelling of wine and fish. She stared into his bulging eyes, focusing on the black, blank depths of his pupils. The knife pressed with terrible slowness – it was taking so long – and there was a rushing in her head as a single drop of blood began to trickle down her neck. Why was it so quiet? Why were his blue eyes so fixed? Then she caught sight of the wall sconce behind him; the flames were entirely still. It was Grandfather. He was saving her from beyond the grave, stopping time. 'Grandfather,' she whispered, afraid to move lest the knife be pressed further. 'I am here.'

But there was no answer. She was alone. With infinite care she reached up and turned Eamon's unresisting hand so that the flat edge of the knife rested against her throat. Time had stopped still, but Grandfather was dead and gone. She took a slow, deep breath and exhaled it, her mind and body flooding with sudden understanding.

'It is me,' she whispered into Eamon's frozen face. 'I am the Talisman.'

7

Soon Nick could feel it whenever Arkady or Alice stopped time. It became impossible for them to catch him unawares, though they tested him constantly. He could even feel it when he was in another room or far away across the house. At that distance he was not caught up in the aura of their manipulations, but he knew that somewhere close by someone had altered the flow of time. It felt like swimming in a river and sensing a different current a few feet away without actually being in it.

He described it that way over dinner one night, and Alice lit up.

'Yes. Remember when I held your hand and said that time is like a river?'

'You held his hand?' Arkady shot a look at his wife. 'When was this?'

'Oh, shut up,' she said. She leaned over the table and gestured at Nick, a leaf of lettuce speared on her fork. 'The River of Time. It seems to flow in one direction, steadily, inexorably. But there are countercurrents and eddies. Ultimately, and in the big picture, it doesn't matter; the river flows to the sea. Those who know the river, and who use it, know that it moves in complex ways, ways that we can use and even change. Our very bodies swimming in the river alter its flow. But we cannot change it for long, and we cannot change the ultimate truth: the river will run to the sea.'

'That is a pretty image, Alice,' Nick said. 'But what are you trying to tell me?'

'And what about this hand holding, I want to know,' Arkady muttered.

Alice rolled her eyes at her husband, then shook her head at Nick. 'I tell you,' she said, cocking her head in Arkady's direction. 'He is hardly worth it.'

Nick leaned back in his chair and twisted his ring on his finger. 'Yes, your wife held my hand,' he said to Arkady. 'What are you going to do about it?'

The Russian shrugged. 'I kill you.'

Nick raised his glass in a salute, and Arkady raised his. They drank.

Alice, meanwhile, was chewing her lettuce with a bored look on her face. She swallowed, dabbed the corners of her mouth with her napkin and propped her elbows on the table. 'If you two gentlemen are finished with your little male-bonding ritual, I would like to continue my lecture about time and rivers.'

Arkady grunted and dug into his salad.

Nick spread his hands. 'I'm all ears,' he said.

'Such handsome ears,' Alice said, cutting a look at her husband over the rim of her glass as she drank.

Arkady glanced up from his troughing. 'Tonight, you pay for that.'

'Goody. Now be quiet.' Alice turned the full strength of her attention on Nick, her flirting clearly at an end. 'Human history is like a river,' she said. 'Billions of souls all living and loving and working and fighting and dying down through the ages, pushing history before them in a powerful flow made up of tiny particles. They make their choices, have their passions. Some are brilliant or powerful or rich or simply lucky enough to make a change for good, a little bend in the river, a slight deviation. Or for bad. Perhaps more often for bad. But, ultimately, it is the vast power and flow of the river that carries them forward.'

'I'm following you,' Nick said.

'Then there is the strange, unexplained fact of us. The Guild. The people who can jump the river's course. Move backwards and forwards along it, more like . . .' Alice paused, thinking. 'More like a water boatman, perhaps, than a drop of water.'

Arkady snorted. 'I am not an insect.'

'No,' Alice said. 'You would say that time is like a harem of beautiful women and you are like a thief who steals in by moonlight. But this is my account, and in my account we are like water boatmen. We can skate here and there on the surface of the river, but nothing we do can really change its overall course, its powerful drive toward the sea.'

'But we all start with a jump,' Nick said. 'Right?'

'Yes. Every single person who can manipulate time begins by first falling out of time. Jumping. We jump and emerge again somewhere further along. Usually it is something drastic that happens to cause the jump. Our lives are at stake. Mostly, it's war. We are fighting, like you were, or we are caught up in war somehow. Less often, we are consumed by an unbearable grief or a drive towards suicide. We lift the knife. But instead of the great courage it takes to plunge the knife into our breast or face death, we tap into this ability, this talent. And we leap forward decades, centuries. Even sometimes a thousand years.'

'So it is a talent.'

'Yes.'

Nick thought about that for a moment. It was inside him, this thing. But he couldn't find it. Arkady and Alice could use it, but he could not. He spoke again, watching Alice carefully. 'Then that's it for most of us. The Guild gives us a pile of money, life is cushy, and we can never manipulate time again.'

Alice pushed a toasted pecan across her plate. 'Most of us *don't* ever manipulate time again. We *can*. We just don't know that we can.'

'Because the Guild makes sure we don't know.' Nick remembered the Frankish butcher's insistence that there was no way to go back. Nobody could. It was impossible, he had said. Nick remembered the old man's sympathy for his first spasms of grief. 'Does Ricchar Hartmut know that we can go back?'

'Ricchar Hartmut?' Alice put her head on one side, searching her memory. 'The Frankish greeter. Was he the man who met you when you jumped?'

Nick nodded. 'Does he know?'

'No.' Alice looked gravely at Nick. 'He doesn't have security clearance. And I know what you're thinking.'

'That you have an honest, well-intentioned man telling your lies for you.'

'Ricchar is a good man. And yes, he is telling lies for us.'

'How do you live with that?'

'Easily. It's about preserving the safety of our members, and the safety of history itself. It's politics.'

'Politics.'

She nodded.

'Was it politics when you had Leo Quonquont and Meg O'Reilly killed?'

'Who?'

Nick narrowed his eyes. Was she lying? 'Two people who were with me in Santiago. You met them. Remember when you saw me and Leo in that market? We were waiting for Meg to come out of the bathroom?'

'No, I'm sorry. I don't remember that. My life is very full.'

'Right.' Nick glared at his untouched salad. It was drizzled with raspberry vinaigrette, a modern concoction that he'd found he simply couldn't stomach. 'Well, it doesn't matter whether or not you remember. The point is that the next day they were gone.'

Alice exchanged a quick glance with Arkady. 'Leo Quonquont and Meg O'Reilly. Was he the Native American who learned languages so quickly? And she was the hungry Irish woman? Yes, I remember them now. I remember hearing that they'd left the compound. I'm sorry.'

'You heard that they'd left. And that was fine with you? You didn't kill them?'

'Of course not.' Alice held his gaze, and her face seemed composed and confident. 'This isn't really about them, is it? You thought the Guild killed them, and yet you didn't yell about it back then. You've taken Guild money for years, lived your comfortable life. What are you really upset about?'

Nick leaned back in his chair and rubbed his eyes with the heels of his hands. She was right, damn it. He wasn't upset about Leo and Meg, or at least not more than usual. He was upset that the Guild had disturbed his peace and quiet. He wanted nothing more than to go back to that comfortable, uncomplicated life he had built for himself on Guild money. His house in Vermont, Thruppenny Farm, his loft in SoHo, his series of lovers. He wanted to forget Leo, forget Meg, forget the Guild. Forget these new revelations, forget the possibility that he might return. He wanted to forget his past, forget . . .

But there was no forgetting the war. Those dreams followed him across the centuries. And the girl with the dark eyes. She was always there, too. Wherever, whenever he was.

'How did your estate, the marquessate, make its money?'

Nick dropped his hands from his eyes and looked at Alice in some confusion. 'Tenant farming. What does this have to do with the Guild?'

94

'Tenant farming? Really? You were a very rich man, my lord. You made all your money from your land?'

'I don't know. It's been years since I thought about it.' Nick shrugged. 'The years of war were good for the landed gentry. Corn prices were high since we were shut off from the rest of the world. But other than that? Investments. Trade, I suppose.'

Alice laid her fork down with a clink. 'Investments where? Trade in what? Sugar, perchance?'

Nick sat up straight in his chair. 'I had no slaves, Alice.'

'Are you sure of that?' She raised her eyebrows. 'You had no investments whatsoever in the West Indies? Come now, my lord. How far away is Falcott House from Bristol? Are you telling me you were a Devonshire marquess and an abolitionist? Don't lie to me, because I already know everything about you, both past and present. You profited, if only indirectly, from slavery. You know it now, but more importantly, you *knew* it then.'

'The slave trade was abolished in 1807,' Nick muttered. 'Everyone knew British slavery itself would end soon . . .'

'Because of you? Because of your labours?'

'It's not a fair argument.' Nick twitched his cuffs into place and laid his hands on either side of his plate, ready to push up and away. 'Believe me, I have suffered over my failings. Besides, what does slavery have to do with the Guild? Are you trying to tell me that the accident of my birth makes me more guilty than you of perpetrating lies? You are the Alderwoman. You can choose to tell us the truth.'

'You were a marquess. You could have chosen to divest your investments. You could have chosen to take your seat in the House of Lords instead of rushing off to a war that didn't need you. You could have worked with Wilberforce and the abolitionists to make a difference. Instead . . .'

Nick sank back into his chair and put out a hand. 'Please.' He sat in silence for a moment. 'Allow me to pronounce my own guilt. I was an aristocrat. It was an inherited burden, and I was not equal to it, Alice. I was not equal to it. I fucked it up. I ran away. I ran away from war, too, when I jumped. Like a coward. I ran away to this barren future. I'm sorry I wasn't an abolitionist. I'm sorry I'm not your man now. And I'm not, Alice.'

Alice pursed her lips, then picked up her fork again and ate her final bite of salad. When she had swallowed, she wiped her mouth with her napkin and looked Nick straight in the eye. 'Perhaps when you go back and are the Marquess of Blackdown again you will have a chance to be our man. A chance to . . .' She paused. 'Unfuck it up in some small way? But remember. The river runs to the sea. You won't be able to change the things that will now seem abhorrent to you. You won't be able to avoid eating sugar made by slaves. You won't be able to avoid wearing shirts sewn by women who are going blind to make those tiny white stitches in your fine white linen. You won't be able to give your sisters the vote or send them to university. You won't be able to halt the march of industry that will destroy the livelihood of your tenants, nor will you be able to prevent the pollution that will kill the fish in your streams. You will know about these things, and you will do what you think is best with the knowledge you have. You will try to protect that which you love and those whom you love. But you will also make choices that go against your principles. You will – yes, you will – you will tell lies, my lord. Just as I do.'

Alice held Nick's gaze for a long time. Then she turned to her husband and pointedly changed the subject.

Nick ate a few bites of his nauseating salad, spiralling into misery as he listened with half an ear to Alice and Arkady's laughing conversation. They had seen a revival of *School for Scandal* last week and they couldn't stop rehashing the best bits between them.

Julia lay for a few breaths beneath the knife. She was the Talisman! She had been the thing that enhanced Grandfather's power. Now it turned out that she could stop time all on her own. If he had known that, perhaps he would have told her more. She swallowed, feeling the flat side of the knife against her throat. Pretend, Grandfather had said. Pretend not to be the Talisman, the Talisman you don't know you are.

Grandfather had left her alone and in wretched ignorance. Grief and anger and panic rose like the three Furies in her breast.

She had no idea how to start time up again. And once it did so, she had no idea how to avoid having her throat cut by Eamon, who would simply pick up where he had left off.

She could slip out from under the knife and run away, leaving time to start up again on its own accord. But then he would know that she was the Talisman. And once he knew, Julia doubted she had enough control of her power to freeze him in his tracks every time he came at her.

She could take his purse. This instant. Take his purse and enough of the family silver to sell. Take a horse from the stables and flee. Perhaps she could somehow gather enough money to leave the country. She could go to live in America, or Italy.

But why should she be the one to run? She had done nothing wrong.

She could kill him. Here and now. Take the knife and plunge it into his heart.

She turned her head slightly and looked out of the window, into the dusk. The treetops were moving in the wind. Time was only stopped here, in this room, and indeed, that was how it always had been when Grandfather did it. A local pause or acceleration, of only a few moments' duration. How long could she hold time back? Perhaps it would simply start up again on its own, at any second, and she would die after all.

Think, Julia, she told herself fiercely. Think about what to *do*. Grandfather had stopped time, and he had sped it up. He had sped it up and made his own death come more quickly. But was it possible to make it run backwards? Perhaps she could wind time back, like yarn into a ball, to the moment before she had so rashly aggravated Eamon. Perhaps it couldn't be done. Grandfather had never done it before, at least not in her presence. Perhaps it wasn't possible. But it was worth a try.

Julia took a deep breath and focused again on Eamon's frozen pupils. Go back, she whispered. Go back.

Nothing happened. She let her breath out and tried to remember how it had felt when Grandfather had played with time. He had always focused on something inconsequential, like dust motes. She closed her eyes and slowed her breathing. Then she opened them and let her eyes rest on a little pagoda in the Chinese wallpaper, under the wall sconce. Grandfather, she thought, recalling his smiling face. Winking roguishly before doing his trick.

There it was. There was the rushing at the back of her head, and time began to reverse, ponderous, reluctant, like a team of oxen being made to back up in a furrow. But it was happening. It was like looking out through misty, rainy window glass. Eamon pulled away and melted down the table to his seat.

Julia closed her eyes in relief and time resumed its forward push. She reached up and touched her throat. The wound was closed over, with no trace of blood. She opened her eyes. Eamon was pushing his food around with his fork. He looked up and caught her eye. 'Penny for your thoughts, kitten,' he said. 'Are you thinking of the talisman?'

'No,' she said, and quietly sliced a medallion of pork in half.

8

Nick woke fighting with his sheets, the dream tearing away from him like a cat's claws, leaving its thin, raw wounds. The room was dark and close, overheated. He cursed and kicked the sheets aside, then went to the window and hauled it up. He leaned out into the night, gulping in cold winter air.

The house was in St James's Square, almost the only residence among embassies and corporate headquarters. The park itself, filled with mature trees, was unrecognizable to him. Back in 1813 the square had been treeless. In fact, it had been entirely cobbled over in white Purbeck stone. There had been a pool at its centre, protected from animals and bathers by an octagonal iron fence. On that last night, Nick had sauntered away from this house across the stones, the ripe full moon following him in reflection across the pool. He had walked away into London, a free man. Now the Guild wouldn't even let him out of this blasted house.

Nick peered up to see if there was a moon now, and indeed, there she was, visible in spite of the bright glow of the city. She showed only the curve of her full cheek to the wintery world. Nick liked the moon best this way – flirtatious. "'Had we but world enough and time,'" he said to her, "'this coyness, lady, were no crime.'" Quoting poetry to heavenly bodies had once been a fashionable thing for a man to do. Now it was ridiculous . . . but *now* didn't really mean anything to Nick any more. He was locked away in this mansion, like an heirloom. Essentially useless in the present, but strangely valuable to the past and future.

It was only when he pulled back into the bedroom and was shutting the window that the rest of the poem stung him like a wasp. He whispered, his breath clouding the glass: "'Time's wingèd chariot . . . deserts of vast eternity . . .'" Then he spoke, loudly: "'Let us roll all our strength and all our sweetness up into one ball, and tear our pleasures with rough strife through the iron gates of life: thus, though we cannot make our sun stand still, yet we will make him run!'"

Nick stared at the white screen his breath had made. He put his hand on the lean flesh below his ribs; his skin was cold, for the window was still half open, but he could feel the heat beneath. His liver. Once upon a time he had believed that his liver was the origin of his courage and hope and love. All three spreading through him, warm and wet, in his blood. He almost believed it even tonight, as the brave heat in the core of him fought against the freezing night air.

Strength and sweetness. The iron gates of life.

Nick slammed the window shut and turned to grab at his clothes, flung across a chair. Fuck the rules, fuck this inertia. He couldn't *not* go down into his city, he couldn't not see what time had done to it.

Walking out the front door of the mansion set off a braying alarm, but let them send the time police after him. He wagered he could lose them for a few hours, anyway. He trotted down the steps as he had two hundred years ago and headed through the bleak predawn for Pall Mall. He was going, of course, to the river. Pall Mall to Cockspur Street, then down Hungerford Street to the Hungerford Stairs. A matter of a few minutes' walk.

But first, as he emerged out of the square and onto Pall Mall, he had to confront the fact that Carlton House, the prince's palace and the glittering hub of the social universe, was gone. He stared at the white buildings that stood on the old palace's gardens. They gleamed in the phosphorous glow of the street lamps like the grin of a skull. This avenue of mausoleums wasn't living, breathing London any more. The city had to be alive and changing and vital somewhere else. Nick glanced up at the moon, then thrust his hands into his pockets and turned left. Find the river, find the city.

He walked quickly through the too-grand grandeur, around the engorged curve of Cockspur Street . . . and there weren't the Royal Mews. Lions, fountains, the towering column – so *this* was Trafalgar Square. And that grand building, presiding over the square – wasn't that Carlton House's portico stuck on its front? That building was sporting Carlton House's façade like a tattered columbine mask! Nick laughed out loud. And St Martin's, which used to thrust its steeple up out of the melee of stables like a drowning arm, now stood exposed, a pretty toy church. In fact, Nick thought, it all looked as if an enormous child had dropped building blocks and stuffed lions and toy buses here.

Walking quickly, he navigated the deserted roundabout at the bottom of the square. A single cab blazoned with an ad for *The Book of Mormon* span past him, beeped a question, then whizzed away into the night. Hungerford Street . . . it should be here.

It wasn't. Hungerford Street no longer existed, far less its noisome stairs down to the river, which had cut between rotting houses swarming with rats. There had been a blacking factory there at the bottom. Well. No more.

Nick set off down Whitehall, assuming he could find the Whitehall Stairs, if they still existed, or get down to the water at Westminster Bridge. His steps slowed as he approached the Horse Guards, where he had been transformed into a fighting man. It looked the same. The single guard standing at stiff attention outside the gates was the only other living person in this street studded with monuments. Nick repressed a mad desire to stop and tell the young man his story. But he only nodded as he passed and kept on walking, all the way down to the new Houses of Parliament, which looked, he thought, like the radiators in his SoHo loft. He turned left and headed across the bridge, reasoning that he could find his way down to the river on the other side.

Eventually, past the enormous wheel and the concrete theatre complex, he found a broad concrete staircase that led him down to where he wanted to be, among the pipe stems and twisted net, the bits of rope and the shattered bricks that made up the river's rough bed. Nick took a deep, happy breath as his feet found their level in the debris. He stood by the Thames for a long time, watching its waters glide at their own sweet will through the mighty heart of London.

It was maybe a half-hour or more later when he finally came out of his reverie. He bent, stiff with cold, to pick up the perfect bowl of a pipe that his foot had uncovered. As his fingers closed around the smooth clay form, the hair lifted at the back of his neck. He was being watched.

Nick took his time. He straightened up with the pipe in hand – it was more intact than he had at first seen; only the end of the stem was broken off. He turned it over in his fingers, this little relic of his own era, then let it fall. He turned and scanned the embankment with a casual air. Men and women were beginning to hurry by on their way to work. A few people were leaning against the railing, looking across the river at the city. Was one of them the Guild's spy? He passed his eyes across two young Asian tourists, the woman looking out toward St Paul's, the man with his iPhone lifted. A jogger taking a rest and swigging from a red bottle. A trio of teenagers in school uniform, smoking cigarettes.

Then he saw him. Not on the embankment, but standing

halfway down the steps to the river. The thick brown hair was the same, and the big, meaty body. This time the suit was an absurd three-piece concoction of pale green tweed. The trousers were plus fours, of all the unbelievable things. Mustard-coloured socks, brown brogues . . . and big, mirrored aviator glasses.

Mr Mibbs.

How he thought he could blend in, Nick didn't know. Or perhaps he wasn't trying to, for when Nick caught sight of him he made no motion to pretend he wasn't staring. Nick almost raised a hand and waved, but that blank, mirrored stare reminded him of how he had felt the first time he had seen the man, all those years ago in Chile. And the way that Leo had warned him away when Nick started to approach. And what Leo had said about Mibbs and stolen babies later on.

Nick turned back to the river. So Leo was right. Mibbs was some kind of Guild official. Probably police, or a spy, though you could hardly describe him as 'plain clothes'. His taste was atrocious.

Well, let him follow. Nick had no intention of going back to St James's Square any time soon. He was playing truant today, and Mibbs was welcome to watch.

That night Julia exulted in her ability. Locked in her bedchamber, long after the household was asleep, she lit five candles around her room so that she could measure the strength of her ability to freeze time. She stood on the bed, holding another candle. For a moment she watched their flames tremble. Then she willed them to stop.

And stop they did.

Excitement bubbled up in her and spilled over, like boiling milk. She gave in to joy, dancing on her bed in the midst of the stalled moment, twirling with her candle held high, its flame still as a painting, her loose hair spinning around her face and shoulders.

"'I drink the air before me!'"

She pointed her finger dramatically and started time again in a wave, beginning with the candle by the door and bringing each flame back to life one by one.

A moment later she lay on the bed, staring at the ceiling, time moving sedately about her. Her soul was rigid with fear. This was rough magic.

At first it was mildly amusing, leading Mibbs around the city. The man was nothing if not persistent, plodding along a block behind as Nick wandered through the streets, getting reacquainted with London. Nick would catch sight of him now and then in a shop window, his hands always flat at his sides, his mirrored glasses glinting in the sun. Then he would forget about him for ten or fifteen minutes at a time. After all, he was in London and there was so much more to pay attention to than one badly dressed Guild thug.

But Nick quickly realized that London wasn't his city any more. Many Georgian houses remained, and many were missing, knocked out like teeth by bombs or Victorians. Those that did remain weren't being used as houses; nobody seemed to live in the centre of town, though the place was teeming with humanity. Nick cut up through Seven Dials and knew for certain: this new city had long forgotten Nicholas Falcott, Marquess of Blackdown, and Nick Davenant was a tourist here, among thousands of other tourists. He stepped into a thronged coffee shop and elbowed his way towards an organic sausage roll and something called a 'flat white'. He paid with his Amtrak Guest Rewards card and wondered, as the espresso machine shrieked, if he would ever board the

Vermonter at Penn Station and rattle over the river and through the woods to his little house again.

After breakfast he stopped counting the things that weren't there, stopped even noticing what remained. He allowed himself to be entirely in the twenty-first-century present, appreciating London for what it now was, not what it had once been. Sometimes a proud blue plaque informed him of where an important person of his generation had lived, but the news of their sober achievements didn't tend to match up with Nick's personal library of information. He smiled to himself, reading that William Lamb, that cuckold and spanker of chambermaids, had apparently gone on to become prime minister in 1834. For a giddy moment Nick imagined himself texting Lamb across the ages: 'omg! u r pm!' And receiving one back: '1834 rocks!'

He wandered northwards, pleased with himself and with the world. The London of his time had petered out just about here, into open fields and pretty villages. How delightful to have missed the decades across which the countryside was desecrated by adipose Victorian sprawl. Now, all that smug, ruddy architecture was venerably antique and crumbling. Nick thought with wicked pleasure of the two or three British generations that had followed his own, and for whom he had developed an antipathy since jumping to the future. They were all pushing up daisies in Highgate Cemetery now. Nick straightened his cuffs and lengthened his stride. He was in the mood for a long walk; maybe he'd go and visit them. Then have a pint in a pub somewhere, and totter home to Alice and Arkady in time for tea. He began to sing under his breath: '"Here I am one and still will be, who spends his days in pleasure! My tailor's bill is seldom filled; he's never took my measure!"'

But when he reached Euston Road, he hit a wall.

It was a wall of fear, and it strangled Nick's little song in his throat. He could look across the streaming traffic to the pagoda roofs of the British Library easily enough. But his heart was slamming against his ribs, and panic seized his limbs. He gasped for air and stumbled backwards. As he did so, the fear dissipated, like mist.

He looked over his shoulder and there was Mibbs, a few yards back, standing in the middle of the pavement. He looked as gormless as a Belisha beacon.

But he didn't have his glasses on.

Nick twisted abruptly to face Euston again. He breathed in and out, forcing himself into a sort of electrified calm. As the light changed, he stepped forward.

And was slammed with terror, exactly like before.

Staggering back, he watched as a few pedestrians crossed over to the library, leaving him behind. They looked happy enough, with their computer bags slung over their arms. Academics, off to spend the day nose deep in books about the past.

It was Mibbs, of course, holding him back with those terrible eyes. Nick wasn't leading him a merry chase through London. This wasn't *A Hard Day's Night*. Mibbs was the master here. Nick simply hadn't realized that he was the one on a leash.

He rubbed the back of his neck and glanced casually over his shoulder. No glasses. Right. Nick turned smartly, following Euston Road instead of crossing it. He kept his gait the same, looked around him with the same interest as before, but every sense was focused now on the man behind him.

So. The Guild could control him through thought manipulation. Leo had described it all those years ago in Chile. Nick felt as if the back of his head had been taken off and a probe stuck into his grey matter.

Nick tested his theory of the invisible cage by trying to cross Euston Road again at the next light. St Pancras Station was right there, like a gothic House Beautiful. If Nick could only get to it, he might climb on a train to France. Run away. He nursed that feeling, feeding it images of good wine and cheese, beautiful French women . . . and tried to propel himself into the street when the light changed. But no. A chasm seemed to yawn over the edge of the kerb. So he stepped away, smiling lightly in Mibbs's direction. The man might be able to control Nick's movements, but he wouldn't get the satisfaction of seeing him sweat.

Nick let the crowds surge past him and across the street, then turned back south, down Judd Street, watching out of the corner of his eye as Mibbs put his shades back on and stepped after him.

Interesting. Glasses back on. So was Mibbs's naked gaze driving him somewhere in particular or only keeping him within the fucking Congestion Charge Zone?

At the end of Hunter Street he stood still for a moment, waiting to see if Mibbs was going to direct him again. But he felt nothing. All right; he was clearly free to roam, within certain boundaries. Arkady and Alice were probably waiting in St James's Square and Mibbs was their equivalent of an electric fence, making sure Nick didn't go far. That was humiliating, to be sure, but it wasn't life-threatening. Nick's battle-readiness faded, and he turned and held up his hands to show that he surrendered. Mibbs was eight feet away. Nick could see himself in those mirrored shades, small and belligerent. He wheeled around again.

Which way? He was facing Guilford Street . . . Guilford Street . . . he searched his memory.

Guilford Street! The Foundling Hospital. It should be right there.

But when he looked to the left he could see that the great curving walls that used to enclose the grounds were gone. Nick crossed the street, staring. Not only the walls, but the imposing dormitories themselves and the grand central hall that had joined them – all gone. Nick walked slowly along the iron fence that now enclosed a large park until he reached the entrance. Here was the marble centrepiece to the grand double gateway that had once stood here. One lonely little relic of the single most imposing monument erected by eighteenth-century benevolence.

The Foundling Hospital had been a favourite charity of his mother's, and Nick well remembered being seven or eight years old and going on visitor's day in the grand Blackdown carriage, his mother glorious in her enormous wig, to look at the children all scrubbed and regimented for presentation. At the end of their visit, they had seen a few women bringing infants to this gateway. Back then the marble had been decorated with a compass rose, and a man stood before it, receiving the little ones. The mothers had to put their hand into a bag and draw out a coloured ball. Two women drew out black balls; they had to take their babies away. The third drew out a white ball, and the man reached out and took the little baby from her with a tenderness that fascinated Nick. The mother left a jet button with her newborn, as identification in case she ever had the means to come back and claim him.

Nicholas's mother stepped forward after the woman turned away and asked the man at the gate if the baby had a name. He explained that all babies were named anew upon being accepted, and Nick's mother said that the child must be named Nicholas, 'for my son, who will be a marquess one day'. She tugged Nick forward: 'Come and see your namesake.' The baby's white-blond hair stood up all around his head in a frothy cloud, exactly like Nick's mother's wig. Nick laughed when he saw it. His mother asked why he laughed, and when he told her, she laughed too. Then they watched as the man entered the new name in a big book: Nicholas Marquess – black button.

Now Nick stood again on the spot where Nicholas Marquess had lost his mother and gained his name, and where Nicholas Falcott had laughed with his mother, the only time he could remember sharing a joke with her. A heartless joke – and yet they had felt so good about themselves, going to see the foundlings. He read the sign adorning the simple iron gate that now opened into the park: CORAM'S FIELDS: NO ADULTS UNLESS ACCOMPANIED BY A CHILD.

Nick put his hand to the gate, wanting to feel the cold of it against his fingers. He peered in at the empty football pitches, the bare trees. Blinking, he realized that tears were in his eyes. Then he felt a pressure on his arm and his feelings lost their footing: He hung over an abyss of fathomless despair, and he felt it sucking him downward . . . he cried out as every joy was lifted from him as gently and as easily . . .

Nick clung now to the iron gates with both hands, his vision narrowing, darkening, a terrible vertigo rushing in his ears. From far away somewhere, chattering, like the sound of children's voices, a fading echo of pleasure . . . if he could just tear through these iron bars, just him . . .

With a last effort he summoned up those calm, dark eyes . . . calm, dark eyes . . . and he forced his own vision to focus. There, just beside him, Mibbs's face. Mibbs's breath on his face. Mibbs's hand on his arm. Mibbs was holding him poised above the pit, as easily as he might hold a spider over a flame, and his eyes burned toward Nick. In a moment the fire would singe the thread, burn it asunder . . .

And then Nick was gasping and cursing before he even

registered that someone had tossed cold water in his face. He twisted, breaking Mibbs's hold: 'Shit!' He blinked water away from his eyes. 'What was that?' He meant the crushing grief. He meant Mibbs's touch.

But by the time he could really focus, Mibbs had melted away across the street, and a young Japanese woman was trying to wipe at Nick's face, prettily accented apologies spilling from her lips. She had dropped her handbag and tossed the contents of her water bottle up and over Nick, and now she was torn between drying him off and collecting her scattered belongings from the pavement. Her arsehole boyfriend laughed and took her picture.

Nick dropped down and started retrieving her things.

'I'm so sorry,' she said, and crouched down, too.

'It's okay.' Nick handed over her pocket-sized *A–Z* street guide. 'I needed the shock. I wasn't feeling well.'

She took the book and smiled at him. She was lovely, but more than that she wore sparkly eyeshadow, and the things they were gathering up were contemporary. A phone. Some ballpoint pens. As she tucked them into her bag, he felt as if he were being tucked back with them into the twenty-first century. His heartbeat slowed.

Ah. A cellophane pack of tissues. 'May I?' Nick extracted one and wiped the remaining water from his face, looking up in disbelief at the boyfriend, who was still going at it with the digital camera. 'Your boyfriend is a jerk,' Nick said as the woman leaned toward him for a pound coin that had rolled between his feet.

She laughed, glancing up, and was even lovelier than before. 'He is my brother,' she said.

'Oh, really?'

'Yes.'

Nick handed her the bag, now fully reassembled. He stood

and put out a hand to pull her up. 'You must find a better travelling companion next time you come to London.'

She held his hand for a moment after she rose; she had that look in her eyes. Nick smiled down at her, well-being seeping back into his soul. She had given him all he could ask for with that warm glance, so unlike Mibbs's terrible blue stare. 'Thank you,' he said, and bowed, like a marquess.

He straightened and watched as she walked away, expostulating with her brother in Japanese.

Then he turned and looked for Mr Mibbs.

He was gone.

9

Julia woke the next morning fired with purpose. She was the Talisman, but what did that mean? A human talisman . . . it made no sense.

After breakfast, she knocked resolutely on the study door. When Eamon called for her to enter, she threw the door open with a flourish and closed it briskly behind her. Then she turned and froze Eamon where he sat in his chair, his mouth open to demand an explanation. He looked like a trout.

'Hold fast to that thought, Cousin,' she said, and strode past him to the bookshelf. There was Grandfather's copy of *Johnson's Dictionary*, pristine in spite of being over fifty years old: Grandfather had considered himself omniscient.

Julia hooked her finger over the binding of the first heavy volume and then the second, dragging them forth from among their friends. She carried them over to the desk, relieved to see that at least the pages were cut. 'Excuse me,' she said, moving Eamon's arm slightly to give herself room. 'I need to look up the word *talisman*,' she explained, as she flipped open volume two. 'Because we need to know what we're talking about, don't you think? Now that the stakes are a little higher?'

She paged through the dictionary, and after five full pages given over to a definition of the word *take*, she found it. *Talisman*. Blast. The definition was three useless words long. 'A magical character.' She closed the book. What did that mean? A magical character, like in a play?

She cracked volume one open, chasing after a new word and smiling when she saw it: *character*. But her smile faded as she drew her finger down the many definitions. 'A mark, a stamp, a representation; a letter used in writing or printing; the hand or manner of writing; the person with his assemblage of qualities; particular constitution of mind.' And then a quote from Pope, to illustrate Johnson's last definition: 'Most women have no *characters* at all.'

'Marvellous,' she said aloud. 'Grand. Look here, Eamon, I believe you will appreciate this titbit of wisdom. What's that you say? Cat got your tongue? How sad.' She slammed the book shut.

Julia hauled the dictionary back to the shelf and pushed the two volumes into place. Then she positioned herself in front of the closed door. '"Hark, hark, the watch-dogs bark," Eamon!' He gaped blindly at her, and she laughed. Then she started time up again.

Words spilled from his lips: 'Get out of here!'

Julia curtseyed low. 'I am sorry to intrude upon you, Cousin. I wondered only if I might search for a word in the dictionary.'

'Get out!'

The problem, she decided five minutes later, as she stared out the window of the yellow saloon, lay in the definition of the word *character*. If she was a magical character in her own right – 'the person with his assemblage of qualities' – then she was in control of her talent. It was hers to use and no one else's. And indeed, she was clearly able to use her power herself. But if she was a magical character in the sense of 'a representation, or a letter used in printing', then her talent could be used by someone else. Writing was a method for channelling meaning from one mind to another, and she suspected that a talisman worked like writing – to channel magic, not to make it.

She was like Ariel, in other words. A magical character in

and of herself, but also bound to do the will of another, should she meet and fall afoul of a Prospero.

Pretend, Grandfather had said. It was the only thing he had ever said to her that might be information about her power, and it was beginning to seem like sound advice indeed.

Julia sighed onto a windowpane, then drew a sweeping *J* in the mist.

Nick pushed open the door to the house in St James's Square, half expecting to find Alice and Arkady waiting for him like angry parents. But the foyer was deserted. Nick headed to the kitchen to make himself some tea and eventually found the two older people in the parlour, sitting cosily around their own tea tray. 'Nick!' Alice looked delighted to see him, as if he hadn't broken her rule about leaving the house.

Arkady twisted round and beamed.

'Hi,' Nick said. 'How are you guys?'

'Fine, fine.' Alice held out a hand and Nick strolled over and took it. She squeezed his fingers. 'I see you have a cup of something – won't you join us?'

Nick settled into the chair that matched Alice's and took a sip of his tea. He eyed his hosts over the rim of his cup. They wore matching expressions of almost comical benevolence. So they were playing Mum and Dad after all, just in an amiable vein. They looked like June and Ward Cleaver, getting ready to deliver the moral lesson of the episode. Don't wander too far from home, Beaver, or Mr Mibbs will control your mind!

'So,' Alice said, 'what did you do today? Go anywhere in particular?'

He gave Alice his thinnest smile. 'Come now. You know what I did. I ran away.'

'But of course,' Arkady said. 'We knew you would. What kind of man would stay, day after day?'

Nick leaned back in his chair and stretched his legs out, crossing them at the ankle. 'So this was a test of my manhood. Well played, me.'

'Bah! Of course it was not a test. I only say, how strange it would be if you did not break free. And you did. Off you went. All my wife does, like a civilized person, is ask where did you go.'

'You know perfectly well where I went. You had me tailed.'

Alice laughed. 'How wonderful that you noticed. You see, Arkady? I told you he would realize. He's very clever.'

'Do you mean to tell me your man was supposed to be subtle?' Nick snorted as Mibbs's villainous yellow socks rose up in his imagination, the hair like Donny Osmond's, the psychedelic Bertie Wooster suit.

'I'm pleasantly surprised, that's all.'

'Okay . . .' Nick frowned, wondering what joy she could possibly be deriving from the misery he had endured by the gates of the Foundling Hospital. 'Whatever. The point is, you know exactly where I went. And you know what happened.'

'Yes,' Arkady said. 'That – how should I put it? – that mishap in Guilford Street.'

'We're so relieved it came to nothing.' Alice leaned forward, her teacup cradled in her hands like an egg. 'We weren't having you followed for the fun of it. It was for your own safety.'

'Is that how you're going to spin this?'

'It's true. Alone all day in London – eventually you were bound to get sucked into your emotions.'

That fear at Euston Road and then that despair on Guilford Street – those had been his fault somehow? Because he couldn't handle London? 'That's bullshit,' he said. 'I'm in perfect control of my feelings. And those feelings weren't my feelings at all. They were forced on me.'

Alice sighed. 'Of course you are in control. Most of the time. But you are a time traveller, Nick, and your emotions are your time machine. That's how it works.'

He raised his eyebrows and stared at her.

She smiled serenely, as if she hadn't just said something unbelievable. 'Normally your feelings are calibrated to keep you in the present, ticking over from moment to moment. But they also can propel you forward and pull you back. Don't you see? We do it with feelings. That's why we keep Guild members away from their homelands. Yearning, nostalgia, loss, loneliness – these are all superhighways back to the past. Your emotions can be overwhelming when you're in a place that once was familiar to you. Without training, without proper understanding . . . well. It can be dangerous. If time is a river, it is a deep and a strong one. It is easy to drown, easy to get swept away.'

'Feelings.' Nick shook his head. 'We do it with feelings.' He snorted, then laughed out loud. 'That's absurd!'

'I don't know why you're being so scornful,' Alice said. 'You should appreciate it. You're from the Romantic era. "Felt in the blood, and felt along the heart . . . the affections gently lead us on."'

'Oh, please. And anyway, I favour the metaphysical poets.'

'Fair enough. But surely you understand; we couldn't let you trot off into London all alone. We needed somebody near you to keep you from slipping away. You were bound to have a moment or two of intense longing for the past. And you did. In Guilford Street.'

Nick blew a long breath out between his teeth. 'I'm sorry, Alice. But your lies don't become you. If those were my feelings, emanating from my heart, I'll eat my hat. And if that spy of yours, that atrocity in tweeds, is your idea of a gentle guiding hand . . .'

Alice's face was as blank as a sheet of foolscap.

'You're pretending to have no idea what I'm talking about.' Nick got to his feet. 'Well, I can't say I'm surprised, not after what I learned about you over dinner last night. The Guild and its deep dark secrets.' A shadow of that terrible despair he had experienced outside the Foundling Hospital fell over him, and he passed a hand over his face. 'This is all bullshit. I'm tired and I need to be alone.'

'Wait.' Alice held a hand out. 'Please. Sit down. Atrocity in tweeds? Who?'

'Your spy. Mr Mibbs.'

'Mr Mibbs?' Alice frowned and glanced at her husband. He shrugged.

'Oh, God, I don't know his real name, but your secret-police guy. That big lummox who followed me. Or rather, who walked me, like a dog, through the city. And then punished me like a dog. Took me down right there in the street. Don't tell me, Alderwoman, that he was saving me from my emotions. Don't try to tell me you don't know exactly what he put me through. For Christ's sake, I thought I would never feel joy again. If it hadn't been for a nice girl who dumped her water over me . . . to be honest, I don't know what might have happened. I don't know if he was killing me with sadness, or stealing my heart, or what. So now tell me your lies, Alice.' Nick shoved his hands in his pockets and prepared to listen. 'Go on. Tell me a different story, one I believe. Explain it all away.'

Alice and Arkady stared up at him like he was a ghost. Then after what felt like a year, Alice said, 'That woman who splashed you, do you remember anything about her?'

'Yes. Sure. She was lovely. Japanese. Her brother was a total dick and kept taking her picture.'

Alice nodded, comprehension writing itself again across her expression. 'Sit down, Nick. No, really. This is very serious. I don't know this Mr Mibbs person. That woman and her brother, they were the ones trailing you for us.'

Nick blinked, thinking about that for a moment, then dismissing it. 'Oh, sure. That's good.'

'No, but really. They were.' Alice was digging her iPhone out from where it was tucked in beside her and turning it on. 'Here.' She held it up to Nick and he saw a map of central London, with the route he had taken perfectly traced out in red through the streets. Then she tapped again at the screen and handed him the phone. There was a photo of himself and the girl, crouching over her purse. 'Kumiko texted right away to say you had a fit in Guilford Street. She said she thought you were about to jump. That would have been a disaster; you are totally untrained. You might have disappeared into the River of Time and been lost. She saved you with that stunt of hers.'

Nick sank down into his chair and stared owlishly at the photo.

Alice kept talking. 'Their names are Kumiko and Shuchiro. They're new, fresh from training. Brother-and-sister team. Twins, actually. Extremely rare, for siblings to jump together. A strong connection. They are very useful to us.'

Kumiko and Shuchiro: the Asian tourists on the embankment. Nick Davenant: total dick. He scrolled back through Shuchiro's pictures. Another of the purse gathering, then one of him gripping the gate, looking weak in the knees. He flipped back more quickly. A picture of him standing at the crossing at Euston Road, then one of him sipping his coffee in Seven Dials. All the way back to a picture or two of him on the banks of the Thames, staring at the water. But not a single one with Mibbs.

He looked up from the phone. 'Where is Kumiko now? I want to ask her something. Can you call her?'

'Yes, of course.' Alice took the phone back and tapped at it. 'Hello, Shuchiro, this is Alderwoman Gacoki. Yes. Thank you for your work today. Is Kumiko with you? May I speak to her please? Thank you.' She nodded to Nick and handed him the phone. 'She'll be on in a minute.'

Nick held the phone to his ear, waiting. Soon enough he heard that accent again, but the voice was stronger, more self-assured. 'Hello? This is Kumiko.'

'Hi, Kumiko. No, this isn't the Alderwoman. This is Nick Davenant. I'm the guy you trailed today.'

'Oh!' She laughed. 'So you knew?'

'No, no. Actually you had me completely fooled. But listen, do you remember, right before you tossed your water on me – was there a man with me?'

'Yes, there was a man. Trying to help you.'

'That was the only time you noticed him? He was dressed ridiculously – you didn't see him earlier on my walk?'

There was silence as she thought about it. 'Maybe I saw him earlier? I don't know. I still think everyone dresses ridiculously in London.'

'Okay . . . but seriously. What was he doing when you saw him with me?'

'Just bending over you. He must have thought you were going to faint. He came forward before we even realized you were in trouble.'

'Did your brother send all the pictures he took? Do you think he might have a picture of that man? I want to show it to the Alderwoman.'

'Just a moment.' He heard her call to her brother in Japanese. He replied, and after a moment Kumiko spoke again in English. 'Yes, we have a picture. He'll send it right now.'

And indeed, there was the buzz of an incoming text message against his ear, and with it he relaxed; there would be proof. Maybe Alice and Arkady would know who Mibbs was and what he was doing trailing after Nick. 'That's great, thanks so much, Kumiko. And listen, thank you for saving me today. You dragged me right back into the moment. I'm very grateful.'

'No problem.' She paused. 'Are you going to be in London long?'

Nick turned his shoulder to Alice and Arkady, as if that would keep his conversation private. 'Maybe, I don't know. I'm not allowed out, you know. You might have to come save me again.'

She laughed, and he laughed, and then he said maybe dinner some night soon, at which point the phone was snatched from his hand.

'Nick is not available for fraternization, Kumiko,' Alice said, on her feet now and frowning at Nick. 'No. Yes. Thank you.' She poked at the screen to end the call and get to her texts. She looked at her phone for a moment, then handed it to Nick again. 'Is this the man you wanted me to see?'

Unfortunately Mibbs's face wasn't visible in the picture, just the back of his head and his hand, clasping Nick's shoulder. Mibbs looked as if he were a concerned citizen, reaching out to check whether the man leaning drunkenly against a fence was all right. Nick shuddered, remembering the terrible feelings that had flooded him at Mibbs's touch. 'Yes, that's him. That man followed me all day long and toward the end of it he started controlling my mind. Which you didn't tell me you people could do yesterday when you were inducting me into the rites and privileges of Level One security clearance. Nor did you tell me that it is possible to force a man into a sinkhole of despair just by touching him.'

Alice was silent, lost in thought, and Nick noticed that Arkady was watching her with a sort of professional detachment, more like an aide than a husband; Alice was fully the Alderwoman now. She reached wordlessly for the phone. Nick held it out, and Alice made another call. 'Venkatesan, this is the Alderwoman. I'm sending you Kumiko and Shuchiro's photos and notes about our guest's journey this morning. He started out from here at around four thirty a.m. and got back half an hour ago. I want all the CCTV footage of him from the minute he left the house until he returned, and I want you to watch for a big, white man who was following him wearing . . .' She looked up at Nick, her eyebrows aloft.

'A pale-green three-piece suit, tweed. Plus fours. Yellow socks.'

'Green suit. Probably always a block or so behind. You'll see Kumiko and Shuchiro throughout, but apparently they didn't notice this man, so he was crafty. Yes. Yes. His name is Mr Mibbs. No. Today. Now. Wait, I'll ask.' She looked up at Nick. 'What kind of hair?'

'Dark. Thick. American-politician hair. But his name isn't –'

She held up a hand to shush him. 'Dark, thick. Yes. American-politician hair. I want you to put everyone on this. Get me a good image of Mibbs's face in half an hour, and all the footage before the end of the day. Yes. Yes. Good. Goodbye.'

'If the Guild has CCTV cameras all over London, why have me followed?' Nick asked as she hung up.

'So we could save your ungrateful butt,' she said shortly. 'A camera can't throw water in your face.' She tapped at her phone, sending Shuchiro's texts and images on to Venkatesan, whoever that might be. 'And they are not our CCTV cameras. We use the government's.'

'They let you do that?'

Arkady snorted and drained his teacup. 'Little priest. They do not even know we exist.'

Nick paced back and forth in the parlour, telling them everything about Mr Mibbs. Except he kept Leo out of the story. He'd betrayed Leo once already. He wasn't going to do it again.

So he told Alice and Arkady he'd seen Mibbs once in Chile, and had experienced the aura of despair that surrounded him. When he realized that Mibbs was following him in London, he'd just assumed that he was Guild police. Then Mibbs started controlling his mind, and finally pressed Nick into that terrible misery. Nick had assumed that this was how the Guild dealt with malefactors.

Alice shook her head. 'We don't do that. We can't. He read your mind?'

'He put feelings into my head. Like my head was a bowl and he was just ladling them in.'

'Those things you describe, they are impossible,' Arkady said.

'They happened.'

'I do not say you lie. I only say they should not be possible with what we know of our talents.'

Just then Alice got an image through from Venkatesan, and they all three clustered around the little screen to see what he had found. It was a short clip of Mibbs walking across the Millennium Footbridge behind Nick. His mirrored shades were on.

'That man is not in the Guild,' Alice said. 'And he certainly hasn't ever been in the compound in Chile. I would know.'

'He was there,' Nick said. 'Clear as day. I saw him. Dressed in a wide-lapel baby-blue suit.'

She frowned, then called Venkatesan again. 'Send all your images to Chile. Find out if anyone has ever seen him there, in the compound. Maybe dressed in blue.' She turned back to Nick.

'He controlled your mind,' Alice said, as she and Arkady sat back down. 'When his glasses were off? So with his eyes?'

'Yes.'

'We can't do that.'

'So you keep saying.' Nick shrugged.

'But honestly, we can't.'

'All right. But you say he isn't in the Guild. That just means he's some other kind of supernatural freak. He has other weirdo talents. What's so strange about that?'

Alice tossed him an impatient glance. 'We aren't super-heroes, Nick, everyone with a different power. Time has rules. We don't understand them all, but this seems far out of the ordinary. I've never known anyone to do what you describe Mibbs doing.'

'Group control of time,' Arkady said to Alice. 'We can do much more in groups. Maybe he was working with some other people. And Nick, he didn't notice.'

Alice frowned. 'That's a possibility.' She turned to Nick. 'If we work together in a group, we can influence someone for a short period of time. But in a carefully managed environment. Not walking down a street in the middle of the city surrounded by Naturals. Even when we work together, we aren't controlling anyone's mind. We are controlling time, in an interlocking series of microenvironments. It is very complex and requires a team of highly trained people. We aren't invading anyone's actual thoughts.'

'Well, he did.' Nick closed his eyes, trying to remember. 'It wasn't exactly my thoughts he was controlling. It was my feelings. I could think whatever I liked, but I felt what he wanted me to feel. Feelings that weren't really my own. Fear the first time, when I tried to cross Euston Road, and a profound despair the second, when he put his hand on me in Guilford Street.'

'Feelings, not thoughts,' she said.

'Right. And I really don't think there was anyone working with him. I kept a relatively close eye on him all morning.'

'Let me try something on you.' Alice stared at him intently, her lips pressed tightly together. Soon her eyelid began to twitch.

He watched her, finding it increasingly difficult not to smile. 'What are you doing?'

'I'm trying to make you feel desperate to kiss me!' She threw her head back and laughed.

Nick grinned. 'Oh, go on, Alice. You run a secret global organization of time travellers. Surely you can get me to kiss you.'

'Well, yes, I probably can.' Alice held out her hand. 'My lord, would you be so kind?'

Nick sketched her a bow and lifted her elegant fingers to his lips. He kissed them, just above the big ring with its yellow stone.

'Please,' Arkady said. 'Can we talk about the serious thing? The bad feeling, and the way this Mibbs person tried to push Nick through it?'

'Yes, of course.' Alice drew her hand away. 'But surely that isn't the scariest thing about Mibbs. Controlling Nick at Euston Road was far worse. In Guilford Street he was just reaching out for a feeling. Taking another time traveller through time with him. We do that regularly. It's how you'll bring Nick back.'

'Yes, yes,' Arkady said. 'But Nick shouldn't have felt what Mibbs was doing. And on top of that, Nick described despair.

Despair, Alice. We can travel on every emotion, every thread of feeling – except despair.'

'Why not?' Nick asked. 'Unhappiness is pretty powerful.'

'Unhappiness, yes. Unhappiness is powerful and we can travel on it if we must. It is not so nice a trip, perhaps. But despair?' Arkady levelled his eyes at Nick. 'Was it unhappiness you felt today? Or was it total? Was it crushing?'

'It was total,' Nick said.

'You see?' Arkady turned to Alice, spreading his hands. 'Despair.'

'What's so impossible about despair?'

'It has to do with how we feel across time, and how feelings stretch across time,' Alice said. 'You think you're the same moment to moment. You're a guy with kind of a wild life story. But you're pretty much just a dude. Right?'

'Um, I guess so.' Nick pictured his gravestone, in some bleak, lawn-mowed American expanse: JUST A DUDE.

Alice continued. 'But in fact, at every instant you are actually in the process of recalling who you were a second ago and becoming yourself again the next second. In each moment your emotions reinterpret you, invent you anew, move you forward – remember, they are your time machine. Despair is different. The self that has no possibility is in despair. It cannot move. It cannot reinvent itself. It sinks into death.'

'That was death? I might have died?'

'I don't know. Might you have? Did it feel that way?'

'Yes.'

Arkady and Alice looked at one another, then back at Nick, their faces sober. 'Where was this place, this spot on Guilford Street?' Alice asked. 'You mentioned it a moment ago. It might be important to what happened.'

'The Foundling Hospital. Now it is a park: Coram's Fields.

But in my old life it was a home for abandoned children. Unmarried women could bring their babies there and leave them.'

Alice stood up. 'We must go to Guilford Street right away. I need to feel this place.' She held a hand out to Arkady. 'It will be hard for you, my darling. But we must go. It sounds like a scar.'

'A scar?' Nick wondered if he had misheard.

'Yes. Like that dashing one over your eye. Except this is a scar in time. A place where, for a long time, for years on end, many people had the same overpowering emotion. So that the place becomes scarred, or turns in on itself. Do you see? There can be no intervention. No one can enter and no one can leave. It is just . . . a place. Not a place in time. It is a place in despair.'

'And you think that spot on Guilford Street is a scar?'

Alice shrugged. 'The gates of the Foundling Hospital, where for years upon years mothers gave over their children, never to see them again? Yes, I should imagine so. Perhaps you felt that despair in that spot on Guilford Street. Or perhaps Mibbs could use that spot to hurt you.'

Nick thought about the feeling he had almost drowned in a few hours ago, and then he remembered the two women who had chosen black balls out of the bag. The way they had turned with their burdens, their eyes staring, terrified, at some future horror. And how the woman who had chosen a white ball had smiled through her tears and pressed her jet button with such passion into the hand of the man who took her baby. That had been grief, but it had also been a searing kind of hope.

As the Rolls-Royce (made now, Nick remembered after a moment of confusion, by BMW) pulled out of St James's Square and onto Pall Mall, Nick closed the window to shut out the chauffeur. 'Before we get back to Guilford Street,' he told Alice and Arkady, 'I want the truth. I had no clue what was happening to me today, nor how to defend myself. I want you to tell me the rules of time. Not the rules of the Guild. The rules of time.'

'"The wreck and not the story of the wreck,"' Alice said dreamily. '"The thing itself and not the myth."'

'Tell me, Alice. No more of this Level One security clearance malarkey. You are the Alderwoman of the Guild. You know everything.'

Alice looked around the luxurious interior of the Rolls. 'Isn't it incredible? A little girl, stolen by a slaver . . . and now look at me.' She shook her head. 'It never stops being unbelievable, Nick.'

'I do not doubt you.'

She settled down into the leather comforts of her seat. 'The Guild is big and terribly, terribly old, but time is bigger and older and very strange. I will tell you what little we understand, but there are things we can't fathom. And there are people out there, not in the Guild. People who think differently about time. People who are trying to learn to use time to control the world.'

'Ah.' So Leo and Meg had been right. There were others.

'The thing we do know, definitively,' Alice said, 'is that the talent always manifests in a jump forward in time.'

'Why? If we can go back, why do we always go forward first?'

Arkady turned from staring out of the window. 'Because, when you face death, you think: what can I do to save myself? What can I do *next*? You are thinking forward, you are hoping – do you understand me? Thinking and hoping forward, into the future. So you pull yourself there.'

'Okay . . .' Nick frowned. 'I guess I understand that. But what about this big secret – that we can all jump back? How does that work?'

'It is very difficult,' Alice said. 'It takes great concentration and training. You must reach back, back into yearnings and memories and feelings of the past. There are some times and places to which we cannot seem to go. We cannot jump in these places we call scars, where the feeling is carved into the very bedrock. We cannot jump to certain kinds of mass events – the destruction of Carthage, for example – events that are so intense, so complete in and of themselves, that they repel the past and the future. And we can't use despair, which is inert. The feelings we use must reach outwards. They must yearn, either forwards or back.'

'But surely everywhere is a scar. Something terrible must have happened in this very spot. Some caveman killed another on . . .' Nick peered out the car window, looking for a street sign. 'Right here on Shaftesbury Avenue, twenty thousand years ago.'

'Yes, certainly. Every inch of the world has been dappled by sadness and happiness. But I'm not talking about individuals and their feelings. Or even individual deaths. Those are drops of water, Nick. Just little drops. We travel on currents, on collective emotion. The feelings of humanity, not singular humans.'

'But on good feelings, not despair. Happiness.'

129

Alice smiled. 'Happiness! So beautiful, but it is effervescent, individual. Hard to use. But yes, we usually choose to travel on what you might call good feelings, because it is more pleasant to do so. But what is a good feeling? Often that's hard to determine. Everyone's loss is someone else's gain. Everyone's bad time is someone else's good time. Let's say I want to go somewhere where they practise human sacrifice. We can sense the fear of the men who lay, generation after generation, beneath the priest's knife. I could travel on that, but I might rather travel on their courageous exultation in having been chosen. Or most likely I would travel on the relief of the people whose world has been rebalanced by the offering.'

'Good lord.' Nick stared at her placid face. 'Are you kidding? You travel on the feelings of whoever is benefiting from torture and oppression? The cannibal who is delighted with his meal?'

'Or the marquess who enjoys sugar in his tea? You are such a true-blue subject of the Enlightenment, Lord Blackdown. It's really quite endearing. Did I use the words *torture* and *oppression*?'

'Well then, what are you saying?'

'Simply this. We can use any swell of feeling produced by a culture, but feelings of completeness, of satisfaction – we prefer them. But really, no matter the flavour of the feeling, it is its movement, its propulsion away from the moment in which it is felt, that we use.'

The car made a sharp turn, and Nick held on to the strap. 'And I could learn to do this?'

'Yes. If the Guild decides to train you. It takes a long time to learn to jump safely and with precision. I cannot tell you how complicated it is, to find the current that will take you where you want to go. Sometimes the most unlikely feeling will whisk you back. Your capacities for empathy must become so finely calibrated, Nick, that it barely feels like empathy any more. Indeed, sometimes you will feel quite heartless.'

'Cry me a river.'

'You choose to scoff,' Alice said lightly. 'But once you get to the past, the difficulty continues. Arkady will take you back, so you don't have to worry about the journey itself. But you will find it difficult once you are there. For one thing, there will be your old self to contend with. And for another, you will not be able to change the future. Or rather, you will only be able to change the smallest things, things that get subsumed back into the big push of the river without making a difference.'

'No killing Hitler,' Nick said.

'No killing Hitler. No giving Queen Liliuokalani back her Hawai'i, no saving Malcolm X, or Joan of Arc, or the princes in the tower. But smaller things – things that are just the normal, everyday stuff of life? Those things are perfectly possible. Fall in love, have children; who cares? You can even kill someone. These are tiny eddies in the river, nothing more.'

'I can kill "someone", but not Hitler? That doesn't make any sense. Has anyone ever tried to go back – or forward – and kill him?'

'There are only a very few individuals who really change the world, for better or worse, Nick. And it is the river that makes important men and women. Who am I to say – maybe if you were to kill Hitler, the river would simply provide another.'

Nick laughed, incredulous. 'Who are you to say, Alice? You're the Alderwoman!'

Arkady slammed his hands down on his thighs. 'Why

when we talk about time travel do we always have to kill Hitler or not kill Hitler! It is to make Hitler a commonplace! The point is this. You are small and the river is big. Live, love, die, my priest. The river will roll on.'

'It sounds to me as if you wish that were true. And you are afraid it isn't.'

Alice and Arkady stared at him, their lips tightly closed.

'Fine,' Nick said, after a moment of cold silence. 'I shall keep my world-saving ambitions to a minimum, and take care not to sire a race of megalomaniacal killers.'

Something close to bitterness twisted Alice's mouth. 'And you think you are not a member of such a race already?'

'The human race, Alice? Yes, I am a card-carrying member.'

The Alderwoman stared Nick down, and Nick saw her beat a burning rage back to an ember. When she shut her eyes, it was not because she ceded the argument. Her eyelids closed, she spoke in the calm voice of a leader: 'We must change the course of our conversation, for we are in danger of fighting over the meaning of history, rather than protecting its flow.' She opened her eyes again. 'Do you have any more questions about the river, Nick?'

He took a moment to let his own anger cool before speaking. 'You say we cannot change the future. What about reversing time itself? Making it go backwards?'

Alice shook her head. 'Absolutely not. The river of human history – it wants to move forward. It must and it will move forward.' Alice fished a silver flask out of her jacket pocket, winked at Nick and unscrewed the cap. She tipped it back and drank. 'I have just taken a sip of good Kentucky rye. Now think about it. You are able to slip backwards in time, just you and maybe a companion, like swimmers through water. Swimming against the current, as I said. But what would it be like to turn the river itself back, and make me untake that sip of whiskey? To make me undo something I have done? I wanted to drink it. I don't want to undrink it. You would be fighting against my desires, my sense of myself and what I have achieved. You would be fighting against my flows of feeling, my own forward motion down the river. Do you see? It would be an incredible skill, Nick, turning back time. An impossible skill. The river is pushing, pressing. It will not allow a single person to do more than create a ripple here and there. The river sweeps forward.'

'If it's impossible to change the river, if we can't turn back time or change history, why send me back to 1815?'

'Ah!' Alice tapped her finger against the end of her nose. 'Clever question! But you see, the history of humankind and the history of the Guild – those are two different histories. They are intimately connected, for the Guild has a single purpose, Nick. A single purpose that drives all of our choices, including our decision to keep our members ignorant of their talents. That purpose is the protection of the grand human story. The protection of the past. We know that one person going back cannot change much. But thousands? We do not know, but we are fairly certain: it would mean chaos. Devastation. That is what we fear. That is why we guard the river, and make sure its flow is true and deep and unchanging.'

Alice's hand was on Arkady's knee, and his arm was round her shoulder. This couple had jumped, like Nick. Been wrenched from their natural time, torn away from everyone they had ever known. But here they were today, sailing through the streets of London in the wake of the Spirit of Ecstasy on the hood of their Rolls-Royce, and they seemed very much at home in their roles as Mr and Mrs Alderwoman. Comfortable, in love, in power. Perhaps they had forgotten the loneliness.

'We all just want to go home again,' Nick said.

Alice chuckled. 'Do you think that's what people want? Do you think that all those Guild members, knowing it is possible to travel through time, would simply settle down back home in the Dark Ages and raise their turnips again, waiting for the plague to get them?'

Nick looked down at his hands, which rested on his thighs. Clean, square nails. The pale half-moons that rose above his cuticles. 'I jumped from Salamanca,' he said, choosing his words carefully. 'A hell of human invention. A hell I helped to make. I have sliced open the throats of boys who should have been home with their mamas. I have ridden my horse over the shattered corpses of men, men of my own army. I have climbed, hand over hand –' He stopped.

Badajoz. The ramparts, piled high with the dead. The days following . . . he looked up at Arkady and Alice, willing them to understand.

'Today,' he said, trying to keep his tone even, 'I was dragged into a more hopeless, more devastating feeling than even the very worst that I experienced in Spain.' He looked blindly out the window for a full minute, then spoke without looking back at Arkady and Alice. 'I'm not saying that I have experienced the worst there is. I know I have not. I know others have suffered far more than I. But today I was almost lost in a whirlpool of despair that was wider than my lifespan, deeper than my admittedly shallow soul. Much larger than the capacity of my heart to beat against it. So.' He turned back to face them. 'I am not interested in your fine calibrations of empathy or your great mission to protect the river of history. I just want to live my own life, and I want to spend it having my own private fucked-up little emotions. I have a new home now, and I would like to return to it. Not through time, but across space. In an aeroplane. Preferably Virgin Atlantic.' He sneered at his own pretension. 'Upper class.' He looked down and twisted the ring on his finger, watching it catch the light. 'I refuse the Summons Direct.'

'You cannot refuse,' Alice said, gently. 'You know that.'

'But I do refuse.'

'You cannot.'

'I will return the money. Somehow. I want out.'

'The money is a token, Nick. Come now. The Guild needs you.'

Nick shook his head. 'I do not care about the Guild, Alice. I am to be dragged back to a time I have already grieved, to kill and perhaps die for the Guild, the same Guild that has kept me from my own God-given abilities. I won't.'

'Why did you kill the French in Spain, Nick?' Alice's voice became even more quiet. '"Cry 'God for Harry, England, and St George'"? Is that it?'

'No.' Nick pointed a finger at the two of them together, safe in their blasted Rolls. 'Damn you to hell for that.' He saw Arkady's body tense, ready itself, and his own body shifted in response, his senses sharpening to encompass the man across the car. 'I am not that man any more,' he said, his voice husky. 'Not that soldier. Everything changes.'

'Nothing changes,' she said. 'Look at you, your fists are clenched. Look at my husband. He is coiled like a spring. You are who you are. The river flows to the sea.'

'I want out.'

'There is no out.'

The car purred to a halt and the chauffeur tapped on the window with his big sovereign ring. They had arrived at the gates.

Half an hour later they were tucked behind a snob screen in the Lamb, a pub at the top of Lamb's Conduit Street that had been there in Nick's time – though it looked different now, with its cubbyholed Victorian interior.

'It isn't a scar,' Arkady said. His eyes were red. He had stood in front of the gates with his arms spread, looking like a saint, tears spilling down his cheeks. Alice had ignored the passers-by who stared, and allowed her husband his time. After a few minutes he had stepped away and then stood with Nick across the street in the shadow of the statue of the woman with the urn. They had watched as Alice padded back and forth in front of the gates like a bloodhound, nose twitching, as if she could smell the past.

'It's something, though,' Alice countered.

'Yes,' Arkady said. 'But there are too many feelings, and a lot of them reach outward to the future. Misery. Excitement. Longing. Crashing over one another.'

'I couldn't tune in to the mystical vibrations,' Nick said. 'But I was there once, in the late eighteenth century –'

'Hush!' Alice looked around, but the snob screen shielded her view. 'For God's sake, Nick.'

'Sorry.' He dropped his voice. 'I was there with my mother when I was a kid. And if it helps, I know we were feeling smug.'

Alice smiled at Nick and sipped her half of bitter. 'Smug, huh? I bet you were a cute little lordling.'

'If you say so.'

She pushed her beer away. 'So it isn't a scar. But what does that mean about today? Arkady, were you overwhelmed with despair when you stood there? Because I wasn't, not at all.'

'No.' Arkady shrugged. 'But all those babies. It made me weep.'

'Yes,' Alice said gently. 'Yes, my tea cake.' She put her hand on his.

Nick put his pint to his lips and let the good, bitter beer

wash down his throat. Arkady was really just a big baby himself, he thought, watching as Alice comforted him. 'Why did you cry?'

'My tears were old tears. Tears I have cried before and will cry again.' Arkady freed his hand from Alice's and steepled his fingers under his chin, his ruby ring glowing like an ember. 'I do not believe that the emotions Nick felt at those gates today were the emotions of the Foundling Hospital,' he said to Alice. 'I think they were the emotions of Mr Mibbs himself.'

'Yes,' Nick said. 'That makes sense. And he put fear into me earlier, at Euston Road. That wasn't some deep historical fear I felt. Unless you can tell me that there was a hangman's tree at the corner of Judd Street and Euston Road at some point.'

Alice glanced at him. 'There might well have been. There is a scar at Marble Arch for that very reason.'

'Tyburn.'

'Yes.'

Arkady spread his hands. 'But Nick said it earlier. The man controlled him with emotions, not thoughts. It is only accident that this happened near the Foundling Hospital.'

'That's an interesting possibility,' Alice said. 'It could be a new development. A new way to use the river. They've discovered it, and they are testing it out on Guild members.'

'They?' Nick raised his eyebrows.

Alice and Arkady regarded him soberly for a moment. Then Alice took a deep breath and let it out through her nose. 'The reason we need you, Nick . . . the reason we are taking you back to your natural time, is that a war is about to begin in that era. It will be a war over the fate of the past, over history itself.'

And so here was the other shoe, dropping at last. He had been right all along. He was here to kill.

Alice continued. 'I told you there were others. People who aren't in the Guild. They don't agree with the Guild's principles. They think we should intervene in history. Try to change it. They are experimenting with the talent, working to learn more about it. Some of the things they have discovered recently in . . .' Alice glanced at Arkady. He nodded. She continued. 'The things they have discovered in Brazil are alarming.'

Brazil! So Meg *had* heard Alice talking that day in the toilets. She had been telling the truth. And Nick was, after all, a dickhead who deserved to have his friends desert him. But Nick's heart lifted. Maybe Meg and Leo were alive, in Brazil. Maybe they had made it.

Alice was looking at Arkady, and Nick followed her eyes. The Russian was staring into some grim distance that only he could see. 'Arkady, my darling. Come back to us.'

The Russian focused again on the little table. Then he wiped his eyes with the back of a hand. 'Yes, yes. Brazil. Beautiful Brazil.'

Alice spoke softly, stroking Arkady's thick white hair. 'I was about to tell Nick about the orphan.'

'The orphan! Bah.' Arkady spoke with loathing in his voice.

Alice turned back to Nick. 'The orphan are a thorn in our side,' she said. 'And they have been, oh, for ever. But things are changing. We can't just continue on, with little skirmishes here and there over nothing. The stakes have become too high. The orphan have found something. A new skill, or maybe even an object of some kind that enhances their power. Whatever it is, we must get it.'

'Wait. You're going too fast. Who is this orphan? Sounds like Oliver Twist.'

Alice laughed. 'Not orphan! Ofan.' She spelled the word. 'The name is a contraction of a Hebrew word – Ophanim.'

'What the hell does that mean?'

'Have you heard of Ezekiel's vision? Of the angels who transport the throne of God?'

'Ezekiel . . .' Nick cast his mind back.

'Ezekiel had a vision of strange angels. Each angel had four faces and many wings. They saw all, could travel in every direction, and they never slept.' Alice closed her dark eyes and quoted: '"And when they went, I heard the noise of their wings, like the noise of great waters, as the voice of the Almighty, the voice of speech, as the noise of an host."'

'Okay,' Nick said. 'So these Ofan, these bad guys. They are deformed angel creatures?'

'Of course not. They are humans, like you and me. It's only a name. It signifies that they are watching, that they can travel the river in whatever direction they like, that they have righteousness and truth on their side. Et cetera, et cetera. Of course we . . .' She smiled. 'We think righteousness and truth are on our side.'

'And Mibbs is one of these Ofan?'

Alice glanced at Arkady. 'What do you think?'

'Maybe,' the Russian said. 'But . . .' He shrugged. 'I don't think so. It doesn't seem right to me.'

'But he must be,' Alice said. 'It's really the only explanation. Maybe those things he could do with feelings – maybe that's their new skill. What else would he be? A lone gun?'

Arkady drank deeply from his pint and wiped his mouth with the back of his hand. 'I don't know. The Ofan, they are cowards. But this? This control of feelings? It does not describe what they are like. They are stupid, careless. Smashing what is good for no reason. Always they chase a fantasy. A fantasy that things can change. Idealists.' He scowled into his beer. 'They do not have enough of the balls to be like this Mibbs.'

'Wait, your enemy is a bunch of idealists? Time travelling hippies? That doesn't sound very scary.'

'Oh, they are scary,' Arkady said. 'They steal our children. They teach them unspeakable things. They fill their heads with dreams.'

'Arkady.' Alice shushed him. 'Please.' She spoke to Nick. 'Arkady really doesn't like them,' she said with a little smile. 'But it is like this. They are a loose affiliation of people who disagree with the Guild and who believe our talents are greater than we know. At various points in time they are very powerful. At other points, they are more disorganized. There are some places in history where we even work in close association with them, where people are both Guild and Ofan at once. But now we have reason to believe that the Ofan have changed, drastically, and are becoming a very real threat. Like I've said, they've found something. They've managed to alter . . . well. You will learn about that from the Alderman in –' She lowered her voice. 'In 1815. This is more his business than mine.' She looked at Arkady. 'I think Mibbs is a clue to what the Ofan can do. Even if he isn't Ofan himself.'

'They have not changed that much, Alice.' Arkady sneered. 'They are still scrambling to find –' He closed his mouth with a snap on whatever he was going to say. Then he drained his glass. 'But we!' He held his empty glass aloft. 'We are the Guild. We will squash them. We have not worked so hard, for so long, to protect the river, only to have them ruin it!' He slammed his empty glass down on the table.

'Yes, my ructious darling.' Alice stroked her knuckles down her husband's cheek. 'And whether Mibbs is Ofan or not, his days of secrecy are over. The Guild is watching for him. I've sent that clip to Chile and soon enough I will send it around the world, and send his description down through time. I'm sure he's hiding somewhere, but when he turns up again, we'll find him.'

Nick leaned back against the carved screen and half closed his eyes, letting the golden glow of the pub's electric lighting shimmer into a semblance of candlelight. The Ofan. He let that name sink into his head. Not 'orphan'. 'Ofan'. Fearsome, many-faced angels. Beautiful, androgynous bodies, wings of shadow and light, eyes bright with visions. Voices rising together like the rush of waters. Straining up, reaching – but cast down by an implacable hand. Down into eternal flame.

Nick closed his eyes completely.

Badajoz.

Two weeks later Arkady and Nick were in Arkady's 1972 MG
Midget. Nick had teased him about driving a Guild car that
wasn't a BMW, but Arkady explained somewhat defensively
that MG had been owned by the German manufacturer for
a few short years in the 1990s. Now they were driving through
Devon on the A396, and Arkady was bellowing Russian folk
songs at the top of his lungs. They had left London at dawn,
Alice standing on tiptoe to kiss them both soundly on the
cheek, like a fond aunt. 'Is that all I get?' Arkady had asked.

'It will have to hold you until you return.' Alice patted her
husband's stomach. 'Perhaps it will make you be good.'

'Never.'

Alice turned to Nick. 'He's all talk.'

'That's not what you said last night.' Arkady twitched his
scarf rakishly over his shoulder.

Alice ignored him. 'Now, as for you, Lord Blackdown.
You are to be very, very good.' She was smiling, but he saw
the grave intention in her eyes.

'Yes, my lady,' he said, sketching her a perfect bow.

For two weeks he had been in an immersion course, with
Arkady serving as tutor. The task was to suppress everything he'd learned at the Chilean compound and the years
following. He had to remember his old self and step back
into the Marquess of Blackdown's shiny, black boots. From
dawn to dusk in Arkady's study it had been 1815: every
word they said, every gesture they made, all their food and
drink and clothing. Nick had disappeared in 1812, but was

travelling back only as far as 1815 because, Arkady said with maddening reserve, 1815 was when the Guild needed Nick's services, and no sooner. But those three missing years were a problem. His excuse was to be a bump on the head and a spell of amnesia. Whatever he didn't remember he could blame on his injury. The trouble was more likely to be what he remembered rather than what he forgot: the twenty-first century phrases and habits that had become second nature. So Arkady drilled him. History, politics, manners. How to signal disapproval and approval. How to stand and how to sit. Boxing, fencing, taking snuff. Almost every muscle must relearn the more arrogant tension of the Regency. Much of it felt effeminate to Nick now, and what didn't felt so aggressive as to border on the criminal. It was a strange mix, to be sure, but Nick found that it was all coming back very quickly.

'I'll remember this man's-world stuff on my own,' Nick had said after only two days of it. They had finally collapsed in the leather chairs at the end of a dreary afternoon spent playing hazard and gossiping about political and sexual scandals two centuries old. 'It's the women I'm afraid of.' Nick worked on untying his cravat. 'I need to remember dance steps and the language of flowers and the names of all of Lady Corinna Alistair's grandchildren.'

'Bah,' Arkady said, flinging his own cravat aside and beginning to tug at one stiff boot. 'I cannot pretend to be a woman and prance about with you.'

'Why not? For God's sake, we look a pair of fools already. Allow me.' Nick reached for Arkady's leg. Arkady extended it and Nick pulled his boot off for him. 'Holy shit, Arkady — your feet stink.'

'Language!'

'Bloody hell, your feet stink,' Nick said. 'Though for your

information, *shit* is one of the oldest words in the English language and was in full circulation –'

'Just get this second shitting boot off,' Arkady interrupted, shoving his other leg forward.

Nick laughed as he tugged. 'Cursing correctly is the highest test of fluency, Arkady. I'd advise you to stick to polite language.'

'*Shitting boot*, it isn't right? But I can say *fucking boot*, yes?'

The boot came off and Nick stumbled backwards. 'Yes,' he said, recovering his balance and tossing the boot away. 'That's right. Who knows why.'

Arkady pursed his lips, committing the information to memory. Then he smiled. 'But women,' he said. 'I can talk about women in any language. And I do not want you, my priest, to worry about the women. It is like, how do you say it? Like riding a bicycle.'

Nick was fairly certain that it was nothing like riding a bicycle. He struggled to extricate himself from his incredibly tight jacket. Arkady smirked at him, offering no help, his arms behind his head, his stockinged feet stretched out to the fire.

Ever since that drink in the Lamb, Nick had played nice and kept his own counsel about most things, including how he intended to behave once he was back in his own time and his old persona. He had no intention of blindly following Guild orders, or slaughtering Ofan just because the Guild pointed and said *kill*. But in spite of his reservations, he was eager to return, and the two weeks of practice had opened the floodgates of his memory. He hadn't even wanted to go out into contemporary London again, and not because he was afraid of Mr Mibbs, who, according to Alice, had disappeared into the river, leaving no trail for the Guild to follow. No, the next time Nick walked down Pall Mall, he wanted to see Carlton House ablaze with lights.

Carlton House and the Royal Mews and Hungerford Street, all restored. The pomp and the squalor, the shine and the stench. Now that he could without choking on grief, Nick let himself long for it, let himself drift through the days leading up to his return on a warm current of homesickness.

And now, finally, they were on their way. Hurtling towards his past in a sports car. Practice was over and the game was about to begin. Soon enough they would be pulling in at Falcott House. Visitors could rent holiday apartments there, and Arkady had chosen one that had been converted from the old kitchens. The plan was to spend a couple of days on the property to accustom Nick to the surroundings, then make the jump back to 1815 when Arkady felt Nick was ready.

Arkady's song ended on a long, warbling high note. He glanced at Nick for approval, but Nick sat thin lipped, staring straight ahead. The warm current ran suddenly cold . . . What the hell was he doing? There is no return . . . there is no return . . . and yet that was the curve of Stoke Hill, and it was rushing toward them fast, far too fast . . .

'Do you recognize anything?' Arkady spoke loudly, over the well-oiled roar of the little car's big engine.

'Yes. Everything.' Nick gritted his teeth against the feeling that the car was hurtling out of control – though the speedometer read only thirty miles per hour.

'I know what you feel, my friend. It is strange. But never mind. Soon you will be home again and all of this' – he waved at the motorway and the cars – 'will seem like a dream.'

'I don't want it to seem like a dream. I like the twenty-first century.'

'You like ten years at the beginning of that century,' Arkady said. 'Do you like the other nine decades?'

'I don't know about anything except the first decade,' Nick said.

Arkady only grunted, and Nick gazed to his left, at Exeter's suburbs giving way to winter fields. It was all entirely familiar, even now that most of the hedgerows had fallen to agribusiness and the villages had all swelled to five times their nineteenth-century size.

Around this next bend and he should be able to see Castle Dar, the Earl of Darchester's estate. But when the MG eased around the curve, the rambling old pile was gone, as if it had never been there. In its place, a massive shed filled with combine harvesters.

Nick forced air into his lungs, and out again.

The girl with the dark eyes had belonged to Castle Dar. She had been walking over from Castle Dar that day. The day his father had died.

Now Castle Dar was gone. Vanished from the face of the earth.

Nick closed his eyes and saw, as clearly as if he were looking at a photograph, the body of his father crumpled on the ground, his head and limbs at crazy angles, like a rag doll tossed aside.

Nick, on Boatswain, had been in the lead, preparing to take the jump first. But his father had spurred up from behind. No final words, no glance; just his horse leaping, a bark from the dog that lurked behind the hedge, a confused cacophony of sounds as the horse landed wrongly and went down. Then silence.

The horse and dog were both shot, the first bullet fulfilling the demands of charity toward a dumb, suffering animal, the second fulfilling some notion of justice. The culprit dog had been young, liver-spotted, Nick remembered for some reason – the pet of a tenant's wife.

His father's body was carried back to Falcott House, met halfway by his running, weeping sisters. How had they known?

Yet there they were. Nick remembered Bella's fingers stroking their father's cold cheek as they walked along, Father's body tied by his reins to a board that had been leaning up against the hedge. Then all four of them sitting in the drawing room for hours, waiting for the body to be washed and prepared, listening to the vicar read from the Bible: 'For I know that my redeemer liveth, and that he shall stand at the latter day upon the earth: And though after my skin-worms destroy this body, yet in my flesh shall I see God.' Nick remembered watching as his mother, her eyes trained blindly on the vicar's face, scratched at the back of her left hand until it bled.

Sometime in the afternoon Nick had managed to sneak out. He saddled Boatswain and galloped off, trying to lose himself in fields he had known all his life. Perhaps trying to fall and break his own neck. But he must not have wanted to die, for at the woods that marked the edge of his father's land – his land – he had dismounted to tighten the saddle girth. That's when he had found himself sobbing into Boatswain's neck, clutching the horse's mane in his fists.

Nick hadn't particularly liked his father, a man whose passions were roused only in competition. The fastest horse, the best brandy, the most expensive snuffboxes. Even as Nick pressed his face into Boatswain's neck he knew he was weeping for himself, rather than for that man, the seventh marquess. He was weeping for his lack of grief. For his guilt and his loneliness. Nick didn't want his father's title. He never had.

But, in the twinkling of an eye, or rather, in the snapping of a neck, he had become Lord Blackdown nevertheless.

His tears subsided. He breathed in Boatswain's scent. Then he felt it. Someone was close by. He looked up, and there she was. Standing in the shadows of the oak trees, her dark eyes candid. She was watching him, had been watching

147

him cry. But instead of shame, a strange peace washed over him as she smiled. It was a smile that seemed to exist outside of rules, outside of judgement. She reached out to him with it, and his grief and panic receded.

It wasn't until she had stepped into the sunlight that he recognized her as Julia Percy, his sister Arabella's best friend. She lived at Castle Dar with her old grandfather, the earl.

Nick could never remember what they'd said then to each other. They must have spoken, but his memory was only of the smile, and of her stepping out of the shadow and into the light, coming toward him and pushing all the bad feeling away, before he even realized who she was. He must have seen her again, after that day, but he couldn't remember. He had left Falcott House at the age of fifteen for Oxford, and he had avoided returning. After Oxford he had gone to London and then to Spain. And then to the future.

Her calm, and that feeling that had come over him when her eyes and mouth had smiled together . . . her eyes and smile had followed him down two hundred years.

Nick wondered if she was buried in the churchyard in Stoke Canon. Most probably she was not buried there. She had been a pretty girl, and he was sure she had grown into a lovely woman. Old Lord Percy probably shot her off at seventeen or eighteen, married her to some baron or earl halfway across the country. She would be buried under that man's name, in his churchyard, in his county. The green lichen on her tombstone would have filled in even that name long ago. I hope you were happy, Julia of the dark eyes, he thought to himself. I hope your husband loved you and I hope your children were healthy and that you lived to see them flourish.

'You are sighing like a furnace, my friend.' Arkady spoke, but Nick kept his eyes closed. 'It is sad to see that Castle Dar is gone?'

'I suppose I'm sad it's gone, yes. But I was thinking more of the people who lived there.'

'Castle Dar,' Arkady said. 'A good name. Almost it could be Russian. I am very eager to visit this castle. We will see it soon, in 1815. Yes, and enter it too, I hope. Will you be happy to see the people there again?'

Nick had no desire to see Castle Dar again, for that would mean seeing it in the nineteenth century, and Nick was still unable to grasp the reality of the return that he was about to make. He hadn't cared much for the blustery old earl, and Julia, at twenty-two, would certainly be married and gone. But still. It was easier to think of visiting Castle Dar than Falcott House, which did still exist and which he would soon be facing. The thought made him feel slightly sick.

'We are here,' Arkady said, slowing and turning the car. Nick kept his eyes closed, feeling the tarmac unroll beneath the car wheels. This must be the long drive up to the house. He pictured it in his mind, the beeches his grandfather had planted, the sweeping lawn dotted with sheep, the windows reflecting back the afternoon sun . . .

'Stop it.' Arkady slapped Nick's thigh. 'Do you want to pull us back out of a moving car?'

'What?' Nick opened his eyes. There it all was. Falcott House, its Palladian symmetry unmarred, its graceful marble dome glowing almost pink in the afternoon light. The trees much bigger, the lawn sheepless, but otherwise . . . 'Stop the car.'

Arkady pulled over. Nick opened the door, leaned out, and vomited his pub lunch onto his ancestral land.

'Nice,' Arkady said. 'Classy.'

Nick straightened up and closed the car door, took the handkerchief Arkady held out and wiped his mouth. He waved his hand in a lordly fashion. 'Drive on.'

*

Arkady parked the MG and together they walked up the broad steps leading to the grand entranceway. A grey-haired woman of about seventy opened the door before they could ring the bell. 'You must be Mr Davenant and Mr Altukhov. I'm Caroline. I have your keys here, but I'm off duty in half an hour, so if you want a tour of the house you'll need to come with me now.'

'We will take tour,' Arkady said, at exactly the same moment that Nick said, 'No thank you.'

Caroline looked back and forth between the two men. 'Well, which is it? Tour or no tour?'

'Tour,' Arkady said, his voice implacable.

Nick sighed.

'The tour isn't so bad,' Caroline said to him. 'It will only be the two of you. Interest in the Second World War is declining, I'm afraid.'

The Second World War? But Nick breathed a sigh of relief when Caroline ushered them into the grand hallway. The graceful staircase remained but thankfully looked unlike itself, since it was flanked by glass cases filled with war memorabilia. Caroline began talking with exaggerated animation about the role the house had played as a nerve centre of intelligence during the hostilities, and when she opened the tall doors that led to the formal rooms, Nick relaxed. The walls and mouldings were all painted a sickly mint, in the thick, industrial paint common to the 1940s, and the rooms were laid out with a series of exhibits about spy activity, local involvement in the war effort and the like.

Arkady and Nick listened politely as Caroline told of Churchill's visit in 1942, of the time a German parachutist landed nearby and tried to burn the house but was caught and kept prisoner in the cellars, and of the annual reunions of the men and women who had worked there across those years, sadly dwindling in number every year. Arkady asked a question or two about the neighbouring Castle Dar: had it been torn down before the war, or had the government used it, too? Nick couldn't have cared less about the answers, and soon their voices were washing over him like so much meaningless chatter.

It was the rooms themselves that Nick was listening to now. They were whispering to him. Their proportions, the quality of the light, the intricately carved mouldings, still beautiful beneath their layers of nasty paint, all begged him to recognize that he was home. While Caroline talked about how Castle Dar had been pulled down for its stone and fittings in 1955, he looked over at the marble mantelpiece. One corner was still ever so slightly chipped from that time he played with his catapult indoors. He closed his eyes and felt the blood rushing to his head. Then a sharp pain as Arkady slowly and deliberately stepped on his foot. His eyes flew open. Caroline was talking about the techniques the government had used to recruit spies. Nick stood on one foot and listened intently.

Caroline told them that, in the upstairs rooms, the National Trust had honoured the eighteenth- and nineteenth-century history of the house, and even had a few objects that had been in the Falcott family at that time. 'I don't know if I can do this,' Nick whispered as they began to mount the stairs.

'You can.' Arkady put his hand on Nick's shoulder. 'You must accustom yourself.'

Nick let his hand trail along the banister as they mounted the stairs. At the top, beneath the dome painted with glowing clouds and pouting cherubim, was a glorious Palladian window, the centrepiece of the house's whole design. Nick knew it showcased a view of Blackdown's famous gardens sweeping down to the banks of the Culm. Except that when he looked out, there were no gardens. The intricate series of interconnected beds had been cleared, and now there was a broad lawn that stretched unbroken right down to the river. In the exact middle of the lawn, his father's Grecian folly, once overgrown with roses, stood out like a lonely tooth. But it had always stood off to the right. Whoever heard of sticking a folly in the dead centre of a view?

Caroline came up behind him. 'Beautiful, isn't it?'

'Were . . .' Nick cleared his throat. 'Were there gardens?'

'Oh, yes. Glorious gardens. But after the death of the last marchioness they went to wrack and ruin. When the house was requisitioned during the war, they ploughed them under. Too easy a target for bombers, you see. And they painted camouflage on the roof. It's still a little hard to find the house from the air,' she said proudly.

'I . . . I see. Was the folly always there? I mean, was it always in that spot?'

'You are a garden buff! No, you are quite right. Drawings of the garden show that the folly stood somewhere over there.' She pointed to the right. 'But they disassembled it during the war, because of the bombs. When the National Trust took over care of the property in the 1970s they found the stones over by the edge of the wood and put it back together again. I don't know why they put it there. Perhaps to keep up the Palladian symmetry?'

'Mm.'

Arkady put his hand on Nick's shoulder again. 'Stop bothering Caroline with your hobby,' he said. 'Let's see the rest of the house.'

Caroline was affronted. 'I am happy to answer all questions,' she assured Nick, turning her shoulder to Arkady. 'If you are interested, there are drawings of the gardens in the pamphlet about the house. The last marquess's young sister made watercolours of them sometime in the early eighteen-hundreds, and they are really quite evocative – though she painted them by moonlight, so they look more ominous than pretty. You can buy the pamphlet in the gift shop.'

Nick thanked her in a strangled voice.

'Let's get on with it,' Arkady growled.

Caroline looked the Russian up and down with obvious disapproval. 'As you wish,' she said stiffly.

Nick survived the next few minutes by keeping his eyes mostly on the floor and humming a marching tune under his breath. But when Caroline threw open the door to the marquess's grand suite, announcing proudly that they were about to see Falcott House's prize possession, his eyes were dragged upward by a force beyond his control. There it was. No bed, no furniture at all, but taking up almost one whole wall was the huge portrait of his family that used to hang in the drawing room in the Falcotts' house in Berkeley Square. It had been painted soon after his father's death, yet it included his father. The seventh marquess was in shadow, to symbolize that he was no longer living. He stood behind his wife. Her body was in shadow, too, but her lovely, grieving face emerged into sunlight. Both parents were gazing with sorrowful pride at Nicholas, Clare, and Arabella, who were shown in full sunlight, lounging smilingly around the Grecian folly, the girls plaiting roses into each other's hair.

Nick stood before the picture, caught in the painted glances of his long-dead sisters. He barely heard Caroline as she spoke but tuned in when he heard his own name on her lips.

'. . . Nicholas, who was the eighth and last marquess, is the young man shown here. It is sad to think that just a few years later he would die in battle, and the title would die with him. You can see his signet ring prominently displayed. The father's hand is in the same position as the son's, do you see? But the ring is missing from his father's hand. That and the red cap trimmed with white fur which Nicholas is holding shows that he is the new marquess –'

'Excuse me.' Nick heard his own voice as if from a great distance. 'Where is the loo?'

Caroline looked at him with real concern. 'Are you all right?'

'He's fine,' Arkady said.

Caroline shot Arkady a look of loathing, which he returned full force.

'It is downstairs, through the gift shop,' she said to Nick. 'We are nearly finished here, so we'll meet you down there, shall we?'

'Yes, fine. Thank you.'

Nick practically ran downstairs, tearing the ring from his finger and stuffing it in his pocket as he went. He charged through the gift shop, which was in what used to be his study, paying no attention to the drab young woman behind the desk. He wrenched open the door to the bathroom and turned on the taps in the sink, splashing his face with cold water; it had worked when Kumiko had done it two weeks ago.

The assistant looked at him curiously as he walked back through the gift shop and out on to the drive, where Caroline and Arkady were waiting. Caroline put her hand on Nick's arm, letting Arkady stride ahead towards their holiday flat. 'I just wanted to say that it will be all right,' she said. 'My husband is just the same as your Mr Altukhov. A difficult man. But difficult men are sometimes secretly the kindest. Upstairs, he told me all about how you lost your family and how you'd always wanted to see the original of that portrait, because the girls look so much like your sisters.' She peered into his face. 'Yes, I can see it. I wonder if you are a distant relative.'

Nick stared at her blankly for a moment. Then a big smile split his face. It was all too absurd. 'No relation,' he said. 'But thank you. Thank you for your comforting words.'

He caught up with Arkady and put his arm round the older man's shoulders. 'Caroline likes you after all,' he said. 'She thinks I should keep you.'

'I do not understand,' Arkady said. 'You were miserable a moment ago and now you're laughing.'

'Send me home, then.'

'You are home.' Arkady produced the key and proceeded to open the door to their flat. 'We jump at dawn. It was not a good idea, spending a few days here in the future.'

'The present.'

Arkady held the door, allowing Nick to enter, then closed it behind them. 'Tomorrow, my lord, this present that you love so much will be the far away future.'

Arkady shook Nick awake an hour before the sun rose. He was as fussy as a valet over Nick's outfit, and then as anxious as a girl over his own. But finally, when the first grey light was filtering through the windows, they were primped and ready in their unmentionables and Hessian boots, their tight jackets and starched cravats. They poked their beaver-hatted heads cautiously out of the door, then stepped into the early dawn like two nervous peacocks. No one was about.

'We stroll down to that bend in the drive,' Arkady said. 'When we are far away enough from the house we jump, then stroll back. As if we are walking up from the main road.'

'It makes no sense,' Nick said. 'We would drive up in a coach, or at least a phaeton.'

'We were dropped off by a travelling friend.'

'Without luggage?'

'We were robbed.'

'My family is not comprised of fools.'

'Your family will be glad to see you. They will not ask questions. And the truth? It is so outlandish that they will never guess it. Believe me, I have done this many times before.'

'And yet still you do not inspire confidence, Arkady.'

The Russian flicked dust from his sleeve and stuck his nose in the air. The twenty-first century was falling from him with each step he took. He looked every inch the elegant and slightly savage Russian count. It was impressive. Nick tried to follow suit and did manage to find his more upright nineteenth-century stride. The two men crunched along in silence for a minute.

'Arkady?'

'Mm.'

'You won't abandon me there . . . here?'

Arkady glanced at Nick out of the corner of his eye, then stopped and put his hand on Nick's shoulder. 'I am your friend, Blackdown. I know you are frustrated that I do not teach you to jump, I do not teach you to freeze time. I only teach you to recognize time play. But believe me, it is for a reason that you are kept without these skills. It is perhaps more dangerous to have the skills. The Ofan can sense time play like we can. If they sensed you shifting time, they would know you were with the Guild. We need you to be clean, ready to infiltrate, to get close to them, to be inside.'

'How am I supposed to do that?'

Arkady grinned. 'You are to use your . . . how do you say it? Your charmingness? The charmingness you have. The charmingness that makes you so good at what you do.'

'What I do?' Nick shrugged his shoulder free of Arkady's grip. 'I don't do anything. I bum around New York seducing women and eating expensive meals. I help some farmers in Vermont. I enjoy myself.'

'Well. Even these little, lazy things. You do them with your charmingness.'

'You mean my charm,' Nick said. 'And I'm not lazy. I work hard at enjoying myself.'

Arkady chuckled. 'Yes, yes. You work hard. But you see, it is more than hard work we need. Any person can work hard. In 1815 you are Lord Blackdown, hero of the war. You are the rich marquess and you have this thing, this *charm*. And you have Falcott House. You are perfect, you see, for what we need. You are the only one.'

'What does Falcott House have to do with it?'

Arkady's expression hardened. 'Something is going on, near Falcott House and also in London. In Devon we need you to be the marquess, magically returned, but secretly alert: What are the Ofan doing down here? In London it is yet more important, what you are to do. You must be charming to the Ofan. Make them want you. You must pretend to join them.'

'I thought you wanted me to fight them.'

'Fighting, spying – it is the same. Do not worry. I will always be near you and I will be playing my part. When it is all over, I will bring you back again to this century.'

'And if I don't want to come back?'

'You must come back.' Arkady's voice was tinged with regret. 'There is no choice. The Guild permits no one to be left behind. Even should you die, I will personally bring your body back to the twenty-first century. Like in that film, you have seen it, yes? It is the First World War, where the soldier goes into the no-man's-land to get his friend's broken body. I am your comrade, like that. The music swells and the guns are shooting, but still he goes forward for his friend –'

Nick held up a hand. 'I haven't seen that film.'

'But I didn't tell you the title.'

'Nevertheless. I don't like war movies.' Nick's tone was abrupt. 'I give you permission to leave my dead body in no-man's-land, Arkady. Please.'

The Russian shrugged. 'Never. I am your brother! But the point is not this foolish movie. The point is that you will come back.'

'Dead or alive.'

'Yes.'

Nick shivered in his stiff clothes and thought about his warm, living body underneath them; scarred, yes, but strong and still relatively young. He didn't want to die for Arkady's cause. He had jumped forward two centuries rather than die for England's cause. *Cowardice. Treason.* Words he used to excoriate himself. Was this cowardice that he felt now, this reluctance to follow Arkady into the River of Time, into this war against the Ofan? Nick packed that thought away. This was no time for memories and no time for self-doubt. He was about to step lightly across an abyss that was centuries deep. He was about to go home.

They followed the bend in the drive, and the house was lost from sight. Arkady stopped and looked around. 'Behind this tree,' he said. 'In your time, would there be anything over there, a building where people might see us?'

'There might always be someone about. Scything the lawn, tending sheep, walking or riding across the land.'

'Hm. Perhaps we jump to night-time.'

'It's probably best. But not too late in the evening. I don't want to wake my mother.' Nick laughed without humour. 'That's a sentence I never thought I'd say again.'

'You are about to say many things you never thought you'd say again. Do many things again.'

Nick didn't reply. He was thinking about dark eyes, trying to stay calm.

'Now then,' Arkady said, stepping off the path and behind the tree, being careful not to get dirt on his shining black boots. 'Are you ready?' He held out his hands. 'Hold tightly.'

Nick gripped the Russian's hands. 'What am I supposed to do? Lie back and think of England?'

'No, you do nothing,' Arkady said, missing the joke. 'I will think of England. You will come along with me as I think. You do not know in your conscious mind *how* to jump, but deep inside, in the heart of you, you know. I could not touch the shoulder of a Natural and drag him with me down through history. But you, you are already a time traveller.'

159

'Okay,' Nick said, dubious.

'Little priest. You must trust me.' Arkady's smile was probably intended to be reassuring, but it was a trifle too wide; with his wild white hair sticking out from under his curly brimmed beaver hat he looked slightly manic, like Christopher Lloyd in *Back to the Future*, a film Nick had finally stopped renting after the girl in the video store started calling him 'Marty McFly'. 'When I reach out to the past, I will feel for it with my heart. I will sense it. When I have found the past in my heart, I will begin to pull myself back. You too will feel it, through my hands. Your heart will open to the feeling. It will come in like the flood. You will come along with me. Do you understand?'

Nick nodded, though really, they were probably both insane: two grown men dressed up like Mr Darcy, holding hands behind a tree, trying to pull themselves by their heartstrings back to the long ago. Mad.

'Close your eyes, then, my friend. Yes, good.'

Immediately Julia Percy was there behind his eyelids, as if she were waiting for him. Closer than usual, emerging from the trees in her yellow dress . . . Nick felt a tug, then a sharp pull backwards. It felt as if his stomach were trying to burst through his spine. He opened his mouth to breathe and found he couldn't. Only the feeling of Arkady's hands and the image of those dark eyes kept him from screaming. Then, abruptly, it was over. Before opening his eyes he breathed, and immediately he was weeping. The air was sweet, sweeter than any air he had breathed in ten years, and it smelled so powerfully of home that Nick began to sink to his knees.

'Goddam it.' Arkady hauled him upright. 'Do you want to ruin your trousers? Pull yourself together.' He shook Nick by the shoulders. 'Now!'

Nick gasped and opened his eyes to a night so black he

could hardly see Arkady beside him. He put out a hand to steady himself against the tree and stumbled as his hand fell through a foot of air; the tree was smaller. It was no longer winter; tiny new leaves were rustling in a slight, cool breeze. Ploughed earth and freshly cut grass and wood smoke . . . He took a few deep breaths.

Arkady spoke more softly. 'Are you all right?'

Nick nodded. 'Yes. I'm sorry. The shock.'

'I must admit you have done better than most.' Arkady allowed some pride into his voice. 'In fact, you have done the best. Most people completely break down. Except for me. Me, I jump back for the first time without a care. I arrive ready for my dinner.'

Nick could not be bothered with Arkady's braggadocio, for through the shifting shadows he had caught sight of twinkling candlelight. Falcott House. Where his sisters and mother were probably sitting down to eat . . . He set off at a run.

'Wait!' He heard Arkady start out after him. 'Do you want to break your leg?'

Nick didn't care. The clean, rich air of home filled his lungs as he ran, leaving Arkady far behind. The gravel of the drive kicked up behind his heels. He vaulted up the stone steps and pounded on the door. 'Mother! Clare! Arabella!'

The door opened to the butler's shocked face.

Nick fell into the doorway, one arm gathering the little butler to his side in a strong embrace. 'Winthrop, you old reprobate. Where is my mother?'

An hour later and a modicum of sanity was restored to Falcott House. It turned out that Mother and Arabella were in London for the Season, but Clare had flown into her brother's arms and stayed there for a full fifteen minutes, crying and laughing and stroking him and calling him by all his childhood names, as servants emerged from every corner of the house to welcome Nick home. Arkady stood to one side and watched it all. Now the Russian was taking himself off to be settled in a guest bedroom. He had explained about their being robbed. Would it be possible to borrow a few things from Lord Blackdown's wardrobe? Or had all his old clothes been discarded?

Nick's mother had not cleared out his rooms after his 'death'; his clothes were as he had left them several years ago, when he departed for the war. 'Be sure to take all the very best things,' Clare said, laughing over her shoulder at Nick as Arkady bowed low over her hand.

'I will endeavour to please you, my lady,' the Russian said, straightening and keeping her hand in his.

Nick felt a rush of anger as he watched them flirt. He frowned, more at the feeling than because of it. The emotion felt so . . . antique.

Arkady went off to raid Nick's dressing room, and Clare tucked her hand into the crook of Nick's elbow. 'I must have you to myself for at least three hours,' she said. 'I want to hear all about your adventures.'

'And I want to hear about yours.'

'That will take two seconds,' she said. 'During the winter I do nothing indoors, and during the summer I do nothing outdoors. And now my tale is done.'

'I don't believe that.'

She smiled. 'Nor should you. In truth I work very hard. Do you wish for some brandy or tea?'

Soon Nick found himself seated beside his elder sister on a delicate sofa in the little blue parlour. 'I'm sure you could not get a good cup of tea in Spain,' she said, picking up the sugar tongs and getting ready to put a lump into his cup.

Nick held up his hand. 'No sugar, please.'

Clare looked up. 'Your tastes have changed.'

'Many things have changed in the years since I left for Spain.'

'Five years is a long time,' she said, 'though the war has aged you more, Brother.' She pursed her lips as she looked at him in that funny way she had that he had forgotten. She handed him his cup, her eyes on the scar across his eyebrow. 'It must have been terrible, the war. And terrible to lose your memory.'

'It was.'

Clare stirred sugar into her own tea. 'We grieved for you. There is a monument in the churchyard in Stoke Canon.'

'It will have to come down.' Nick was surprised to hear the resolution in his voice. And of course it shouldn't come down – he was only going to disappear all over again when this task was done, and break her heart once more.

'Yes, tomorrow.' Clare smiled. 'We will smash it to pieces, you and I.'

'You can wear a chip of it in a locket, to remember how I conquered death.'

'Arrogant! As if I would carry it around like a fragment of the one true cross.'

'I don't see why not.'

Clare's smile became a grin. 'Of course, Mother must be informed that you are returned.'

'I shall send for her in the morning.'

'Yes . . .' Clare appeared to consider it, but Nick knew his sister and could see she had already come up with a plan. 'It would be a shame to ruin Bella's Season, though, wouldn't it?'

Nick shrugged.

'Well, it would, even if you don't realize it, man that you are. If Mother knew you were here she would pack Bella up in the space of an hour and kill three teams of horses in her rush to get to you. Best to simply inform her that, by the time she is reading our letter, we are already on our way to her. It will take me a few days — maybe four — to ready the house and myself for a trip to London. Will Count Lebedev be disappointed to return to London so quickly?'

Nick straightened his cuffs. 'Lebedev will do as he is told.'

'Oh, will he, my lord?'

'Yes, he will.'

She sipped her tea and beamed at him over the edge of her cup. He had missed her, deep in his marrow. 'Clare,' he said.

'Do I look older to you?' She said it lightly, but he knew it was an important question. She was twenty-nine years old. Back in the twenty-first century, that was still considered young. Here and now, she was well past her youth. Her beautiful hair was bundled up beneath a frilly white cap. His sister was a spinster.

'When did you put on caps?'

Clare took a delicate sip. 'Last year.'

Nick was silent, not knowing what to say. Would his old self have been silent, too? Clare seemed to think so.

'I can see what you are thinking, Nick, and I assure you, I want to hear no words about it.'

He nodded. 'As to whether or not you look older,' he said, 'I always think of you as a kid, dragging me behind you into trouble.'

'A *kid*?'

'I'm sorry.' He had slipped up already. 'A kid. It's . . . it's soldiers' cant for a child. I meant that I always see a young girl when I look at you.'

'That's kind of you. But I know my age. And I no longer expect to be married.' She looked at him closely. 'Your scar. How did you get it?'

'This?' He touched his eyebrow, the ramparts of Badajoz looming in his memory.

'Yes.'

'A taproom disagreement.'

Clare frowned, but said nothing.

'I think you are beautiful,' he said, both to break the silence and because it was true.

'Thank you. I suppose I should learn that when you ask for compliments, the compliments you receive always sound like false coin.'

'You never used to be this self-doubting.'

'Your death changed everything. We have not known how to be happy for three years.' Between one breath and the next Clare was crying.

Nick gathered his sister into his arms, pushing the wretched cap from her head and stroking her hair. 'Hush,' he said. 'Hush now.'

She gripped his shoulders and wept for a moment, then she pulled away and rearranged herself on her chair. With her face turned from him, she replaced her cap carefully back over her hair. 'Oh, dear.' She wiped her eyes with her napkin. 'I am sorry. It is such a shock.' She looked at him again, her eyes a little red. 'Such a lovely, lovely shock to see you, Nick. I'm afraid I lost control.'

'I am glad you could show me your tears. It makes me feel . . .' He stopped, surprised to discover that the feeling was pride. It was in relation to the emotion that had surprised him a few moments ago, when Clare had been flirting with Arkady. Except that he wasn't angry now.

'It makes you feel like you're home again? To have your sister dissolve into tears like a ninny?'

Yes. It had to do with being home. He realized it now. These feelings had been waiting for him. Waiting here in this house, like ghosts. These were the emotions of that man he would have become, had he never jumped. He had left home so young and gone to the wars and then to the future. He had become someone else entirely. A modern man. Half an American. Yet here they were, that other man's emotions, roiling inside him. The Marquess of Blackdown. A proud man. Inflexible. Competitive. Like his father.

Nick didn't care much for his nineteenth-century self, but he smiled into Clare's eyes, even as he tamped the marquess down. 'Yes. It makes me feel that I am home.'

'I am sorry to welcome you in such a fashion. I haven't wept, oh, in years. Mother has been desolate without you. She lost all her vigour. She never entertains any more, and it took all my ingenuity and Bella's combined to get her to take our sister to London.'

'Why aren't you with them? Surely you could have participated in the Season as well. You aren't so old, however much you may hide your hair beneath a cap. As I recall, the only unmarried men in the neighbourhood are the vicar and old Lord Percy. You should be in London.'

'Lord Percy is dead. They buried him two weeks ago. The new earl seems vile. Everyone says so.'

'I'm sorry to hear that.' Nick thought for a moment about Lord Percy, the bombastic old earl. He had been a powerful man, healthy as an ox, and as much a part of Castle Dar as the stones themselves. 'I didn't realize Percy even had an heir. I seem to recall him talking about being the last of his line.'

'That's the worst thing about it,' Clare said. 'The estate was entailed after all. Apparently old Lord Percy had been trying to break the entail ever since his son's death, that's how much he hated his successor. But to no avail.'

Nick found he didn't really care about the new earl. Julia

Percy had to be married by now, and that was his only interest in Castle Dar. And he found he didn't want to know
anything about whom she might have married, or when. 'I'm
sorry to hear that,' he said. 'An unpleasant neighbour will be
a burden.'

'Yes.' She put her teacup down. 'There are bigger questions facing us, though.'

'Oh? What are they?'

Clare didn't speak.

'Clare?'

She raised her cup of tea, then replaced it untasted. 'Perhaps you have considered it already. It concerns the succession
here at Blackdown.'

'What of it? I have returned.'

'And I am so glad you have, Nickin.'

He thought she might start crying again, her eyes were so
sad and happy all at once.

'But we thought you were dead,' she went on. 'We . . . You
left a will.'

Nick went still. So he had. Before leaving for Spain he had
drawn up a will bequeathing all of Blackdown – the house
and its lands, its system of tenancy, all its cares and all its
income – to his capable elder sister. Until this very evening
Clare had thought herself an independent woman.

'Oh,' he said.

She nodded. 'Yes. And believing you were dead . . . well,
let's just say you came back in the nick of time.'

Nick of time! Nick swallowed a laugh. His sister had no
idea how pertinent her pun was. 'Were you about to sell up
and move to Bath? Has my return banjaxed your dreams?'

'Is that more soldiers' cant? You needn't laugh at my having dreams, Nick.'

'Oh, God.' Now he felt like a scoundrel. And he couldn't

explain his laughter or his language, not without telling her the impossible truth. 'I'm sorry, Clare. I'm not laughing at you. Tell me what's happened.'

'When you died the marquessate became extinct, and the Blackdown estate turned into saleable property, like any other. And I . . .' She took a deep breath, and to his surprise he realized that her hands were trembling. 'Oh, dear. Well, it's best to get quickly over rough ground, isn't it?'

'Are you telling me that Blackdown is sold? Lock, stock, and barrel?'

'No. Not yet. And I was never going to sell it all. But I was planning to put quite a large segment of it into trust. The papers were to be signed next week. So you see, you did come home at exactly the right moment.' She squared her shoulders, almost as if she were bracing herself for an explosion.

And indeed, he could feel the ghostly marquess building up a head of steam, could even taste the aristocratic outrage in his mouth: rusted metal. It must have been that man's outburst that Clare was expecting. He let his gaze rest on his elder sister, saw the courage in her calm self-possession. She who had learned her arithmetic and her history by listening at the keyhole to his sessions with his tutor, and then doing his lessons for him every evening. She who had taken the beating when it was discovered that Nick didn't, in fact, know into how many parts Gaul had been divided. His anger dissipated as fast as it had built. 'It should have been yours anyway,' he said, and put his teacup down with a clatter. With the bright noise a rebellious joy burst in his heart. 'You are the eldest and, by God, I will sign it over to you in life as I did in death. Blackdown shall remain yours. It always should have been.'

Clare blinked. 'I don't understand what you're saying, Nick. You cannot gift it to me. You have returned. Blackdown is yours and it cannot be otherwise.'

'I'm saying I don't want it, aren't you listening?' The words came tumbling out of his mouth. 'You take it. Take it and sell it all. I don't care. I will renounce the title and give you the whole estate.' Nick had to bite down on the urge to tell her everything. Once upon a time, a man went and lived in a future age. In this future, the human race had walked on the moon. Buildings scraped the sky. Mechanical carriages travelled four times faster than the fastest horse. There was no primogeniture.

But he couldn't tell her. She was right: the choice wasn't his to make. His ebullience died instantly, like a man shot through the head. He was left staring at her blank, white face and he knew his own was equally expressionless.

She probably thought he was mad.

'Nick –'

'Please, Clare. Give me a moment.' He turned from her, twisting in his chair to look out of the window. Outside the soft night was brooding over the awakening earth. The commons. He could feel it out there. The ancient will of the land to be free of him.

'Nick?'

He turned back slowly, gathering himself together again.

'Shall I pour you another cup?' She spoke as if nothing had happened, and held the teapot, that most benign weapon of civilization, poised above the china.

He breathed in, then out, and summoned up a small smile. 'No thank you, Sister. I'm sorry I . . .' He fought the phrase *stressed you out* and came up, after a panicked trawl through his memory, with the correct expression. 'I am sorry I discomfited you. I quite literally forgot myself in Spain, and I am afraid I forgot myself again just now. Of course I will not, indeed cannot, renounce my title. I am glad to be home, and I am eager to take up the reins again.' He inclined his head to her. 'And I am quite willing to apprentice myself to your greater knowledge of how to manage this blasted place. Are you willing to serve as my steward? Alongside Mr Cooper, of course.'

She set the teapot down again. 'Mr Cooper ran off with a seamstress from Tavistock. Mrs Cooper is now the house-keeper at Castle Dar.'

Nick paused, assimilating that information. 'And you were selling land because you need the money? The land . . . it isn't in good heart? What are the problems?'

'No, it isn't for the money.' She shook her head. 'Or rather, it is for the money, but mostly it's because every-thing has changed, including money itself. All the silver's drained away to China and India, and now into the war. There's hardly enough silver left in Britain to make a child's rattle! They're overstriking foreign coins, asking us to accept slips of paper and thin little tokens that represent nothing at all.'

Nick raised his eyebrows. 'My apologies, but I have no idea what you are talking about, Clare.'

She looked at him curiously, her head on one side. 'I sup-pose you are more familiar with lead than with silver. But honestly, Nick, you will have to start noticing the way things are if you are to make Blackdown a success. The weight of a coin in your hand will tell you everything about the trouble we're in. And not just here. All over Britain. Nothing adds up. It's a different time now.'

'I know it is,' Nick said. 'Believe me. And I want to learn from you.'

'So humble!' But her smile was sad.

'Tell me what happened,' Nick said. 'Just tell me the truth.'

'All right.' She glanced down, then up at him again. 'You know, you are like the old Nick again. The way you were before Father died. Kind. I wouldn't have thought war would do that to a man. Open his heart.'

Nick blinked, confused. 'I thought we were talking about the degradation of British coinage. What does that have to do with my heart? Or with the estate, for that matter?'

'Nothing. Nothing at all.' She sighed. 'Except that I am glad you are more like your old self. It makes it easier to tell you the state of things here. You have heard, perhaps, of the riots a few years back? The Luddites? But I am ahead of myself. After you left, we began to lose tenants. To America. To the wars. Two men didn't come back from Spain. Ben Tucker and Red Wycliff. Jonas Hill came back and he seemed physically fit but . . .' She paused.

'He was unable to work,' Nick said.

'Yes. And one day he just went away.' She searched his face, her eyes lingering again on his scar.

He reached up and touched it, and her eyes shifted away. 'It's just a scar,' he said. 'It matters not how or why or when.'

'The war –'

'Was terrible. The land is underworked, then?' He turned the subject firmly around, like a plough at a furrow's end.

'Yes.' She followed his lead. 'We lost more men to the manufactories than we lost to the war; they came one by one to say they were going. It wasn't that they weren't well treated here. It was that you were dead, or rather, that the marquessate was dissolved. Suddenly Blackdown was only acreage. The men felt free to put off their fathers' shoes and strike out on their own. Off they went, filled with hope. But then there were the riots, and one of our men who had left to work in the north was killed. Executed actually.' She drew a shuddering breath. 'John Stock.'

'Good God!' John's face flashed before Nick's eyes.

'Yes. He was executed with sixteen other men in York a

little over a year ago. For machine breaking. His brother Asa was transported. Their wives and children came back to us here.'

'Are there no men left at all?'

'There should have been, but the year before last there was the magnificent harvest, so by the time of John's execution the tenants were in such low spirits, eight families left en masse for America.'

Nick had to search his brain for why a magnificent harvest would crush morale. The answer came slowly. 'Rents,' he finally said.

'The corn, Nick, I wish you could have seen it. By July the stalks were bent with the weight of the seed. It was as if England was Eden, with the fruit of the earth bursting forth in praise of creation. But the more enchanting the country-side, the more fecund and rich, the more the tenants fell into despair. They harvested that magnificent crop in fear. It was the same all over England and it was as clear as day: The price of corn must fall. In June it was at a hundred and seventeen shillings a quarter. A year later, Nick, imagine; it had fallen to just sixty-nine, and it remains so! The tenants could not make their rents, so of course I dropped them, but with John executed, the war over, and all of Russia poised to drown us in corn, everyone knew the prices would not rise again soon. And Blackdown cannot survive on low rents, at least not if it is to remain what it is.'

'So the men left.'

'Yes. The strongest and best farmers, of course. They pooled their resources and bought land in America, in a place called Ohio, and they left with hardly a fare-thee-well. They have named their new town "Blackdown", but they own it, Nick.'

Nick raised his eyebrows. Blackdown, Ohio. Hilarious. He

wondered which dark, Satanic box stores were built, in the twenty-first century, on his tenants' pleasant pastures. 'So who is left?'

'Some twelve men who can work hard. And of course there are the old men, and the women work in the fields when they must, although they don't like it.'

'You have been carrying this burden all on your own? I don't suppose Mother has been of any help.'

'No,' she said flatly, and they paused for a moment, thinking of their mother. When Clare spoke again her face seemed to yearn toward him. 'Everything has changed, and not just because you are dead. Were dead.' She smiled at her mistake. 'It's as if you left a hundred years ago.'

'Yes,' Nick said. 'I know.'

'War kept us rich, Nick. I see that now.' Clare's voice was low, hesitant, as if she were telling him a shameful secret. 'Those men who went to Spain went as sacrifice to Mammon. And the manufactories. They eat people. They eat them up and demand more. They are spinning gold up there on the looms, but there never seems to be enough money, and the people are wretched. And we, we grow gold down here! In 1813 we grew enough corn to feed the world, but the people cannot live.' She looked down at her tightly laced fingers and deliberately untangled them, placing her hands on her thighs and straightening her spine. 'At least Napoleon is locked away on Elba and the war is finally done. We may be poorer, but we are at peace.'

Nick swallowed a laugh. For God's sake, he knew that Napoleon would escape in a few weeks' time! He knew the name of the battle that was to come, knew its outcome, knew the name of every war that would follow down across two centuries. Wars to make this one look like child's play. Waterloo! Forty-seven thousand casualties in a few hours. Forty-seven thousand,

and for what? So that Sweden could win the Eurovision Song Contest in 1974? Nick bit the inside of his cheek to keep the laugh in. Yes, Clare, look behind you! The past is melting away, and the future is catching you up in its pantomime.

'Are you all right?' She had that wary look in her eye again.

Nick smiled, forcibly packing the Technicolor future back into the recesses of his mind. 'Yes. I am merely thinking of Napoleon. Of the war. Now tell me. How does all this translate into you selling Blackdown?'

Clare reached up and adjusted her cap, then folded her hands in her lap. 'When you died,' she said quietly, 'it was as if a curtain had been pulled aside from a great truth. In France and in America they know it. Our day has passed.'

'Our day?'

She nodded.

He said nothing.

She continued, her voice a little stronger. 'I mourned you; you will never know how I mourned you. But then I thought that if anything good could come of your death, it was this: Blackdown was now . . .'

'Free.' Nick said it roughly.

'I was going to say "unencumbered".'

'Oh, let us speak plainly, Sister. Without me Blackdown is free of almost three centuries of bondage – more if you count the centuries it belonged to the Pope. Visiting the iniquity of the fathers onto the children unto the seventh generation.'

'You put it far more harshly than I ever thought to.'

'But it is what you meant.'

She sucked in her cheeks and regarded him for a long moment. 'I thought that there must be a way to bring free men back to free land. Bring them back and not indenture land and men both to the same master. Have you not read of Robert Owen's manufactories at New Lanark? It is possible to make a profit without sacrificing human dignity. He has proved it up there. Well, farming is not so different from manufacture. Why could we not do something similar at Blackdown? So I thought to invite a group of decommissioned soldiers and sailors –'

'You wanted to found a model community.' The laugh burst out before he even knew it was coming, fast and harsh. 'By God, you have become a Benthamite!'

'Have you not seen the returning soldiers and sailors?' Clare leaned across the space between them and clasped his hand. 'Nick, they have fought our war, but they have no homes, no work, no food. They have scars, like yours; they have been wounded inside, too. All they know how to do is fight the French. Now they fight themselves, and us – they fight in the streets, over scraps.'

'They are dogs.' Nick withdrew his hand and squeezed his eyes shut against Clare's shocked silence. 'I don't mean that. There are good men among them.' He thought, for some reason, of Tom Feely and his cheeses, far away and in the future. He opened his eyes. 'But they are not little orphan children, Clare. You cannot take them in and mother them.'

'No, of course not, Nick.' Clare leaned back. 'And I was not meaning to turn Blackdown into an almshouse. Far from it. I wished to transform it, make it fit the modern age. After Mr Cooper absconded I engaged a new steward. With his help I devised plans that would put our arable acreage into a trust. For twenty years the men would work the land much as our tenants do now, but the money they pay to me would go towards buying the land, do you see? At the end of twenty years they would own the land in common. The great farm would produce everything the families need to survive, and the extra would turn a profit that would be divided equally among them.'

'Yes, I see,' Nick said. 'And after twenty years? Your noble soldiers would be living the high life, to be sure. But where would *your* money come from? What would happen to Falcott House?'

Clare frowned. 'That doesn't matter now. It isn't going to happen. You are returned and with you the entail.' She smiled lightly. 'Back to sewing fine seams!'

Nick twitched his cuffs into place and with that gesture the marquess finally boiled up, hot and angry, in him. The marquess knew exactly how to feel about this situation, and exactly what to say. Nick let him blow: 'Robert Owen is a visionary. But who are you, Clare? What experience do you have? None. You intend to sign your land – my land – away to a pack of rascals fresh from the carnage of war. The same men who laid waste to Badajoz are to lay their bloody hands on my acres?'

Clare's expression retreated as he talked, and when she spoke her voice was devoid of feeling. 'No, Nick, not any more. You are returned and the land is safely entailed. Unto the seventh generation, et cetera.'

'And I am the eighth marquess, Sister.' Nick sneered, whether at Clare or at himself, he was not sure. 'The eighth benighted marquess! With quite enough iniquity to curse another seven generations. So your little dream must wait three centuries more.'

She said nothing to that. Her face was now as calm as an open palm – it was the same empty look she used to turn upon their mother when the dowager marchioness was in temper. But the marquess was at full throttle now, and Nick couldn't check him: 'Who is this radical new steward, Clare, who wants to throw Blackdown to the dogs? For it is he who has put these ideas into your head, isn't it?'

Clare answered flatly, but Nick, who knew her so well,

could hear the anger crackling around the edges of her words: 'I believe you know him. He served with you in the Peninsula. His name is Jem Jemison.'

Well, shit. Nick collapsed back, raking his fingers through his hair, and the marquess fizzled away.

13

Julia crept out at dawn and saddled her mare, whom she had not seen for a week. Marigold whickered when Julia entered the stall, nibbled Julia's fingers with her lips as she put on the bridle and flirted sideways as Julia stood on the mounting block. Then she danced a gavotte all the way down the drive, tossing her head and whinnying. 'Will you be quiet?' Julia glanced back at the house, but there was no enraged Eamon leaning from an upstairs window in his dressing gown. She reached down and patted Marigold's neck, and the horse whinnied again. 'I'm glad to see you too, you idiot. Now be quiet.'

Marigold settled and soon Julia guided her along a path that cut into the woods to the right of the drive. The early morning was clear and cool, shot through with birdsong. The forest knew nothing of dead grandfathers and dreadful, mad cousins. It seemed timeless. Timeless! Julia's heart rose to her throat. Her powers still felt unreal.

Julia looked up into the oak trees above her and listened to the whispering of their new leaves. Oak trees carried magic. Everyone around here knew that, though not many people would admit to believing it. On Midsummer's Eve the men from the village came to Castle Dar and demanded a great oak log of the earl, which he was obliged to give. Then they went to Falcott House and demanded an oak log of the marquess. That night, in the village, a bonfire would be lit to honour the turning of the season. It was just a bonfire, every-one said, just an evening's revelry. But the logs had to be ancient oak and nothing else; it had always been that way. That was magic, or at least the traces of it.

But Julia was convinced that, Talisman or no, her ability to manipulate time was not magical. What she could do, what Grandfather had been able to do, this twisting of the threads of time – it didn't feel otherworldly or even very strange. It felt like making music – a talent, a gift, one that had to be honed to reach its full beauty. She was untrained, because Grandfather hadn't known she had the talent. He had thought she was a talisman, an instrument through which his own power was magnified. He thought she needed to be protected so that others couldn't use her. If he'd known that she also had the ability to manipulate time, he would have taught her how to do it, how to develop her skill. He would have trained her to protect herself.

Unless . . . Julia allowed the doubt that had been knocking at the door of her heart ever since she had frozen Eamon at the dinner table to enter. Unless Grandfather *had* known, and had simply kept his knowledge to himself. If that were true, it would mean he had deceived her, day in, day out.

Julia forcibly ejected the doubt. She just couldn't believe it of him. He had loved her.

Marigold emerged from the woods into the sunlight. Horse and rider stood gazing over the fields to Falcott House, an elegant Palladian structure glowing in the morning sun, the River Culm sparkling along below its magnificent gardens. Falcott House, where she had spent so many happy hours with Bella, her childhood friend. But Bella was gone to London, and Julia couldn't ride down to that empty house and demand sanctuary.

Julia looked around, and a shiver of memory passed through her. This spot, right here at the edge of the woods – this was the place where she had seen Bella's brother, crying. Nicholas Falcott, the young marquess.

It had been ten years ago, on the day that the seventh marquess had died. Word had come in the afternoon that John Falcott had fallen and broken his neck. Grandfather had ridden over immediately to offer his help and his condolences. He told Julia to stay at home. 'No place for a child!'

But she had sneaked out – of course she had. Bella was a child, too, and Bella was at Falcott House, suffering. She would need her friend. Julia could almost feel Bella calling to her. So she had set out walking through the woods.

When she had emerged just here, she had seen Bella's older brother standing in the shadow of the trees. He was all bony elbows and knees. His arms were around his horse's neck, his face pressed into its mane.

Julia had taken a step backwards, intending to steal into the shadows and return the way she had come. It would be terrible if he saw her. He was clearly here to be alone. But when the horse pricked its ears and whickered, Bella's brother looked up as well. There was no hiding. Julia stepped forward into the sunlight. He had looked at her intently, not seeming to care that his cheeks were wet with tears. She smiled. It was the only thing she could think to do. They exchanged a few words. She offered him condolences for his father. He said he was obliged to her for her sympathy.

Then he had mounted and ridden off toward the river, and Julia had turned back to Castle Dar.

Now that gangly boy was a man three years dead. His bones were in Spain, and his monument stood beside his father's in Stoke Canon.

Julia stared across the meadows to Blackdown. There was smoke coming from the chimneys; she supposed the servants were keeping themselves warm. The family was not at home. A sad little family it was, now that the marquess was gone. Bella had always been full of news about his exploits at Oxford

180

and later in London. After he enlisted, she showed Julia the letters that came from Spain, bursting with descriptions of the camps. He wrote about rabbit hunting, about how he and his friends would run packs of Spanish greyhounds across the dry plains, then eat rabbit stew by the light of the moon and stars. He was a convert to greyhounds for hunting rabbits, he said, but wasn't sure they would suit the fox hunt. He wrote of Lord Arthur Wellesley and his staff, the revelries of winter camp. But there was never any description of battle, which left Bella frustrated. She wanted blood and gore.

Then the letters had stopped coming.

Julia sighed and patted Marigold's neck. 'Shall we run?' she whispered. Marigold tossed her head. Julia encouraged her to a quick trot and then a canter. The horse whinnied, loud and shrill, and stretched out, her long strides eating up the sweeping green meadow. Julia laughed in answer, relaxing into the rolling rhythm of the ride.

Nick awoke before the rest of the household and knew immediately where he was. He was home. He pushed back the linen sheets. How could he have forgotten the glory of heavy linen? No more cotton for him. He would find just such thick, glorious sheets, by hook or by crook, when he went back. If he went back.

Swinging his legs over the edge of the bed, he looked out of his bedroom window, over the mist-shrouded gardens, down to the river, which was glowing silver in the predawn light.

Arkady had been right. It felt good to be the marquess. And it was funny – this morning he could barely remember how he'd felt a few weeks ago and two hundred years from now, his suspicion of the Guild, his anger. Or even how he'd felt yesterday, when he was talking to Clare. The way the title had revolted him, his desire to give it up. It must have been some version of the bends – entering the past too quickly. His emotions had been scrambled. Well, he felt fine now. So what if he was here to spy on people, perhaps even kill people? So what that Jem Jemison was installed as the new steward? Nick could handle it. He was Blackdown, he was here, and here was home. He stretched and stood, warmth spreading through his limbs.

Arkady popped out of his bedchamber as Nick strode down the hallway on the way to breakfast. 'Today we begin our investigation,' he said. 'Shake your sister off.'

Nick looked the Russian up and down. His borrowed nightshirt barely skimmed his bony knees, and its full sleeves didn't reach his wrists. 'You look like a girl who has outgrown her pinafore, Arkady.'

'Bah. The nightclothes of this time. So undignified.'

'Indeed. I recommend that you dress yourself before emerging from your lair.' Nick twitched his cuffs. 'As for your plans, I'm afraid I must disappoint you. I've just been reunited with my sister, the world smells good for the first time in two centuries, and I intend to spend a few days forgetting your existence. Today I am going to beat my bounds, and if I catch sight of your unkempt white hair anywhere in my path, why, I'll scalp you. What day is it today, Monday? I do not wish to think about the Guild or the Ofan until Friday. Oh – and on Friday, Count Lebedev, this household is going to London.' He held his hand up to quash Arkady's response. 'You cannot bring me back and not expect me to care for my family. My young sister is having her first London Season, and my mother is with her. We will be going to London and joining them. You said that the Ofan are at work in London, too; we will begin there, and finish the job in Devon later. Is that understood?'

'You are quick to slip back into your aristocratic arrogance, Blackdown.'

'You told me I would enjoy it.'

Arkady looked at him soberly for a moment, then slapped Nick on the back. 'Yes. I did say it. And I like to be right. Up to a point. Enjoy your freedom. Then yes, London is a good place to start. As for me, I make myself scarce. Hunt the Ofan. Perhaps I will cultivate the acquaintance of your so lovely sister.'

Almost before he realized what he was doing, Nick found himself grabbing Arkady with both hands by the thin cotton of the nightshirt and dragging his face close to his own. 'If I did not know your devotion to Alice, Arkady, I would challenge you for those words.'

The Russian raised his brows high and let his eyes drop down to Nick's two fists. 'My old friend Nick Davenant, he was a blasé fellow,' he said in a constricted voice. 'But Lord Blackdown has a temper.'

Nick released him and took a step back. He was shaken. 'I apologize,' he said. 'But . . .'

'But?' Arkady brushed his nightshirt into place with the same care as if it had been one of Weston's finest jackets.

'My sister is not a modern woman.'

'And you? You are a modern man, Nick Davenant.'

'Am I? I'm not so sure.'

'If I trifle with your sister, what will you do?'

'I will horsewhip you.'

'Ah.' Arkady bowed. 'And now, my lord, we have both threatened to harm each other over women.'

'Have we?'

'Yes.' Arkady's smile was a little sad. 'When you flirted with my wife? I said I would kill you. I joke. But you . . . you are in earnest about your whip. Nevertheless. Now we are true friends. Come to me.' The Russian gathered Nick into a bear hug and kissed him soundly on both cheeks. 'My brother.' Then he stepped back into his bedchamber and snapped the door shut.

Nick stared at the closed door, flexing his hands. The marquess was triumphing. Indeed, Nick had been the marquess since the moment he had awoken this morning. Maybe it was best that way. A month ago he had been a New Yorker with a house in Vermont, a twenty-first-century Casanova with no responsibilities beyond his own pleasures. Today he was a Georgian aristocrat, the lord of a vast estate. His concerns were bound up with tenants, farming cycles, investments, virginal spinster sisters and oversexed Russian noblemen. Perhaps he needed nineteenth-century feelings to handle nineteenth-century situations. He couldn't lay his title aside, neither legally nor, it seemed, emotionally. So be it. When they sent him back to the twenty-first century, then he would become Nick Davenant again.

Or perhaps he could find a way to stay here. Arkady had said the Guild would drag him back to the twenty-first century, but all the rules of the Guild seemed to be malleable. Perhaps he could simply be the marquess for ever.

Half an hour later Nick stood on the front steps, his belly full of ham and eggs from the home farm. A lunch stolen from the kitchens bulged in his satchel, and his none-too-supple buckskin breeches were warming up nicely. His toes were happily at home in an old pair of country boots made especially for his feet. He carried his favourite fowling piece, in case he scared up any game. He would take a long walk all round the periphery of the estate. Greet whichever of the tenants were left. Maybe take a detour into the village and pay his respects to the vicar.

'My lord.'

The voice came from behind him. A northern voice. Jem Jemison's voice. Nick turned, and there he was.

He was dressed as a civilian, not as a soldier. Of course. But it surprised Nick. Somehow he had pictured Jemison still in those sun-faded, dust-dulled regimentals. The only true scarlet left had been their armpits and beneath the white straps that crossed their chests. X marks the spot.

'Jemison.' Nick held out his hand.

Brown hair and eyes as black as a Spaniard's. They used to tease him about that. But Jemison was unteasable. Nick remembered watching him in the firelight, as the men laughed all around them, making cruel fun of one another. That thin, alert face in the flickering glow, like a fox's mask when it turns and watches the baying pack of hounds that chase it.

It was only when he felt Jemison's hand in his own that Nick remembered; he was a marquess and Jemison a commoner. He pulled his hand away and nodded instead.

Jemison's mouth twitched – was he amused? But then he bowed, with precision. 'Welcome home, my lord.'

'Thank you.' Nick looked the man up and down. The last man he'd seen before jumping. Well, the second to last. For Nick had certainly seen the Frenchman, seen the look in his eye.

'I killed him,' Jemison said.

Nick blinked. 'Excuse me?'

'Why?' Jemison looked puzzled.

'I mean, what did you say?'

'The dragoon. I killed him.'

'I see. Thank you – I suppose.'

'No need to thank me. I didn't save your life.'

'No. Of course not.' It was a heavy debt, owing a man

your life. Jemison wasn't claiming those dues. He was up to something, though.

'He fell, you see, after you disappeared,' Jemison said, his voice flat. 'He lunged to kill you, and then when you weren't there he overbalanced and tumbled. I crushed his head with my rifle butt.'

Nick nodded, his eyes never leaving Jemison's. Painted into that blunt portrait of a death was the thing Jemison was really telling him. He had seen Nick disappear, and he wasn't going to pretend he hadn't. 'Are you the one who blabbed about my disappearance?'

'That was Peel. Everyone thought he was crazy.'

'And you didn't corroborate his story, I take it.'

'I keep myself to myself.'

'Where is Peel now?'

'Dead of a fever.'

Nick rocked back on his heels and looked up at the sky. 'So you are telling me that you are the only one left alive who saw. Peel and the Frenchman are both dead.'

Jemison shrugged. 'I'm not telling you anything.'

Tell no one. The third rule of the Guild. And yet here was this man, this enigmatic Natural northerner. This man who had been with him at Badajoz. Nick sucked in his cheeks, remembering standing beside Jemison on the city wall on the third day of the sack. Down below in the square two soldiers of their own regiment were dragging a girl out of hiding, calling to their comrades who were lounging, drunk, in the shadow of the gallows Wellington had erected to try to scare the men out of their mad rampage. So far it wasn't working. Jemison had turned to Nick with those knowing black eyes and said, conversationally, 'I bet you five guineas we can shoot them both and not hurt the woman.'

Those black eyes were looking at him now, with the same

look. Nick heard himself speak, as if from a distance: 'When I disappeared, I –'

'My lord.' Jemison held up his long, narrow hand, and Nick closed his mouth. 'I'm not telling you anything. And you're not telling me anything, either.'

Nick raised his eyebrows. The man was bold.

Jemison nodded once, as if in acknowledgement of that unspoken judgement. Then he bowed, turned, and walked away across the lawn.

Nick strode up along the line of trees that marked the edge of Darchester's land. It was still early in the morning; the dew sparkled on the grass and the sky was blue. But the pleasant walk he had anticipated had turned into a pilgrim's progress, and Nick feared the Slough of Despond lay dead ahead. For God's sake, to come face to face with Jem Jemison of all people. Not that he disliked the man, by any means. But Jemison *knew*. He had been at Badajoz, and then he had seen Nick disappear at Salamanca. So now Nick was in his debt after all. Not because Jemison had saved his life. This debt was a far stranger encumbrance than that most brotherly of bonds. Jemison had protected Nick from his own impulse to share. No secrets, no promises, no pledge, no collateral. No return.

Nick looked at the ground as he walked. Bright, tender, green English grass cropped short by sheep. So different from the tough, blue-green grass that carpeted American lawns. Nick had never thought to feel it again – the particular way that wet turf gives beneath the feet, welcoming you, then springs back beneath the heels, pushing you away again.

All those years in America and barely a complicated feeling. He hadn't been home for twenty-four hours and already nothing was simple. The marquess was battling for ascendancy. Clare, who had been about to sell Blackdown, was now dispossessed by his return. And Jemison. That thin hand held up against Nick's story. That curt nod, and the way that Jemison had turned and left, as if it were his own land across which he walked so lightly.

A sound made Nick look up. A horse was nosing its way out of the little path that emerged from the trees up ahead. At first he could see only the horse's head, but then the entire animal stepped delicately into the sun, and its rider was revealed.

Thank God. A woman. Something to distract him from himself.

Her black riding habit was unrelieved by any colour except for a splash of white at her throat. The early-morning sun was shining behind her, so that he couldn't see her face or determine the colour of her hair, which was coiled and netted. She was looking away from him, down the long slope towards Falcott House, and he could make out the pure line of her cheek, her neck, her breast. The rest was camouflaged by her full skirts.

The mysterious lady held her horse's reins lightly in one gloved hand. The mare tossed her head, but the lady's hand remained resting at the pommel. Nick felt a rush of erotic pleasure: her small hand, the powerful animal. She trusted the horse, and her own control over it. Nick had spent ten years in the republic of tight jeans and bikinis, and he had come to like it there very much. But it was good here, too. He stepped forward, intending to present himself, but, without ever realizing he was there, she urged her horse on and was soon flying over the fields in the direction of the river.

The mare neighed once, shrilly, hallooing the joy she felt in the canter, and Nick heard the rider's responding laugh.

He stood, hands on hips, watching them go. The mare's pretty black legs flashed, her hooves kicking up clods of rich earth as she stretched to run as fast as she could. The lady sat her like a queen, her lovely bottom (and this Nick could now see, for the habit was tucked most advantageously) lifting with the horse's gait. Would she come back this way? Nick watched as horse and rider grew smaller, slowing as they reached the river, then walking along it back up toward the line of trees. There was a path there, also, that led along the river to the village; they still might choose to come back this way. He waited. The lady and her horse disappeared into the woods. No matter. This was clearly her morning ride.

He would be here tomorrow, perhaps on a horse of his own. He wasn't looking forward to the painful process of getting reaccustomed to the saddle. He didn't want to think about the aches and pains that were coming the way of his own lovely bottom.

14

'What did you do today?' Nick asked Arkady over brandy, after Clare had left them for the evening.

'I sat all day in the inn yard in Stoke Canon and listened to conversations. Mostly they were talking about you.'

Nick smiled.

Arkady did not. 'You enjoy yourself too much, playing the great lord,' he said. 'Remember, you are here to do a job.'

Nick sipped his brandy. 'The way I see it, I am doing my job. The job I was raised to do. I am the marquess.' He looked out of the window at the perfectly dark night. 'I know that this way of life is passing. Is already past. Factories are rising, the railway is coming. But you cannot bring me back here and not expect me to take up the old ways. You said that I would enjoy being the marquess again. But it isn't enjoyment that I feel. It is simply . . .' Nick swirled the amber liquid in his glass. 'It feels right. I am home.'

'Listen to me.' Arkady set his brandy balloon down on a table and leaned forward, his sharp elbows propped on his sharp knees. 'When I said you would enjoy being the marquess, I also said that it was nothing but a fantasy, yes? You know what comes, what is coming. You are a traveller in time. No more for you the wallowing like a happy pig in the pleasures of the present. It is not for you, or for your sisters, that you are here, dressed like that. It is not for your family or your tenants or your title that you stand there, drinking brandy that was laid down before Marie Antoinette's pretty head rolled beneath the guillotine's blade. It is for the

Guild. It is for the Guild that we return and put on these costumes.'

'You said the Guild wanted me to be an aristocrat. It's why they let me keep my ring. Even as they dispossessed me, they knew. Now I have remembered. This is my home. My family. My land.' Nick twisted the ring on his finger. 'I am Blackdown.'

'Bah!' Arkady clenched his fists, then opened his long-fingered hands very wide. 'You are Nick Davenant! Do not forget this! This time we have come back to, it wants you. Like the siren who sings. You are giving in. I said to Alice, perhaps he is too weak. But she said no, that you are strong.'

'I never wanted this,' Nick said quietly. 'I asked to be sent back to Vermont. I told you I wasn't right for the job.'

Arkady's face softened into compassion. 'Do you think I don't feel for you? I, too, lost all when I jumped. Remember, it was I who taught you to feel time, my priest. To feel it slow and stop and speed up again. I taught you to step outside the stream. I taught you that beautiful sensation. Try to feel it again now, how the time is dragging you along. Feel it. Can you? It is moving your limbs, moving your thoughts. Remember you grabbed me by my sleeping clothes today?'

Nick did remember how the marquess had flared up in him. And with the exception of that brief hour in the morning when he had allowed Jem Jemison to rattle him, Nick had given in and been the marquess all day long. Ogling horsewomen. Walking his lands. Greeting his tenants. Inspecting the home farm. He felt the marquess in him now, angry and affronted. He let him speak: 'I grabbed your nightshirt – which in fact is my nightshirt – because you deserved it.'

Arkady looked at him, his blue eyes very serious. 'No.' He shook his head. 'Do not give in. Come back to me, Nick Davenant.'

Nick stared at his friend, his lips pressed tightly together.

The Russian's voice was quiet. 'You think you are a singular man, an individual, Nick. A great marquess, second only to a duke, yes? You think that you control your own feelings. But *time*, Nick. Time is all around you. Volga: the Queen of Rivers. Mississippi: the Father of Waters. Amazon: the River Sea. The River of Time is a thousand times greater than these. As wide and deep as the universe itself. If you try now, you will feel how you swim in it. It holds you up. It feels good. But it can pull you down. Wear your dandy clothes and drink your brandy. But do not give in. Do not drown.'

'Could I drown? What do you mean? Stop speaking in metaphors.'

The Russian sat back. He pulled his own ring up to the knuckle and pushed it back down, then again. He was searching for words, something Nick had never seen him do before. 'Metaphors, they are all we have.'

'Whatever,' Nick said. 'Surely you can speak plainly for once. You want me to be the marquess but not be the marquess. Why?'

'Alice told you that we travel on feelings. Your feelings, they are your time machine; she said this to you.'

'Yes.'

'And you think you understand this. You have jumped, with me to guide you. You have reentered the river in your natural time. You are remembering the feelings of this era. And you think, "I am the Marquess of Blackdown! I remember!" Bah. Little you, little tiny man. You do not remember. The river – it is the river that remembers you! It flows all around you, through you; it drowns you. Unless you respect its power.'

'"Little tiny man"! Now I hope *that* is a metaphor, Arkady . . .'

But the Russian was not to be distracted. His half-lidded eyes gazed somewhere over Nick's shoulder. 'Human emotion. Millions of souls, together they make the mood of a certain time. It doesn't matter that they disagree, that they hate, that they fight. All together they create it, this thing. This epoch. Times of war. Times of famine. Times of wealth and happiness. The mood of an era. What is stronger than that?'

'Is that what you do to us, those of us who jump and never learn the truth? You drown us in the new era, so that we never reach our potential?'

The Russian's eyes snapped back to focus on Nick. 'I have not thought of it that way,' he said. 'You make it sound bad. I believe that it is humane, what we do. But yes. Exactly. We drown Guild members in their new time.'

'And I came up for air, didn't I? For the first time, back in 2013, when you stepped on my foot in the drawing room. I was feeling backwards. I was looking at the mantel and seeing the place where it was chipped. I was beginning to touch the past.'

Arkady nodded, smiling. 'You have many feelings, Nick Davenant. You are a passionate man, behind that solid English garden wall. It is good. But you stirred time then with your longing for your home. Also, do you remember? You stirred time in the car when we were passing Castle Dar. You are not trained – probably you could not have jumped. But imagine if you had? A man enters the past in mid-air, sitting two feet above the ground, and travelling at sixty miles an hour.' He laughed. 'Road pizza!'

Nick stared at the fire. His talent wanted to express itself, it wanted to be trained. But they were keeping him ignorant.

Arkady reached across the space between their two chairs and gripped Nick's shoulder. 'My friend,' he said. 'Do you think I like it? The lies and the secrets? I do not like it. But believe me, it is the only way. The past *must* stay the past, Nick.'

'Why?'

'To protect the future.' Arkady spoke with conviction, and with the frustration of a teacher for a wilfully stupid student. 'It is obvious.'

'But *why*? *Why* is the future so precious?'

Arkady shook his head. 'My priest,' he said, and his voice was strangely loving. 'Simply believe.'

'I am no priest.'

Arkady sat back. 'No, you are not a priest. And belief is not simple. But try. I ask you: stay afloat. Remember. This era wants to drown you, wants to claim you. Swim in the river. But do not drown. We are here to fight the Ofan, and I don't want to lose you to your marquessing. You are Nick Davenant, of the Guild.'

Nick looked for a moment into Arkady's pale eyes, then nodded. Yes. He could feel it now. The strong pull to be someone he might have been, to be swept away, to be the Marquess of Blackdown, war hero, protector of women, benevolent squire – and nothing else. At first it would feel good to let go. It would feel good to forget Nick Davenant, forget the twenty-first century, forget the blasted Guild. But Arkady was right. It would be to drown in his personal tempest. 'Those are pearls that were his eyes . . . Sea nymphs hourly ring his knell.'

Arkady stood up, suddenly all energy. 'Enough of this! I can smell him, on the wind, our Ofan whom we have come so far to find. He is somewhere nearby. But he is lying low. Who can he be? All day I listen to the peasants, talking of you. They talk of nothing else. How sad that you lost your memory, how wonderful that you are returned, how glad your poor mother will be. I hear nothing, nothing at all to help me.'

Nick swirled the brandy in his glass. 'Perhaps I am Ofan.'

Arkady whirled and pointed a long finger at Nick. 'Do not joke about such a thing. The Ofan!' Arkady spat the word out. 'They killed my daughter, did I tell you?'

Nick whistled a low note. 'No, you most certainly did not.'

'Well.' The Russian passed a hand over his face. 'They did. My poor Eréndira. But. It is in the past.'

'How terrible for you and Alice. I'm so very sorry.'

'She was not also Alice's daughter. She was born before I knew my Alice. Eréndira was the child of a lover I had in South America, how shall I say – many, many years ago. She was a brilliant girl . . .' Arkady blew his breath out through his teeth and squeezed his eyes shut. 'But enough of that. Enough.'

'I'm sorry.'

'My brother, it is I who am sorry to burden you with this long-ago pain of mine. But now you know. We do not joke about them. If the Ofan are trying to set up their business here and now, in little Stoke Canon, I will find them.'

Neither man spoke for a long while. Nick stared into the shifting light of the embers and Arkady, standing, stared through the window. When Arkady broke the silence, his voice was peevish. 'Your English peasants, they are not very friendly.'

Nick chuckled. 'I hope you didn't call them peasants to their faces.'

Arkady turned from the window, his hands spread. 'I did not get the chance to call them anything. I drink their beer and eat their food, and no one will talk to me. I am a foreigner and a stranger.'

'But you listened.'

'Yes. To the chatter about you, I listen. A little about the new earl, Lord Dar-something?'

'Darchester.'

'Yes. There is a new earl, and he is hated. I thought, perhaps he is Ofan, so I push my chair back to hear the conversation that is happening behind me. I learn that he is an ugly man, an old man. But already, they say, he has a young mistress. The peasants, they know the mistress before he came. She is young and beautiful but they say she is the daughter of a whore, perhaps. This bad mother is why she will be with the ugly earl.'

Nick frowned. He didn't remember any woman with that story in the village. 'A local girl?'

'Yes, so they said. But I think an Ofan would not have a mistress that local people know; he will not take that risk. This is not our man.'

'I wonder if it was the earl's mistress that I saw today. I saw a girl when I was out walking.'

'Pretty?'

'I think so. I was quite far away and the sun was behind her. But she was shapely. She could ride like a Valkyrie. I wouldn't have thought she was an old man's mistress, but it's been so long. I can no longer read the women of this time.' Nick took a swallow of brandy. 'If she is his mistress, perhaps she is open for a little dalliance.'

'You will steal your neighbour's mistress? Is that the sort of man you are, back here in the past?'

Nick grinned. 'No . . . not steal. Maybe just borrow?'

'Bah! To be unmarried! I tell you, it is hard to be married to the Alderwoman. She knows everything. My leash – it is very short. I so much as smile at a girl in this time, she will know it two hundred years later.'

196

'You wouldn't have it any other way, Arkady.' Nick drained his glass and stood. 'Don't try to fool me.'

He was surprised to see the Russian blush. 'Yes. I love her like I love my own life. She is my heartbeat.'

15

The next morning Nick was down at the stables at dawn. He'd left orders for a hunter to be saddled, and he was delighted when he saw that it was Boatswain who was waiting for him in the yard, a groom by his shoulder. When he heard Nick's step he looked up and tossed his head, whickering and stepping to the side. The groom held him firm. 'He has missed you, my lord.'

Nick took the reins and stroked the stallion's neck. He let that spicy scent of horse and leather fill his nose. 'How are you, old man?' He reached into his pocket and fished out a carrot. Boatswain took it daintily from his master's palm. Nick turned to thank the groom, but Boatswain would not tolerate the shift of attention from himself and blew snot all over Nick's hand. Nick accepted the cloth the groom handed him and looked Boatswain in the eye, seeing the horsey amusement there. 'I'd forgotten about you and your tricks.'

Boatswain snickered, pleased with himself.

'He's sixteen now, my lord, but at heart he'll always be a colt.'

'I hope so. Thank you for readying him for me.'

Nick mounted. He hadn't been on horseback in years, and it felt good, though he knew he would suffer for it later. 'Now then, Boatswain,' he said. 'Let's see what you can do, and more to the point, what I can do.'

They set out at a canter, and Nick relaxed into the easy gait. Boatswain was older and heavier; Nick could feel the difference in the horse's stride. It was a cold, overcast morning, not as sparkling as yesterday. He urged his mount on, his heartbeat quickening as he thought of the mysterious woman in black. He wanted to be at the pathway into the trees when she appeared. A dalliance would be the perfect thing to smooth the transition back into this time. The perfect thing to keep him from drowning. Boatswain picked up his pace, breaking into a gallop, and Nick's body shifted to accommodate.

'Like riding a bicycle,' Arkady had said about women. But Nick was as anxious as a fifteen-year-old; what would she be like? He had left for Spain when he was twenty, and before that he had sown his wild oats among the demi-monde and willing serving wenches. And for years now his lovers had been twenty-first-century women.

Boatswain was flagging, and Nick let him slow to a walk. Why was he even thinking about this woman at all? He couldn't actually sleep with another man's mistress; it would be ungentlemanly in the extreme. And if she wasn't Darchester's mistress, she was another man's wife, or a virgin, at which point ill manners tipped into villainy.

In the end, he convinced himself that he wasn't riding out to see the mysterious woman in black. He was riding his estate, getting to know his horse again, and if he happened to meet a neighbour, so much the better. Nevertheless, when he reached the path that led back into the trees, he dismounted and let Boatswain graze while he leaned against a tree and . . . if he was being honest with himself, he was waiting. But he wasn't being honest with himself. So he wasn't waiting. He was resting.

Marigold was calmer this morning and accepted her carrot with dignity. She capered only a little as they cantered down the drive, and she picked her way along the woodland path quietly. But before the trees gave way to fields, the horse pricked her ears. A bright whinny sounded from somewhere up ahead, and Marigold answered, breaking into a trot.

Julia pulled her back and stopped. Someone was up ahead, there where the path entered Blackdown land. Perhaps it was the Falcotts' new steward, Mr Jemison. Or were the Falcotts themselves back from London? Julia hoped so, fervently. Perhaps she could wangle an invitation to stay, and that would prove to the village that she was still worthy of their friendship. Otherwise . . .

Julia frowned up into the oak leaves above her head, tears pressing against her eyes. Otherwise she would have to leave Castle Dar, leave Stoke Canon, and go . . . where? To Scotland, to her mother's family? She didn't even know how to find them.

But leave she must, unless something miraculous were to happen, and soon. That had been patently obvious yesterday when she had ridden through Stoke Canon, hoping to stop and talk to people, hoping to let them know that she was still Julia Percy.

Instead, she had received only a few distant hellos, and no offers of conversation. She had kept her pride down the length of the High Street, greeting averted faces as if they were the smiling neighbours she had known all her life. But the minute she was out in the fields again she had set Marigold's face for home and let her gallop all the way.

Once back in Castle Dar, Julia had packed two bandboxes with a change of clothes and her jewellery, then unpacked them again; the servants would discover what she was planning if she left luggage sitting about. Meanwhile, let the townspeople indulge themselves in an orgy of recriminations, old and new. "'And whosoever shall not receive you, nor hear your words, when ye depart out of that house or city, shake off the dust of your feet!"' Julia spoke the words into the mirror. The sentence began bravely enough, but by the end she was weeping. How could she shake the dust of this house from her feet when she felt that she was crumbling away to join it? She knew no dust in the world but this dust.

So this morning she was riding, not away, but around, trying to collect her thoughts and make a plan.

The horse up ahead whinnied again, and Julia gave Marigold her head. She held her own head high and her spine straight. Whoever it was that waited there, Julia Percy was ready.

He was standing in the same place, the same big bay stallion beside him. His hair, which had been fair, was several shades darker. She would never describe him as all elbows now. He was taller by a head and broader in the beam. Instead of crying he was leaning at his ease against a tree. He had a lazy, distant look in his eye and he was almost, but not quite, smiling.

She had the distinct impression that he was waiting for *her*. She didn't think she liked it.

So she reined Marigold in, stared right back at him and asked the bluntest question she could think of. 'Are you not dead?'

She had the satisfaction of knocking that knowing look from his face. His eyes flew wide.

Then she saw him recognize her, and it was her turn to be disconcerted. It was the strangest thing. He recognized her, and his whole face, even his body, transformed. His mouth lost its smile, but the skin around his eyes crinkled, and his eyes themselves lost that weary, faraway look. 'Miss Percy,' he said. 'Julia.'

His voice was different. Deeper, a man's voice. His accent was strange, too. Flattened here and there. Like the accent of someone who has returned home after years abroad. Which was, after all, nothing but the truth. He had gone to Spain. But had he returned from Spain, or the land of the dead? They had mourned him for dead. Now here he stood, fully alive, his recognition of her making his eyes change from rainy blue-grey to a warmer, darker, more disturbing colour. A feeling rather than a colour. Her horse shifted beneath her. She was holding the reins too tightly as she looked down at the miraculously returned Lord Blackdown. She forced herself to relax. 'My lord,' she said, inclining her head. 'Welcome home.'

It was Julia Percy. Nick didn't recognize her for a moment, but then there she was. His heart began pounding. The girl who had seen him through so much. He took a step forward, his mouth opening to say God knows what, when she spoke.

'Are you not dead?'

He was stunned for a second, simply by seeing her, and by the shock of her question. Impossible to explain that he was returned from an unimaginable future. So he said her name. 'Miss Percy. Julia.' It felt wonderful, speaking her forename out loud after so many years, the way the tip of his tongue only lightly touched his palate, once, in the middle of the word.

He stepped forward and held both hands up to help her dismount. She put her gloved hands in his and leapt down lightly. She stood just to his shoulder, her hair the colour of walnut liqueur.

'You are grown,' he said, ridiculously.

'And you have come back from the dead. I believe you have more to explain than I.'

'You're right,' he said. 'It is a tale. But first please allow me to offer you condolences on the death of your grandfather. He was a good man.'

'Thank you, my lord. It is a great loss. He mourned your death, you know. We all did.'

Nick twisted his ring on his finger. 'It is rather awkward, to have been mourned, and then to return. Not that I complain. There is a comfort in knowing that people mourned you. But the monument in the churchyard –' He stopped. He was blathering.

Silence fell, except that the birds were deafening and each shifting move the horses made pointed out that he had no idea what to say to her. What was considered polite conversation between a young woman and a man? His mind was blank. 'Boatswain's still alive, too,' he said, and then wished he could swallow his tongue.

'So I see.' She turned to her black mare. 'This is Marigold.'

He reached out his hand, and the mare nuzzled his fingers. 'She's beautiful.'

The animal snorted and stomped her hoof, tossing her head in Boatswain's direction.

'She is an incorrigible flirt,' Julia said.

'I fear Boatswain is not very chivalrous.' Nick felt ashamed for his horse. The old stallion was quietly munching the long grass, twitching his ears at Marigold, but showing no interest.

Marigold put her nose in the air, whickered and pawed the ground.

'Enough,' Julia told her, and reached into her pocket for a carrot. 'He doesn't like you. Sometimes we must face life's disappointments head-on.'

'Shall we ride together awhile, Miss Percy?' Nick found himself reaching out and taking her gloved hand again. He hadn't encountered that frustrating but entirely thrilling sensation of holding a woman's hand through a layer of thin leather in so long he had forgotten entirely about it. It really was scandalously erotic, the way you could feel the heat of a woman's hand through her glove.

'I shall be missed at home.' Julia glanced down at their joined hands. 'My cousin, the new earl . . .'

Her cousin. Julia was still living at Castle Dar.

Nick went cold.

So Julia was the mistress. She was the woman the villagers had been talking about. They all thought she was sleeping with her cousin.

Julia searched his face and understood. 'Ah, I see you've heard the gossip.' She drew her hand away and took a step back.

'I have, and I don't believe it. No one who knows you would believe it.'

She put her chin up. 'You know me not at all. And those who are gossiping have known me my entire life.'

But she had been with him all along, all through the years. 'We . . . we were children together!'

'Hardly, my lord. You avoided Bella and me like the pox.'

'Be that as it may, I believe I know you, and I know you are not his mistress.'

'No. I am not.' She looked him in the eye.

She reminded him of modern women. The way she stood so confidently, the way she met his eye like an equal, the way she spoke unblushingly of the sex she was not having with her cousin. But her situation was clearly taking a toll on her courage. He could tell by the way she clenched and unclenched her left fist.

Nick glanced up for a moment into the trees, wondering what to say next. He savoured the cold air in his lungs. Then he looked down again at the woman standing before him. She was proud. And she was quietly desperate.

Last time they had met here, they had both been children. He had been the desperate one that day, the younger one, despite their ages, and somehow she had calmed him, soothed him. He had then carried her with him through the years as a misty memory.

Now her eyes were deep, storm-tossed. She needed him.

He bowed. 'I am at your service,' he said. 'Tell me how to help you.'

A smile broke across her face, and Nick realized that until this moment he had been seeing a pale shadow of Julia Percy, dimmed by her own defensive courage. Glad colour rushed to her cheeks and she burst into speech. 'Thank you, my lord. It has been the worst of times . . .'

Her voice washed over him. He was here again, where he never thought to be, and Julia Percy was alive. She was struggling against the ridiculous strictures of her age, but it was *her*. Nick watched her as she spoke: her dark hair and eyes, her vivid face . . .

God! The river was dragging at him full force, and he had to fight his way back. She was still speaking, and he held on to her voice until it broke through and made sense.

'. . . but Eamon is difficult. He does not allow me to go abroad into society, and I have not been able to convince him that I need a chaperone to maintain my reputation.'

'I don't understand; he doesn't let you out? Is he mad?'

'I believe he is.'

'Why has Clare not asked you to stay at Falcott House?'

'Clare is at Blackdown!' She frowned. 'I thought her gone to London with Bella and your mother.'

'She helped them settle in London but she prefers the country. She has been at Blackdown since just after your grandfather's death. I am shocked to learn that she has not contacted you.'

That open face shut its doors again – slammed them, rather. 'Oh.' She put her hand on her horse's pommel. 'She has heard the gossip. She believes it.'

'No. I am sure she has not, would not.' Nick put his hand over hers. 'Do not go riding off just yet, Julia.'

She whispered, and he knew it was because if she spoke any more loudly she would either shout or cry. 'Of course she believes it. I rode into the village yesterday. I saw their faces. What they believe of me, of my mother –'

'They!' Nick scoffed. 'Give Stoke Canon a man, a woman and a slightly irregular situation and it will serve you a steaming bowl of scandal broth before an hour has passed. They will sing a different tune once you are at Blackdown. As for Clare, she is not such a ninnyhammer, but if she is, then she must simply change her mind. In any case, I am taking you back to Blackdown right now. I will not have you return to Castle Dar.'

He was amazed to see her sad eyes glint with humour. 'So speaks the great marquess.'

She was teasing him from out of the depths of her fear. He smiled. 'Why shouldn't the great marquess have his say? I have to be good for something. Riding roughshod over my sisters is one my most venerable duties.'

That small sparkle faded. 'I thank you for your kind invitation, my lord, and believe me, I accept. I accept wholeheartedly. But I cannot come with you at once. Although the scandal is baseless, Eamon has reason enough to want me at Castle Dar. If I come with you now he will simply demand me back.'

'Demand you back? You're a full-grown woman. You can do as you choose . . .' Even before the words were out of his mouth, Nick realized that the sentence he had just spoken only made sense after two centuries of struggle that had yet to happen.

'Where exactly have you spent these past three years, my lord? Among some Amazon tribe?'

'In all honesty, I cannot say,' he said, and it was almost true. 'I – I had amnesia.'

'It must certainly have been somewhere quite different from England.'

'It was.'

She simply looked at him. She, who had known him as a child and now saw him as an adult. Nick couldn't believe how good it felt to have that gap bridged. How good it felt just to have those ink-dark eyes rest on him, even with that quizzical look in them. 'Then I'll kill him,' he heard himself saying. 'If he won't allow you to come to Blackdown with me now, I'll kill him.'

She laughed. 'You will have to make up your mind between the two options you give me. Either I am to do just as I please and walk out of the front door, or you are to kill him and carry me off like a pillaged sack of flour!'

She was right. He did sound like a maniac. He needed to get control of himself. Himselves. But he didn't want to. Her laugh was enchanting. It was the same one he had heard yesterday as she galloped away towards the river. He wanted to kiss her. He Nick Davenant, and he Nicholas Falcott. For once they wanted the same thing.

He dropped his hand from where it rested on hers, to keep himself from grabbing it and pulling her to him. 'What do you propose, then?'

She looked down the fields towards Blackdown. 'I had been planning to run away. I could affect a bolt to London and come to you instead.'

Nick sucked in his cheeks. 'But that would cement your bad reputation, and frankly it would besmirch my name as well.' He smiled. 'And since I am as pure as snow and as guileless as a dove . . .'

She snorted. 'Oh, indeed.'

The snort did it. Nick was lost. He stared at her like a mooncalf. Why shouldn't he fall down on one knee right here and ask for her hand? He *was* Blackdown, at least partially. And she was an earl's granddaughter. If it weren't for the Guild, he wouldn't even hesitate. He would be expected to do it. Do it and then live happily ever goddam after, day following day.

'My lord?'

He blinked.

'Is something amiss?'

'I . . . need to think.' He stepped closer to her. 'I need to think, and I need to consult with Clare. Don't run away. Don't do anything. Just meet me here tomorrow.'

Her eyes widened, and he realized he was looming over her, demanding that she meet him again, unchaperoned. For God's sake, the nineteenth century! It was ridiculous. 'To make plans,' he said, stepping back.

'Of course.' She put her nose up, affecting not to have misunderstood him. Perfection. 'That is, if Clare raises no objection to you trysting with the whore of Stoke Canon.'

'I shall be here, Julia, never you fear. Now let me toss you up.' He put his hands at her waist, felt the delicious swell of her hips, and in spite of all his instincts, which urged him to pull that beautiful derrière back against himself, he placed her neatly in her saddle, allowing his hand to rest for just a fraction of a second on her thigh.

She looked down at him, her eyes grave. Then, without saying anything more, she turned Marigold back toward the path through the woods. The horse made its careful way through the trees, soon disappearing into the shifting shade. Nick stood stock still, staring after them. Then he yanked Boatswain's head up from the grass, threw himself into the saddle and galloped all the way back to Falcott House.

16

Julia rode slowly through the woods. Blackdown was back from the dead. And just in time to help her.

She had recognized him immediately, but the longer they talked the less she could see the boy in the man in front of her. By the end of their conversation she had felt she was talking to a stranger. His eyes crinkled when he smiled. What had been dimples were now two deeply carved lines. He had a scar across his eyebrow.

Well, he had been in the wars, hadn't he? He had been lost for three years. He must have been terribly injured, not to know himself for that long. Terrible things could age a man.

This new Blackdown was unsettling. The distance in his eyes had suddenly became a nearness that seemed to sear right through her. The strength she had felt in his arms when he helped her into the saddle. He was grown.

As was she. Twenty-two. Almost on the shelf, that's how grown she was.

In other words, the years had flown. Time had passed. There was nothing strange in that.

Yet there was something off-kilter. Time had passed, but it had passed *wrongly*. Blackdown looked older than he should. And she, who had never seen the world, never been to a ball more grand than an impromptu minuet at a neighbour's — she realized, in his presence, that she had not ever truly stepped across the threshold into adulthood, despite being too old to be young.

All her problems seemed to be about time.

She ducked her head to avoid a low-hanging bough. Do not borrow trouble from tomorrow. That had been Grandfather's motto, and look what good it had done. It turned out that yesterday's trouble had been brewing in Stoke Canon ever since she'd arrived. Some suspicion of her mother's virtue, long buried, but ready to burst forth. The chicken-and-the-egg conundrum. Was she bad because her mother was bad, or was her poor dead mother being vilified only now that the daughter was in trouble?

Julia laughed bitterly. Because now she was, indeed, living down to her reputation. She had, after all, agreed to meet Blackdown again tomorrow. Julia would be the first to admit that she had been raised largely by accident, but it was wrong for a young woman to sneak off and meet a man alone in the woods. Even she knew that much about propriety.

As for Blackdown, he was no paragon. He had put his ungloved hand on hers when she reached up for her pommel then left it there for ages. And then when he had tossed her up, for just a moment that hand had rested on her leg. She had looked at his hand, both times. The ring that had looked too big when he was young now suited his strength exactly. His hand was beautiful. More beautiful than the rest of him.

Did he believe she was Eamon's mistress?

Marigold emerged from the woods and broke, unasked, into a trot. Julia welcomed the jolting gait. Maybe it would bring her back to herself. Because it didn't matter what the marquess thought. What mattered was that she now had an invitation to Falcott House, the invitation that she desperately needed. The grandeur of his title and his home, the unquestionable virtue of his sister and her chaperonage – her honour would be salvaged. All she had to do was find a way to leave Castle Dar.

*

'So. You disobey me.' Eamon stood in the doorway, watching her climb the steps.

'Good day, Cousin.' Julia found that the sight of him no longer nauseated her.

'Get in here.' He reached out for her arm as she walked up the steps.

She jerked it away. 'Unhand me. There is no need. I am coming in.' She swept past him into the dark hallway, stripping off her gloves and unpinning her hat. She laid them on the footman's chair and turned to face her fulminating cousin. 'What is it you want of me?'

Eamon's tombstone teeth gleamed in the dim light of the entrance hall. 'I have found the talisman,' he said.

Julia raised her eyebrows. 'Really? Have you stopped time?'

'No, but I will soon enough. Come. I want to see if you recognize it.' He led the way into the study, and Julia suppressed a gasp. The piles of strange items that the servants had collected for Eamon had all been cleared away. Everything of Grandfather's, all his stones and books and knick-knacks, was gone. The room was bare and the desk entirely clear, except for one small, colourful box sitting in the exact centre of the leather desktop.

It was the lacquered Chinese box that Grandfather had shown her years before.

Eamon picked it up and handed it to her. 'Have you ever seen this box before?'

'No,' Julia lied. She held it lightly. 'What is it?'

Eamon looked at her, long and piercingly, and Julia returned his gaze. Apparently satisfied, he took a piece of paper out of his pocket. She could see that it had a line or two of Grandfather's writing on it. '"July the twenty-first, 1803,"' Eamon read out loud. '"Solved in forty-eight seconds."'

Julia turned the box over in her hands. 'It requires a solution?' She hoped her voice sounded innocent.

Eamon snatched it out of her hands. 'Yes, stupid girl. It is clearly a magical box of some sort. There is either something in it or something in the opening of it that must unlock time. I found it in a hidden compartment in this desk – devilish clever, but I found it. This box, and a worthless miniature of some mulatto.' Eamon dug carelessly in his pocket and extracted another square of paper. He handed it over and Julia gazed down at a remarkably realistic painting, smooth as ice. It depicted a young woman's laughing face. The woman's skin was darker than English people's, her hair a deeper black, her eyes a clearer blue. Indeed, the colours of everything in the picture, including the slice of sky behind her head and the yellows of her dress, seemed richer than any Julia had seen before. She turned the painting over, but there was nothing written on the back. The paper was slick; Julia had no idea how the paint could possibly adhere to it. She held it back out to Eamon, but he waved his hand. 'Keep it if you like.'

'Might not this picture be the talisman?'

'Give it back!' He snatched the painting and studied it. 'Perhaps, perhaps . . . but how?'

'If Grandfather hid it with the box, perhaps they are to be used together.'

Eamon frowned at her, suspicious. 'You suddenly seem very eager to help, Julia.'

'As you know, Cousin, I do not believe there is a talisman. I believe Grandfather's talent died with him. But if this trinket will satisfy your quest for one, I shall be delighted.'

'There is a talisman.' Eamon pushed the painting back into his pocket, oblivious to her sarcasm. 'I am sure of it. It is this box. But the note is puzzling. The box must be manipulated in a certain way for exactly forty-eight seconds? Could that be it?'

Julia knew very well what the note chronicled. Grandfather had been looking at his stopwatch while she had tried to solve the puzzle. She had thought herself defeated, for the box never opened. But clearly she had, in fact, succeeded, and he had been testing her speed with it. Why?

Eamon was half twisting the box one way, then twisting it back and half twisting it another. He was clearly afraid to disarrange it. 'How does it work?' he muttered to himself. 'What is the secret?'

Julia cleared her throat. 'Cousin, may I please leave you to this?'

Eamon looked up at her blindly, the lacquered box sickly bright in his pale fingers. Then he nodded. 'Yes, yes. Go. Run along. In fact, I don't want to see you for the remainder of the day.'

And I hope to never see you again, Julia thought as she left the room.

Nick leapt from his horse, tossed the reins to a waiting groom and ran from the stable yard to the house. He began yelling for Clare before he was even properly inside.

She came running, her face pale. 'What is it? Are you ill?'

'I am completely well,' he said, 'but what in the devil's name is wrong with you?'

'With me?' His sister drew up short. 'Have you hit your head again?' She came forward, hand outstretched to feel his forehead.

'There's nothing amiss with me.' He pushed past her and strode ahead into the drawing room, then turned and pointed a finger. 'But you need a damned good explanation for why you haven't been to see Julia Percy, when you must know that her reputation is in tatters. The new Lord Darchester is keeping her locked up like a prisoner. Or are you deceived by the slander?'

'Heavens.' Clare sank onto a settee. 'I feared that something was terribly wrong over at Castle Dar. There has been talk among the servants that the new earl might be mad. Their footman is betrothed to our kitchen maid and she said that –'

'I see. You feared something might be wrong. And you heard from the servants that the earl is mad. So instead of helping our family's friend and neighbour, you spent your time weaving plans with Jem Jemison for the destruction of Blackdown.'

Clare thinned her lips and took a moment to respond. 'Mr Jemison has left Blackdown, you will be pleased to know. He has gone to London.'

For some reason this only enraged Nick further. 'So now I must find a new steward? Wonderful! And why didn't he tell me of his decision to leave? I am the marquess –'

'I hired him when you were dead,' Clare said sharply, her temper finally flaring. 'And so he came to me this morning and told me he was leaving. He is in London trying to find another way to care for the soldiers of *your* regiment.'

'Oh, they were *my* soldiers, were they, who were going to swarm like locusts over my land? You didn't tell me that yesterday. And now you imply that I am the rich man of the parable, that I turn them from the door like Lazarus the leper! I understand you, Sister. You imply that I am a negligent boor, and perhaps I am. But you are no better. Explain to me about Julia Percy, and why you have abandoned her!'

Clare stood still, allowing his rage to crash around her, her face rigid. 'You have been away too long. You forget: you cannot simply burst into the home of a belted earl on the strength of servants' gossip and demand that he hand over a member of his family.'

Nick threw up his hands. 'Of course not. Perish the thought that it might be possible to rescue Julia from the clutches of a madman. Shall I tell you why? It is because he is a lord of the realm and his accusers are servants. And because she is a woman, with no rights of her own.' He rounded on Clare, pointing a finger at her nose. 'I tell you, Clare, the world has to change. You women must stop regarding yourselves as chattels.'

At that, Clare put back her hands on her hips and laughed. 'Your bump on the head certainly changed you, Nickin. You accuse me of destroying Blackdown for a dream of brotherhood and equality – meanwhile it appears that you have been transformed into a Godwinite!'

'Perhaps I have been. As should you.'

Her laugh died, but her eyes smiled at him. 'What happened to you in Spain?'

'Never you mind.' Nick crossed his arms over his chest. 'Now explain yourself, woman.'

'A Godwinite, but still pig-headed! Of course I have been to visit the new earl, and to see Julia. Do you think I am heartless? She adored that crusty grandfather of hers, and she must be devastated without him. I arrived home from London the day after the old earl died, and I went immediately to Castle Dar. I was turned away, but I returned the next day and again the next. The other women of the parish have also tried to call. We left cards, we left invitations, we even went as a group and sought to be admitted. The men have gone, too. Although we could tell it pained good Pringle to do it, we were all repeatedly turned away.'

Nick glared at his sister, then strode away across the room and back again. 'Talk, talk, talk,' he finally said. 'Gossip and talk. The good people of the parish fret and worry: "Oh, poor Julia." Then, my dear sister, do you know what they do when they are home again? They tell vicious stories, and they relish every word. Did you know, Clare, that everyone thinks she is Darchester's mistress? After only a fortnight?' He nodded at her. 'Oh, yes. I suppose you are not privy to the more salacious rumours that fly about the village, due to your being . . .' He paused. 'Due to . . .' He finished lamely.

Clare sat back down. 'Due to the fact that I am a spinster, you mean? You have ranted like a lunatic for ten minutes, and now you choose to mince words? I am a spinster and a noblewoman. As a result, no one ever tells me anything. Why don't you come down off your high horse, take a seat and let us have a rational conversation about this problem. I am indeed appalled to learn that our neighbours think so badly of Julia, and I am ashamed that I have not done more to try to see her and find out the truth of her situation. But let us not lose our heads. Tell me what you know, and together we shall find a way to secure Julia's freedom.'

Nick glowered.

She patted the seat next to her and raised her eyebrows at him in the time-honoured gesture of an older sister. 'Sit,' she said.

'As you wish.' He collapsed down next to her, draped one arm around her shoulders, and stretched his legs out. He tried, unconsciously, to shove one trainer off his foot with the toe of the other, and looked in some surprise down the length of his body, past his jacket and breeches to his tall riding boots. 'I am in all my dirt,' he said, remembering suddenly that he really ought to change out of his riding clothes before conversing with a lady, even if that lady happened to be his sister.

'Yes, you are a barbarian,' Clare said. 'Now tell me.'

Nick let his head fall back against the sofa. He spoke up to the ceiling. 'I rode to the wood and encountered Julia riding over from Castle Dar,' he said.

'I thought she was a prisoner.'

'She is, to all intents.'

Clare sighed. 'I don't mean to doubt you, Nick, but are you certain she is in such dire straits as you imagine? After all, she was riding about. When did you even have the chance to hear village gossip? You returned only the day before yesterday.'

'Count Lebedev overheard the news of Julia's supposed disgrace bantered about the inn yard, of all places. And I know Julia is in danger because she told me she was, and I believe her.'

Clare nodded. 'Julia is a dramatic little body,' she said, 'but she is not a liar.'

'What do you mean, a dramatic little body?' Nick sat up straight and swivelled to face his sister.

'Oh, nothing. But when Julia was younger, she and Bella were forever brewing up mischief of one kind or another. You must remember, Nickin. She was always over here, underfoot. They did terrible things.'

Nick did have a vague memory of his little sister and her friend charging up and down the staircases yodelling like beagles, but he had hardly been interested in girls three years his junior. 'How terrible could two little girls be?'

Clare laughed incredulously. 'I will not even deign to answer that question. Except to remind you of the time, a few years before Papa's death, when they let the pigs into the kitchen garden. Arabella did not care for carrots and they thought to ruin the year's crop.'

A memory floated back to him of little Bella at teatime, the rest of the family feasting on her favourite cake while she sat weeping, with nothing but a big carrot on her plate. 'Julia was behind that prank?'

'Oh, I don't know whose idea it was, but she was certainly caught red-handed alongside Bella, exhorting the pigs to root up the gardeners' hard work. Of course the poor animals were simply running wild all over the garden, trying to escape two screaming girls.'

'Papa must have been enraged.'

'I'm surprised they both survived into adulthood,' Clare said. 'When they were discovered in their mischief-making, Bella lied or cried like any normal girl, but Julia stood like a queen and took her punishment. If she felt the accusation was just, she condescended to apologize for her actions. But if she felt the accusation was unfair, the scorn in her eye was withering. If she hadn't been such a loving child, and so obviously in need of mothering, I believe Mother would have come to fear her.' Clare sighed. 'I hate to think of someone of her spirit suffering confinement and perhaps . . . worse.' She turned an anxious face to Nick. 'You don't think there is any truth in the gossip? That she is his . . . ?'

'No.' Nick stood and paced the room. 'No. The girl I met today was no one's mistress, willing or unwilling. But she was anxious about her own safety, and she did agree that she should come to us at Blackdown. Apparently she cannot get away from this cousin of hers. He seems to have some hold over her. It's enough to drive me mad with worry for her.'

Clare looked at him thoughtfully, her lips pursed. 'Hmm,' she said.

'Hmm what?'

'Just hmm.'

Nick twitched his cuffs into place. He had never been able to hide anything from the all-seeing older-sisterly powers of Clare. Of course that went two ways, and therefore he knew exactly what she was thinking when she said 'hmm'. And she was perfectly right. This morning Julia had plucked his heart like it was nothing more than a strawberry hiding under a leaf. He loved her. He, Nick Davenant, né Nicholas Falcott. Or was it Falcott né Davenant? In any case, there it was. He was in love with a woman two hundred years in his past.

Not that he was going to admit his feelings to Clare, or indeed to anyone. So he scowled. 'May we please concentrate on how to get Julia from there to here?'

Then, from across the room, Nick and Clare heard a delicate cough, and the Russian rose up from a leather armchair that faced the fire. 'If I may offer my services?' The paternal benevolence of his smile encompassed them both.

'For God's sake, Lebedev. Don't you know it is rude to eavesdrop?'

'I beg your pardon.' Arkady examined his fingernails. 'But I was happily dozing in this chair when you two barged in and began your so interesting conversation.'

'Clare, I apologize for the count. If anyone is a barbarian, it is he.'

Clare turned sparklingly to Arkady. 'If you would care to join us, Count Lebedev? I'm sure your suggestions will be most welcome.'

'I thank you.' He bowed, shooting Nick a triumphant glance, then strolled across the room. 'The problems of your neighbours are tiresome. I came here to fry, how to say it, bigger fish?'

Nick rolled his eyes. 'I am desolate to learn that you find our society tedious and our problems beneath your interest.'

Arkady brushed past Nick. 'May I?' He indicated Nick's old seat beside Clare, and Clare nodded. Arkady disposed himself gracefully and looked from one sibling to the other. 'The rank of marquess, it is higher than the rank of earl, am I wrong?'

'So what?' Nick crossed his arms over his chest.

'This phrase, "so what",' Arkady said. 'It does not sound quite correct.' He looked darkly at Nick.

'I don't give a rat's arse,' Nick said. 'You understand me perfectly. I repeat: so what?'

Clare laughed. 'Calm yourself, Nick, and do exert yourself to speak like a gentleman. The count is only trying to help, and you are behaving like a bear.'

Arkady spread his hands. 'You have been forgetting yourself for three years, Lord Blackdown. Your sister said you have changed. You admire Godwin and his wife Mary . . . Mary . . .'

'Wollstonecraft.' Nick ground the name out.

'Ah, yes. You have been keeping company, perhaps, with revolutionaries? And, shall we say, enlightened women? Such exciting thoughts they think, these men and women who dream about the future. But please recall: what is in the brain of a normal aristocrat? He goes to a dinner party. Is he thinking that the women are the equals of the men? Does he want to end the slavery? No. He worries: who is sitting below me at the table? To that man, he shows only his nostrils. Who is sitting above me? To that man, he smiles and smiles.'

'Please,' Nick said. 'Get to your point.'

Arkady inclined his head. 'If your English aristocracy is anything like our Russian aristocracy, your neighbour the earl will welcome you, the marquess, with bows and scrapes. He thought you were dead. That made him the highest aristocrat in miles and miles. Down he looked upon everyone. But now you have returned. He will not like it, but he must look up to you. I predict that he will accept a visit from you and your sister.'

'Of course.' Clare pivoted on the couch. She was practically in Arkady's lap. 'You are right. We shall wear our finest apparel, stink of ambergris and disapproval, and stay only fifteen minutes. We shall suggest to him that if he does not stop trampling on his cousin's reputation, society will shun him.'

'If I may be permitted to join you?' Arkady smiled at Clare. 'I have much interest in this Castle Dar. I have heard, oh, many tales about it. It has a very interesting atmosphere. Almost . . . timeless?' Arkady caught Nick's eye over Clare's head and gave him a meaningful look.

Nick had to admit it was a plan. It did not involve riding up to Castle Dar on a fiery white stallion, fighting the earl with a broadsword and then carrying Julia away into the sunset. But then again, it would probably work. And if Arkady got to hunt Ofan on the side, that was fine, too. 'Yes,' he said. 'We go tomorrow afternoon.'

'Why not this afternoon?' Clare asked.

Nick thought of Julia, and the possibility of a meeting up by the woods tomorrow morning. Once she was at Blackdown, he would never see her alone; she would always be with Clare, stitching or some other nonsense. 'I have said tomorrow afternoon; it is decided.'

Clare regarded him coolly, then turned to Arkady. 'Do you know, Count, I think he is in danger of falling in love with our imperilled Miss Percy.'

Arkady crossed his arms. 'I think you are right.' He, too, favoured Nick with a long, serious look. 'And I don't like it.'

Nick slammed out of the room.

17

Julia on her horse. Julia dressed in jeans and a T-shirt, curled up by the fire in the Vermont house. Julia bent back over his arm . . . Nick flipped over, pulling a pillow onto his head. It was three in the morning and he was wracked by lust. His body and soul were on fire with it.

Yesterday on the hillside the marquess had managed to gain the upper hand, and his idea was simple. Marry her. Settle down and raise little marquesses. The marquess was living in a comedy. Nick Davenant was tied to the Guild and therefore he was living in a tragedy. But this scene, in which the hero is tormented by desire, was the same in both scripts.

It was the thought of her waist. Of how it had felt in his hands when he had lifted her into the saddle. How she might strain upward to kiss him, if she were to kiss him. How his hands might drift down from her waist . . .

Good grief.

She is a gentlewoman, he told himself. A lady. Bred to save her virginity and even her kisses until marriage.

Even her kisses, Nick, he told himself from under the pillow. You can't kiss her if she comes to meet you in the morning. You shouldn't even hold her hand. Those are the rules and you know them through and through.

'Through and through,' he said out loud. 'Shoe and glue. Brew and blue. Tutu.'

He groaned. The last time he had tried the rhyming game it had ended with his thinking of Julia. Way back in the twenty-first century, when the thought of Julia used to calm him down. Now she inflamed him.

She probably thought he was marriage material. Maybe she even wanted to tempt his kisses. That was how it worked. A kiss and then a proposal. A girl in her position expected to get married, to dutifully offer up her virginity on her wedding night, to have children and be a respected lady. Getting herself married off to the boy next door might seem like the perfect happy ending to her. Goddam it, it *was* the perfect happy ending.

Nick groaned again as the wedding-night scenario unrolled its luxurious details, like Cleopatra out of a carpet.

He would stay home tomorrow morning. He would stay home tomorrow morning. He would stay home . . .

Morning found him walking towards the woods, rain dripping from his curly brimmed beaver hat and from the capes of his greatcoat. Gore-tex, he thought to himself. Wicking fabric. He had high-tech rain gear in his hall closet in Vermont. Yet here he was, dressed in clothes that smelled when they got wet. Wool and linen and leather and fur and cotton. Animal and vegetable. Natural dyes. Hand-stitching. He breathed the clean air in through his mouth. The rain tasted pure on his tongue. Perhaps Julia would stay home and solve his problem for him. She hadn't said she would come. She certainly shouldn't come. If she was a good girl, a lady . . .

She wasn't a good girl or a lady. She was Julia.

She would come.

He looked up, almost expecting to see her up at the edge of the wood, waiting for him. But the line of trees, black in the rain, cut blankly across the horizon like a wall.

Julia hung back under the boughs, watching him come towards her. He looked severe in his hat and greatcoat, and he was walking with deliberate purpose, as if striding across the field to a duel. Or perhaps he was coming to tell her that he now believed the rumours.

She took a step or two back into the trees. She wasn't sure she could bear to hear those recriminations on his lips. There was still time to turn and walk away. But he was making short work of the distance. She saw him look up and wondered whether he'd seen her. She was wearing her red cloak, for she had no black one. But if he did see her he gave no sign and simply marched inexorably forward.

God, he was a fool. No fool like an old fool. He was only supposed to be a few years her senior, and if you counted by birth year, that was true enough. But in another way he was nearly twelve years older, and in yet another way he was unfathomably older – so old, in fact, that he shouldn't even have been born yet. Yet, in spite of it all, here he was, squelching through the fields like some pastoral swain off to meet his shepherdess. Fortunately she wasn't there, and he was later than he had been yesterday. Maybe she had some sense. It would be good if one of them did. In spite of the cold rain wilting his cravat and spotting his boots, in spite of the knowledge that he was a damned idiot, and in spite of the fact that he was clearly heading arrow-straight towards supreme folly, he burned for her.

'Damn.' He cursed aloud. Then he looked up again, and there she was, her red cape like an ensign against the black bark of the trees, her face lifted to the rain. She was so beautiful that he stopped in his tracks. Then he couldn't help it. He frowned, but he stepped forward, and his hand was reaching out for hers.

She could sense his foul mood as he came closer, and perversely, it drew her out of the trees. She put her chin up, and her hood fell back. She didn't replace it. The cool rain on her face felt good. She didn't know why he was coming towards her looking so ferocious, but if he thought he could scare her, he could think again. Then he looked up and his eyes fastened on hers and his frown deepened. But he closed the space between them in a few short strides and his hand in its brown glove reached for hers. 'Julia,' he said, and his voice was rough.

She put her black-gloved hand in his and curtseyed, her back straight. 'My lord.'

He looked down at her, holding her hand lightly in his. Now that he was close she could tell that he was angry with himself and not with her. He said nothing.

'You are thinking you should not have come,' she said.

'Yes.'

'You invited me. It was for me to accept or decline. If you had not come, and I had, you would have been breaking every rule of good society.'

He smiled grimly. 'By inviting you I broke every rule of good society, and you know it.'

'Yes, I do know it,' she said. They stood for a moment, looking at their entwined hands. She could feel the banked energy in his fingers, even as they held hers as gently as a bone-china teacup. She lifted her eyes. She intended to say that she knew he was here only to make plans, but instead she said, 'I am glad you came. I –'

Suddenly he was kissing her. Perhaps he could not have helped it. Her rain-wet mouth, her red cloak, the dark trees, the smell of the earth, and most of all her dark eyes looking so candidly into his, those eyes that had haunted him for centuries . . . Before she could finish what she was saying, he gathered her into his arms and his lips found hers.

At first it felt innocent, if only because of the cool rain-water on their faces. Her lips, fresh with rain, trembled beneath his like the leaves trembling above their heads. Her nose tucked perfectly against his, and he pulled her still more tightly against him. Even through their layers of wet clothing he thought he could feel her heart fluttering, but perhaps it was his own heart, or simply his own blood singing in his ears.

Then he pulled back, just a little. Her sweet breath washed warm over his face, and nothing was innocent any more. They were back among the trees, and she was up against the smooth trunk of an ancient beech, her arms around his neck as he kissed her open mouth and reached into the opening of her cloak and around to pull her narrow waist closer to him. His hat was knocked from his head; her dark hair was half spilling down her shoulders. He kissed her face, her closed eyes, her chin, and down her neck. She cried his name, and it sounded so perfect on her lips – Nicholas. 'Say that again,' he breathed in her ear, feeling her shiver and arch more firmly against him. 'Nicholas,' she whispered. He flicked his tongue lightly around her ear, and she swayed and seemed to lose her balance. He caught her delicious bottom in his hands and brought her gasping against his thighs. She pulled his head down for another kiss.

Then, as if by mutual agreement, it slowly began to end. Perhaps it was the change in the light as the rain stopped. Or perhaps it was that there were only two choices, and one of them was unthinkable. In any case, like sleepers slowly waking, they pulled clingingly apart until they stood facing one another again, her hand in his, gazing down together at their fingers.

'Julia.'

She didn't look up but pulled her hand from his. 'Say nothing.'

'How do you know what I would say?'

She brushed her hands down her cloak, and it fell closed again across her black dress. 'I just do not want you to say anything.' She looked up. 'Let it be.'

'I am not free,' he said.

The shock came to her eyes immediately, and he stumbled to explain.

'I don't mean –'

She held her hand up and turned away. 'I asked you to say nothing.'

Nick reached for her and managed to capture the edge of her cloak. She looked back over her shoulder. 'Yes?'

'You are right. You asked me to be silent and I was not able to. For that I apologize.'

'I accept your apology.'

'I do not, however, apologize for kissing you, Julia. That, I had to do. I don't regret it.'

She wheeled and faced him fully, twitching her cloak from his fingers. 'If you had apologized for that, Nicholas Falcott,' she said, 'you would at this moment be sporting a black eye.'

That made all his desire come surging back. 'You are gallant, Julia,' he said roughly. 'A champion. I fully intend to kiss you again one day.'

'Oh do you?'

'Yes, I'm afraid I do.'

She stared at him for a moment, and when she spoke her voice was low and vibrant. 'The road to hell is paved with such intentions, my lord. It will be a cold day in that place when you kiss me again.' She turned and stalked away.

'Wait,' he called. 'I must inform you of another matter.'

She stopped without turning. 'Yes?'

'My sister and I have devised a plan for your release from Castle Dar. Clare, my friend Count Lebedev and I will be arriving this afternoon at four to confront your cousin. We intend to be disgustingly imperious. I shall be the grand marquess, and Clare shall be the outraged lady of virtue. Lebedev will fill in as necessary. The intention is to shame your cousin into releasing you.'

She turned her head and showed him one haughty eye. 'Thank you, my lord,' she said, stiffly formal. 'I shall be ready.' She snapped her head back round and walked away, her red cloak brilliant against the wet green leaves.

Nick watched her go, half expecting her to turn again, but of course she did not. When she disappeared round a bend in the dripping tunnel of trees, he retrieved his hat from the ground and absent-mindedly brushed its pile into place before jamming it on his head. Well, he'd gone ahead and kissed her. Because it was the only thing to do. Because rules are made to be broken.

There was a rustle in the tree above him, then something fell, ricocheting off his hat. He watched as the small missile bounced once and came to rest near his toe. Nick bent and picked it up. It was a perfect little acorn, still with its jaunty cap. One of last season's. It must have held on until this spring rain knocked it down. It was like Julia. Small, brown and lovely. Filled with a compact, passionate promise. He tucked it in his pocket.

He set off towards home, kicking at the ground and cursing the dragoon whose raised sabre had sent him crashing into the twenty-first century. He doubly cursed the Guild, which had first made it impossible for him to return and now made it impossible for him to stay. If, instead of jumping, he had somehow survived the war and returned home, he might at this moment be safely buckled to Julia, well on the way to the smug, fat contentment that was his birthright. Instead he had been hurled forward, out of Julia's life, and then back into her life like a bloody bolt from the blue. He had just this moment bruised her pride, if not her heart, and he might well have destroyed his own chances for happiness into the bargain.

He kicked a clod of mud and cursed when it proved to be a cowpat. 'I hate myself,' he muttered, hopping on one foot while trying to wipe the toe of his boot on the grass. 'Sometimes I just hate myself.'

18

At three forty-five Julia was waiting upstairs in the Yellow Saloon, where callers were usually received. She alternated sitting with pacing back and forth in front of the windows, looking for the first sign of the carriage. Would they come? He'd said they would, but that had been in the wake of him kissing her. Perhaps he had gone away and thought better of it. After all, she had stolen away to meet him, she had recklessly kissed him back . . . when they were supposed to be planning how to save her reputation. How stood her reputation now? Julia closed her eyes. The world was very small, and it was easy to trip over things, easy to close doors for ever. Easy to trap yourself.

That was why she hadn't wanted him to say anything afterwards. She hadn't wanted the kiss to resolve immediately into debts, duties . . . or awkward explanations of why he couldn't, why he wouldn't. She had just wanted him to be silent. Just wanted the kiss to be a kiss, a floating moment in time without repercussions.

Instead, he'd spoken. 'I am not free.' It was strange, but his saying that had made the notion of freedom seem suddenly sordid. It had made her feel like he was perfectly free and it was she who was tainted, guilty, unfree. And perhaps now he did finally believe that she was no better than her reputation. A loose woman.

Well. Best not to borrow trouble from earlier today, either. Julia sighed and turned her mind to more immediate problems. If he did come, it was important that the plan should work, and she wasn't sure strategic snobbery and appeals to propriety would do the trick. Eamon was currently obsessed with the lacquered box and much less interested in Julia than he had been. He might already be willing to let her go. Or he might be enraged by the pomposity of his neighbours and refuse.

She heard a sound and went to the window. She couldn't yet see the carriage, but she could hear the horses' hooves and the wheels on the gravel. She turned and looked some-what wildly around the room. Soon Nicholas would be here, in this room. The man she had kissed in the rain. Desire had held her in its hand today, and she had yielded, as a ripe peach yields to the teeth. She wanted to be back with him in the woods, she wanted to feel his rough cheek against hers, his hair tangling in her hands, his hot kisses on her throat.

Julia closed her eyes and took a deep breath. Her temper had always been her besetting sin. Now she knew that anger and desire were drawn from the same well. He had gripped her strongly, kissed her harshly, and she had met him with equal strength. Then he'd made her angry, and her anger had felt good, as good as the passion.

The sound of the approaching carriage grew louder and Julia opened her eyes. For a moment she simply stared, and then she laughed; an ostentatious red-bodied coach was bowling out from under the trees, a gilded coat of arms on its doors. The coachman was in full Blackdown livery, and he was driving a perfectly matched four of chestnuts. It was all very splendid, and utterly ridiculous for an afternoon visit among near neighbours. She laughed again as the coachman deftly avoided the bump in the drive. But her laughter died in her throat as the horses swept the coach up in front of the house, and she was biting her lip by the time the coachman climbed down, opened the door and lowered the step with a flourish.

Clare's foot emerged first, clad in a satin shoe, and then the rest of her, her gloved hand grasping the coachman's for support, her calm face tilted to look up at the house. She wore an elaborately ruched chocolate-brown spencer over a dress of rust-red net, its deep hem richly embroidered in browns and blues and golds. Her red turban sported a glorious dark blue ostrich feather affixed with a golden brooch. She looked so magnificent as to appear slightly theatrical, which Julia knew to be the goal.

Next to emerge was a tall, older man with a full head of wild white hair. This had to be Count Lebedev. He stood beside Clare and looked at the house with a slight sneer, one hand on his hip, the other clasping his black beaver hat, which Julia could see had a garish red lining.

Finally, after what seemed like a year, Blackdown climbed out of the coach. He was a few inches shorter than the Russian but dressed identically, in a blue superfine coat with bright buttons, buff pantaloons and tasselled Hessian boots. The men's snowy cravats were even tied in the same stiff and intricate oriental style.

She reached out and put her hand against the glass, covering the party of visitors with her fingers for just a moment. She let her hand drop, and the three callers reappeared. As if he sensed her, Nick turned his head and looked straight up at her window. She held her chin high. He nodded to her curtly.

The trio paused together and gazed at the house, rather like three generals surveying a battlefield, Clare with unruffled certitude, the Russian with contempt and the marquess with impassive determination. Without speaking to one another, they moved towards the door and out of Julia's line of sight.

She now simply had to wait, and hope that Eamon would receive his guests in the Yellow Saloon.

Pringle tried to turn them away at the door, as he had been instructed. But his obedience to his master was suitably overwhelmed by the sight of Nicholas Falcott, returned so gloriously and miraculously from the war. The young marquess was sadly weathered by his years spent in the hot sun, but he was so finely dressed, and his elegant Russian friend was a true dandy, Pringle could tell. After some debate, he agreed that the earl might be persuaded into receiving his guests.

Five minutes later he returned. The earl would see them in the Blue Drawing Room. 'Which is in and of itself a miracle, my lords and lady. But not Miss Julia. He orders that she must wait upstairs. She will not be permitted to join you.'

'Where is Miss Julia?' Clare put her hand on Pringle's arm. 'She is expecting us.'

'In the Yellow Saloon, my lady.'

'Does she yet know that she is not to come downstairs?' Clare asked.

The butler shook his head.

'Then I shall go up to her,' Clare said, all brisk efficiency. 'You may explain to the earl that I insisted upon seeing my old friend and would not take no for an answer. I'll then bring her down to the Blue Drawing Room. I shall simply tell his lordship that I couldn't bear not to see her.' She turned to Nick and Arkady. 'Good luck, gentlemen. I'll be down with Julia in a trice.' She caught up her skirt in one hand and ran lightly up the stairs.

Pringle led the men across the entrance hall, but after only a few steps Arkady held up his hand. 'Hush.' He cocked his head, as if listening. 'Do you feel it?'

'Feel what?'

Arkady mouthed the word so that Pringle could not hear: 'Time.'

Nick concentrated. Perhaps he did feel a little tremor, a tiny sensation. But nothing definite. He raised a quizzical eyebrow, and Arkady nodded.

'Give us a moment please, Pringle?' Nick looked to the butler, who stepped discreetly away.

'That is time play?' Nick whispered. 'But it's so faint. It doesn't feel right.'

'Yes.' Arkady looked all round the room. 'Someone is thinking of playing with time. They have not yet done it, but they are making the surface of the river ripple with the power of their feelings.' Arkady paused again, wrinkling his nose as if at a bad smell. 'But as you say, it doesn't feel right. Something is very strange here.'

'So what do we do?'

'Keep your eyes and ears open. Someone here is dangling their fingers in the river. Perhaps we will discover who it is. Perhaps this so-reclusive earl is of interest after all.'

Arkady strode towards Pringle, and with a flourish the butler pulled open the huge mahogany double doors that led to the formal rooms of Castle Dar. 'The Marquess of Blackdown. Count Lebedev of St Petersburg.' Pringle sang their names into the echoing, dark vastness of the Blue Drawing Room.

Where were they? Julia paced the Yellow Saloon, tamping down the desire to go in search of them. She had half a mind to freeze time and go downstairs to see what was going on, but then she heard a light step running up the stair. Julia opened the door just as Clare reached it. Julia cried out at the sight of the familiar face, and Clare hugged her.

'Oh, poor Julia!' Clare pulled away, gripping Julia's shoulders. 'Nick told me what you have been suffering. I did not realize the gossip was so cruel, but that is no excuse for my negligence. I hope you can forgive me.'

'Please, it is nothing. I am just so glad to see you, and to see that you believe in me.' Julia hugged Clare again. 'Where are the others?'

'There is a fly in the ointment. They are downstairs with your cousin in the Blue Drawing Room.'

'But we never use that room. It is a silk-lined barn. The servants probably haven't dusted it in a month.'

'Nevertheless, that is where the gentlemen are. Your cousin did not want you to be informed of our visit.'

Anger bit Julia, hard. 'He is a toad,' she said, spitting the word out. 'He makes me his prisoner, allows the gossip to grow – and only for his own perverse pleasure in seeing me suffer.'

Julia barely heard Clare's words of condolence and continued apology. She wanted nothing more than to stop time. She could do it. She could feel the desire to do it building at the base of her skull. She could march downstairs and into the Blue Drawing Room, drop her deepest curtsey to Lord Blackdown and his Russian friend, who would be standing like two statues. She could pull her arm back . . .

But if the men awoke to find Eamon with a painful handprint on his cheek, where a moment ago there had been none? Eamon was stupid, but it wouldn't take him long to realize what she could do.

With a powerful effort Julia quelled her rage. And inspiration struck. 'The priest's hole,' she said slowly, remembering the secret closet on the landing built during the Dissolution to hide not a priest, but an abbess. It contained spyholes overlooking the Blue Room from high in its east wall. She

jumped to her feet, pulling Clare up with her. 'If Eamon
wants to pose as the evil guardian and pretend that we are all
trapped in a "horrid" novel, then let us play along!'

Clare laughed. 'Last time we played in the priest's hole, I
had agreed to be a queen held for ransom in a tower. You
and Bella were to rescue me.'

'It wasn't a tower,' Julia said. 'Please, Clare. You were
locked in the hold of a pirate ship.'

'Was I? I spent the time reading by candlelight, I'm afraid.
As I recall, I spent a full hour in that closet, waiting to be
sprung free.'

'Ah, yes. Indeed. That can be explained. You see, you
agreed to be the queen, so long as we didn't distract you from
your reading, but the game relied upon Nick agreeing to be
the pirate. Once we had you in place, we went to convince
him. His refusal destroyed all our pleasure in the game and
so . . .'

'You abandoned me there.'

'Yes,' Julia said, laughing, 'I'm afraid so.'

Clare stood and brushed her skirts smooth. 'Shall we complete the scene today, but with some of the parts transposed?
I believe you will find that Nick is now eager to play.'

A few short moments later, Clare, Julia and a candle were
ensconced in the priest's hole. Each woman had her eye
pressed to one of the peepholes in the wall.

At first it was hard to see anything in the drawing room, for
the heavy blinds were drawn against the daylight, and only a
few candles burned here and there. As their eyes adjusted, figures slowly emerged out of the gloom. The gentlemen must
only recently have entered the room, for they were still standing, showing their profiles to the peepholes. Eamon was
dressed in rusty black, and he cut a disgraceful figure com-
pared to the others. His fingers were ink stained, and Julia

could see that his neck cloth, tied in the simplest of knots, was also smudged with ink. The men were clearly in some sort of stand-off, for none of them spoke, and Nick and Arkady each wore an expression of outraged shock.

'Eamon has not wasted any time in offending them,' Julia whispered. 'Look how vexed they seem.' Clare nodded, without taking her eye from the hole.

Eamon had taken up his belligerent stance, the one that made him look like an affronted piglet. His head was thrust so far forward that it looked as if it must topple off his shoulders. His feet were planted primly but firmly, the toes pointing at ten and two o'clock. His hands flexed and unflexed at his sides, and he was slowly changing colour, from a rather repellent shade of poultice pink to a far more alarming shade of red. The Russian, who stood with one booted foot placed elegantly forward, was clearly fascinated, for he slowly lifted his quizzing glass to his eye and surveyed Eamon up and down. He then sneered so broadly that the women could see the curl of his lip.

Finally Nick broke the silence. 'I *beg* your pardon?'

'The woman.' Eamon spat the words out. 'Where is she? Pringle said there would be three of you. Two roosters and a hen. Two boars and a sow. Two dogs and a bitch. Where is the damned bitch?' His voice rose. 'Is she spying on me? Have you sent her to find my secrets?'

Clare clutched Julia's hand and looked at her, eyes huge in the candlelight.

'I told you so,' Julia mouthed.

'But he is unspeakable, Julia. Unspeakable.' Clare's whisper was urgent. 'We must get you away.'

Julia pressed her friend's hand as they both turned back to their peepholes.

'If you had friends,' Nick was saying, his voice as calm as the earl's was loud, 'I would ask you to name your seconds.

No one speaks of my sister in that fashion. However, since you have no friends, and since you are clearly ignorant of the dignities and responsibilities that come with your new title, I shall merely request that you alter your tone with me, sir.' He crossed his arms over his chest. 'I await your apology.'

Eamon stood goggling at him, his mouth forming soundless words.

'This man.' The Russian gestured at Eamon with a disgusted flick of the wrist. 'He is a snorting wild boar. In Russia, we kill this animal like vermin, and yet here he stands, an earl.'

'He has been an earl for but a few weeks, Count Lebedev,' Nick said, speaking to his friend as if Eamon were nothing more than an interesting exhibit, and not a living man growing more enraged with every passing second. 'You see, he was never intended to inherit. The old earl lost his son, and this cousin crawled out from under a rock somewhere. We must endure him.'

It was then that all hell broke loose. Eamon reached up to the mantelpiece and grabbed a china statuette of Shakespeare leaning contemplatively against a tree, and he smashed it against a nearby table. He brandished the base of the figure, which now sprouted two graceful legs and a stump, all ending in razor-sharp edges. 'Leave my house!' the earl screamed, charging at them with his weapon.

Clare gasped, and Julia acted without thinking. She began to stall time, focusing all her powers of concentration out through that tiny peephole and down onto the gentlemen below. But almost immediately she felt something, someone, fighting her. Eamon! He must have divined that she was the Talisman, must have found a way to use her strength against her. The worst had happened. He was using her. She concentrated her attention, straining against him until she thought her head would burst.

He was pushing back against the strength of her will. She watched through the peephole as time slowed and Eamon's motions became ponderous, but try as she might she could not stop time altogether. Her head hurt with trying, and she managed to slow the scene only a fraction more, before her concentration snapped as if it were a dry, dead stem. She pulled back from the peephole with a gasp, clutching her head.

The pain faded almost immediately. She turned quickly to Clare, who was still pressed to her peephole. They had to run. Further away than Falcott House. She had to leave the country. Eamon knew!

She grabbed at Clare, whispering her name, but her friend did not respond. Clare was frozen in a moment in time. Her hands, spread against the wall on either side of her peephole, were still as death. Julia glanced at the candle. It didn't move.

Eamon had stopped time. He had overpowered and used her. She was the Talisman and he was channelling his will through her.

'Oh my dear God,' she whispered, and slowly put her eye back to the peephole, letting her shaking fingers rest on Clare's unmoving wrist.

The earl was suspended in mid-air, his absurd weapon held triumphantly aloft like Excalibur itself. 'That wasn't part of the plan,' Nick said. He turned to Arkady and was shocked to see that his friend was shaken and sweating. 'What's wrong with you?' He helped him to a seat.

Arkady pointed at Darchester. 'That man is something extraordinary. He is as mad as your King George, but he is powerful. Didn't you feel it?'

'I felt you stop time. It took you long enough. The blasted

fool was about to slice my face off with Shakespeare's codpiece.'

Arkady wiped his forehead. 'You are too inexperienced to understand what happened here. *He* tried to stop time first. I had to fight him. I won. He is not strong enough. Few people are strong enough to win in a duel with me. But still he is very strong. I could feel – he should have been able to fight me, if he were trained. Perhaps he is inexperienced, or perhaps it is that he is crazy, or it is both things combined.'

'All right . . .' Nick wasn't quite sure he understood what Arkady was saying, but it was clear they were in some sort of mess. 'What the hell are we going to do now?'

Arkady was not to be rushed. He was calmer now, and contemplated the earl with a scholarly eye. 'I don't understand. Why is he now frozen? If he can freeze time himself, he should also be immune to being frozen. Remember how I trained you to notice when I stopped time? And then you could avoid being frozen with it? And yet you see him there. Even the spittle. It is like ice on his lips.' He stared up from his chair at the earl, suspended in mid-leap. 'He cannot be Ofan. The whole purpose of Ofan resistance to the Guild is knowledge, education. An Ofan would know everything about his talent. He would know everything about how to use it.' Arkady propped his head in his hands and stared again at the immobilized earl. 'This untrained maniac. He distresses me. Never have I seen anything like him. So strong the talent, and so ignorant the man.' Arkady walked up to Darchester, peering at him closely. 'Are you Ofan?'

The contorted face said nothing.

'Let me kill him.' Nick heard the words leave his mouth, and realized he meant them. 'I want to!'

Arkady turned, laughing. 'The warrior priest! Why do you want to kill him? You who are so squeamish?'

Nick raked his hands through his hair in frustration. 'You brought me here to kill Ofan. You uprooted my life to bring me here for this task. I will gladly begin right here and now and crush this serpent for us all.'

Arkady rocked back on his heels, that scholarly gaze turned on Nick, now. 'Ah. I see. It is the woman. You will kill for a girl, but not for the Guild. This Julia, she beckons to you with the pretty looks and it makes you disloyal.'

'Do not speak of her that way.'

'What way?' Arkady looked him up and down. 'You do not wish to hear her spoken of as a woman? Nor you as a man?' The Russian smiled, and for the first time Nick disliked him. 'You are the great marquess now, is that it? The protector of virgins? You who were so recently the tomcat?' He shook his head. 'I'm afraid I do not believe it, my priest. This very morning, I saw you heading towards Castle Dar. I saw the flash of a girl's red cloak against the trees. She is yours already.'

Nick got one punch in before Arkady was on him, tumbling him off his legs and pinning him back against the chair. 'Ah, Nick,' he said, almost dreamily. 'You are romantic. I like it in you. But you cannot hit me. Not me, your old friend.'

'What makes you my friend, Arkady?' Nick's face was so close to the Russian's now that he could see his own face reflected in his pupils. 'You expect me to die for a cause I know almost nothing about. You mock a woman I hold in great esteem. You make obscene suggestions about her to my face. Then you claim friendship with me?'

Arkady's eyes were sparkling with delight by the end of Nick's speech. He leapt to his feet, hauling Nick up with him. 'Yes! You are so impassioned. Almost like a Russian. There is no priest in you now. I embrace you.' He did so. 'No man is a man until he is made weak by a woman.' Arkady pulled back and held Nick by the shoulders, gazing tenderly into his eyes. 'Kiss me.'

'I am not made weak by a woman, and I will not kiss you.'

'Bah. You lie.' Arkady smashed his lips against Nick's unresponding mouth. He pulled back, grinning. 'You are a man. We will save her. Why? Because it is beautiful and romantic to do so. We will fight this maniac like the men we are – with our fists. Why? Because it is beautiful and romantic to do so.' Arkady released Nick and turned to face Darchester. 'Are you ready? I am about to set him free. Prepare, Nicholas Davenant, to defend yourself!'

Nick couldn't help but laugh. 'You are entirely insane!'

The Russian turned a wild, joyous face back to him, and then the earl was upon them, howling, and slashing with the broken statuette. Arkady and Nick milled in with their fists. Nick saw Darchester's spittle, mobile again, fly from his lips, and then felt his own coat, shirt and skin sliced open just above the elbow. 'Damn you to hell!' He charged, head bowed like a ram's, fists pumping. Meanwhile Arkady stepped behind the earl and caught him as Nick knocked him backwards. Darchester got one more slash in before Arkady grasped his wrist and squeezed until Darchester squealed like a pig and dropped his weapon. Nick laughed in Darchester's enraged face, only to have his shin viciously kicked. 'You little shit sack!' Nick yelled, and Darchester began laughing in his turn. Hauling his arm back, Nick delivered a perfect right cross to the earl's jaw. Eamon's head snapped back and he fell, senseless, to the ground. Nick rubbed his fist. 'That felt wonderful,' he said. 'I haven't done that in centuries.'

'Hush.' Arkady prodded the crumpled earl with a boot. 'Time has started up again. You are the marquess. You know nothing of centuries.'

And indeed, the room was suddenly full of cheering servants, and then Clare and Julia were there, too. Clare hugged Nick. He looked over her shoulder to find Julia's dark eyes upon him. He had no idea what it was that he saw in them.

19

'What do you think of this one?' Arabella Falcott held aloft a wicker hat that managed to be lushly feminine and disturbingly pagan at the same time. Its crown and brim were so sharply curved, and its trimming so abundantly floral, that it looked like a stag's antlers protruding from a rose bush.

Julia displayed her own choice. This was a parasol of such minuscule proportions that one would have to be a leprechaun to make any real use of it. But ultimately, after much argument, Bella's wicker hat was acknowledged the winner. The game, which had been going on all morning up and down the stalls of the Western Exchange, was called 'find the most ludicrous thing'. With the triumph of the wicker hat, Bella was now ahead by seven points. Julia laid the parasol down with a sigh. 'I admit defeat. Your eye for the vulgar is far better developed than my own. Now I must stand you an ice at Gunter's.'

Bella crowed her triumph, and the young women turned away from the stall, much to the relief of the deeply insulted attendant.

Half an hour later they were seated in Berkeley Square, watching a waiter dodge horses and pedestrians to bring them their ices. After several weeks in town, Bella was an old hand at all things Gunter's, and she ate her rye-bread ice with a blasé air. But this was all new to Julia, and her first taste of bergamot ice was a revelation. It was cold but creamy, sweet but tart. The exotic flavour and delicate perfume made the perfect complement to this upliftingly glorious day in London.

It had been three weeks since Grandfather's death, and a week since she had been her cousin's prisoner. Now here she was in London for the first time in her life. Bella, her oldest and best crony, was beside her, and they were seated at the very centre of a world designed to delight the senses, eating the most delectable sweetmeats ever concocted by human hand. Julia was dressed in the highest kick of fashion – albeit all in black. The beautiful mourning clothes were a gift of the dowager marchioness. Upon receiving the news that her son was alive and that he planned to bring Julia to London along with his sister and a Russian nobleman, she had arranged for Julia to have a black walking dress, a black carriage dress and a black evening gown ready and waiting.

Julia took another spoonful, sat back in her chair and gave herself over to pleasure. She banished all thought, except appreciation of the moment and relish of this most beautiful of beautiful spring days. The town houses around the square sparkled white in the sun. Brightly painted high-perch phaetons pulled by prime horseflesh dashed by on the way to Hyde Park. They were driven by gentlemen of the first stare and carried ladies dressed in all the colours of a spring garden. The oval park itself was full of mamas and nursemaids and scampering children, a few strolling couples, the dedicated patrons of Gunter's, and of course, weaving through it all, the ever-nimble waiters, carrying aloft their silver trays of sugary iced confections. Julia sighed and wished it could go on for ever – but the dancing shadows cast by the overarching plane trees made the scene feel like a flickering dream, and she had to eat her ice quickly or it would melt.

Bella stuck out her tongue and flicked the last of her ice off her spoon. 'What shall we do next?'

'Surely licking your spoon is bad ton, Bella.' Julia eyed her own with temptation but set it back in her empty dish.

'You are still afraid of London. I have learned that rules are made to be broken. Although you must pick and choose which ones to break, and when.'

'Hmm. Which rules have you been breaking, pray tell?'

'Nothing very serious.' Bella stood and brushed out her green cambric skirt. 'Licking my spoon. Going alone to Vauxhall Gardens. Tying my garter in public.'

'Be serious.'

'How do you know I'm not being serious?' Bella held her hand out and pulled Julia to her feet. 'Let us take a stroll around the square and I shall tell you all about it.'

Bella was small, with black hair and hazel eyes. She looked nothing like Clare and Nick, who were both tall and fair. Luckily, there was an uncanny resemblance to a great-great-aunt on her father's side. The dowager marchioness, always terrified of What Other People Might Think, had rescued the dour portrait of that otherwise forgotten ancestress from the attics and hung it prominently at Falcott House; nobody was going to accuse her of playing her husband false. Still, Bella's family nickname was 'Changeling'.

She was a mercurial young woman, mostly full of fun, though sometimes a darker thread appeared in the bright fabric of her personality. A fervent Romanticist, Bella had committed whole swathes of *Werther* – in German, which she only partly understood – to memory. She could often be found painting by moonlight or sitting at the piano, plunking out the tune of a dreary *lied* with one finger and paging through her German wordbook with the other hand, discerning the meaning of the lyrics. Sometimes she was not to be found at all, for every now and then she took herself off for a long, solitary walk, preferably when the weather was threatening. She was firmly forbidden to wander off by herself in London, but as she now explained to Julia, it was a rule that was impossible to obey. 'I have the *wanderlust*, you see,' she said, careful to pronounce the word correctly. 'I just can't help myself. Some days I wake up, and I must simply follow my own footsteps and see where they lead.'

'You came here to find a husband, Bella. Not to explore the underbelly of London.'

'I know.' Bella squeezed Julia's arm to her side. 'I shall. The Season is excessively entertaining, Julia. The men are ridiculous and the women are worse, but . . .' She cut her eyes sideways at her friend, one black eyebrow winging up. 'There are some good apples in among the bad.'

Julia glittered with intrigue. 'Have you discovered any particularly good apples?'

'It depends on whether you prefer them tart or sweet.'

Julia thought of Blackdown striding angrily up the hill in the rain. 'I think it's possible to find an apple that is both tart and sweet,' she said.

'Oh.' Bella's eyes crinkled at the corners when she laughed – much like her brother's. 'It sounds like perhaps you have come across just such an excellent fruit. I must hear all about him.'

Julia pressed her lips together. She didn't like to think of Blackdown's rainy kisses, not since that scene in the Blue Drawing Room.

'Ah.' Bella nodded. 'And Julia becomes a clam.'

They were rounding the north corner of Berkeley Square, which meant they passed the Falcotts' London town house. Bella raised her hand and waved, though Julia could see no one – the windows reflected back the trees and the sky. Then she saw a pale hand rise to the glass of a second-storey window. 'Is that your mother?'

'Yes. She watches all day when I am out without her, simply waiting for me. Now that Nick is back, she is ten times worse. You'd think she would have rallied with the news of his return. But instead she is even more tormented, because she fears losing him again. Last night she stayed up until three awaiting his return from his club.'

'He was out until three?' Julia slowed her steps.

Bella sighed. 'I know. Aren't you consumed with jealousy? Imagine such freedom! But in actual fact, he was out until even later – or should I say earlier? For it was only that Mother finally gave up and went to bed at three. She came along the hallway weeping, convinced he was dead again, and I had to gather her up and tuck her in like a child. I am surprised we did not wake you.'

Julia hadn't heard anything. She had lain awake late thinking over her own problems, only to fall into a dreamless sleep just before two. 'Do you think the marquess came home at all last night?'

Bella kicked a pebble with her silk slipper, and it skittled away into the grass. 'Call him Nick, Julia, like you used to in the old days. It's so dreary, hearing his title on your lips like he's something special all of a sudden. Lord, I hope he stayed out all night. Imagine if you were a gentleman and you arrived home after three years. Not just any three years, but years when you didn't even know who you were. Suddenly it turns out you are not a wandering, penniless soldier, but a great lord with a vast fortune. You discover that you have a town house in the heart of a throbbing metropolis, and everything you see is yours for the asking. Would you spend your first night at home *at home*, if you know what I mean?'

Julia knew exactly what her friend meant, but she wasn't going to commit to it yet. 'I'm not sure.'

'Peagoose.' Bella pinched the skin on the back of Julia's hand. 'Doesn't blood run in here any more? I mean that he must have gone out with all his old friends, wining and dining and wenching the night away. At breakfast he denied it. He said he'd been with the Duke of Kirklaw, catching up on old times. But I don't believe him. Kirklaw is a terrible bore. Nick was carousing, I'll wager you anything. Just imagine. The jollity, the gay abandon, the laughter and song. I wish I were a man or . . . or . . .' Bella subsided.

'Or what?'

'I don't know. A woman who could do those things.'

'A member of the demi-monde?'

'Well,' Bella said, 'why not?' She tossed this shocking statement off lightly, half an eye on Julia. Julia smiled at her friend's daring but was terribly distracted. She could not now rid herself of the image of Nicholas Falcott, his arm round a beautiful woman. The woman was spilling out of her clothes and kissing him, and he had a bottle of champagne raised high in his other fist. Was he that sort of man? A rake? He had been a bit of a roaring boy before he went to war. Bella clearly thought he still was.

Rake, dandy, Corinthian . . . it didn't really matter what kind of man Blackdown was. Now she knew something far more important about him, something awful. Blackdown was involved somehow in a much larger world of time manipulation than Julia had dreamed possible. And he was bound up with his terrifying friend, the Russian count.

The kiss seemed distant now, like a dream that fades to nothing. Indeed, as she looked around her everything seemed dreamlike. Berkeley Square, Gunter's, ices, pretty dresses . . . it was all just a passing vision and would be washed away with time.

Time.

Blackdown and his friend were able to manipulate time, like her.

She could barely make sense of what she had seen and

heard during that amazing sojourn in the priest's hole. It had been the Russian who pushed against her while she tried to stop time. But, thank God, the Russian hadn't realized that she was his adversary. He thought it had been Eamon. She needed him to keep thinking that. For as long as possible.

The count was searching for 'Ofans', people with talents like hers, and the Russian wanted to stop them. In fact, he wanted to kill them. Blackdown wanted to stop them, too; he had even offered to end Eamon's life right there.

But Blackdown wasn't exactly the Russian's bosom friend. He had been angry at the count, frustrated with him. There had been that tussle, when Lebedev had insulted her honour. Julia had discovered that it isn't, in fact, pleasant to be the object of a fight between men. Especially not when the man who is defending you is trounced. The count had easily over-powered Blackdown, though Blackdown was tall and strong and a soldier.

Fear tickled up her spine. She had escaped Eamon only to gain a far more formidable enemy. Julia allowed herself to concentrate on the Russian. He was a wiry, powerful man, well over six feet tall. But his physical strength was not what really frightened her. The Russian seemed coldly intelligent, and he seemed implacable. There would be no time to explain, were he to discover her talent. He would discover the truth, and then he would kill her.

Indeed, Blackdown must be a killer, too. He had said that the Russian had brought him home to kill the Ofan people. People like her. And he must be good at killing in order to have survived the war in Spain. He had a scar on his face. His kisses had ranged from gentle to fierce. She wasn't so much of a fool as to think that the passions of love and the passions of war were unconnected.

But love was not something she could allow herself to

contemplate, not after what she had seen through the peephole. Thank God Blackdown thought she was just Julia Percy, just a girl with whom he had whiled away a luscious hour. Not even an hour. The fact that he had kissed her might even protect her, for perhaps now she was just one of many others in his list of conquests. A face in the crowd.

He did seem to have lost interest in her since that day. She had been whisked away from Castle Dar in that ridiculous travelling coach. The Russian and Nick had stayed behind to deal with Eamon and had not come back until late. Then the marquess had told her, quite formally, that after some discussion Eamon was content to allow her to accompany the Falcotts to London.

Since that moment Blackdown had kept a strict distance from her. He was never alone with her, and he never addressed her directly. While their entourage of coaches had made its slow way from Devon to London, the marquess had ridden his bay hunter rather than joining the ladies in the travelling coach. Indeed, it was only when Julia chose to ride Marigold for an hour that he had decided Boatswain needed a rest. He had bowed to her, his eyes remote, and had taken her place inside the coach. It had been a relief, in fact. She couldn't think clearly when she was near him.

Now he had been out all night, doing God knows what while she lay awake worrying about the future. The future and the past and the present and all of time itself. Worrying for her very life.

'Julia? Julia!' Bella was peering at her. 'Did I shock you so dreadfully?'

'What?' Julia realized that her steps had slowed until she was almost standing still. 'What were you saying?'

'I was talking about becoming a lady of easy virtue. And you go meandering off into your own thoughts. What kind of friend are you? Are you so ready to see me sacrifice my good name?'

Julia frowned. Joining the demi-monde; it was the fantasy of a silly child. 'Don't be ridiculous. It's nothing to joke about. Just a few days ago I was wondering what I would do to keep body and soul together if I were forced to run away from my odious cousin before reaching my majority. Very little stood between me and just such a life.'

'But would you?' Bella's voice thrilled with intrigue. 'Would you really turn to prostitution, if the alternative were death?'

'No.' Julia raised her chin. 'Of course not. I never would.' She looked out over the square rather than meet Bella's eyes.

Bella hugged Julia's arm close. 'Liar liar, brimstone and fire. You would, you know. We all would.'

'I do not care for this conversation, Bella.' Julia's scowl deepened.

'Oh, please.' Bella pulled Julia along briskly. 'Stop pretending to be a prude, because I know for a fact that you are not. Who spied on the stable hands as they washed themselves, then broke her arm falling out of the hayloft because she leaned out to get a clear view of Martinson's you-know-what?'

'His cock,' Julia muttered. 'You taught me that word, Arabella Falcott. Now who's the prude?' She sniffed. 'Martinson didn't have anything worth looking at, let me tell you.'

'Ha! Indeed. Welcome back to yourself, Julia Percy. This is exactly the sort of conversation we have had every day since we were thirteen years old.'

'We are not thirteen now.'

'No,' Bella said, 'we certainly are not. That is why we must talk about these things without blushing.' She fixed Julia with a serious gaze. 'It means "half the world", you know.'

'What does?'

'Demi-monde.'

Julia stopped, bringing her friend to a standstill. 'But of course it does. I never thought of that before. How remarkable. Half the world.'

They had now walked back around to the Gunter's side of Berkeley Square. Carriages were lined up outside the shop and gentlemen were procuring ices for ladies, then leaning against the park railings and chatting with one another while the ladies ate without alighting. 'Look at them,' Bella said.

Julia looked. She began to see that each woman ate her ice differently. Some scraped the ice onto their spoons, others scooped it. Some took big bites, some little. Some allowed the relish they had for the treat to show on their faces, others appeared bored or even disgusted. Quite a number of them, she realized with a start, must have ordered their ice to match their gowns. 'People can't help but look ridiculous while they are eating,' she said.

Her friend looked at her blankly for a moment and then started laughing. 'Oh, Julia.'

'What?'

'You are watching them eat.'

'Well, of course I am. Look at all the flavours I have yet to try.'

'Do you know what I see when I look?'

'You are probably looking at the gentlemen.'

'Not at all.' Bella gestured at the scene as if she were discussing a painting in a gallery. 'Look at that lovely woman in pink, with the high-poke bonnet.'

'I see her.'

'Is any other woman looking at her? Now look at that beautiful creature in the dark blue spencer. Are any other women looking in her direction?'

Julia began to follow the eyes of all the females eating ices.

A woman's eyes slid unseeingly over one lady, to alight happily upon another. Waves and greetings were exchanged between two ladies across the body of another woman who stared straight ahead, as if she were alone on a mountain top. 'Oh!' Julia said. Suddenly her vision cleared and she could see, as if a veil had been lifted. All the women were eating ices, but only some women were acknowledged to exist, while others were subtly . . . spurned. Made invisible. Except that Julia could see them. It was like magic.

'Yes,' Bella said. 'Half the world. Now you can see it.'

Julia looked at her friend with awe and something like pride. 'How did you work it out? Surely your mother didn't . . .'

Bella snorted. 'My mother thinks a girl should reach her wedding night as ignorant as a fluffy duckling.'

'I know. Remember when she had the brass to tell a pair of sixteen-year-old girls that she had found all three of her children in cabbages?'

'How could I forget? And when you asked her to describe harvesting cabbage babies, she revealed that it is a dangerous matter, because apparently cabbages grow in trees.'

'I love your mother,' Julia said, 'but her innocence – of vegetable life – is truly amazing.' The smile faded from her lips. 'I've missed you, Bella.'

Bella pressed her hand. 'I know. When we marry we most likely will not see one another from one end of the year to the next. We shall simply have to find husbands with neighbouring estates. It shouldn't be too difficult.'

They walked on in silence for a moment. Physical distance hadn't been what Julia meant when she said she'd missed Bella. Neighbouring estates wouldn't mend the rift that now yawned between them. They could talk about men and sex and prostitutes until the cows came home. But time, and Grandfather, and the problem of being the Talisman . . . the problem of Blackdown and the Russian and the mysterious tribe they were hunting . . .

Pretend, Grandfather had said. Tell no one.

Julia felt the warmth of her friend's arm tucked against her side. The arm felt sturdy, and her friend was true. But Bella, London, this day . . . it was all light and shadow. She could trust no one.

As they came again to the corner graced by the Falcott town house, Bella spoke. 'I shall have to introduce you to a friend of mine. I met her on one of my walks. She showed me what I showed you today.'

'Is she a prostitute?'

Bella dropped her voice. 'Of course not. But she believes in education. Of all kinds.'

'I am beginning to believe in education myself,' Julia said. She looked into Bella's eyes and wished her friend could read her mind. 'Thank you,' she said. 'You have taught me something today.'

'You are most welcome,' Bella replied. 'Now – shall we go home to Mother?'

20

Nick had indeed been with the Duke of Kirklaw the previous night. The butler had delivered a note at midday: 'White's tonight – Kirklaw.' Nick had groaned, crumpled the note and tossed it back onto the silver salver. Back in America, his friends were ambivalent at best about their high-school reunions, and now Nick knew why. The thought of going to his father's club and strolling down memory lane with three dozen Georgian Tories – he would rather eat ground glass. But like his American friends, who once a decade found themselves travelling to their hometowns in order to compare weight gain and hair loss with people they had never intended to see again, Nick realized around dinnertime that his steps were carrying him towards the grand building in Mayfair.

Before he even mounted the stairs he was hailed by the bow-window set, including Beau Brummell, who saluted him through the glass. Nick nodded to the prince of dandies, took a deep breath and prepared to greet many of the men he had known in his old life.

The doors opened onto warmth, light and a low roar of welcome. Nick's apprehensions lifted from him as easily as the greatcoat that was removed from his shoulders by a servant. A glass was pressed into his hand, a toast was raised. Bonhomie flowed like wine, and the wine tasted like nectar. Nick was passed through a crowd of men ranging in age from eighteen to eighty, their hands grasping his, their pale faces shining with benevolence. The sound of their laughter was like a tune he had once loved but had forgotten. The weight of an arm over his shoulder, the gentle humour of a lewd joke, the good wishes passed on from someone who couldn't be there. The smells soothed: beeswax, tobacco, leather, booze, musk and cologne. The sounds delighted: bass, baritone and tenor voices; glasses clinking; cards shuffling; dice clicking; fire crackling. This was the very perfection of good living, good drinking, good feeling. Nick found himself casting about for the river, its pull, its depth all around him, but it simply wasn't there. It was like he was suspended in warm honey, and he wondered if this place was some paradisiacal twin of Tyburn, a scar, a place where time and feeling turns in upon itself. He made his slow way through the crowd, guided by smiles and halloos and fragments of fraternal conversation.

At dinner, Nick shared a table with nine bachelors of his own generation, each as genial as the next. Steak had never tasted so good; it was perfectly aged, with a sensuous chew and a yielding, buttery taste. He found himself raising his glass and calling out in a loud voice, 'Beef and liberty!' This was his only error; it was the rallying cry of the Sublime Society of Beef Steaks, a Whig club, and White's was firmly Tory. For a moment he felt a vibration of doubt move through the room. But approval was strong for Nick tonight, the miraculously returned hero. He was forgiven his gaffe almost before the words were out of his mouth, and the drop of uneasy feeling dissipated without a trace into the unguent of brotherly love. And so the evening slipped along, the hours told by glasses of wine. It was only when the clock struck midnight that Nick realized he had seen neither hide nor hair of Kirklaw.

The snuff was being passed when a footman tapped him on his shoulder. The duke, apparently, awaited Nick in a private chamber. Nick got to his feet and bade his companions a tender farewell. They chorused their goodbyes. His brain pleasantly fuzzy, his stomach handsomely full, Nick followed the bewigged footman up the stairs and into a private drawing room.

Kirklaw was not alone; two other men stood by the mantel, each looking expectantly towards him. Good Lord. The one on the left, the bald one, that was Baron Blessing. And the one on the right was the Honourable Richard Bonnet. Nick strode forward. 'Blessing! Bonnet!'

He was brought up short by their chilly bows. 'Blackdown,' Blessing said. And, 'Blackdown,' Bonnet echoed. Then, 'I'm not Bonnet any more. My father is dead. I'm Delbun.'

'Delbun,' Nick said, bowing.

Kirklaw came forward, hand outstretched. Five years had transformed the duke. In 1810 he had been twenty-two but had looked sixteen, pale and scrawny. The man walking towards Nick now was well padded, and although Nick knew he was only twenty-seven, he looked indeterminately middle-aged, with a high colour and a receding hairline. His face was set in an expression that could clearly tip towards the pleased or the displeased without disrupting the general aura of smug self-congratulation. He took Nick's hand. 'By God, you've changed, Blackdown. Look at you! What happened?'

'War,' Nick said. 'Then I was lost . . . in Spain.'

'Yes, yes, we've heard. Your memory.' Kirklaw stepped back. 'And very glad we are to have you returned to us, aren't we?'

'Very glad,' said Blessing.

'Indeed,' said Delbun.

'It was quite a blow when they told me you were dead. Quite a blow.'

'A blow,' confirmed Blessing.

'You don't have a drink, Blackdown. We're drinking brandy; it's the good stuff, from my own cellars.'

'Thank you.'

Kirklaw turned to a sideboard. Nick stood looking at Blessing and Delbun and they looked back. Surely old friends should talk to each other? But they were stiffly silent, and Nick wasn't going to yammer like a ninny. So he waited, letting his collar and cravat decide the arrogant angle of his head.

Kirklaw handed Nick a glass and raised his own. 'While deeds of glory stimulate the brave, and laurels spring upon the hero's grave!'

'Deeds of glory!' Blessing said.

'Deeds!' Delbun echoed.

Nick held his glass aloft and let his gaze slip from lord to lord to lord as they drank. The three men were uncomfortable, their anxiety made the more obvious by the congenial buzz of conversation that still ebbed and swelled from the floor below. These men wanted something from him, and they weren't sure how to ask. Nick set his glass down, put his hands in his pockets and waited. They would get to the point sooner or later.

Kirklaw plucked a cigar from a box, twirled it between his fingers and made a show of sniffing it. 'Finally can get these from Spain, thanks to gallant boys like you.' The duke's nails, Nick noticed, were bitten to the quick and his blunt, raw fingertips stained with tobacco. He tapped a toe and tossed the cigar from hand to hand. 'Back from the wars, back from the wars, back from the wars,' he said in sing-song. 'Little Lord Blackdown is back from the wars.'

Nick found that his hands, in his pockets, were clenched. But at the heart of one fist, that little acorn. It calmed him, and he managed to extract his other hand from his pocket in a peaceable manner, lift his glass, and take a sip of brandy. 'And you, Kirklaw? What have you done with yourself these past five years?'

'Oh . . .' Kirklaw waved his cigar airily. 'Politics, my boy. Have a hankering to be PM one day.'

Nick raised his eyebrows and scanned his memory. He wasn't entirely sure, but he didn't think that particular honour was waiting downriver for the man.

'Of course, that is in the lap of the gods! You are far more interesting. I would ask you to tell us a tale or two, but really, we are still inundated with stories from Spain.' The duke grabbed up a copy of *The Gentleman's Magazine* from the table beside him. 'Why, almost every day we must read a letter from a gallant soldier to his dear mama, the last she ever heard from him before he died for king and country. And the simple Spanish! How they adore us.'

'Glorious times,' Blessing said. 'Rule Britannia!' He raised his glass.

'Glorious,' Delbun agreed.

They drank.

'And you were there, in the midst of it all, Blackdown,' Kirklaw said, tossing the paper aside. 'Why, when you think of it, when we were lads, the army was no place for a nobleman. What did Wellington call the soldiery?'

'The scum of the earth,' Nick said.

'Indeed. The scum of the earth. What a thing to say!' Delbun downed his brandy in a single swallow, coughed and set his balloon aside. Then he sat down. 'When you hared off to join up, I must admit it – I thought you were crazy.'

'We all did,' Blessing said, also sitting.

'You weren't entirely wrong.' Nick disposed himself in a straight-backed chair.

'Maybe so,' Delbun said. 'But what I wouldn't give to be in your shoes now that the war is over. The country's gone army-mad. Heroes everywhere you turn. Falling from the rafters like spiders. Women can't get enough of them.'

'My God, the women.' Kirklaw remained on his feet. 'They are denatured by army fever. Why, my own sister, the other day, read out loud to me from her *Belle Assemblée* – and was she reading to me of fashion? Or gossip? Or cucumber treatments? Would you believe, she lisped whole sentences about the disinterested patriotism of Great Britain in flying to the aid of Spain. Not to say she's a bluestocking. Pretty girl, my sister. Do you know she is eighteen this year?'

'Please.' Nick raised his hand. 'I am only just returned. I am not yet thinking of marriage.'

'And I wasn't offering.' Kirklaw's glance was hard and bright. 'Your own sister, the little Lady Arabella – she is hawking her wares to good effect this season.'

'Good effect,' Blessing said. 'Fetching girl.'

'She's hardly a girl.' Kirklaw's expression slid towards the cruel. 'Somewhat overripe, I'd say. Now, now – don't take offence. I meant no offence. I've cut a caper or two with her at Almack's.'

'Oh, you have, have you?'

'And I'm still not offering!' The duke laughed and fished an evil-looking device from his pocket. 'There's another sister, isn't there, Blackdown?' He snipped the end off his cigar. 'Not your marriageable sister, no. Your spinster sister. What is her name? The Lady . . .'

'Clare.' Nick knew Kirklaw knew her name full well. He narrowed his eyes. Somehow, through this talk of sisters, they were coming to the point. 'Her name is Clare.'

'Lady Clare.' The duke lit his cigar from a candle with a series of minuscule, moist little puffs. 'Lady Clare, Lady Clare, Lady Clare.' His face disappeared behind a cloud of smoke, and when it emerged the expression hovered between disapproval and disgust. 'I suppose she told you of her mad plan.'

Ah. Nick glanced at Blessing and Delbun. They sat tightly

in their seats, and they were right to be anxious. The talk was bumping up against slander. 'Yes. I know of it,' Nick said carefully. 'It has come to nothing, however. I am returned.'

'Of course, of course.' The duke pinched at the wet end of his cigar with a stained thumb and forefinger. Then he popped the cigar back in his mouth and visibly chewed on it. Nick looked away.

'You disapprove of her plans, then,' Delbun asked. 'Just want to make sure of that.'

Nick frowned. 'I fail to understand how it is any business of yours.'

Delbun looked to Kirklaw for backup. The duke disappeared into another cloud of smoke. His smile appeared first. 'What Delbun means is that we are glad you are returned and Blackdown is saved. There are so few of us left, after all. All the king's newly created titles swell our ranks, of course, but meanwhile the real aristocracy is dwindling away.'

'Dwindling,' Blessing said.

'Why, when I heard what was in train for Blackdown, I almost offered for Lady Clare myself. With my influence your title could have been brought out of abeyance for our second son, perhaps, and the entail re-established.' Kirklaw gazed down on Nick, clearly waiting to be thanked.

The crystal curve of Nick's brandy balloon rested lightly on his fingertips, its perfect, fragile arc catching the light. He remembered the intensity of Clare's dedication to her dream, and the grace with which she had yielded it when Nick returned. The seconds ticked by.

'It was the least I could do,' the duke finally said, as if Nick had thanked him. 'Not that I did do it. I seem to be almost offering for both your superannuated sisters tonight! But you understand me, of course.'

'Of course.'

'Now.' Kirklaw leaned his elbows on the back of Delbun's overstuffed chair. 'Lady Clare owed her scheme to the interventions of a new steward, or so I heard. A man by the name of . . .' Kirklaw snapped his fingers, pretending to search his memory.

'Jem Jemison.'

'Yes, that's it. This Jem Jemison.'

'Not a married man, I take it,' Blessing said.

Nick turned his head slowly and stared at the baron until he saw a flush of red climb up from his collar.

'Now, Blackdown,' Kirklaw said. 'Blessing isn't suggesting . . .'

'Isn't suggesting what?'

'Isn't suggesting anything,' Blessing said.

'Yet,' Delbun said.

And there it was. The threat. Out in the open, like a hart breaking cover. Except that a hart is beautiful. 'I've forgotten,' Nick said. 'Is this what we do, we lords of the realm? Do we spend all our time slandering females?'

'Blackdown . . .' Kirklaw's tone was a warning.

'When I left,' Nick interrupted, swirling his brandy in his glass, 'we were all young men.'

'Rakehells,' Blessing said, a little bashful.

'Yes,' Nick said. 'Such larks. We never spared a thought for sisters, or stewards, or whether or not stewards were married.'

'We were young,' Delbun said.

Nick sipped his brandy and let the burn spread across his tongue before speaking again. 'I left Great Britain in 1810. Five long years ago. Like Odysseus, I sacked Troy. Like Odysseus, it was a long and strange journey that brought me home again.'

'Well now, Blackdown, that's a romantical way of thinking,' Blessing said. 'You were only in Spain.'

Nick continued. 'And like Odysseus, I have returned to find that the reputations of the women in my household are in danger. I find that you have called me here neither to welcome me nor to re-establish our old conviviality. Instead, you are panting with concern over my sister's choices, and my sister's virtue, a sister you would disdain, yourselves, to marry.' The three men stared at him. They had each of them become repellent, in ways that had nothing to do with the composition of their features. Nick suspected that had he stayed with them instead of going to war, he would have hardened into just such an anxious ugliness. 'I would be grateful if you would stop amusing yourself with my sisters' good names and come to the point.'

'Would you? Would you indeed?' Kirklaw frowned, got the cigar out of his mouth and worried at its wet, frayed end with his fingers. 'All right, then, here it is without roundaboutation. The point is this. Jem Jemison. He's come to London, now that you have put paid to his plans for Blackdown. He's here, and he's making a damned nuisance of himself. Rabble-rousing in Soho and the East End. Drumming up opposition to the Corn Bill.'

'So? What does that have to do with me? Or with Clare?'

All three men laughed. 'Everything!' Blessing said. 'Your name is linked with his! This scheme of your sister's; people want to know if you are turning against the politics of your fathers. They want to know if you support her, if you stand against the aristocracy, against everything we represent!'

'They doubt me? The men below seemed to have no anxiety on that front.'

'They don't doubt you yet,' Kirklaw said. 'But they could well come to doubt you. You are in a precarious position, Blackdown.'

'Ah.' Nick smiled. 'Yes. I forgot. You brought me here to threaten me.'

'We are not threatening you; the future itself is threatening you! Have you not been reading the papers? The Corn Bill is going to save your sorry hide. Now that the war is over, it's the only thing that can keep prices high.'

'I've been in Spain, you may recall. Saving your own sorry hide.'

'Oh, spare me, please.' Kirklaw thrust his ruined cigar back between his teeth and spoke around it. 'You went to Spain to escape your responsibilities. Don't play the great hero with us. While you were marching about like a toy soldier, we grew up. We shouldered our responsibilities. We sat on our cold seats in the House of Lords and we served this country. And now you come back without the foggiest notion of the dangers you face as a lord of the realm, as a brother to your wayward – yes, your wayward – sisters. The dangers you face as an Englishman.'

'Do you dare to rebuke me because you outrank me, Kirklaw? I only ask because it has been so long since I have studied the *Peerage*. I've heard it is the best thing in fiction the English have ever done.'

The three lords stared at Nick from matching pairs of blue eyes, their faces as flat as a row of Wedgwood plates. Then Kirklaw blinked and flushed. 'Fiction? *Fiction?* Without the Corn Bill fixing the price of our corn, our days are numbered. The manufactories are already squeezing us, stealing our workers. And the merchants are buying our titles with their whey-faced daughters and their filthy money. Once foreign corn starts pouring in, we will have neither the money nor the influence to keep men on the land. Do you want America, or France, to happen on English soil? Are you ready, at best, to become a commoner, who must make his leg to the richest tailor in town, or at worst to see your sisters' heads roll as you wait your own turn for Madame Guillotine?'

'And your Corn Bill? It will save us from those unimaginable fates?'

'It certainly will,' Blessing said. 'Indefinitely.'

'If it passes,' Delbun said.

Kirklaw waved a dismissive hand. 'The bill will pass, handily. But it is unpopular with the lower classes. To say the least. And your Jemison –'

'He is not my Jemison.'

'Your Jemison,' the duke said insistently, 'is at the heart of the trouble. I need you to denounce him. You are known to be my friend, and you cannot be both my friend and his.'

'Surely one returned soldier cannot tarnish the reputation of a duke.'

'No, but one marquess can.' Kirklaw pointed a wet finger at Nick. 'Your peers are ready to accept you as a hero, as a leader. They are ready to hand you their trust and their admiration on a plate. But that could change. I am merely warning you of the thin ice upon which you stand. If the people rise up after the vote – and they will – and if you have not stood up and made clear your loyalty to your party and your class, your peers will turn on you. They will blame you for the unrest. Then they will turn to me, and they will think, How could Kirklaw be friends with that man? The mob or me. That is your choice.'

The mob! Nick pictured Tony Soprano bursting into the House of Lords and shooting everyone dead with his ArmaLite AR-10. He chuckled. 'You want to ride the coat-tails of my eminence, don't you, Kirklaw? And if you cannot, you will bring me down in a fit of pique.'

'I will not be the one to bring you down. I only warn you that fame is a fickle mistress. Your fair-weather friends downstairs might come to learn of Jemison's association with Lady Clare. They might come to learn that he served with you in

267

the Peninsula. That he fought side by side with you. It could be said that you sent Jemison on from Spain to be the steward at Blackdown. It could be said that you are a radical, like Byron, who wishes to see his own class degraded, destroyed. Like Byron, you think the mob speaks the sentiments of the people.'

'That club-footed reprobate has fathered a child on his own sister,' Blessing said. 'If you don't stand against Jemison soon, people might say that you are little better than he, that you condone Jemison's corruption of Lady Clare. That you would welcome the issue of a tallow chandler into your family. For that is what Jemison is. A tallow chandler's son.'

Nick laughed out loud at that one and twitched his cuffs into place. 'Between the tallow chandlers and the incestuous noblemen, it's a wonder Albion hasn't sunk beneath the waves. I'll have you know, Kirklaw: Byron will be remembered when we are all rotting away in our family vaults. As for the tallow chandler, Jemison the Elder provides candles to the navy. His candles have illuminated the battle plans of Sidney Smith and Horatio Nelson. He is a wealthier man than any of us here.'

Kirklaw curled his lip. 'Our great admirals use waxen candles, surely.'

Nick clapped his hands. 'Oh, well done, Your Grace. You have bested me. How dare I suggest that the great Nelson ever had to smell burning fat!' He got to his feet. 'My Lord Gossip.' He bowed to Blessing. 'My Lord Calumny.' He bowed to Delbun. 'And Your Grace of Slander.' He made an elaborate leg to Kirklaw. 'I believe we have said enough to one another this evening. I thank you for your hospitality, and I bid you goodnight.' He drained his brandy balloon with a flourish.

'One moment before you go, Blackdown.' Kirklaw went

to a leather writing case sitting on an escritoire, opened it, and drew out a heavy sheet of paper. He spent a moment perusing it, then handed it to Blessing, who handed it to Delbun, who handed it up to Nick. It read: 'George Augustus Frederick, the Prince of Wales, Regent of the United Kingdom of Great Britain and Ireland, To Our Right Trusty and Well Beloved Nicholas Clancy Falcott, Chevalier, Greeting.'

Shit!

A Writ of Summons.

Nick looked up to find Kirklaw watching him with a smirk, pinching at that wretched cigar. 'You are to appear in the House of Lords in your robes the day after tomorrow,' he said. 'Whereupon you will take your oath of allegiance and make your maiden speech in favour of the Corn Bill.' He reached into the case and extracted a sheaf of papers. 'This is your speech. It repudiates Jemison and those like him, and calls for immediate passage of the bill. It praises me, your old friend.' He shuffled through the pages and found a passage, which he read out loud. '"I fought in Spain, at the head of a gallant company. I can tell you from experience that Jem Jemison is a coward. But I can also tell you, as a leader of men, that I know how to recognize courage and fortitude in any man."' Kirklaw looked up. 'And here you gesture at me. I shall look surprised, and you shall ask me to stand. Then you say, in ringing tones, "The Duke of Kirklaw is just such an exemplar of British manhood! I put my faith in him, the faith of a soldier and an Englishman!"'

Nick suppressed a smile. 'You expect me to read that, out loud, in the House of Lords.'

'I do. And I believe, when you consider the alternatives, that you will.' The duke handed the papers to Blessing, who handed them to Delbun, who handed them up to Nick.

'I don't have robes.'

269

'You will find that Ede and Ravenscroft have your father's robes put away. Like your title and the duties you owe to your family, your estate and your class, Ede and Ravenscroft have been waiting for you.'

'And if I do not appear?'

'The choice is entirely yours, of course.'

'Oh, of course.'

'May I offer you another drink, or have you had enough?'

Nick looked down at his empty balloon, then up and into the eyes of his former friend. 'Oh, fill her up,' he said. 'Smuggled brandy makes blackmail go down much more smoothly.'

Kirklaw bowed, acknowledging the hit. Finally flicking his shredded cigar into the fire, he grabbed the bottle up from the table where it had been left and strolled over to Nick. 'Welcome home, my old friend,' he said, tipping brandy into Nick's glass.

The house was silent, except for the patter of raindrops on the windows. Julia lay on her bed, trying to distract herself with a novel. She had declined an invitation to join Clare, Bella and the dowager marchioness on a visit to their second cousin Lydia. It hadn't been hard to say no: Lydia was a famously bad-tempered old woman who lived in unfashionable Kensington. She had many cats, three parrots and a silent husband. Bella said the husband was probably stuffed, for he always sat in the same place and never said a word. Julia had waved them off without a shred of regret.

Thinking herself alone in the house, she had gone into the drawing room to read, only to find Count Lebedev stretched out asleep between two gold bergère chairs that he had pulled into position, his knees ridiculously supported by the harpsichord bench that he had placed between them. There he lay, snoring, his boots casually ruining the exquisite blue-and-gold silk jacquard upholstery. Julia indulged herself in a good, long contemptuous stare. This was the man of whom she was so afraid, the man who was hunting her down. This boorish man, who clearly gave not one pin for the dowager marchioness's delicate sensibilities; she doted on those chairs almost as if they were her children. Surely Blackdown couldn't actually like this Russian miscreant?

Well. Julia flared her nostrils. What Blackdown liked and didn't like was no concern of hers. She knew full well what she thought of the Russian. If ever the day came that he was looming over her with a knife, she would spend her last moments smirking in his face and treasuring the memory of him like this. His mouth was gaping open, his long limbs were splayed and slack, and best of all, his snore was high and piercing, something like the choking gobble of a tom turkey. She closed the door silently and headed up to her room. She had a Minerva novel and was well launched into its third, splenetic volume. If she didn't finish it now, perhaps it would at least send her to sleep.

But an hour had passed and the trials of the perpetually fainting Matilda Weimar had neither come to an end nor dispatched Julia into the arms of Lethe. She found herself staring out of the window at the rain, her mind going in circles. The rain made her remember the kiss. The kiss made her think about Blackdown, and thinking about Blackdown made her wonder what bound him to the horrible snoring Russian downstairs. Debt? Honour? Friendship? Or was Blackdown some sort of slave to Lebedev's time manipulations?

Julia repressed the thought. Thank heaven she had witnessed that scene at Castle Dar, for now she knew that if she so much as imagined playing with time, the Russian might sense it. And if he sensed it, he would think she was one of those he was hunting. Would he skewer her on a sword, or shoot her? Or he might choose more subtle methods. Her saddle girth might be cut or a finial might be knocked from the roof of the house just when she was walking below – did this house even have finials?

Finials! For God's sake. Julia clenched her fists and tried to stop thinking at all, which made her hear the rain against the window. And the rain made her remember the kiss.

'Botheration!' She threw her book across the room and felt a fierce sort of pleasure when a badly stitched parcel of pages broke free and fell out. She hoped it was the part where the Countess of Wolfenbach is locked in a closet giving birth as the corpse of her lover bleeds all over her gown.

Julia jumped from the bed. She should have chosen boredom at Cousin Lydia's over fretting isolation in this ominously pensive house. It was almost as if the house were haunted, and she could feel the vibrations of a restless spirit. But that restless spirit was her own.

She needed a more active distraction than the damp sentiments of Matilda and friends. She could not go downstairs where the count was sleeping, and she could not go out. Nowhere to go up but up. She would explore the top three storeys of the house.

She slipped out into the hallway. There was Bella's door, and Clare's, and in the centre, the dowager marchioness's grand suite. The marquess was, of course, entitled to claim the master suite as his own, but he had refused to displace his mother. There was the count's bedroom – Julia stepped past quickly, her heart in her throat. Beside that, Blackdown's. Every impulse urged her to go in and explore. She did put her hand on the cool porcelain knob, and turned it just a little, enough to know that it wasn't locked. But she didn't turn it all the way, and with firm steps she went past that last, most fascinating bedchamber.

The next floor up contained some empty rooms, some locked rooms and the old nursery. It was bare but for an elegant dapple-grey rocking horse with a mane and tail of real white horsehair. Julia spent a few minutes with him, imagining Clare and Nick and Bella as children, playing on and around him. She had always envied them their siblinghood, their togetherness. Had they shared this beautiful toy, or had there been tussles, tears? Julia stroked the horse's wooden nose, knowing that had he been hers, she would have had trouble sharing him. She would have ridden him for hours, a bandit queen, her sword – no, her bow and arrow – repelling all attackers. She gazed into his dark eye, enlivened by one painted white dot. He kept his secrets and wouldn't tell which fairylands he had conquered in his time. So she set him rocking with a tug of his thick tail. 'Gallop apace, you fiery-footed steed,' she whispered, and climbed the stairs to the topmost floor.

Servants' quarters, which she ignored with the same fastidiousness with which she had marched past the bedrooms two floors down, and attic rooms, which were locked. At the end of the corridor there was a narrow, curving staircase leading still further up. Where did it go? The house on Berkeley Square was only five storeys tall, and this was the fifth. She put her foot on the first step and looked up. Watery sunlight was streaming down and she could hear the rain pattering on glass; there had to be a cupola, invisible from street level. She climbed higher, around the curve of the stairs, her hand on the thin wooden railing. Then, when she was halfway up, she sensed it – someone was up there. She stopped still. The count? She climbed one more step. A servant? She held her breath, listening. A small, rustling sound – a page being turned. Whoever it was seemed to be reading. Not the count, she thought. He didn't have the soul to steal away to the top of a house to read in the rain.

Then she knew. It was Blackdown.

She should have been terrified of him, now that she knew he was an Ofan-killer. But this wasn't terror that sent her climbing silently still higher. It was something else. Her heart was beating so fast and so hard that she was sure it was booming out like a drum. Then she could see him. The staircase opened directly into the cupola, which was a simple glass room, more rectangular than square. A deep, upholstered bench, like a wide window seat, was built around all four walls and liberally tossed with cushions. Blackdown was lying along one side, one leg stretched out, the other bent at the knee, his back propped up by big pillows. The book he held was tiny, its pigskin binding white. He held it in one hand, his other hand behind his head. She watched him read, hardly daring to breathe. If he looked up – when he looked up – he would see her head almost at floor level. She would look like a kobold popping up out of the earth. Should she try to descend, or simply keep climbing? She couldn't decide, and in the end, her predicament was too ridiculous. She laughed.

He looked up and for just a moment his eyes, as grey as the rain outside, were blank with surprise. But then he sat up 'Hello.'

'Hello,' she said. 'I did not wish to disturb you.' She started to go back down the stairs.

'No.' He put his book down quickly on the floor, took two light steps over to the stairwell and reached out a hand. 'Come back.'

She put her hand out and he took it, pulling her gently up and into the glass room. 'Oh.' She looked around. The rainy city stretched out on all sides; it was like being a bird up on a chimney, except that the falling rain never reached her. 'How magical.'

His fingers were warm around hers; no leather between them now.

'Please,' he said gently. 'Do sit. I wish I had refreshment to offer you. But I neglected to procure Madeira and biscuits before coming up here.'

She sat and looked down on Berkeley Square, all grey and green and misty. 'What a perfect place,' she said. 'I had no idea it was here.'

He sat down next to her and took her hand again. 'It is

something of a secret,' he said. 'Everyone knows of it, but no one thinks to come up. I was almost afraid I should discover it had been blown away in a storm, or dismantled. But when I climbed up here this morning I found all just as I had left it. This book even, still here.'

'What is it?' She was grateful that they were talking of nothing, but there was her hand in his, and as they talked their fingers intertwined of their own accord.

'John Donne,' he said. 'His early works. I had forgotten that I was reading them here before I left for Spain. Now I find they are useful to me.' He glanced at her for a moment. 'Personal liberty and social responsibility,' he said. 'Do you ever think about those things?'

She smiled. 'Oh, all the time.'

He squeezed her hand and said nothing. He seemed troubled in spirit.

'I have not read Donne,' she said after a moment.

'No, I wouldn't suppose that you had.' His fingers slipped more intimately in among hers. 'His early poems are not . . .' He seemed to be searching for the right words. 'I suppose they are not considered appropriate for . . . young ladies.'

Julia's eyebrows flew up. 'I see.'

'Are you always careful of your purity, Julia?' His voice was soft, his eyes half lidded.

What was he asking her? She withdrew her hand a little, but he kept it firmly in his own. 'Of course,' she said automatically, for it was the only possible answer. But as she said it she remembered that it had been she who pulled his head down to hers for a second kiss. 'Or rather, I think I am. I mean . . .' She looked at her hand, caught in his. 'Of what are we talking?'

He smiled, almost sadly. 'My apologies.' He let go of her hand. 'I am out of practice with gently reared young ladies,

I'm afraid.' He opened his other hand. In his palm was, of all things, a small, brown acorn. He must have been holding it all along. He bent and placed it carefully on top of the book, next to the gold-embossed word on the cover: ELEGIES. He traced that word with one finger. 'Of what are we talking?' He repeated her question dreamily. Then he sat up straight, turned, and his eyes were intent upon hers. 'Do you protect yourself against knowledge? Against feeling? Do you always do and feel what you are told? Are you always safe? Or do you yearn to know, to feel, more?'

'I yearn to know more,' she said, and it felt as if the words were bursting from her, so desperately were they true. But then she sat silent, not knowing how to proceed.

His hand came slowly up, almost as if he feared he might scare her away. '"License my roving hands,"' he whispered. '"Let them go . . ."' He stroked her cheek, so softly that it felt like the raindrops that weren't falling on her skin.

'Nicholas,' she murmured, hearing the catch in her voice. She was in his arms, and he was kissing her tenderly, his fingers tangling in her hair. He ended the kiss and simply buried his face in her hair, his hands stroking her shoulders. His rough cheek was against hers and she breathed in the scent of him.

He pulled back and looked again into her eyes, one hand slipping around to rest at her waist, the other cradling the back of her head. 'We seem to meet in the rain,' he said.

'Please . . .' She put her hands on his chest. At the moment, she didn't care who he was, or whether he was in league with the Russian. 'Kiss me again, Nicholas,' she said. 'I want you to.'

Again his eyes were sad. 'You sweet, lovely woman,' he said, and then those sad eyes seemed to flash and she was pressed against him roughly.

His hands slipped down her back, pulling her still closer.

They twisted in her hair, turning her head now this way, now that, as he kissed her mouth, her face, her ears. She pressed against him, her own hands pushing inside his jacket and around, feeling the strength of his back through his linen shirt. But she felt he was controlling himself even as he seemed to devour her. What would it be to feel him give in? She wanted him to! She wanted to bring him to that edge and fall off it with him.

She gripped his shoulders, arching her back as he trailed kisses down her neck, and then his hands were moving firmly, up along her ribs to her breasts, pushing them up until they were tight against the muslin of her dress. His mouth descended, taking her nipple through the muslin and gently biting it. It stiffened deliciously between his teeth and she closed her eyes and cried out.

Then his mouth was hot, sucking through the muslin, one hand gripping her bottom, the other reaching up and pulling her dress down until her other breast was entirely free. Julia toppled back against the cushions, and his mouth descended on her naked breast; she had never felt anything so entirely real. Her head was thrown back on the cushions and her hands were lost in his hair, grasping his head as his tongue flicked roughly over her nipple, and then his teeth again, biting gently, pulling away, and his breath strangely cold on her breast as she breathed his name.

But he was easing his body away from hers, pulling her dress back up, stroking her hair and kissing her face and then kissing her fingers and sitting beside her, calming her.

She wanted him to continue. Why wouldn't he? She opened her eyes slowly, knowing that she would feel awkward – even ashamed – the second she saw his face, and indeed, those sad eyes were smiling ruefully down into hers and she felt the heat in her cheeks. 'Damn,' she said. She sat up quickly, her hands moving to cover her cheeks. 'Damn damn damn.'

He sat beside her, one arm around her waist, the other taking a hand and bringing it to his mouth. He kissed her fingers, and then her lips. 'You are beautiful,' he whispered. 'I love the corner of your mouth.' He kissed it. 'And this sweet little place where you frown, right between your eyes.' He kissed it. 'And your beautiful eyes themselves. Close them. Let me kiss them.'

She closed her eyelids. His soft mouth pressed gently against one and then the other. He was teasing her away from passion, and she could feel it ebb, just like the rain, which was falling more patchily now.

'There,' he said, tracing her mouth with one finger.

She opened her eyes. He was entirely rumpled and handsomer for it. They had kissed again, again in the rain. Again he was pulling away. But now she knew more about him. She reached out a finger and traced the scar that crossed his eyebrow. Then she leaned forward and placed her own kiss on his mouth. 'I admire your scar,' she said.

'It is not a happy memory,' he said. 'The getting of it.'

'How did you come by it?'

'At Badajoz.' His voice was flat.

'I haven't heard much about Badajoz,' she said carefully. 'It was a siege?'

'I am glad you don't know. I wish no one knew.'

'Tell me?'

'The man who fought beside me when finally we stormed the city, who climbed with me, up . . .' He stopped and searched her face. What did he see there? Whatever it was, he chose to continue. 'We climbed into Badajoz on a ladder of our own dead, Julia. A man ahead would fall, shot by the French who were picking us off from above. That man would become the next rung. Do you understand?'

She put her hand on his. 'Yes.'

His eyes deepened. 'But of course you know. You were there.'

'What do you mean?'

He stroked her hair back from her brow and let his eyes wander from her eyes, down her face and body, and back up. 'Julia. That day. So long ago. When you saw me and Boatswain. I was weeping.'

'For your father's death.'

'I wish I could say it was for his death. I was weeping for myself. I did not want to be Blackdown. But I already was Blackdown. Then there you were. Do you know . . .' He drew his hand down her face, causing her to close her eyes. She opened them again when his hand withdrew. 'Yes,' he said. 'That look.' He touched her lips with his finger. 'I am afraid I have used you for years. Carried you into battle with me. Used you to fight back the memories. You, stepping out of the woods at my darkest hour. Smiling at me.'

'That was your darkest hour? The day your father died?'

'When I was that young, yes, that was my darkest hour. I have had darker since.'

Julia touched the scar again. 'You got this scar climbing into the city?'

'No.' His eyes went blank. 'It was later. Once we took Badajoz. In the aftermath.' He reached up and grasped her exploring fingers, bringing them down to his mouth.

'You don't want to tell me,' she said. 'Did you do something terrible?'

'Yes,' he said. 'It was terrible. But it was the only thing I could do. It was right.'

His face was still strange to her. Rough, broken even, with that scar. But she was coming to understand it. 'I don't care what you did then,' she said. 'I like your scar now.'

He grinned, the light returning to his eyes. 'Other women have liked it, too.'

'Don't tell me that!'

He laughed lightly, and she turned her face away. How could he change so quickly?

'Oh, come.' The laugh was still in his voice. He reached for her, but she held back. 'I'm sorry,' he said. 'You're such an innocent. I was teasing you. I take it back.'

She turned her face to him again. 'I cannot help that I am innocent.'

'I like it.'

She put her chin up. 'Other men have liked it, too!'

His eyes flashed dark, and with a quick jerk he pulled her against him and kissed her. She kissed him back fiercely, but he pulled away. 'You wicked girl,' he said. Yet he was smiling as he said it, a real smile instead of that wretched knowing one. 'You make it hard to stop kissing you.'

'I don't want you to stop.' She put her hand on his thigh. 'I am not that sweet girl you thought about all those years. I'm glad she could help you. But she isn't me. You made her up out of the shadows and light of that afternoon.'

'I know it,' he said.

'I want you to keep kissing me, Nicholas. Why won't you?'

'Last time I kissed you, you didn't want to hear about my reasons for stopping.'

She looked at her hand on his leg. 'I know your reasons.' She pushed her hand up his thigh, feeling the way the lean muscles swelled.

He put his hand over hers to stay it. 'Stop that,' he said. 'My reasons are very simple today. We have to call a halt now or we won't be able to.' He bent to the white book on the floor, and the acorn still perched on top of it. 'The acorn is mine,' he said, palming it. 'But read these.' He handed her the book. 'Ignore the one called "Julia"! Donne didn't like his Julia, whereas I like mine, very much. But I think you will find the last poem informative.' He stood up. 'I'll go downstairs now. You stay here for a while, then come down when you are sure I've had time to be elsewhere. And, Julia?'

She looked up at him.

He tossed the acorn into the air and caught it. 'I said I would kiss you again, and I did.'

'Oh!' She made as if to throw his little book at him, and he ducked, laughing, and ran lightly down the stairs.

22

Julia frowned at her reflection in the mirror. For an hour or more she had stared at the ceiling, then at her reflection, then out of the window, then at her reflection again. Eyes, nose, mouth. Neck, arms, breasts. Hands. Belly, sex, thighs. Knees, feet, toes.

Trouble.

But now the clock and her troublesome body were both telling her it was almost time to go down to dinner. Her dress was laid out upon the bed; her combs and ribbons were on the dresser. Everything was in waiting. Julia rang for the maid.

When she was dressed and the maid dismissed, Julia pinched some colour into her cheeks. The clock ticked loudly but slowly. If she went down now she would be a mite early. If she was early, she would have to watch his face as he entered. If late, she would have to watch his face as she entered. These seemed like completely different possibilities, and yet no matter which she chose, she would still have to see Blackdown over dinner, she would have to talk to him, she would have to look at him and pretend that nothing had ever happened. That had been easier before, when they had only kissed once, under a tree in the rain. She had struggled with her desire after that, but ultimately she had managed to pack it away. Or so she'd thought. Give her Blackdown alone in a pretty little glass room high up over the square, and it turned out that her neatly folded desire was a jack-in-the-box, ready to spring up.

In the end, it happened that Julia and Blackdown met at

the top of the stairs. He smiled when he saw her, and his expression was neither knowing nor distant, but simply his own. She relaxed and fell into step beside him.

'Have you read the poem?'

'Not yet.'

'Enough excitement for one afternoon?'

'Quite!' She swept past him, enjoying the sound of his laughter tumbling down the stairs after her.

The dowager marchioness and Bella were dining in Greenwich tonight, and staying the night as the guests of Lord and Lady Latch, which meant that the table was set for only four. When Nick and Julia entered, Clare and the Russian were already seated and chatting away in that light manner they had. Julia could not understand how Clare could bear the count, but she seemed actually to like him. The Russian got to his feet and bowed when Julia entered, and Clare explained that he had been telling her about how best to escape wolves in Russia. 'It is all nonsense, of course,' she said. 'But he claims that they cannot bear the sound of French. All you must do is speak French to a wolf, and he will run away.'

'It is true, I swear it,' the count said, pulling out Julia's chair but never turning his attention from Clare. 'Do you speak French?'

'A few words.'

'A few words, they are enough for a wolf. Here, we try.' He leaned across the table towards Clare and growled.

'*Bonjour*, Monsieur Wolf,' Clare said. '*Comment ça va?*'

The Russian whined and yipped like a puppy in pain. 'There, you see?' He grinned at Clare, and Julia thought his big teeth were rather lupine. 'Very simple.'

Julia looked at Nick to see what he thought of this display. His face was a careful blank. She looked back to her empty plate and prepared herself for an uncomfortable evening.

Once they were served, Nick turned the conversation to the Corn Bill and engaged Clare in a heated conversation about its merits and failings. The Russian was so clearly repelled by political talk that Julia wondered if Nick had chosen that topic on purpose, to keep his friend from conversing with his sister. Indeed, the count tried several times to intervene.

'The Corn Bill! Bah!'

He was ignored.

'The Corn Bill, it is as good as passed. Why do you care, Blackdown? You have more important things to think of.'

Nick turned his shoulder and continued talking to his sister.

'It is rude to make ladies talk about politics!'

Clare stopped what she was saying mid-sentence. '*Mal chien!*' She pointed at the Russian. '*Mal!*'

The set-down had the unfortunate effect of forcing the count to talk to Julia. He turned with a barely repressed sigh and asked her how her day had been. She said that she'd had a lovely time reading. Had he had a restful day?

'The English rain. So unpleasant. I slept. But tell me . . .' His voice dwindled away. 'Such dark eyes you have.'

'My grandfather had dark eyes.'

He gazed for a moment more into her eyes. 'Poor girl. And now you are an Ofan.'

She started involuntarily. How did he know? She had done nothing whatsoever in his presence to indicate that she could manipulate time, too. But still somehow he knew!

But his blue eyes were limpid, and his smile was benign.

An *orphan.*

He had called her an orphan.

She cursed herself for the fluttering fear which might so easily have exposed her secret. 'I am grateful for your sympathy,' she said, her voice coming out high, like a child's. But let him think her foolish. It was better than the alternative. She cleared her throat discreetly. 'And thank you for the part you played in freeing me from my cousin.'

'It was the pleasure.' His perfunctory nod was meant to make it obvious that he had found saving her a chore. But Julia knew otherwise. The Russian was fascinated by Eamon; he thought Eamon was Ofan. And he pursued that interest now, to Julia's intense discomfort. 'This cousin you have. This new earl who replaces your grandfather. How well do you know him?'

'Hardly at all.'

'Since your grandfather's death? You have not come to know him any better?'

'He is not an outgoing man.'

'Perhaps you notice strange things about this cousin?' He spoke as he might to a child, asking simple questions in a friendly tone. 'Perhaps he has mysterious instruments in his study? Perhaps he speaks and acts oddly? Is there anything, any unusual object, that particularly he treasured?'

Julia bit her lip. So the Russian was looking for a talisman too. Grandfather had said that there might be others, besides Eamon, who would come and ask questions of her. Pretend, he had said. Never tell. Pretend. It was Count Lebedev Grandfather had been warning her about. Count Lebedev and . . .

And perhaps Blackdown.

The count leaned towards her. 'Well? Was there anything, anything at all?'

'No,' Julia said, willing him to feel that she was telling the truth, pushing with all her might against his suspicion. 'Nothing like that.'

Somewhat to her surprise, he relented. 'No, of course there wasn't.' He let his disappointed gaze rest on her for just a moment more before he turned his shoulder and dug into his dinner, eating quickly and paying her not one more moment's notice.

Julia forced herself to pick up her knife and fork and eat, forced herself to think of anything at all other than Ofans and time and the blasted Talisman – which was herself!

Nick. His voice. He was still speaking to Clare.

He might be searching for Ofans, too, and he might be just as dangerous as his Russian friend. But he had said she was his Julia, up in the cupola. Surely that meant he cared for her. She clung to the sound of his voice and the words he was speaking as if they were flotsam and jetsam in a shipwreck.

'Let us say for the sake of the argument that these Corn Laws hung in the balance, and you could choose which way the vote would go, but at a price. Would you be willing to sacrifice your good name for your convictions?'

'Do you mean to ask if I would actually . . . ?'

'No.' Blackdown spread his hands in a gesture of denial. 'Of course not, Clare. I'm talking about whether or not you would be willing to be . . .' He paused. 'To be shunned. If you could have the vote go the way you wanted, but you knew it would make people talk about you, revile you . . .'

'Some people always say bad things anyway,' Clare said. 'And there is always another club. Vote for the Corn Bill, you make one set of friends. Vote against, you make another. If White's expels you, what do you do? You go to Brooks's.' She smiled. 'Perhaps you will go to Brooks's of your own accord one day.'

'Yes, that is true enough for me. But you are a woman.'

'What iota of difference does that make?'

'I believe that, for women, there is only one respectable club.'

'Ah.' Clare reached up and adjusted her cap. 'That is tediously true. How unkind of you to remind me.'

'I didn't mean —'

Clare reached out and patted her brother's arm. 'For goodness' sake, Nickin. I am teasing you. You have asked me a hypothetical question. Don't let it tie you in knots.' She turned to Julia. 'What do you think?'

Both siblings were looking at her now, awaiting an answer. Even the Russian glanced up from his food.

'Would I sacrifice my good name for my convictions?' Julia considered, remembering the feeling of hollow desolation that had come over her in Stoke Canon when she realized that the town had turned against her. How precarious her hold on life had felt, as if she were teetering on the edge of a cliff. 'I don't think I have a reputation to trade any more. At this point my good name depends on yours, Clare. I discovered last week that my neighbours have been waiting all my life for me to prove that I am . . .' She blinked, remembering with searing clarity exactly how it had felt when she had pressed her naked breast to Blackdown's mouth.

She folded her lips together tightly and fought against her desire to look at him.

'It is ridiculous,' Clare said, taking over. 'Women are all chained together by this thing called reputation. If I sacrifice mine, I destroy Julia's.'

Blackdown banged his hand on the table, and the noise made Julia jump. 'It is ridiculous, yes!' His voice was loud and angry. 'In time the dark ages will be understood to include our own!'

Clare and Julia both laughed, and Clare got up and kissed him. 'Oh, Nickin, I do think you should join Brooks's sooner rather than later. Or start your own club. And let me join it.'

He glowered and stuffed a bite of fish into his mouth, but Clare stood with her hand on his shoulder and smiled at Julia. 'My brother has returned from Spain a changed man. He believes that women should control their own destinies. Such a rare beast. Do you think we should put him on exhibit at the Tower of London, alongside the lions and tigers?'

'Please, ladies, do take control of your blasted destinies and save me a headache,' Blackdown said, wiping his mouth with his napkin and looking decidedly frazzled. 'I have been back in England for a few short weeks, and all I seem to do is worry about women and their godforsaken reputations. Rise up and claim your rights and leave me in peace!'

The Russian interrupted their laughter, and what he said was so absurd and so kind that it took Julia a long moment to remember that he was her enemy. 'Anyone who would doubt Julia Percy's good name? That man is a fool.' His voice was harsh. 'Just look into her eyes.' He pushed his chair back from the table and stalked from the room.

23

Nick stood on the top step and took his time adjusting his hat to his satisfaction, enjoying the sight of Arkady, already in the street, scowling and tossing his stick from hand to hand. 'Surely this could wait until tomorrow, Arkady. It is well past midnight.'

'Tonight you begin your service to the Guild. You should be eager, like the young hound! But you worry over your hat like a woman. Come! We will be late.' Arkady turned and started walking.

Nick walked lightly down the stairs, glanced up at the stars, then sauntered after his friend. 'I do hope we are taking a hackney? Or are you going to jump us to the twenty-first century for a tube ride? Because I for one am unarmed.'

'Do not be a coward. I have a cudgel.' Arkady slapped the heavy brass knob at the top of his stick into his palm. 'A hack! The tube! I spurn them both! It feels good to be alive when there is danger. The stars and the moon, they shine. The city may stink but she is very beautiful. She smiles on us. We are her kings, her masters. In all ages she recognizes us and welcomes us as a lover.'

'Hmm. The stinking city welcomes us both as her lovers. What a vision. You are a terrible poet.'

'Pah!' The Russian snapped his fingers. 'That for your criticism.'

They went down Berkeley Street towards Piccadilly, then east towards the City. Arkady wasn't wrong. The night was beautiful and perilous, and as he walked Nick felt an answering courage flow through his veins. Footpads, cutpurses, highway-men and all the other Georgian bad guys – Nick was ready for them. Why did that readiness feel so much like happiness?

Julia. That was the answer. She had come to him in the cupola and he had drawn out her sighs like spun sugar. Nick surrendered to lascivious thoughts. Why not? He was home again, London was filthy and dangerous again, he was alive. What better way to celebrate than to imagine the delicious deflowering of Julia Percy?

For a while Nick and Arkady walked in silence. The streets were dark but they weren't sleeping. Here and there small groups of men were making their way homeward. Now and again a woman, leaning in a doorway, made clear what she was offering. A dog barked and was answered by another, and out of the corner of his eye Nick saw a rat slip over the cobbles in the shadow of a crumbling wall. When they reached the Strand, the street grew more crowded. Down side streets to the south they could see the Thames – it was at low tide, and the night-fishing boats, each with its dancing lantern, crowded the centre channel. The long, sloping banks were dotted here and there with people, some tending small fires, others combing for treasure among the rocks and bones and broken pipe stems that littered the mudflats.

Out of nowhere, a clutch of children appeared, scarcely older than infants. They trotted at Nick and Arkady's heels, begging for money. The stars ignited their hungry, hopeful eyes. Nick was about to toss them a few coins when he remembered that to do so could well make him a target of older children or even adults, watching and waiting in the shadows.

Nick looked sideways at Arkady, the man who had brought him back here. The Russian's smile was as tranquil as the slender moon. He turned a ragged child gently aside with his stick. He did it expertly, lifting it slightly under one thin arm and redirecting its steps. It was as if the child were a cat that had sidled up, hoping to be stroked. The child turned to try again, its little face lifted up, but Arkady's stick was in the way and Nick watched as the child's face lost its look of hope and closed in. The children fell behind, their pleas turning to shrill little curses as the two tall aristocrats strode out of their lives for ever.

'You ask no questions,' Arkady said, breaking the silence. 'That is unusual for you.'

'I have learned that I will receive no answers.'

'Yet I have told you I am taking you to a rendezvous far from gracious Mayfair. I lead you into the dark City, to meet strangers. You are either very brave or very stupid, my friend.'

'That's easy. I am very stupid.'

'Don't you want to know where we are going and why?'

'Oh, no.' Nick waved a hand. 'Lead on! You see, I have realized that I am but a humble pawn. I play on several different chessboards, it's true, but I am always a pawn.'

'What other chessboards? There is only one. The Guild's.'

Nick smiled. 'You have brought me home, Arkady, to this sunset of the aristocracy. You have given me back my name, however temporarily. So unless you're going to tell me that the Prince Regent is a time traveller, I'm afraid I'm bound to play on his chessboard, too. Did I not tell you? He sent me a Writ of Summons. I am to appear in the House of Lords tomorrow.'

'Was that what you were going on about at dinner? My priest, how dreary!' He laughed. 'Maybe it is the sunset of the aristocracy, but money – it is always high noon with the money! That is why the Corn Bill – it passes. People suffer. Decades later it is struck down, but oh dear – it is too late to save the Irish!' Arkady yawned. 'This is the foolery of Naturals. It has nothing to do with you, and there is nothing you can do that could change it.'

'I was planning to vote for it.'

That wiped the smile from Arkady's face. He stopped walking and stared. 'What? But you know it is terrible, this bill!'

'Ah.' Nick twitched his cuffs. 'I thought you said it didn't matter what I did. I thought you said the bill was boring.'

Arkady's stare softened. 'You are pulling the leg! You trick me!'

'Perhaps.' Nick smiled. 'You're afraid that things *can* be changed, Arkady, admit it. That the Ofan can change things. That I might change things. You don't want me to think for myself in case I screw up the future.'

'Is that what you think?' Arkady set out walking again with a jaunty swing of his stick. 'That you could change the world? I laugh at you.'

'All right, but if I can't change anything, why do you care? You clearly don't want me to play even my small role in British politics. Why?'

'I do not care. I only tell you, it makes no difference. Vote for the bill and stain your immortal soul, or vote against it and make the saints smile. How you vote? It tells me if you are a good man, but it does not *matter*. The Corn Bill will pass. People will starve. The barons and earls will be rich for another generation. But you? You are bound to the Guild. This is why I do not want you distracted by these small turnips.'

'Potatoes,' Nick said absently. He dug his hands into his pockets and found the acorn. They were walking around St Clement Danes. Nick glanced up at the fairy church, its tiered steeple standing black against the slightly less black sky. Oranges and lemons say the bells of St Clements. Arkady was right, of course. Turnips and potatoes. Oranges and lemons.

Apples and oranges. What did Nick's little problems – his prince, his unsavoury ex-friends, his sister, his onetime comrade in arms – have to do with the River of Time? And yet the Writ of Summons, Kirklaw, Clare and Jem Jemison – they were real. He couldn't just ignore them.

Arkady ranted on. 'Say that somehow you convince one hundred other lords to vote against this bill that protects their money and their power. Say the bill does not pass. You, Nick Davenant, have changed history! But what happens? Do the poor get rich? Do the hungry eat? No. If bread is cheap, factories pay lower wages. Your Corn Bill? It is a fight over who gets to use the poor as a golden goose.' Arkady jerked his head towards the Thames. 'They are down there now, the poor, picking through the bones. They will be there for ever.'

Nick looked down the crooked street to their right and caught a glimpse of the river. 'That's your precious eternal history, then? A riverbed of bones and garbage?'

'Bah!' Arkady gripped Nick's arm and spoke, hot and angry, in his ear. 'The river flows to the sea, Nick Davenant! You are a servant of the Guild. Act like one.'

Nick wrenched away. 'Well then, can the Guild write a note to my other master? "Dear Prince George: Please excuse Master Nick for not participating in historical events today. He had to defend the River of Time from angels with four faces who want to take it over." I hope that will work, Arkady, because otherwise I'm expected in the Lesser Hall of the House of Lords tomorrow.'

Arkady threw up his hands. 'Go, then! Go and be damned!'

Nick made Arkady an elaborate leg. 'Thank you, Lebedev. I am grateful for your permission. Now, may I push your beneficence an inch further and ask where we are going?'

The Russian glowered at him and ground the words out like sausage meat. 'To a ball.'

Nick was shocked into silence for a moment, but then he laughed. 'A ball! Who does that make me? Cinderella? Or Prince Charming? I suppose you are the fairy godmother?'

'There are other characters,' Arkady said. 'The unpleasant sisters. The pumpkin.'

'I do have big feet . . .'

'But your head . . .' Arkady considered him. 'It is also big. And your hair. It is red. I think you are the pumpkin.'

'My hair is not red. It is light brown.'

'It is . . . what do they call it? The strawberry yellow.'

'It most certainly is not!' Nick was horrified. His hair was not as dark as he would have liked, but it was not strawberry blond, not by any stretch of the imagination.

Arkady laughed. 'My priest! I have discovered your vanity!'

'Hair is your vanity, Arkady, not mine.'

'Yes.' The Russian stood tall. 'My hair is very beautiful. Always it has been beautiful. When I was young, it was the shining black. Women, they loved it. Now it is the bright white and still, women –'

'Yes, yes, the women. I know. Tell me about this ball.'

They were walking now along Fleet Street, coming up upon the debtors' prison; a few voices called out from behind the barred windows, begging alms to pay for their keep even at this hour of the night.

'It is the yearly celebration for Guild members who live in and near London.'

'Why is it here, in the City?'

'Ah! You are not so stupid. That is a good question. Consider. In the twenty-first century anyone who is rich can be powerful, yes?'

'I suppose so. They must also have ambition and intelligence. But money opens all doors.'

'Exactly.' Arkady twirled his stick. 'But here and now, in

Britain in 1815 . . . Would you, Lord Blackdown, nod to a man simply because he was loaded down with gold?'

Nick looked down the length of Ludgate Hill to where the smoke-blackened dome of St Paul's rose like an ominous moon. The City would change almost beyond recognition across the coming two centuries. Empire would swell it, then German bombs would flatten much of it. Then it would rise again, in glass and steel. 'Of course I would not,' he said. 'I could not. Nor could you.'

'Indeed. That is why the ball, it is here. In 1815 Guild members are wealthy, they are educated – as it always has been and will be. But they are forever outside of English society. Guild members – they cannot say who their parents are. They make their way without a name. They are foreigners. You will never find a Guild member at Almack's or White's. In the City, that is where you will find them.'

Nick shrugged. 'Fine. Are you worried that I will sneer at them? You know me better than that. I have not drowned and I will not now. I like the coming egalitarian world, Arkady. I approve of it.'

'Yes. It is a pretty vision, this egalitarian world you speak of. But I wonder. Will you approve of what comes after your beloved 2013?' Arkady slowed his steps, his boots ringing on the cobbles. He spoke more quietly. 'But we are not talking of the coming world. We are talking about the Guild. Remember what most Guild members think: *There is no return.* But you and me? We are from the future. So you do not say to anyone that you are in the Guild. Tonight you are a Natural who arrived in 1815 by living through 1813 and 1814. Lord Blackdown, he knows nothing of time travel. I am your loud friend Count Lebedev. I too am a Natural. We are the so illustrious guests of Monsieur Bertrand Penture.'

'Got it,' Nick said. 'Pretend to be an ignorant toff.'

'Yes. And the Guild members there, they too will be [pre]tending. The party will appear to be a gathering of foreign merchants and their wives. Monsieur Penture, he imports from the Orient. His ships have returned from China, and now his investors, they are all richer than they were before. They have a party. We come to the party. Everyone is happy.'

'And that's all? You dragged me back two centuries to send me to a party where I am to pretend to know nothing?'

'Ah! No! And now we get to it. Tonight we begin to find a traitor. The Ofan are strong in London. Penture, you see, he is the new Alderman. He is ambitious. He wants to chase the Ofan out of the nineteenth century. But first he must know who is who. Who is good and who is bad. Before the war, there must come the spying, and so we need you. That is why we come out tonight.' Arkady took Nick's arm. 'Tonight you begin. It must be tonight because tomorrow, I am gone.'

Nick looked at Arkady in some shock. 'Where are you going?'

'Back to Devon, but of course. I must go back and ask questions of this Lord Darchester, the mysterious and sadly crazy earl. He is, perhaps, the key to what we seek.'

'The Ofan,' Nick said. 'And the skills they are developing. Mr Mibbs.'

'Yes, the Ofan. But not Mr Mibbs – I do not believe he is important, this man who dresses funny.' Arkady waved a dismissive hand. 'Alice, she is concerned. But me? These things you say he can do – they are not possible. Making people feel things. Controlling emotion. This is not Ofan behaviour.'

'It happened.'

'Bah. Forget about this Mibbs. He is far away in the future, following some other nice-looking young man. We are here, now, and so are the Ofan. You have a job to do in London, and I have a job to do in Devon. I must know how great is

'You're kidding me.'

Arkady released Nick's sho[ulder] no, I am not! It is funny, yes?' himself. 'But it is still very seriou[s] war with the Ofan must soon s[tart] information. One of the guests Blomgren. She is a traitor to the great courtesan who has recently l[eft] to replace him in her affections.'

'That is . . .' Nick struggled to That's what it is. I won't do it.'

Arkady seemed genuinely puzzled you are not here to kill, after all? You a[re] you choose a toy gun over a girl? I tol[d] when we jumped. I told you why we wa[nt]

'You most certainly did not.'

'I did. We want you for your charmin[g] know all about how you are the tomcat Vermont, but of course we do. So many lo[vers] is the thing your Nelson said with the expects . . . expects . . .''

'"England expects that every man will do muttered.

'Yes.' Arkady smiled his approval. 'It is the Guild.'

Nick stared at the Russian, then turned asid[e] ately spat. 'I will *not* be your lightskirt.' He turne[d] 'I bid you goodnight, Arkady.'

'Don't be ridiculous – look, we are here n[ow] nipped Nick to his side with an iron grip and kn[ocked] cipitously on a huge, black door set directly ont[o] Hill. It opened immediately, and a butler who m[ust have] been seven feet tall ushered them into a hallway

talent of this earl. I m
of him. It should not take
for two weeks, perhaps, I am
must work.'

Nick sighed, packing away
over the Mibbs affair. It was h
with any clarity; so much had
Nick's understanding of what e
they were for. Since that day Ni
the flow of feeling and lived fo
Indeed, his emotions had been
return that he had almost drowr
Arkady, sex-obsessed pain in the as
his faithful guide, leading him forv
dangers. Maybe the old buzzard was
just a guy in a crazy outfit. 'All right,
put my shoulder to the wheel. But
about the Guild in this time. How ar
nize Ofan? And what do I do with the

'My priest.' Arkady put his arm arc
and his voice was tender. 'Your job is nc
the James Bond, who knows everythin
car and the licence to kill. No. You hav
precise job to do for us.'

Uneasiness tingled along Nick's spine.

'You are attending this party because yo
with a taste for women.' Arkady squeezed l
'You have heard that a certain woman will
party. And you come because you are looking

Nick stopped in his tracks. 'No!'

Arkady's starlit eyes sparkled. 'But yes, my
we have dragged you back in time!' He put his l
laughed.

overflowing with men and women. Through an open door Nick could see a sunken ballroom lit by hundreds of candles, aswirl with sumptuous ball gowns.

'I won't do it,' Nick said as they handed over their hats and coats.

Arkady steered him into the crowd. 'Your newfound purity is charming, of course.' He smiled beatifically. 'But you must not be afraid. She will be gentle with you.'

24

The receiving line moved slowly. By the time Nick and Arkady had made their way through the grand double doors and stood at the top of the steps leading down into the ballroom, Nick was in a searing rage. Arkady had a tight, lordly smile tucked up neatly under his nose, and Nick knew he ought to have just such a sour-lemon expression pinned to his own face. They were, after all, noblemen condescending to join commoners. Well, the commoners would have to make do with his terrible scowl.

So the Guild had chosen him to be their stud, their boar, their bull, their goddam rooster in the henhouse. Now Nick felt like killing. He had a tiepin. He could take it out and stick it into Arkady's jugular. As for this Ofan whore he was supposed to tup for the good of the Guild . . . Nick's imagination failed him. Never in his life, either before or after his jump, had anyone had the stunning nerve to frame him as a gigolo. Sold, and sold as a prostitute, to a prostitute.

A few weeks ago Nick might have thought this assignment would be fun. Maybe. He couldn't really even recall who he had been a few weeks ago, and two hundred years in the future.

It was John Donne's fault. He should leave this party, march on down to St Paul's and punch the statue of a piously shrouded Donne on the nose.

Nick had been in perfect control of his emotions, holding Julia at arm's length. But then she had risen up out of the floor, just when Nick was reading that bit about America.

And before a lamb could shake its tail . . . no. He needed an American animal. Before a raccoon could wash its dinner, they had been in each other's arms and halfway to paradise. Paradise or Gretna Green or Las Vegas. Wherever he could marry her and live happily ever after with the greatest possible efficiency. Nick frowned to himself. America! Home of American girls. Raised on promises. Make it last all night. He'd liked those girls, liked them a lot. But now it seemed that this Devonshire acorn *was* his America, his newfound land, even though he'd stumbled across her in his own past and in his own backyard.

Except that now Arkady had dumped the Whore of Babylon in his lap and told him it was his duty to service her in the name of the Guild.

The crowd in the ballroom was staring at him, of course. The two aristocrats had arrived. All those faces turned upward to where they stood at the top of the stairs leading down into the ballroom. Each and every person here knew, apparently, that Nick was looking for sex. Well, they could stare all they liked. He wasn't going to give them a show. He wouldn't talk to a single woman all evening.

Finally, Nick stepped forward to meet his host. Bertrand Penture was a man of about Nick's own age and height, handsome in the Gary Cooper style. Nick nodded. 'Penture'.

Penture's bow was precise and perfunctory, only just deep enough to acknowledge Nick's rank. 'My lord.' His French accent was slight, and it tinged his words with honey, but there was nothing sweet about his expression. Nick could see it in the man's strange, pale green eyes: Penture disliked him. And Nick found himself responding, his lip curling in a scornful smile, his eyes flickering down the man's immaculate evening dress and back up again.

'Ah, Penture, you old undertaker.' Arkady pushed in between

them, his voice booming out over the crowd. 'Wonderful news about the shipping venture. I was afraid I would lose my trousers.'

Nick raised an eyebrow. 'The count is afraid to lose his trousers, but he is always happy to trick his friends into losing theirs. You must be careful, Penture. Before you know it this Russian will have you dancing the cancan on a tabletop.'

Arkady barked, but Penture's expression did not change. 'I am not given to making or enjoying jokes, my lord,' he said. 'Especially not jokes made at the expense of people for whom your English is not a mother tongue. Besides.' He lowered his voice. 'The cancan is a dance not yet invented. You are clearly an ass, but please try not to be a fool.'

So this was the Alderman of the Guild in 1815, a few months before the battle of Waterloo: a humourless, supercilious Frenchman. For a second Nick forgot that, back in the good old twenty-first century, he liked the French. Something deadly must have flared in Nick's face, for Penture, without taking those strange eyes from him, spoke softly, for Nick's ears alone. 'Watch yourself, Mr Davenant.'

'I am in perfect control,' Nick said in a normal tone of voice. 'In spite of the greatest possible provocation.'

Penture's nostrils flared. But when he opened his mouth again, he spoke as the host welcoming important guests. 'Please enjoy yourselves in my home, my lords. I hope I have time to speak to you later.' He bowed and turned to greet his next guest.

'Well,' Nick said as they descended the steps. 'He's a prick.'

'He put you in your place,' Arkady said. 'But I am glad you have rediscovered your sense of humour. I introduce you to the woman now, yes?'

Nick turned to the Russian with a public smile, but with private venom in his voice. 'Do not speak to me. In fact, do not even come near me. You may find your own way home tonight. Goodbye.' Without a backward glance he slipped sideways into the crowd.

'She has the yellow hair and tonight she wears a blue gown,' Arkady called over the heads of several partiers. 'You cannot miss her.'

Nick did not reply. He headed straight for the tables where drinks were being served.

Fifteen minutes later he had relaxed, and could even admit to himself that the ball was agreeable. It was easy enough to avoid speaking more than a few words to women. No one admitted belonging to the Guild, of course, although everyone here was clearly fabulously wealthy. The clothes and jewellery were at the teetering pinnacle of fashion. The women were far more elegantly dressed, in fact, than many members of the ton. It was a grand spectacle. And they all talked of the glorious shipping venture as if it were real – as perhaps it was.

Nick scanned the crowd. His eyes caught on a face. A woman at the centre of the crowd. And another face, a man's. Dark faces. Nick felt some distant part of himself pricked by what he hadn't even noticed a moment before; that not everyone at this party shared his skin colour. Of course they didn't; this was a Guild party. And yet now that Nick had noticed it, he found that part of him – perhaps it was the marquess – could see nothing else. He leaned back against the table and tried to forget it, tried to watch, as he had a moment before, people laughing, dancing, bowing and curt-seying, the silks and satins worn by the women shifting beneath the glittering chandeliers, the more sober colours of the men's clothing punctuating the scene, like rocks in the midst of a swirling, sunset-drenched sea of sumptuous cloth. But as he sipped his champagne he let his eyes rest on a handsome dark-skinned man, who was bowing, and signing the dance card of a white woman, the man's hand on the woman's elbow . . .

Suddenly that distant part of Nick was very near, nearer than breathing; the river was pouring through him, crashing like a flood, sweeping him away. Tom Molineaux was fighting Tom Cribb at Shenington Hollow, and Nick was in the crowd, with ten thousand other men, his voice hoarse after hours of yelling. It was the thirty-fourth round, and Molineaux's hand had been broken for the last fifteen. But now Cribb was going to win. Both boxers were drenched, their bare hands wet and red, their battered bodies running with sweat, their feet caked with blood-churned mud. Molineaux was weaving, swaying into unconsciousness, and the crowd was howling for Cribb's imminent victory, howling for Molineaux's defeat. Nick's betting slip was clutched in his hand; he was set to win big on Cribb but he didn't want the show to end – no one wanted the show to end. Nick and the crowd howled with one voice as Tom Molineaux crashed to the ground and Tom Cribb raised his battered face and open, streaming hands to the sky . . .

'Do you dance, my lord?' The words were soft in his ear.

The river retreated, like a fast-ebbing wave, sucking him back with it then beaching him in the ballroom. He gasped for breath and stared wildly at the woman who was there beside him, her hands reaching for his.

'My lord, you must breathe. Yes, that's it. Breathe and look at me.'

The orchestra was tuning up – the dancing was about to begin. A thousand candles caught the facets of a thousand jewels scattered in the hair and on the hands and around the throats of the women below. His own diamond tiepin winked, answering the general sparkle.

'Holy shit,' he whispered. He gripped the woman's hands. 'I was fine, and then . . .' He found he didn't know how to explain what had happened. 'The river swept me away . . . not in time, but in myself. To someone I used to be . . . a fight . . .'

'Ah,' she said. 'Yes.'

Nick held on to her hands as if they were a lifeline.

'People are watching us,' she said softly. 'Can you pretend to be recovered? I shan't leave you.'

He dropped her hands. 'Yes, yes of course.' In saying it, it became true. He straightened up and twitched his cuffs into place, casting a severe glance over his shoulder at a man who was openly gaping. Then he turned back and really looked at her.

Blonde, blue dress.

It was her. It had to be her. A woman somewhat older than himself and almost his own height, her white-blonde hair arranged in an elegant coil, a few curls artlessly loose at the front. Her blue gown was far more demure than most that graced the ballroom. Around her neck, square-cut diamonds flashed in the candlelight, and he saw others glinting among the curls that were so perfectly disarranged around her ears. Her oval face was a palette of whites and palest pinks, her violet eyes moonlit and fathomless.

'You are Alva Blomgren,' he said.

'Yes,' she said. 'And now that you are yourself again, we can get on with our acquaintance. Let us dance.' She turned on her beauty like stadium lights and opened her arms.

'Ah,' he said, stepping back, all his offence at this situation recalled. 'No. I do not dance. Besides, madam, we have not been introduced.'

Her slight smile didn't grow, but it seemed to deepen. Perhaps it was something she did with her eyes. In any case it was clear that she was laughing at him. 'But how foolish that you refuse,' she said, and now he heard the faint accent. It was like the tiny bubbles that float up through champagne. 'You are Lord Blackdown and I am Alva Blomgren. We must play our parts. You have come here to . . .' She paused. Damn it if the palest, most delicious shade of pink didn't stain her porcelain cheeks. 'To dance with me.'

He allowed his gaze to travel from her toes up to her eyes. 'You should not listen to gossip,' he said.

'Perhaps not.' Her blush had faded. 'Still, I will dance with you.' She took his glass from his hand and set it down on the table behind him. 'And I will call you Nick.'

'Without my permission?'

'Oh, come.' She put her long fingers on his shoulder and reached for his hand. 'Dance this next waltz with me.' He put his right hand in hers and his left at her waist. He felt the warmth of her through her gown, and her scent was in his nostrils. Something bright. Not the smell of a bordello. 'Yes,' she said softly. 'Like that.'

He allowed himself a moment to feel her in his arms before dropping them. 'I have said I do not dance,' he said quietly. 'And you may not address me as Nick.'

'Oh.' He was surprised to see kindness and understanding in her eyes. 'Then we will simply talk. And surely I do not need your permission to address you by your name.' She took his arm and began to stroll with him around the edge of the ballroom. 'I shall address you however I choose. You don't have to call me anything. But still we will be friends.'

'I don't like you,' he said bluntly, though he was beginning to suspect that perhaps he did like her.

'Ah.' She peeked at him sidelong, out of those glorious violet eyes of hers. 'You are very sure of yourself, my lord.'

He looked over the heads of the people getting ready to

dance, then back down at her, allowing a smile to touch his lips. '"My lord"? I see you are learning your place.'

'That sounds remarkably like flirtation . . .' Alva squeezed his arm. 'Why don't you like me? Is it because I am a courtesan?'

'No.' He flushed and hated himself for it. 'No. You may do as you wish. It is but a small matter to me.'

The waltz began, and immediately the edges of the room became too crowded for strolling, as the circle of dancers colonized the floor. Non-dancers began to spill out of the doors into adjacent rooms and onto the terrace. Nick found himself outside with Alva. She led him to a balustrade that looked down over the small garden. Others milled around them, and she spoke softly, close to his ear. 'It makes no difference to you if I am a courtesan? A whore? But surely it must. You think that you could perhaps have me for a price. Or you think that I want you only for your money. It makes friendship seem impossible. You see, it comes immediately between us, this small matter of my profession.'

Nick turned to her, and the crowd pressed him close. He could feel her breath on his face. 'I did not come here seeking you,' he said. 'I know that you have been told that was my intention, but it is not. I have no need of a mistress.'

She closed the space between them. Her left hand rested on his thigh, as lightly as a butterfly. She whispered, her champagne voice filling his head with a rush of bursting bubbles. 'But what if . . . I am seeking a master?'

Then his cock, goddam it, was at attention. She smiled – he knew she smiled, because she was so close that he felt her lips, feather-soft against his cheek, as they curved. Her fingers moved – a single, delicate stroke, up the length of his poor, idiotic cock. 'The notion seems to agree with you,' she whispered.

'God.' He wrenched sideways to face the balustrade. 'Leave me.'

Her sigh was a soft sound, half regretful, half amused. 'Well. This is a brave night to cool a courtesan. I was only teasing you, my lord. If you do not want to be my lover, I understand.' Turning, she leaned forward over the railing and looked out into the garden. 'In fact, it will be good to be just friends. But we must be friends.'

'Why, for God's sake?' He looked sideways at her white-blonde head, the elegant curve of her back as she bent, her elbows propped on the railing. 'I don't need friends. I certainly don't need a friend like you.'

She tipped her face up. Her expression was full of warmth. 'Yes, you do. That incident back there in the ballroom should prove it to you. You are barely in control, and you need friends badly.' She reached out and touched his face – the scar that crossed his eyebrow. 'Poor Lord Blackdown. You don't really understand anything, do you?'

'No, I don't. I wish you would explain yourself.'

She looked out again over the lawn. 'But I am very simple. I am not what needs explaining.' She met his gaze squarely. 'Do you understand what I am saying to you? I am not what needs explaining.'

Recognition of what she meant slid into place. Excitement coursed through his veins. It wasn't sexual excitement … it was pure intellectual energy. She had answers. 'Yes. Yes, I think I do.'

But at that moment they were interrupted. 'Alva!' A huge, drunken Englishman, as ugly as a side of beef, his eyes spilling tears, pushed himself between them. 'Alva, my angel. My goddess.' He grasped Alva's hands in his enormous, hairy paws and stood weeping down upon her like a bulldog snuffling over a tiny spaniel.

'Excuse me,' Nick said, outraged. 'I was speaking to the lady.'

The man turned his heavy head. It took a long time for his drunken red eyes to focus on Nick, and when they did, a new flood of tears washed over his cheeks. 'Oh, no. No. You are handsome!'

Nick raised a repressive eyebrow, but the man was long past all subtlety. With a wail he hurled himself forward, and Nick was only just able to put his fists up before his face to combat the assault. But the man wasn't coming in for a fight; he was coming in for a hug. He gathered Nick to his broad chest as easily as if Nick had been a small child, and he clasped him tenderly, rocking back and forth and keening, head lifted to the stars. 'I'm so unhappy!' Then he collapsed, weeping into Nick's shoulder and grabbing at his jacket in huge handfuls. 'She'll never love me. Never. My Alva. My angel. My goddess.'

Nick stifled a shocked laugh and patted his back. 'Save me,' he mouthed over the man's shoulder.

Alva nodded, sparkling with her own suppressed laughter. 'Now, Henry,' she said, peeling the man easily away from Nick with her elegant hands. 'Enough of that. There, there. Hush now.' She produced a handkerchief from nowhere and wiped his woebegone face. 'You must calm down, my dear. We've talked about this, do you recall? You promised there would be no more of this.'

The giant stood calmly now, but new tears continued to seep from his eyes. 'I love you, Alva. I can't bear it. He's handsome.' He pointed at Nick. 'You told me there was no one else.'

'I told you I have no lover, Henry.' Alva peeped at Nick as she said this. 'And that is true. But someday I shall, and you must be strong. I can never be your wife.'

'But, Alva, I love you.' Henry's voice was sullen now, like a petulant child's.

'That's enough, Henry. Go home,' Alva said firmly.

'Oh, Alva.' The tears began all over again. He reached for her. 'My angel. My goddess.'

Alva spoke sharply for the first time. 'Henry. Stop it!' To Nick's shock and delight, she hauled her long arm back and slapped the huge man soundly across his face.

Henry's tears stopped as if they had never fallen. 'Alva.' He put a hand up to nurse his check. 'My . . . my . . .'

She stood facing him, her hands on her hips. 'Your what? Which is it? Am I your angel or your goddess? Because angels are different from goddesses, Henry.'

Her mountainous admirer stood staring at Alva for a long moment, and then tears began slowly welling up again.

'Oh, for God's sake.' Alva threw up her hands. 'Go home, Henry. Go home. Before I slap you again.'

'Alva.' Henry half reached for her, but then, with a broken sob, he turned slowly and lumbered away.

Nick couldn't help it. He clapped. 'Brava! Well played. Marvellous.'

Alva came back to the balustrade, a more natural smile on her mouth than he had yet seen. Interestingly enough, it downgraded her beauty to mere prettiness, but it made her seem more real. 'I have recently lost my lover,' she said. 'And I am suddenly beset with suitors.'

'I am sorry for your loss.'

Her eyes brightened, surprised. 'Thank you. That is kind of you, my lord. I apologize for Henry. I hope he didn't ruin your jacket.'

'It can be mended. In any event, it's not every day that I am complimented on my looks. And please.' He smiled. 'Call me Nick.'

Alva opened her mouth to say something, but they were interrupted again, this time by Bertrand Penture. 'Excuse me, Miss Blomgren.' He bowed, and Alva curtseyed, grimacing slightly at Nick as she did so, though by the time Penture straightened up her face was a mask of beautiful disinterest. 'I am afraid I must steal your companion from you.' Penture turned to Nick. 'If you would accompany me, my lord? I would like you to try a cognac I have saved for just such a special guest.'

Nick bowed. 'Of course, Monsieur Penture. It would be my pleasure. Please allow me to make my goodbyes to this lovely creature, and I shall be with you shortly.' He winked broadly at the Frenchman and was pleased to see a look of revulsion flit across Penture's stony face.

'Of course. A footman will direct you to the study when you are . . . finished.' Penture curled a lip and left.

Alva and Nick watched him until his black back disappeared among the revellers. Then both began speaking at once.

'I –'

'We –'

They both halted, amused, and then Alva carried on. 'We have not concluded our interesting conversation.' She laid a hand on Nick's arm. 'You may find me in Soho Square, if you decide that you do, after all, need friends.' She turned to go.

'Wait.' Nick caught her hand. 'I don't want to be your lover, but I do want to be your friend. I want . . . I want to learn from you. I am beginning to think that I like you very much indeed.'

'Thank you.' She squeezed his hand.

'One more thing, Alva.' Nick looked searchingly at her face. 'Henry couldn't tell if you were an angel or a goddess.

But I think I know.' He felt her hand twitch in his, just once. 'You are an angel, aren't you? A very specific kind of angel.'

She lifted a finger to her lips. 'Shh.' With a twist and a flurry of blue silk, she was gone.

25

A footman waited just inside the doors that led to the terrace. 'If you will follow me, my lord,' he said. He was a short man, with a thick accent that Nick couldn't place. He led Nick across the ballroom, where dancers were forming for the next set, through a door on the other side, down a long hallway and up a flight of stairs. Finally, they reached a small, inconspicuous wooden door, and the footman knocked three times slowly, followed by a pause, and then four times, fast.

The door was unlocked from the inside, in a series of soft clicks that sounded, to Nick's ears, like the mechanism of a computerized lock. Eventually, it opened. Penture stood looking at them. 'You are alone?'

'Yes,' the footman said.

'No one followed you?'

'No.'

'Good. Come.' Penture stood aside and Nick followed the footman in, glancing back to see that yes, on this side the door was smooth, gleaming metal, inset with a lock that looked like it belonged to a bank vault.

It was a large, windowless chamber, much older than the house that now surrounded it. A small fire in a large fireplace created a pool of light against the far wall; otherwise the chamber was lit only dimly by a few flickering wall sconces. A massive, carved Jacobean table ran down the centre of the room, set around with a melange of sleek modernist chairs. The floor was mosaic, clearly Roman, though Nick could not see what was depicted in the centre. Only some naked arms and legs and the head of a snake emerged from the shadows under the table. The vaulted ceiling was Norman, the walls hung with tapestries that, to the extent that they were illuminated by the wall sconces, seemed to depict the horticulture of tulips in be-windmilled Dutch landscapes. Hanging above the centre of the table was a grotesque chandelier of white hand-blown glass, which Nick recognized as the twenty-first-century work of Dale Chihuly. A few candles gleamed somewhere in its bulbous interior but shed no light outward. Beneath it, a vase of white tulips seemed to flush with their own light, like phosphorescent sea creatures in the gloom.

It was, Nick thought, one of the ugliest rooms he'd ever seen, for all that each individual part of it was refined and rare.

People were emerging from the shadows to greet him. Arkady – Nick could tell him by his great height and shock of white hair. And that was Alice Gacoki the Russian had tucked in by his side; she was dressed in a twenty-first-century business suit: black slacks and jacket, and white shirt. The other two were unknown to him: a middle-aged Asian man dressed in a shimmery gold fabric that seemed to move almost as a liquid, and a woman in a farthingale and stomacher embroidered all over with Tudor roses.

'Nick.' Alice hugged him and began to introduce him around. 'Arkady and Bertrand you know already, of course.' She grasped the fingers of the man in gold. 'This is Alderman Ahn Jun-suh, from the mid-twenty-second century.'

'Call me Ahn,' the man said, disengaging from Alice and shaking Nick's hand.

'Nick Davenant.'

'Great to meet you.'

'And this,' Alice said, putting a hand on the footman's shoulder, 'is Mürsel Saatçi. He is playing the part of a servant tonight. In fact, he is Bertrand's secretary and the corner-stone of the Guild in this era.'

'Davenant.' Saatçi gripped Nick's hand; he had an eager, friendly air.

Alice turned last to the other woman in the room. 'This is my friend Marjory Northway. She is our head of intelligence for the mid-fifteenth century in Britain, though she some-times works further afield. In fact, she made a three-month case study of you, Nick, leading up to your summons. She gave you a glowing recommendation.'

This woman with a ruff the size of a hubcap had spied on him? Nick peered at her, but it was impossible to see past the Elizabethan costume. Her face was painted white as paper; her lips and cheeks were cherry red. A heavy rose scent wafted from her.

Her eyes glittered and her mask cracked open in a smile, revealing a set of startlingly perfect white teeth. 'Hi, England,' she said, her southern drawl exaggerated. 'How's them cheeses hangin'?'

The awful truth yawned beneath him like a trapdoor. When he'd last seen this woman, she'd been dressed in jeans, her brown hair pulled back in a ponytail. She had been waving out of the open window of her BMW as she pulled away down his driveway, early in the morning. Out of his life for ever. Or so he'd thought.

The cheese inspector.

Those straight white teeth, shining in that red, red mouth. He had taken her to bed, for God's sake, to keep himself and Tom Feely out of the FDA's leg manacles. Did everyone in the room know that? He glanced at their audience. They were watching as if this were a play. Very well then. If they wanted a play, they would get one.

He quirked a smile at Marjory, letting her see he knew she

knew he knew, and that he was mildly amused. He took her hand. 'I hope I rewarded your months of hard work,' he said. 'Tailing a farmer around Vermont. I'm sure the fifteenth century is much more exciting.'

She sank down in a graceful bob. 'I was amply rewarded, thank you.' Her accent faded back again to its original twang, which he now heard as quaintly English. She had never really been in disguise; indeed, her half-rusted old car had even been a BMW. He caught a glimpse of those white teeth again as she flashed him a coy smile from the bottom of her curtsey.

He raised her up. 'I'm so glad.' He turned to the others, Marjory's hand still in his. 'I'm delighted to meet you all,' he said to their expectant faces. 'But especially my lovely spy.' He bowed to her, wishing that he had a hat to sweep from his head. 'I am flattered that I passed your inspection.'

'With flying colours.'

He kissed her hand.

The group laughed; apparently the scene had pleased them. Nick laughed with them, but he was really laughing at himself and his own internal contradictions. Why was he so enraged at being asked to whore himself out to Alva, who was lovely and compassionate? He had quite happily serviced the cheese inspector to save Tom Feely's farm, and the cheese inspector was much less charming.

Nick turned to Penture, a self-deprecating smile still haunting his lips. 'Now then, Alderman. Miss Northway has decided that I make the grade. Tell me what you want of me.'

'But of course,' Penture said, and opened his hands to encompass everyone in the room. 'Shall we sit?'

They all pulled out seats. Nick's was a little wooden chair that looked as if it had been cut from a cardboard pattern and hinged together with brass brads. He tipped it at an angle to admire it. It was enchanting.

'You like it,' Saatçi said, pulling out his own seat, a Saarinen tulip design not at all to Nick's liking. 'That is a very unusual chair. Breuer designed it in the 1930s for a college dormitory. Eventually the college threw the old chairs away. I rescued this one from a skip. It was broken, so sad.' Saatçi reached out and touched the pretty golden wood. 'I brought it back here and mended it – I sanded away all the graffiti.' The little man blushed. 'Graffiti like that I have never seen! But now he is clean and new.'

Nick settled down into it. 'But it's so short.'

'The college was for women.'

'Ah.' Nick stretched his legs under the table, enjoying the thought of generations of students sitting on this hard seat, cramming their heads full of knowledge. Carving their desires into the yielding wood. Desires that had been sanded away to a blank prettiness. Nick's enjoyment faded. He looked around the table at the men and women gathered to tell him about his mission. 'All right,' he said. 'Let's get this party started. What do you want of me?'

'I am glad you are eager to cooperate,' Penture said. 'Let us begin with this man you call Mr Mibbs. I would like you to tell us all about him, if you please.'

Nick glanced at Alice, then told the gathered Guild elite everything he knew, again excluding Leo.

'He controlled your emotions, you say,' Penture said when Nick was finished. 'To the point that you feared for your life.'

'Yes. He seemed to be trying to kill me with despair.'

'Kill you with despair? But we cannot use emotions as weapons. And we cannot use despair at all.'

'So everyone keeps telling me.' Nick smiled. 'Nevertheless, he came at me with despair. But I am a jolly fellow, and I survived.'

Penture folded his hands on the table, gazed at Nick for a

moment, then turned to Alice. 'There has been no sign of Mibbs in the London of your era since that strange encounter?'

'No,' Alice said. 'Nor anywhere or anytime else. He has disappeared.'

Penture nodded. 'Very strange indeed. This man who can do things with the river of feelings that we cannot. This man who can harness the one emotion that repels us.' The Frenchman's strange green eyes were intent upon Nick. 'I assume that you are telling us the truth about your experiences.'

'I am.'

'Do you think he is Ofan?' Ahn asked Penture.

'Perhaps. Perhaps not.'

'I do not think so.' Arkady scowled. 'The Ofan spout their nonsense about knowledge and happiness. They dress like the hobo bums. They would not even think to try to harness the despair.'

'Arkady,' Alice said. 'We have had this argument many times. You must accept that Mibbs is probably Ofan, that he is the clue to what the Ofan are doing. The Ofan you hate, the revolutionaries who killed Eréndira – they are dispersed. The revenge you want – you aren't going to get that, darling. Vogelstein must be dead. And now things have changed. The stakes are too high for us to fight the Ofan on your terms. We must fight the Ofan as the Guild, and because we want to protect the river. Not because you are a heartbroken father who wishes to revenge his child.'

Arkady pushed his chair back and stood. He raised his face to the grotesque chandelier for a long moment, then looked down at his wife. 'From you,' he said quietly, looking at Alice. 'From my wife I have to hear this.'

'I am speaking to you as your Alderwoman,' Alice said, her voice quiet. 'And I am speaking the truth.'

'Sit, Altukhov,' Penture said gently.

The old Russian looked around the room. No one said anything. After a long moment, he folded himself back down into his chair and clasped his white hands in front of him, staring fixedly at his ring. Alice put her hand on the table near him, where he could see it, but she made no move to touch him.

After a moment of respectful silence, Penture turned back to Nick. 'Alice and Arkady have assured me that you are loyal to the Guild and that you are ready to join forces with us in our battle against the insurgent Ofan. Is that correct?'

Nick didn't answer.

'I saw, when I came to collect you, that you have met your target. I assume this means that you are taking on the duties that Arkady explained to you.'

Nick again said nothing.

The Alderman leaned back in his chair, and a lock of black hair fell onto his forehead. His mouth was a stern line. He really was movie-star handsome, but less Gary Cooper, Nick decided, more Gregory Peck. 'Is this the silence of considered thought, of petulant resistance, or of imbecility, Mr Davenant?'

'Nick —' Alice began.

Penture held up a hand to silence her.

'I reject the assignment,' Nick said. 'When I agreed — reluctantly — to help the Guild, I believed I was joining you as a soldier, not as a gigolo.'

Penture let a thin smile touch his lips. 'I am sorry if you had any misapprehensions about your assignment,' he said. 'But I'm afraid you don't have a choice in the matter. Miss Blomgren's bereavement is a chance we cannot pass up. She is in need of a new lover. You have the status and the wealth to appeal to her.'

'Surely there must be other ways.'

Penture made an impatient Gallic gesture, as if he held a bird in his hands and was setting it free. 'You are enraging! This Englishness!'

'I told you,' Arkady said, not looking up. 'He is a priest.'

'Alva Blomgren is the most beautiful woman in London and a fabled courtesan,' Penture said to Nick. 'She is also the head of a ring of Ofan who have established themselves in Soho Square. We have known about her activities for a few years, but until recently there was no need to crack down on the Ofan; they seemed a harmless enough group of dissidents. Laughable, even, with their wild notions. But now things are different. It is possible that we must purge the world of the Ofan once and for all. But first we must learn more about what they are up to. We need you as a spy, not a killer.'

'I'm not interested.'

'Oh, for the love of God!' Alice rolled her eyes. 'First Arkady and now you – behaving like children!'

'Let me tell you about Alva,' Penture said. 'She jumped from 1348 to 1790, a teenager, suddenly free of her plague-wracked medieval village. She was the brightest new recruit the Guild had seen in decades. Everyone thought she was destined to lead. The Alderwoman at the time, my predecessor, was Hannelore von Trockenberg. A genius. Under her governance the Guild was as powerful as in any other age. She never showed favour to anyone. Except Alva – Hannelore loved her. Alva was always at the Alderwoman's side. But then . . . it is hard to believe, even now . . . Alva informed us all that she was not interested in a Guild position. That she would use her yearly stipend to open a high-class brothel in Soho Square. That she had already covertly established herself as a courtesan of the highest calibre.'

Nick raised his eyebrows. 'That's quite a departure. Why did she do that?'

Penture shrugged. 'Who can say? But Hannelore's rage was boundless. It was as if her own daughter had turned to prostitution. After that Alva was no longer in favour. She continued to receive her stipend, as prescribed by Guild law, and she came to the larger Guild functions, but if Hannelore heard her name, or saw her face, she would rage for days. We all began to spend our time making sure the two women never met. Then, a few years ago, Hannelore was dying. She asked to see Alva. Alva came. They spent an hour together. When she left, Hannelore called us to her bedside. Me, Saatçi and one other. She said to us: "That woman is a traitor, she is Ofan. And if she is Ofan, then the Ofan are now a danger to the Guild." It was soon after that we realized . . .' Penture paused. 'That we realized the damage the Ofan have actually done to the river.'

Nick twitched his cuffs into place. 'I am sorry that you find yourselves in a sticky situation with your ancient enemy,' he said. 'And I am flattered that you think my towering prowess as a lover will breach the defences of a woman you have described as a sexual, entrepreneurial and political mastermind. But I hope you will forgive me when I say that you are fools. Sex only makes people more like themselves. A powerful, secretive woman becomes only more powerful and more secretive in the throes of passion. Whereas an easygoing, gullible fellow like myself, confronted with a woman like Alva Blomgren?' He shrugged. 'She would have me singing Guild secrets from the rooftops, and I would come away having learned nothing from her.'

'Why do you think we haven't told you any Guild secrets?' Arkady growled.

Penture held up his hand, silencing the Russian. 'So this is why Arkady calls you his priest. You are belligerently pure.' He shrugged. 'So be it. I cannot force you into her arms. And perhaps you are correct that she would not sing her secrets in the midst of passion. You are wiser than I thought. But however you go about it, your assignment is to infiltrate the Ofan and learn Alva's secrets. Let's see . . .' He looked around the room. 'What skills does our friend Mr Davenant have besides womanizing? Cheese making? Will he perhaps succeed in gaining Alva's trust with a fine wheel of Cheddar?'

'Actually, he's good at farm management in general,' Marjory Northway said brightly. 'He owns a couple of other organic operations in Vermont.'

'Well there we are.' Penture turned to Nick. 'I'm sure the most intriguing woman in a glittering era of fashion and romance will be transfixed by your tales from the tilth. Anything else?'

Nick scratched his head. 'That is about the best of it. Of course, I can also kill Frenchmen in hand-to-hand combat . . .'

Penture's eyes gleamed. 'Ah!' He flexed his hands, cracking his knuckles.

'Boys . . .' Alice let her exasperation show. 'Please, play nicely.' She turned her shoulder to Penture and addressed Nick as if he were the only person in the room. 'Please listen to me. However unsavoury you find the job, I'm afraid we must insist. If you can do it without sleeping with her, all well and good. None of us cares.'

'I care,' Arkady said, finally looking up from his clasped hands. 'Do it for me, Nick!'

'It must be you, Mr Davenant,' Penture said.

'Ah.' Nick turned and pointed at the Frenchman. 'Now we are getting somewhere. This isn't about sex, and it isn't about killing. It isn't even really about Alva. It's about me. Why? Why must it be me? Why drag me out of my happy complacency to do this small job for you, a job you could get anyone to do? Why *me*?'

Penture's eyes flickered. 'Because,' he said, softly. 'Just because.'

Nick shook his head. 'You'll have to do better than that.'

'Don't push it to this, Nick,' Alice said.

'To what?' Nick rounded on her, his anger finally taking over. 'Empty threats and non-information, that is all you have offered me. Give me one good reason why I shouldn't just join the Ofan myself.'

Alice thinned her lips as she looked at Nick, her own beautiful face grim with disappointment. Then she turned to Penture with a weary sigh. 'We are in your era, Alderman. Not mine. How do you want to proceed?'

Penture narrowed his eyes. 'There are times, Nicholas Davenant, when you must choose sides. Times when, even though you do not have all the information, you must decide to act for one cause or for another. Now is one of those times. I am going to help you make your decision. The right decision.'

Penture nodded to Saatçi and the tension in the room mounted. They were all suddenly anxious – he could feel their shared emotion spread like an oil slick through the room. And then it changed, moved . . . shimmered from simple feeling to a fully active manipulation of time. The air around him seemed to be thickening – it was the depth and breadth of time compacted into space. The others were all getting to their feet. What were they doing? Ah – Saatçi had an ornate silver pistol in his hand, worthy of a Hollywood cowboy. He passed it to Penture, who calmly raised it and aimed between Nick's eyes.

'Oh my God.' Nick scooted back in his too-small chair and spread his hands. 'This is a farce. What is that thing, something out of a Wild West show?'

Penture pulled the trigger.

In the same instant, time hardened around Nick. He was frozen, but he was horribly conscious. The others stood beside their chairs, and he could feel the force with which they were each directing their talent at him, keeping him motionless. The gunpowder flashed as it ignited, and bright smoke mushroomed slowly. Then the bullet emerged and began to move through the air toward Nick's head. Penture laid the gun down on the table and spoke. His voice was chillingly regular in its speed. How did he *do* that?

'As you can see,' he said, 'this bullet is travelling towards your head, Mr Davenant. If we do not pluck it from its course, it will kill you. You will experience your death quite slowly, as the bullet first touches you, then pierces your skin, and begins to flatten out as it bores through your skull. By the time it blows off the back of your head you will of course no longer be able to experience what is happening to you. I suggest that you choose sides now. Blink if you agree.'

Alice spoke with embarrassed urgency. 'Nick, my good friend. I'm very sorry it had to come to this. We like you very much, and admire you. But you don't have a choice.' Nick listened to her and watched the bullet crawl towards his head. He was curiously unafraid.

The bullet began to deform as it sped, slowly, through the air. Fascinating.

So many conflicting loyalties. The Guild, his sisters, Julia . . . even Kirklaw and Jemison. And now there was Alva. They were right about her – she was an enchanting woman, and she had already staked a claim in his affections. It wasn't her beauty, and it wasn't even the fact that she had rescued him from that moment when the river had rushed through him, dragging him back to that memory of group rage, that collective desire. It was because she had offered something – sex – and stepped away, unfazed, when he had refused. Like a gentleman. She hadn't slandered his sisters, or reminded him of all that he owed her, or pointed a damned gun at his head. She hadn't tried to tie him down with duty or debt. Instead, she had told him that, if he wanted one, he had a friend. And then, for no reason other than that she seemed to like him, she had revealed her greatest secret. She was Ofan. Instead of warning him that he must keep his mouth shut, or telling him that he was now bound by some blood brotherhood of shared knowledge, she had put her finger to her lips and twirled away. As if she trusted him – he, who was so obviously a Guild spy.

The bullet was close enough now that, had he the use of his limbs, Nick might have plucked it from its course himself. But apart from his eyelids, his captors wouldn't let him move a muscle.

Well, he thought, as the bullet got so close that he couldn't focus on it any more, there is nothing like staring your own slow-motion death in the face to bring clarity to a situation. He had no intention of being the Guild's good soldier and vicarious Lothario, but the time for argument was at an end.

He must pretend to do their bidding. He must learn everything he could about the Ofan and tell none of it to the Guild. Yes, Bertrand Penture, he would choose a side. The side of the angels.

He blinked once, and just as the bullet touched his forehead, as lightly as the kiss of a raindrop, Penture reached out, took it, and put it in his pocket. With a rush of blood in his head, Nick felt time resume its normal course. The air in his lungs came out in a whoosh and he collapsed, gasping for breath.

Everyone was silent, waiting for Nick to regain his dignity. Saatçi poured him a drink from a decanter and put it next to him. When he could breathe normally, he downed the contents of the glass without even noticing which liquor it was that burned his throat.

Penture watched Nick drink. 'You are a brave man,' he said.

'I enjoy melodrama.' Nick set his empty glass down on the table. 'That was rather cheap melodrama, mind you, but at least it captured my attention. I applaud you all.'

Nick was shocked to see Penture smile, a big, natural smile. It transformed him from a grim politician into a dashing ruffian, with a deep dimple in one cheek – from Gregory Peck to Cary Grant. 'I thank you,' Penture said. 'I was an actor in a former life. I am glad that our little performance was able to convince you of your loyalties.'

Nick put his hands together as if in prayer. '"Behold the handmaiden of the Lord."'

'My priest!' Arkady proclaimed. 'I told all of you that he would come around.'

For her part, Alice reached across the table and took Nick's hand. 'Thank you, my friend. Please forgive us.'

Fat chance, Nick thought to himself. But he said otherwise: 'Really, there is nothing to forgive.'

26

Julia stood by the window of her bedchamber, holding the little white book of poetry in her hand. But she wasn't reading. She was watching Count Lebedev. He was standing down there in the dark street, tossing his stick from hand to hand and scowling up at the door. And here was Blackdown coming down the stairs, his hat at a rakish angle. It was after midnight, and they walked away down Berkeley Street like two alley cats, off for a night of fun.

Bella was right. It was dreadful to be cooped up. Julia glowered at the men's receding backs.

But if the cats were away, Julia thought, the mouse could play. She was determined to practise her time tricks again. She knew, from what she had learned through the peephole, that her skills needed training and honing to become more powerful, but she also knew that she could never practise while there was the faintest chance that either Nick or Lebedev might be home, or might come home.

Stroking its binding with one finger, Julia examined the book she held. It was smooth and small and filled with some secret that was locked up inside it. If she squeezed it, she might feel a heartbeat. Kisses and caresses. Poetry. Pleasant distractions designed to while away the hours.

She glanced up at the window. The men were no longer in sight.

Julia tossed the book onto her bed. What she needed was real knowledge. She had to become a scholar of time, and since she didn't know whom to trust, she had to tutor herself, devise her own lessons, be an apprentice without a master. Or rather, time itself would have to be her master.

She picked up a silver penny from her dressing table. 'Georgius III Dei Gratia,' she read in the flickering light of the candle by her bed. She could make sense of that. 'George the Third Thank God.' She contemplated his squashy profile and the silly wig on his poor, deluded head. The other side, with the crown floating over the number *1*, was less legible. It read 'MAG BRI FR ET HIB REX 1800.' She didn't know what that meant, except the date and the *rex*. She had been seven in the year this coin was struck. Now she was twenty-two, and all alone with a gift as big as a kingdom and as mighty.

She closed her eyes to clear her thoughts, then opened them again, regarding the penny not as an object but as a flashing moment in time. She tossed it gently into the air. It took no effort at all to freeze it. Julia kept it in her sights and walked around it, reading again the heads and then the tails side. She turned away and heard it clatter to the floor. She bent to pick it up. The count had kept Eamon frozen for a long time while he talked with Blackdown. He'd even turned his back on him. Julia tossed the penny in the air again, and again she froze it. She turned her back. Down it fell. 'Blast.'

An hour later, Julia could keep the penny frozen for a full fifteen minutes while she stared out of the window watching for Blackdown and Lebedev, straightened pillows, counted backwards, closed her eyes, and thought of other things. She could freeze time in a circle around her, projecting in a pie shape, or focus the effect on a tiny space, just around the coin itself. Finally, she tried her hand at keeping the coin frozen while reading, but her excitement upon picking up the little book was so great that the penny slipped before she even cracked the cover. Besides, she was exhausted. Controlling time took energy and concentration, and she had achieved a great deal tonight already. Now, she told herself, for lesson number two. Literature. She forgot about the penny, sat down on the bed and took up the book.

It looked remarkably like the demure white prayer book that the vicar had given her in celebration of her confirmation. Those weekly visits to the vicarage for three months leading up to confirmation when she was thirteen were the only formal education Julia had ever received – and it had disgusted Grandfather. 'Get them young,' he'd said every time he saw her practising her answers. He'd been even more disgusted by the prim little book. 'Pap,' he'd spat. 'Sugar water.' The next time he had come home from London he had brought her an old, graphically illustrated edition of *Foxe's Book of Martyrs*. 'As an antidote,' he'd said. He'd stomped away, leaving her to pore over gory woodcuts of burnings at the stake, disembowellings, the glorious rewards of heaven and the fiery torments of hell.

She thought of Grandfather as she read again the golden letters spelling *Elegies*. It wasn't that he hadn't interested himself in her education. It was just that it was haphazard and followed his whims, whatever he was interested in at the moment. She had to read, in order to follow him in his reading, so he taught her how. She had to write, in order to write to him when he was away, so he taught her how. His library was at her disposal, but if she asked for anything particular from London, any new book of verse or a specific novel or collection of essays, he would invariably arrive home with a book about the Antipodes or the western wildernesses of America. 'Read that out to your old ancestor,' he would say, and slump down in his armchair, light a cigarillo and watch her through the smoke as she flipped between the pages, reading aloud descriptions of wild savages and mountain lions.

Occasionally he would get her to write him a composition. 'Call this one "Little Girls Must Never Lie",' he said once, when she was ten or eleven. 'Two hundred words by tomorrow afternoon.'

The next day she stood up before him and read her composition to him. 'Ahem!' She cleared her throat. '"Little Girls Must Always Lie", by Julia Percy.'

He guffawed. 'Minx!'

She curtseyed and continued: '"Little girls must always lie. Their grandfathers are such great bullies that lying is their only hope of survival. If a grandfather asks, 'Did you eat the last of the mincemeat pies, little girl?' the little girl who truthfully answers, 'Yes, Grandpapa, I did,' will then have to endure hours of storming rage as Grandfather vents his spleen upon her. But the little girl who says, forthrightly and without a quiver, 'No, Grandpapa, *you* ate the last of the mincemeat pies and have simply forgotten it,' will need only wait two hours before her Grandfather has bullied the poor cook into making a new batch. And then she may eat them all again, just as she did yesterday."'

At this Grandfather gathered her up, kissed her and told her she was a pearl beyond price. 'But that was not two hundred words, my little kangaroo. It was only a hundred and eighteen.'

'How can you tell that, Grandfather? I knew it but hoped you wouldn't notice.'

'Oh, it is just a trick I have. I wager you have it, too. Let's see. I shall give you a composition, shall I? I have not prepared one, so it will have to be something from my memory. Listen, but do not try to count my words. Don't even think about counting. Just listen. Are you ready?'

'Yes.'

'Let me see. I must think of something. Just a moment.'

Grandfather searched his memory with an exaggerated rolling of his eyes and scratching of his head.

Julia laughed.

'All right, yes,' Grandfather said. He flexed his hands and cleared his throat. 'Listen to this.' He began, speaking quickly: '"The history of all hitherto existing society is the history of class struggles. Freeman and slave, patrician and plebeian, lord and serf, guild-master and journeyman, in a word, oppressor and oppressed, stood in constant opposition to one another, carried on an uninterrupted, now hidden, now open fight, a fight that each time ended, either in a revolutionary reconstitution of society at large, or in the common ruin of the contending classes."' Grandfather stopped and looked at Julia. 'Now then, how many words was that?'

'But what does it mean?'

'What does it mean? Why, nothing! At least, not yet. Don't worry about that. How many words long was it? Come, I know you know.'

'Seventy-one.'

'Exactly so! You see, you can do it, too.' His eyes were suddenly sad, and he hugged her again, tightly. Then he set her from him and patted her cheek. 'Now. Run away. I have things to do.'

Julia went away puzzled. The words he had recited transfixed her as she listened, the blood rushing at the base of her head. When he was finished she knew exactly how many words he had spoken, as if she had counted as they ticked along. But she hadn't counted. After that she could always do it, if she wanted to. She never did want to. It was a useless trick.

A useless trick. Counting words without counting them, solving stupid puzzles quickly . . . that was nonsense. When she had a very real talent. And no training. No knowledge.

Had he *really* not known that she could manipulate time, just like him?

Julia blinked, and was surprised to realize that she had tears in her eyes. One fell on the pristine binding of Blackdown's book. She wiped it, and then her eyes.

The book sat in her lap, innocent looking.

The last poem. That was the one Blackdown had recommended. The last shall be first. She had to start her education too late and backwards in every way. She held the book close to the candlelight and opened it at the back, flipping through a few pages of verse until she found the title. '"To His Mistress Going to Bed",' she read out loud. She kept going, silently.

Then she laughed. So this is what boys got to read. So much better than Matilda Weimar, forever fainting in the shrubbery.

She read the poem again, and again. When she had arrived for the third time at 'Full nakedness! All joys are due to thee,' she heard men's voices in the street. She was so startled that she froze time in a wide circumference, without even considering her actions.

Then she sat on the bed in an agony of fear. What had she done? Surely those men were Arkady and Blackdown, home again, and if so, they would not be caught in the moment. Indeed, they would know that someone inside the house could freeze time. They might even now be opening the front door, ready to come and kill her. She squeezed her eyes shut, listening.

But there was no sound at all. She got to her feet, and each small sound she made struck her ear like a thunderclap. She peeked around the curtain.

Thank God. Down in the street three men stood looking up at the house, as still as statues. Two of them were strangers to her, workingmen in rough clothes, one with a paper in one hand and a stub of graphite in the other. The third was dressed like a gentleman. Julia's heart started beating again. Three men, frozen stiff, and none of them Nick or Arkady.

She put her hand to the glass and leaned closer. But the gentleman – she knew him. His eyes shone in the glow of a dark lantern that he held up high, its shutter open. The thin cheeks, the saturnine brows.

It was the Falcotts' steward, Mr Jemison.

27

'I believe we *all* need a drink after that,' Marjory Northway said, and there was laughing agreement around the table.

Saatçi got up and did the honours – 'Since tonight I am dressed as a footman,' he said.

As he worked his way round the room, the Guild members talked eagerly about what they had just done in controlling the bullet. Each wanted to brag about the part he or she had played; no one wanted to listen to anyone else.

'You talk as if this is the first time you've done this,' Nick said into the clamour of voices.

Silence fell.

'Ah.' Nick put his hands behind his head and grinned at them. 'This *is* the first time you've done this.'

'You remember, Nick,' Alice said. 'We talked about it.'

'Talked about what?'

'It was when you were being followed by Mibbs. We wondered for a moment if he had used some new Ofan skill on you. Arkady said it might be group time control, and I told you about what they'd been up to in Brazil. The Ofan have really been making headway with it and we've learned a few of their tricks. So you were perfectly safe. We practised last night.'

'On a living subject?'

No one said anything. Saatçi came past with the bottle and Nick pushed his glass forward. 'Better make it a large one.'

Ahn got to his feet. His gold clothing shimmered in the candlelight as he raised his drink, supporting his right arm with his left hand. 'Nick, in Korea we turn our backs to those of higher rank when we drink. Here, among these comrades from around the world and across time, it is impossible to say who ranks the highest. But tonight you have shown your-self to be a prince.' He turned his shoulder to Nick. '*Gun bae!* To courage!'

'To courage!' Everyone drank. Nick drank, too, although what he had endured had not required courage; he'd had no choice but to face the bullet.

Arkady got to his feet and raised his glass. 'I give you a Russian toast. To Father Frost and the Snow Maiden!'

'Make a toast that's about Nick, Arkady,' Alice said. 'Not about you.'

'Wait.' Nick got to his feet. 'If we are toasting women, I have one.' He cleared his throat. '"Here's to the charmer, whose dimples we prize . . ."'

Alice groaned.

Nick smiled at her and carried on. '"Now to the maid who has none, sir. Here's to the girl with a pair of blue eyes, and here's to the nymph with but one, sir!"'

Everyone laughed, and drank.

Except Penture. The Frenchman sat back in his chair, swirling his brandy in his glass. When the laughter was done he got to his feet. 'To our once-beloved sister who has turned against us, and against whom we have turned. Alva Blomgren!'

'To Alva,' Nick echoed, and clinked glasses with the Alder-man, and then with the others, who toasted as if to a dead friend: 'To Alva.'

Penture put his glass down but remained standing. He leaned over the table and waited until he had everyone's attention. 'Now,' he said, 'I'm afraid we must tell Mr Davenant about the future.'

It was as if a cold wind had blown through the room.

People shifted in their chairs, and Nick watched as Alice transformed from a relaxed friend among friends to a tightly controlled Alderwoman among colleagues.

He glanced back at Penture and found that those flat green eyes were bent on him. 'What do you know about the future, Davenant?'

Waterloo? The scramble for Africa? The Hoover Dam? The Cultural Revolution? The Beatles? AIDS? 'A great deal,' he said. 'Mostly useless.'

'No. Not what's coming. What is. What does the future mean to the Guild? What does the Guild mean to the future?'

'The Guild protects the future from the past,' Nick said. 'You protect the flow of history from the Ofan, who think it is possible to change the river, and change the future.'

'That is the theory. If history is a river that flows to the sea, the Guild is the guardian of that flow. But recently . . .'

The Alderman paused and looked down at his hands, which rested on the table. He wore a heavy golden ring with a polished purple stone. It looked very old, almost crude. Nick twisted his own ring on his finger. Arkady had his hand around the stem of his glass, and that enormous ruby winked in the dim light. And Alice's pale yellow stone; Nick couldn't see it, for her hands were in her lap, but she wore it always. Ahn's hands were on the table; he wore what looked like a plain gold wedding band on his ring finger. And Saatçi? Marjory Northway? Their hands were out of sight.

Penture covered the fingers of his left hand with his right, obscuring his ring. 'The Guild has always protected the river of history, Davenant, since time immemorial.'

'Can time be immemorial for the Guild? Surely you know everything, back to when we were hunting woolly rhinos in the Dordogne.'

337

'Have you ever met a caveman?'

'Yes.' Nick pointed to Arkady. 'There he sits.'

Arkady nodded, accepting this as an accolade.

Penture smiled thinly. 'I mean a real caveman. I know the answer; you have not. Any single person's window of travel is about a thousand years back, give or take a century or two. If you were to jump back to the Norman Conquest, you might meet someone from the age of Christ, so we can talk to people from the past across a gap of roughly two thousand years.'

'So I could jump forward almost as far as the third millennium?'

Penture said nothing. The silence around the table was complete.

'My greeter jumped forward from Charlemagne's empire. Ricchar Hartmut,' Nick continued.

'Yes, we still get people from a thousand years ago who jump to the twenty-first century,' Alice said. 'Like Ricchar. But after the turn of the twentieth to the twenty-first century, the travelling begins to get very difficult. People make shorter jumps. People who jump from the twenty-first century . . .' She shook her head. 'It gets harder and harder to jump forward, Nick. We don't know why. Usually people make an initial jump like you or me. Several hundred years. Well beyond their natural life spans. But recently, people who jump from their natural time in the twentieth or twenty-first centuries can only make a small leap. A few decades at most. It's very awkward; their spouses and children might still be alive. And for those of us who know how to travel in time, jumping past the twenty-first century is almost impossible. It takes incredible energy and concentration, and we have to find very specific places where we can latch on to a current that will carry us there. It's as if there isn't any feeling further on downriver that we can recognize. It's as if the entire future is becoming a scar.'

'And this is new? You used to be able to go to the future more easily?'

'No, not exactly,' Marjory said. 'It was always harder to jump after the twentieth century. Like the Alderwoman said, it's scarred up in the future. Once you're there it isn't all that pleasant. Things are rough further along. Very rough. But we used to be able to go there. And some people were still making their initial jumps there, poor things.'

Nick watched as Alice reached out to Arkady, beside her. He took her hand and stroked it. 'What's changed,' Alice said, 'is that after a certain date, we cannot jump at all. It is like hitting a moving wall. No matter where we go, no matter how hard we try, we cannot penetrate past a certain date. We don't know if the Guild exists any more after that date. If humanity itself exists.'

'Wait – after a certain date? What date?'

Everyone turned to Ahn in his glimmering golden clothing. 'Today the Pale is at the nineteenth of December, 2145,' he said.

'The Pale?'

'The barrier. The moment after which we cannot jump.'

'*Today* it is at the nineteenth of December? What was it yesterday?'

'The twentieth.'

'And tomorrow it will be the eighteenth,' Marjory said.

Nick looked from face to face. 'What are you saying?' His voice came out a hoarse whisper.

'We are saying that the future has turned around,' Penture said. 'It is pushing back, consuming the past. Day by day. Our time is getting shorter and shorter.'

Everyone was looking at Nick. Everyone's hands were

now on the table. Everyone, he noted in his rising panic, was indeed wearing a ring. He pushed back his little chair and stood up. 'What the hell are you people talking about?'

'The future, Nick,' Alice said. 'It is pushing the river back against itself. Against us. Like a tsunami.'

28

Julia looked down at the three men, frozen at her whim. They were fifteen feet away or more – much further than she had thought her powers could extend. In the bedroom to the left, Clare was probably frozen in her sleep. If the effect spread up as well as out, the servants upstairs were frozen in their narrow beds. And the mice in the walls. Julia crossed her arms, hugging her ribs, feeling her breath flutter, her heart beat. It was a fearsome gift she had. To pluck herself out of time and stand alone, at the centre of a great stillness.

She let time start again and watched as the three men picked up where they had left off, the one writing on his paper, Jemison and the other man looking at the door in the narrow beam of the dark lantern. Then they moved on to the next house. Julia watched for ten minutes as the lantern bobbed slowly all the way round the square, winking out for long periods as the trees blocked her view, but moving steadily on. When they got back to the Falcott mansion, Jemison closed the shutter on his lantern, shook hands with the other two men and waited as they walked away down Berkeley Street. When they were gone, he turned back and looked up at the façade.

Julia ducked behind a curtain, peering out again cautiously. Jemison stood with his hands on his hips, scanning the house. Then she heard a window scrape open, and something must have been tossed down, for Jemison bent and plucked an object from the dust near his feet. He held it up to show that he had found it, and it caught the light of the moon: a key. He moved away around the house, towards the side kitchen entrance.

Julia grabbed her candle and, shielding its flame with her hand, she flew to her bedroom door and wrenched it open.

There was Clare beetling down the hall, wrapped in a dressing gown and carrying her own candle in a holder with a glass shade. She stopped when she heard Julia's door open, then turned slowly. 'Oh. Hello, Julia.'

'Hello, Clare. Are you sleepwalking?'

'I'm . . . hungry. I'm going down to raid the kitchens.'

'You threw a key down to Mr Jemison!'

'Ah. Yes. Yes, I did.' Clare frowned. 'And I must go to meet him in case he runs into difficulty. Go back to bed. Forget you ever saw anything.' She started off down the hall again.

'I'm coming with you.'

Clare turned, exasperated. 'Go to bed!'

'No! I'm not letting you meet a man alone. Who knows what might happen?'

Clare leaned forward, holding her candle out to illuminate Julia's face. 'Who knows? You don't. And that is how I want it. I insist as your hostess that you return to your bed.'

'Don't be a fool. No friend worth her salt would let you scamper off in your nightgown after a man. Your steward, Clare, for God's sake! Wait for me there.'

'It is you who is being foolish . . .'

But Julia was already back in her room, awkwardly shoving her feet into slippers and scrambling into a wrap while trying to keep her upheld candle from lighting her hair on fire. When she came back out into the hall she was relieved to see that Clare was waiting, her face a picture of frustration. 'You are a pest, Julia Percy.'

'Good. You clearly need one.'

Clare stalked away down the hall like an angry lioness and Julia followed after, excitement beginning to buzz through her veins. Clare was having a clandestine affair with her steward. And Julia was saving her from her folly. It was like when the Countess of Wolfenbach –

Julia stopped walking. This very afternoon she had been half undressed in Blackdown's arms, and happier than she had ever been in her life.

'Full nakedness. All joys are due to thee.'

'Clare . . .'

Her friend turned.

'Perhaps it is better that I leave you alone?'

'I wish you would.'

Julia nodded, once. 'I shall, then.' She turned on her heel.

'Oh, for pity's sake, you ninny!' Clare grabbed Julia by the arm. 'Come along. Better you accompany me than go back to your bed imagining that I am down in the kitchens among the onions, locked in an embrace with Mr Jemison.'

'Well, wouldn't you be?'

Clare pulled Julia along the corridor, so quickly that Julia's candle guttered out. 'I know it is impossible for you to imagine, my dear, but men and women can make more together than babies. I am going downstairs in the dead of night to talk to Mr Jemison about an impending riot.'

'A riot!'

But Clare said nothing more as they descended the stairs, and soon enough she pushed open the door to the basement kitchens. Mr Jemison was standing there eating an apple, his lantern and his leather satchel on the stocky kitchen table beside him.

He swallowed hurriedly when he saw Julia.

'I couldn't stop her,' Clare said, setting her candle next to his lantern on the big kitchen table. 'She insisted on protecting me from you. She will keep our confidence, though, will you not, Julia?' It was an order, not a question.

'Yes, of course.'

343

Julia found herself the subject of Jem Jemison's consideration, and it was disconcerting. His eyes were as dark as her own, and they scanned her slowly, critically. Finally, he sighed. 'What's done can't be undone,' he said, and bowed. 'Miss Percy.'

Julia inclined her head. 'Mr Jemison,' she said.

'Let me help you with that,' Clare said, and Julia watched with some shock as a lady eased a steward out of his coat and hung it over a chair.

Free of his heavy coat, Jemison looked even thinner than before; Julia wondered if he ate only apples. 'I brought you the latest,' he said to Clare, opening his satchel and removing a mismatched stack of papers. He held them in his long, narrow hands for a moment and smiled at Julia, including her. 'Have you heard of the Corn Bill, Miss Percy?'

'We talked of it only this evening, over dinner.'

'Did you? With Lord Blackdown in attendance?' He glanced at Clare. 'I must hear about that. But meanwhile . . .' He divided the pile of papers in half and handed a sheaf to each of them. 'You'll see that things are heating up as the vote draws nigh.'

'When is the vote?'

'It could be any day now. Perhaps tomorrow. Perhaps next week. It depends upon when all the lords are finished giving their speeches.'

Clare rolled her eyes and began flipping through her stack of papers, scanning them quickly and laying them on the table as she was finished. Julia glanced at her stack. It was a collection of broadsides and sheets from a newspaper called *The Political Register*. The top one was a broadside with verses printed on it, entitled 'British Freedom'.

Clare looked up. 'I can see, just from a glance,' she said. 'There will certainly be a riot when the bill passes. Listen to this: "Bread! Bread's our right! – Bread's our need! Like air and water – ours as yet! Bread! Bread! We *must* – we will have bread!"'

'The tide is turning,' Jemison said.

'What have you got there?' Clare looked over Julia's shoulder.

'"And free we're born,"' Julia read aloud, '"to sow the corn, and free, when ripe, to reap it. And when we do, the ruling few, are free to come and eat it!"'

Jemison laughed. He had propped his narrow behind on the table and now he leaned at his ease in this kitchen that wasn't his own. 'I hadn't seen that one. May I?' She let him have it and he read it over, chuckling to himself and eating his apple.

'But the bill might not pass,' Julia said. 'Surely if it's so wrong . . .'

'Oh, it will pass,' Clare said. 'No doubt about it.'

Jemison glanced up. 'What is ironic is that if we still had an estate to work with, the Corn Bill would have helped our little dream, Clare.'

Ah. So he called her Clare when his guard was down. 'What dream?' Julia asked it softly.

Clare shrugged. 'A small-scale one. Jemison and I were going to turn Blackdown into a model farm. Soldiers and sailors returning from the war with nowhere to go – a new system of cooperative farm management that would slowly do away with tenancy and put the land in the hands of those who work it. But it was just wishes and horses. And who knows? The Corn Bill might have helped, Jem, but it also might well have squashed our plan. So many things might have squashed it.' She reached out and touched the round haunch of an apple in the bowl. 'So many things did squash it. Best, perhaps, that it didn't happen.'

'And now here we are in London,' Jemison said brightly.

'Where those same soldiers and sailors will be smashing windows and dragging fat lords into the streets and dancing the hornpipe on them in a few days' time.'

Julia raised her eyebrows. 'Surely not!'

'Oh, you don't know our London mob,' Jemison said. 'A venerable creature, the mob. And it won't be the lords' houses, alone. Whole parishes will feel their wrath. Three London parishes have refused to organize against the Corn Bill, and can you guess which ones they are? St Mary-le-Bone, Hanover Square and St James. Tomorrow Westminster is delivering 42,473 signatures against the bill. But the great men of Mayfair? Who get their money from rents, rents they can keep high if the price of corn is fixed? Not a single name. Not one.'

Julia said nothing. What could she say? She felt like a milk pumpkin, raised all alone under a protective cloth, fed rich, unnatural food and grown pale and strange as a result.

Jemison seemed to understand. He put a thin hand on her shoulder in a brotherly gesture. 'All this talk, this heightened feeling, it's about more than the Corn Bill,' he said gently. 'It's important because it's about the future, Miss Julia, when we shall have fellowship among men, and common property, and fair wages. But before all that, we must have a cheap loaf. Grub first, then ethics! That's why we fight the Corn Bill so fiercely.' He gestured to the papers. 'That's a few weeks' out-pourings only. This bill, you see, it's turning the tide of feeling. It's so bloody cynical that everyone can see it, pardon my language. When the lords pass the bill, it will be like they are saying to their tenants, "Yes, Joe, I'd rather see you starve than make a living. Now pull that forelock and bend that knee."' He squeezed Julia's shoulder. 'You will see the future when they pass that bill, Miss Julia, if you are still in London. You will see the future begin.'

346

'Maybe,' Clare said. 'The future has begun many times before and hasn't come to much.'

'Doubter.' Jemison shook his head. 'Why are women such doubters? It really brings a man down.' He took a broadside and struck a pose, one hand uplifted with the paper so he could read it, the other, with the apple core, balanced on his hip. '"UP, man of reason! Rouse thee UP! AROUSE thee for the strife!"' He waved his apple core suggestively in front of his trouser flap, grinning at Clare. '"Be UP and doing – for the world with mighty change is rife!"'

'Enough!' Clare laughed and snatched the broadside from Jemison's hand. 'I'm sorry, Julia. Mr Jemison is . . . well, words fail me.'

He turned that happy grin on them both, then brought the apple stem-end toward his mouth and began eating the core. Julia stared. 'Learned to do that in Spain,' he said, mouth full. 'Not enough to eat.' He stuffed the last of the core in his mouth.

'He's just trying to shock,' Clare said, looking bored. 'It means he likes you, believe it or not.'

'I'm suppose I'm flattered.'

'He can behave like a gentleman when he must.'

Jemison swallowed. 'Can't. Tallow chandler's son.' He licked his fingers.

'Rich as Croesus,' Clare said. 'Just playing at being a working-man.'

Jemison reached for another apple from the bowl on the table. 'Sticks and stones, my lady. Sticks and stones. So. Tell me. What did your brother have to say about the bill?'

Clare sighed. 'He was all in a twist about it. I honestly don't know what his opinion is. I don't know what to make of him in general.'

'What do you mean?'

'He's changed. I don't know how he thinks any more.'

Jemison polished his second apple on his breast. 'War changes a man,' he said carefully. 'He was at Badajoz. No man who lived through those days will ever be the same again.'

'What happened?' Clare's voice was soft, pleading.

But Jemison only glanced at her with those dark eyes. 'No, my lady. That's between a man and his God.' He put the fruit between his lips, and the bright, jolly sound of a crisp apple yielding to the teeth filled the room.

'You probably know Nick better than I do, having served with him.'

'I'm sure I do,' Jemison said. 'But I don't love him, and you do, and that's a different kind of knowledge. So tell me.'

'It's like he's two different men. I wish you could have heard the conversation when I told him about almost selling Blackdown. At first I thought he was more excited by it even than I. But by conversation's end, it was as if he were the oldest, goutiest, most backward old duke in the Upper House. Ranting at me!'

'That doesn't surprise me. He's a brave man, but I suspect he always felt guilty about leaving Blackdown. Now that he's back he'll dig right in like a tick.'

'Don't talk like that about him. He's my brother. I know you hate him and are sorry he's returned –'

Jemison's eyes flew wide. 'Is that what you think?' He laughed. 'Good God, woman, I almost wept, I was so glad to see him, landlord scum that he is!' He put his apple to his mouth for a bite but lowered it again, and spoke softly. 'If I could tell you what I've lived through, side by side with your brother. What our eyes have seen. And then at the last, when he . . .' Jemison was holding the apple in front of his heart; Julia could see the red of it between his fingers. 'And not to know where he had gone, or how . . .' His eyes were focused on a distant horror.

'Jem?' Clare touched his knee.

'Yes. Enough of that. I'm sorry. Tell me more. So half of him is the great lord, storming around his estate. And the other half?'

'The marquess seems to think that women should be the equals of men. He claims to be a follower of Mary Wollstonecraft.' Clare crossed her arms over her chest. 'What do you make of that, Mr Glorious Future of the Workingman?'

Jemison took a big bite and chewed his eyes merry. 'I think he's mad,' he said with his mouth full.

'Yes, or maybe you still have some thinking to do.'

'"UP, man of reason! Rouse thee UP!" . . . mercy, mercy!' Jemison cowered, laughing, beneath Clare's brandished papers.

'But how will Blackdown vote?' Julia asked.

'He won't,' Clare said. 'He won't take up his seat.'

'No, no, Clare! You have heard the truth, and out of the mouths of babes!' Jemison waved his apple at Julia. 'Which of the two marquesses will vote on the Corn Bill? My Lord Backward Looking, or My Lord Forward Looking? He's taking the oath of allegiance tomorrow, so he's planning to have a voice.'

'He's taking the *oath*?' Clare looked astounded.

'Yes, indeed. Prinny sent him a Writ of Summons and by God he's answering it. Word is, he's supposed to give his maiden speech on the Corn Bill. Nobody knows which side he's on.'

'Well!' Clare propped her own behind on the table beside Jemison's. 'I never.'

Julia looked at them both in some confusion. 'What's so strange about Blackdown's voting?'

'It's like I said.' Clare leaned back on her hands. 'He's changed. He left for a Spain a scapegrace. I would have laid money on his never entering the House of Lords. Now he's so much more serious in his demeanour. And his face! Maybe it's that scar, but he looks older than he should. As if he's seen something terrible . . .'

'He has,' Jemison said. 'Believe me. He has. And when he disappeared –'

'What do you mean?' Clare turned to him, eager.

Jemison's face closed in and he stood away from the table, walked away a few steps and turned back. 'You know as well as I. He was lost in Spain for years on end . . .'

'Yes. And he's told me nothing about that, either.'

Why had Jemison closed in like that? There was something he knew about Blackdown that he wasn't telling. Julia stared at him, willing him to tell. Infusing him with her own powerful desire to know everything about Nicholas Falcott.

Jemison turned his head slowly towards her. When he met her eyes, she extended herself fully to him, flooding him with her need, her passionate curiosity. She pictured him opening his mouth and speaking . . .

'Young lady,' he said. His voice was quiet but firm. 'Pray, what are you doing to me?'

Julia drew back, blinking. 'I beg your pardon?'

'I think you know.' He laid his apple core on the table and walked toward her, his eyes very intent. 'I want you to stop.' He took her hand, and she felt his resistance to her will in his very fingertips. 'I am a free man, my dear. And I do not choose to tell you anything about Lord Blackdown.'

Clare looked quizzically at Jemison and then at Julia. 'What on earth are you talking about?'

'It's nothing.' Jemison came back to his position beside Clare, but his eyes were still on Julia. 'Miss Percy was just looking at me so appealingly. I had to explain to her that Lord Nick's secrets and mine are our own. To share when and with whom we choose.'

Julia stood rigid. Had she really just penetrated Jemison's mind with her own emotions? That wasn't a normal thing to do. Normal people couldn't do that. And yet . . .

She had done it once already today. She had done it at dinner, and she hadn't even realized it until just now. She had done it when she had extended herself to the Russian and made him trust her. She had put her trust in herself into his head, and he had accepted it as his own emotion. Believed it. He had even sung her praises at the end of the evening.

And now she had tried to make Jemison talk to her, tried to make him tell her his secrets. She had done it thoughtlessly. But he was right. She'd intruded on him. Put her own feelings into him and tried to make him act on them.

It was a terrifying power. No, it was *another* terrifying power. She cowered in her own skin, yearning for Grandfather, yearning for a friend.

Some time later, Clare touched her arm.

Julia came back to herself. 'I'm all right,' she said. 'I was just wool-gathering.'

'Wool-gathering! How could you, while we were talking about the possible destruction of this house by a mob of angry Londoners!' Clare laughed, but Jemison was concerned for her, she could tell. His dark eyes seemed to see right through her.

'Let's go back to bed, my dear,' Clare said. 'It is very late, and who knows when Nick will return. He mustn't find us consorting in the basement with a radical tallow chandler, dressed only in our nightclothes.'

Julia picked up her burned-out candle. She wished Nick would find her tonight. Even his disappointment or his anger would feel like human contact. Even the fact that she couldn't tell him about her talent, even the terrible fact that she must hide it from him at all costs . . . being with him and keeping secrets from him felt better than this loneliness.

Jemison levered himself back into his coat and tucked a third apple into its pocket. 'Goodnight, then, and Godspeed.' He sketched them both a bow. 'Let's hope the marquess votes against the bill and makes himself a hero. There are some lords' houses in Berkeley Square that will certainly draw the ire of the crowd after the bill passes. I won't be able to protect this one if they turn their rage in its direction.'

Clare nodded. 'I shall do my best to convince him, but the choice must be his.'

'Yes.' Jemison picked up his lantern. For the first time his voice was cold. 'The precious marquess must make his own choice.' But the sparkle returned immediately, and his grin flashed in the glow of his lantern. '"UP men of reason . . . !"'

He opened the kitchen door with a flourish and was gone.

29

From some hidden pocket, Ahn produced what looked like a silver card case. He placed it on the table in front of him and said, 'First image.' A three-dimensional, fully coloured moving image appeared, hovering over the length and breadth of the table. It showed a city in flames, and the sky boiling with red-and-black clouds. A great ruined dome rose in the centre. With a start, Nick recognized St Paul's Cathedral, half blasted away. 'London, 2145,' Ahn said. 'In my time, Nick, the world is in crisis. The Guild is in disarray. The Ofan have taken advantage of the confusion and are gaining in power.'

Nick whistled. 'Did they cause this destruction?'

'Second image.' A new picture replaced the spectre of London. This time it was the Guild compound near Santiago, also entirely in ruins. 'No,' Ahn said. 'The Ofan didn't cause it. Humankind has reached this state unaided.'

'I suppose I'm not terribly surprised,' Nick said, and no one contradicted him.

'Close image,' Ahn said, and the picture of the Santiago compound winked out. Ahn put the card case back in his pocket. 'As perhaps you know, the Guild tries not to interfere with the vast movements of human history. The opposite, in fact. But the Ofan have their beautiful dreams.' Ahn steepled his fingers. 'In my time, ecological devastation and a world war have made it impossible for the Guild to maintain its operations on a global scale. The Ofan find it easier to gain members among those few who are unfortunate enough to jump into our desolate world. Using their knowledge of the future, they are travelling back and trying to establish powerful cells in earlier eras. This era, and this city – Georgian London – is just such a stronghold. They are doing their best to dig in deep here and now, because they believe they can influence some things in the early nineteenth century that will pan out much later on. Their goal is to intervene in human history, keep the earth clean and safe; to prevent that ecological devastation, that terrible war . . .'

'And that's wrong, why?'

Ahn let his steepled fingers interlace. 'It would be nice if we could go back and fix our mistakes,' he said carefully. 'Apologize and try again. But that isn't the way it works. This new horror, this turning back of time itself? It must be because the Ofan have meddled with the future. That is the only possible explanation. The Ofan have changed something, who knows what. It could be anything at all. And now the future, as terrible as it was, has turned on us, like a cornered tiger. That is worse, surely, than simply trying to survive the difficult times ahead.'

Nick looked up at the bulbous chandelier glimmering with the light of hidden candles, then back at the Alderman of the future. 'If you can't jump past the Pale, how do you know it stays bad? What if it's some sort of salvation? "The world's great age begins anew, The golden years return, The earth doth like a snake renew" – that sort of thing.'

'You would not think that if you saw what it is like. If you felt the pressure, the storm of time blowing towards us, catastrophe piling ruin upon ruin . . .'

'My daughter,' Arkady said in a broken voice from across the table, as if he had not been listening to Ahn, 'my Eréndira . . .'

Ahn glanced at Arkady, then passed a hand over his face, clearly glad to be interrupted.

'My Eréndira was in Brazil. She was part of a group that was trying to pierce the Pale, to learn what lies beyond it. The Ofan were reaching towards it, pushing, working together. I do not know exactly what happened, but they lost her. She alone had managed to jump beyond the Pale, and then – she could not return. They could sense her trying, trying . . . and then they lost even that faint image of her.' Arkady looked at Nick, and his blue eyes were like two empty holes right through his head, with the sky shining through.

'I'm sorry,' Nick said.

Arkady didn't reply. He wasn't listening to Nick. Indeed, he wasn't really even in the same room. 'They simply lost her,' he said again, and his voice quavered like an old man's. 'Then I got a call one day when I was at the Santiago compound. She had reappeared. Not in Brazil but here, in London, in 1793. She was dying. I flew to London. I jumped back. I found her with the Ofan, in a house in Chelsea. They were the followers of that coward Ignatz Vogelstein!' He spat the name. 'It was the Ofan who were with her, those riff-raff! Not her own papa! But I got there in time to kiss her, in time to say goodbye.'

Alice put her hand on her husband's shoulder but he shrugged it off.

'She could not speak. I could only hold her. She died. Her beautiful hair, it had turned white, like mine. Her face was young but her hair was white, and her eyes! Despair like that? I have never seen it. And in the eyes of my own child . . .' He wept, his face uplifted for all to see the tears. His big hands, open on the tabletop, shook helplessly.

There was silence around the table as Arkady wept, and Nick realized that there were tears on his own cheeks as well, for Eréndira. *She* had been courageous.

There were other emotions in the room, emotions directed at him, and Nick felt strangely immune to them all. He could feel the power of these men and women's collective fear and grief, their sense of failure, their rage. Alice, whom he had come to admire and enjoy. Arkady, whose strange definition of friendship maddened and delighted him. And the others, even the cheese inspector. Even Penture. They were all well-intentioned people who loved the Guild and were willing to do anything to save it. They feared the Pale, but more than that they feared the end of their fraternity.

Penture spoke into the thick atmosphere, and his voice was hushed and serious. 'Now, Nick Davenant. Now that you have joined us, accepted your duty, and we have told you of the terrible things that will happen downriver, you must be told what we really want you to discover while you are in the arms of Alva Blomgren.'

Everyone around the table went very still.

Ah. Nick tipped his chair back on to its hind legs.

Saatçi reached over and tapped Nick's shoulder. 'The chair!' he whispered in tortured tones.

'Sorry.' Nick righted himself.

Penture waited, with a frown for Saatçi, until all was quiet again. 'A story has travelled up and down the river in recent weeks,' he said, 'among those few who have seen the future. The rumour is this. There is something, somewhere – an object of some description – that can save us from the disaster that is coming closer with every passing day. Something that magnifies our talent, perhaps, or something that can alter time mechanically. We do not know. Is it big or small? Is it from the future – from beyond the Pale itself? Some advanced technology? Or is it from the past? The more credulous think that it has magical powers. Others believe that it is from outer space, or that a nuclear accident has mutated something already known. Still others are sure that it is God's work: the salvation of humankind from Armageddon.'

'What do you think it is?'

Penture allowed a small, pinched little smile to touch his lips. 'I do not even allow myself to believe that it exists. Our talent has never relied upon objects. It is located in our emotions, in our connection to the feelings of other human beings down through time. But this much is clear. If it exists at all, the recent escalation in Ofan activity suggests that they might have it in their possession, or they know where it is and are working to retrieve it. Perhaps the object is in fact to blame for what has happened to the future. Perhaps it is something terrible, not something good. But if there is such a thing, the Guild must have it. We must not let the Ofan learn its powers. We must either find it before the Ofan do, or if they have it already, we must get it back from them.'

'And you think Alva might have this thing, this . . .'

'People are calling it simply "the Talisman". And if there is any Ofan up and down the river who knows what and where the Talisman is, that Ofan is Alva Blomgren.'

30

The next morning after a cup of coffee and a bite of toast, Julia curled up in a winged armchair in the library, trying to untangle a snarl of embroidery thread for Clare. Instead, she found herself blinking dreamily at the fire. She hadn't slept after returning to bed, or at least not until she'd heard Blackdown and Count Lebedev return, soon after dawn. Then she had awoken again only an hour later, from a confused dream that fled the moment she tried to recall it. So she had risen, rung for the maid, dressed in her diurnal black gown and taken her hussif down to the library . . . but now the armchair was so comfortable, and the fire in the big fireplace so cheerful. She nodded off into a delicious slumber.

Delicious except for that annoying sound . . . Julia opened her eyes, just as something white flew past her chair into the fire.

She leapt to her feet with a gasp, sending the little workbag and the thread tumbling to the floor, and span to face the room.

'Holy . . . !'

It was Blackdown, and he was staring at her as if she were a ghost.

Julia looked at his shocked face, and then at what he was wearing, and she collapsed back into her chair, laughing.

'Oh, for God's sake.' He came forward with a sheaf of papers in his hand, bending to scoop up what she'd dropped. He slumped down into the chair that was pulled up in front of the fire beside hers. 'You scared the hell out of me. I didn't see you there. What are you doing?'

Julia wiped her eyes. 'I was untangling that snarl for your sister.'

Blackdown looked at the thread and then at the hussif. He held the pouch up with a grin, displaying the sloppy J.P. picked out in irregular Berlin work. 'Was this made by your own fair paw?'

'No, most certainly not – I could not set a stitch to save my life. Bella made it for me when she was twelve.'

'Why even carry it, then? Just to appear a lady?'

Julia rolled her eyes and held her hands up, and he tossed it to her to her, along with the threads.

She caught them, and stuffed the now more tangled mess down in among the few little treasures she carried in her hussif instead of sewing notions. 'I carry a few keepsakes in here. A memento of my grandfather; it's a stone insect, actually. And a funny twisty ring – nothing but a fairing – the only thing I have that was my mother's.' She tied the ribbon around the hussif, glanced at Nick and started laughing once more. 'But at least I am trying to make myself useful as well as ornamental. What are you doing? No – answer me this. What are you wearing? You look like an enormous maypole.'

Lord Blackdown looked down at his brilliant red robes banded with three broad stripes of ermine and gold. 'I know. Isn't it hideous? They were my sainted father's, and his father's before that. The old buzzards at Ede and Ravenscroft had them in storage. It seems *they* knew I was coming back.' He jerked his thumb, gesturing behind him to the table. 'There's the hat. And the stick.'

Julia twisted in her chair and looked at his accessories. 'Oh, dear.'

'Yes.' He slumped further down and frowned at the fire.

'So you are going to take the oath?'

'How did you know?'

'It's all over London, apparently.'

'Oh, God.' He pushed a hand into his hair. 'I can't tell you how unhappy that makes me.'

'Why do it, if you find it such a burden? Most lords don't darken the door. My grandfather stopped going years ago. According to him, arguing a point in the House of Lords is like speaking to the dead, in a vault, by the glimmering of a sepulchral lamp.'

'I'm sure he was right.' Blackdown stared into the fire for another moment, then he rolled his head to the side and looked at Julia. His morose expression transformed into a sleepy smile. 'You're pretty,' he said.

She raised an eyebrow. 'You're ridiculous.'

'Come sit on my lap.' He patted his thighs. 'I'll be Santa Claus.'

'Who?'

His smile faded. 'Oh. Right . . . Father Christmas?'

'Are you foxed, my lord? Why would I want to sit on Father Christmas's lap? And anyway, you look nothing like him. He wears green, and he's fat and has a beard.'

His arm snaked out and hauled her, yelping, out of her chair. 'Stop being pernickety. Come and snuggle up.'

After a few moments of elbowy rearrangement, they were both settled in Blackdown's chair, Julia's legs over his, his arm around her shoulders, his sheaf of papers stuffed beside him. 'Mm.' He pressed her close. 'Your hair smells good.' His other arm found its way around her waist. 'And this feels good.'

'And you feel like an unfortunate cross between a sheep and a stoat.' She stroked one of the ermine bands that crossed his crimson chest. 'You smell musty.'

He put his head back against the chair and looked down

his nose with mock-solemnity. 'I'll have you know that these robes are the sign of my great dignity and magnificence and superior . . . superiority.'

'Well, then.' She moved to stand up. 'Best if I leave you in majestic isolation.'

'Oh no!' He pulled her firmly against him. 'If I have to take the oath of allegiance, I need to be drunk . . . on kisses.'

'I am not going to kiss you here, at nine in the morning, with the door unlocked.'

'No? But what if I kiss you?' He suited actions to words.

She smiled against his mouth, and a few delightful minutes ticked away.

It was Blackdown who pulled back. 'Have you ever made a paper aeroplane?' he whispered.

'A what?'

He tugged a piece of paper from the sheaf that was wedged beside him. Both sides were covered in big, loopy writing. 'A paper aeroplane. A glider, made of paper.'

'No. And what is written on that paper?'

'Nothing important. Here, let me show you.'

Julia was tucked lusciously up against him, her head resting on one shoulder, and he was able, with his arms around her, to demonstrate folding the piece of paper in half, and then in a series of angles, until it looked like the head of a spear. 'That's a paper glider,' he said. 'You hold it like this, by this cluster of folds here underneath. You aim it . . .' He pointed it at the fire. 'Then you give it a little shove . . .' Nick sent the glider winging into the fire. He made a sound like the wind as it went, and then a crashing sound when it wedged itself between two logs and went up in flames. He immediately began making another. 'This one's for you.' He folded it carefully and put it in her hands. 'That's right. Pinch it there, and then aim it . . . and let go.'

She watched as her glider floated away from her and into the flames. It sat for a moment on some embers, the undersides of its wings glowing pink. Then all at once it became a miniature inferno. She laughed and grabbed his knee. 'Make me another one.'

They worked their way through the entire sheaf, sending glider after glider into the flames. Soon it became a rule that they must kiss until each glider was finished burning, and they both became adept at sending their gliders into cooler corners of the fire. But when Julia sent one deliberately outside the fireplace altogether, Nick sent her after it. 'You won't trick me into losing my virtue that easily,' he said.

After she had tossed it onto the fire and turned round, she found him standing and brushing his robes into place. 'That's it,' he said nonchalantly. 'That's my entire maiden speech, burned up. Like the Battle of Britain.'

'That was your maiden speech?' Julia stared at him.

'That's right.'

'But what will you do? Do you have it memorized?'

'No.' He straightened the robe on his shoulders, then smoothed his hair with a hand, looking at himself in the mirror that hung over the mantel. 'Mahvellous, dahling,' he said to his reflection.

'Nicholas Falcott! Be serious. What will you say instead?'

He turned from the mirror, and for just a moment he managed to look dignified. 'That I would prefer not to.'

An hour later Blackdown was gone, and the hallway was filled with the bustling return of Arabella and the dowager marchioness from Greenwich. Julia watched as box after box was unloaded from the carriage that waited at the front door, Arabella overseeing the whole operation; her mother had rushed upstairs, claiming a headache.

362

'All that for one overnight visit?'

Bella gestured to a neat pile of three blue bandboxes. 'Those are mine. The rest . . . Mother's.'

'Perhaps that is a good sign. She is interesting herself in society again.'

'Yes.' Bella looked doubtful. 'Perhaps.'

When the last box was in, Bella asked one of the footmen to hold the horses and the coachman to come inside. He entered, his hat in his hand, and Bella addressed him and the remaining footman with great warmth. 'I want to thank you both,' she said, 'for sending that madman on his way just now. I would have been quite anxious without the two of you.' She fished in her reticule, took out two coins and handed one to each man. 'If I were a man, I would stand you both a drink, but you will have to raise your glasses to yourselves.'

The coachman bowed and left to drive the coach round to the mews, and the footman returned to organizing the luggage. Bella took Julia's arm. 'I'm so glad to be home, I cannot tell you. Greenwich was a bore.'

'At least you were able to leave the house and see the sunshine. Remember you are talking to a creature who must hide in the dark, wearing black, having miserable feelings for six months before she is allowed to wear the most odious shade of purple.'

'You are allowed to leave the house. Now and then. If you're very good.'

Julia sighed. Sedate walks in the company of servants did not count, in her book, as freedom, and she knew Bella did not count it as freedom, either. 'Anyway,' she said, 'even if it was boring I want to hear every tiny detail. Come and tell me everything.' They mounted the stairs. 'And it sounds as if you had at least one thrill – what was that about a madman?'

'It was the strangest thing. It happened just now, as we

climbed down from the carriage. A man walked right up to Mother and addressed her. He was very formal, and exceedingly dour. Dressed expensively but in the most outmoded of fashions. At first we thought he must be an old acquaintance of Father's or something, and Mother greeted him politely enough. But then he began to insist that there was a baby hidden in our house! A baby, can you imagine? He demanded that the baby be given to him. When Mother assured him in the kindest possible way that there was no baby and had been no baby in the house for twenty years, he became quite obstreperous, and demanded to see a man he called Altukhov.'

'Altukhov? That sounds Russian.'

'Yes, isn't it curious?' Bella opened the door to her bedchamber and invited Julia in. 'For of course we do have a Russian in the house, and what are the chances of that?'

'Then what happened?' Julia sat in one of the two little chairs that faced the window looking out onto Berkeley Square.

'The footman was very firm, and told the man to move along, that he had the wrong house, that he was bothering their ladyships, and all of that footmanish sort of thing that they say.' Bella unpinned her hat, took off her pelisse and tossed them together with her reticule onto her bed. 'It seemed at first to work, for the man appeared to calm down.' Bella checked her hair in the mirror and settled herself in the other chair. 'But then' – she turned towards Julia, her eyes alight with humour – 'I realized that for the whole time that the footman had been talking, the man had not been listening at all. He had been standing like a moonstruck cow, gaping at Mother as if she were a heavenly apparition. Which you must admit she never is, not even on her best days.'

'Your mother is a beautiful woman,' Julia said dutifully.

'Have it your way.' Bella flared her nostrils. 'In any case, Mother stared back for a moment, and then – I wish you could have seen it – she clutched her breast and moaned. She stumbled up the stairs to the door, calling back to Coachman to drive the man from the door like a leper! Which Coachman did, by bellowing and flapping his arms at the man until he turned and walked away.' Bella laughed. 'She actually said "like a leper", and her voice turned biblical. And Coachman . . . he looked like an apoplectic rooster!'

'But that's all terrifying! Thank goodness Coachman was able to drive the madman off.'

Bella sighed. 'I know, I suppose I ought to have found it frightening. Do you think there's something wrong with me? But honestly, Julia, at least it was exciting.' She slumped down in her chair just as her brother had done in the library an hour earlier, and stared out of the window. Julia stared, too. Although she wasn't actually incarcerated in London as she had been at Castle Dar, the effect was the same, for aside from her brief outing to Gunter's she had barely left the house. And yet, for all that the minutes moved as slowly as cold treacle, her life was far too exciting. Exciting – or perhaps she was simply insane, and was even now in the grip of a delusion that she could manipulate time, and that two lords were pursuing her with deadly intent. But . . . Julia smiled to herself. One of those lords was – to call a fig a fig – on the high road to becoming her lover, and she knew that he was real, for if she closed her eyes she could still feel that ermine beneath her fingers and taste his kisses on her lips.

Bella interrupted her reverie. 'I think things are drearier now because my value has gone up.'

Julia opened her eyes. 'Whatever do you mean?'

Bella's arms hung down over the arms of her chair like a rag doll's. 'Oh, before Nick's miraculous reappearance I was a wealthy match, but the title was extinct, so I didn't bring with me a connection to a powerful family. Any man who showed interest in me was either a fortune hunter, which was thrilling in a piratical sort of way, or else he truly admired me, which was flattering and sometimes even slightly tempting. Now that Nick is home, my stock in the marriage market has risen, and suddenly the most dreadfully important and boring men are monopolizing my time.' She sighed. 'You see before you a valuable commodity.'

'Surely you enjoy that. You are in London to catch a husband, remember?'

'I suppose.' Bella propped her slippered heels on the windowsill. 'If only there were someone I liked.' She reached out for Julia's hand. 'I wish you were out of mourning so that you could join me. At least then I would have someone to laugh with over it all. Mother is blue-devilled, and Clare refuses to participate in the Season.'

Julia took her friend's hand and swung it between their chairs. 'You should be glad I can't participate,' she said. 'I was raised by wolves. Or rather, by a wolf. I don't know how to dance, or play the harp, or anything.'

'All you have to do is learn how to simper. A good simper disguises all blemishes.'

Julia snorted. 'You wouldn't know how to simper if your life depended upon it.'

'That is why all the other girls go flying off the shelf and I am left behind, gathering dust in the shop window.'

'You just said you were a valuable commodity.'

'Ah. Do I contradict myself?' Bella wiggled her toes and squeezed Julia's fingers. But her expression was thoughtful. 'I wonder if Count Lebedev knows this Altukhov?'

'Ask him during dinner.'

Bella flopped her feet apart and then together. 'Wouldn't

it be thrilling if the count were involved in some infant-smuggling scheme, and we were the ones to expose it to the eyes of the world? But we cannot ask him. He is gone.'

'What?' Julia sat up straight in her chair, pulling her hand from her friend's.

'Yes. The footman said so. I told him to alert the count about the maniac, in case he did know anything about an Altukhov who might be hiding a baby. But Lebedev is gone. And not just for the day. He loaded up the second-best coach and drove off this morning, early.' She put the back of her hand over her brow. '"Of joys departed, not to return, how painful the remembrance!"'

'Oh, Bella, be serious! Where is he gone? Is he ever coming back?'

'How should I know?'

Julia had to will herself to remain in her seat and not climb the walls. Devon. That was the answer. Julia knew it. Lebedev was gone to Devon to investigate Eamon. To find out if he was Ofan. When he got there it would take the Russian five seconds to realize that Eamon was a buffoon, with no more power over time than a broken pocket watch. And when the count knew that, he would start wondering: Who else had been at Castle Dar that day?

Bella was eyeing her with some trepidation. 'Are you well, Julia? I know you are chafing after all this isolation, but please don't start talking about lepers.'

Julia forced herself to smile. 'I'm fine.' She placed her shoulders back against the chair in a semblance of relaxation and turned a rigid smile on her friend. 'Tell me more about Greenwich. With whom did you dance?'

Bella shook her head. 'You can't fool me, Julia. It is high time that you kicked over your traces, and I'm the one to help you.'

'Oh, no!' Julia curled her feet up under her and held on to her chair's arms with both her hands. 'You are far too corky, Arabella Falcott, and I won't be led astray by you.'

'But, my dear,' Bella said, with real concern in her hazel eyes. 'You would do the same for me, were I in your shoes. And take it from me: You are curling up at the edges.'

At eight thirty the following morning, Nick set out for Soho Square without a pang of guilt, although he had just sold his mother a bag of moonshine about how he was going again to the House of Lords. He was sorry to lie to her, but she had cornered him in the breakfast room and ranted about some gentleman who had the misfortune to look strangely at her upon her return from Greenwich. She had even set the coachman on the poor man.

Alva had told him to find her in Soho Square – no address, no description of the house. He supposed he would just turn up and wait. Kicking his heels in the square seemed as reasonable a way as any other to escape one's whingeing mother on the one hand, and the House of Lords on the other.

He had survived yesterday's ignominious ceremony by remembering Julia crammed into a chair with him, sending paper aeroplanes into the fire. He was able to keep a private smile on his face all through the parading and hat doffing and bobbing up and down. The smile slipped when he had to get down on his knees to present his Writ of Summons to the Lord High Chancellor, but he had soldiered on, reading the oath of allegiance and signing the test rolls. Finally he was conducted by Black Rod to his seat among the other marquesses. They had welcomed him with a collective 'woof', much like the simultaneous sneezing of a row of bulldogs.

He had been allowed out of his ceremonial robes after that, but the day was just beginning.

The Corn Bill would clearly pass; nearly everyone was in

support. And yet it was as if they knew that history would prove them wrong. Each peer wanted to go on record explaining himself, and for each the explanation was nearly identical: I must keep hold of my wealth, yes – but in addition and more importantly, England must remain the same. The future threatens. The past is safe.

It had all sounded uncannily familiar.

Kirklaw, sitting with the other dukes, kept staring at him, willing him to get up and make his speech. Nick turned in his seat so that he couldn't see him. But there was Delbun with the earls, and Blessing with the barons. Nick stopped looking at faces and began counting types of knots in neck cloths.

Just when he had thought he would slide from his seat and expire from boredom, Baronet Burdett had presented the House with forty thousand and more signatures from Westminster in opposition to the bill. England, Burdett had argued, must meet the future by making everyone free and equal, without restriction. His speech was met with jeers and really, Nick thought with sympathy for the poor, kindly looking man, it was like asking a pack of hyenas to voluntarily knock out their own teeth. Burdett's speech so enraged one viscount that he had leapt to his feet, declaring that he wanted to strangle the baron right there in front of everyone. The viscount said they might as well roll England up like a scroll, and go home and wait for the mob to level the city. This was good stuff, and Nick leaned forward, hoping that something energizing might happen now, but it all simmered down again and an old earl got up and began to speak in a particularly soporific drone about how the poor like to be hungry.

He had looked away, and then he felt river rushing all around him, around them all – rushing at full flood. And he the only living man, afloat on a broken spar, among the drowned.

Nick stood up at the next opportunity, bowed to the men seated near him and then left. Arkady was right. This was no place for a man who knew the future.

Kirklaw had leapt to his feet and scurried after him, catching up with him just outside the door. 'You didn't give your speech.'

'No.'

'Will you yet? The vote won't come for several more days.'

Nick had thrust his hands into the pockets of his greatcoat and found the acorn there. 'I don't think so, Your Grace.'

Kirklaw nodded, once. 'Well, then.'

'Indeed.'

They had bowed coldly to one another and gone their separate ways, Nick out into the world, the duke back into the chamber.

Nick had sent the carriage home with his robes, and then he strolled alone up Whitehall in the light of a spectacular sunset, tossing the little acorn from hand to hand. He couldn't feel the river now. The spring evening was alive with birdsong and breezes, which, for this half hour anyway, blew the scent of meadow grasses in from the surrounding farmland and carried away the stink of human strife and struggle.

Nick tossed the acorn high and caught it low.

Now he stood beside the decrepit statue of Charles II in the centre of Soho Square. Two boys and a dog were driving a lowing herd of cattle along the east side, past what had been, in the eighteenth century, the notorious White House brothel. It was probably still a brothel, Nick thought, then saw a man in fine but decidedly rumpled clothing open the door and slip out into the morning sunlight. He stood on the step yelling at the cows that blocked him from entering the street. So it was a brothel – but the 'skeleton room' and sinking sofa and other contraptions for which the White House had been famous in the last century – Nick didn't think they would be in the style of calm, elegant Alva Blomgren. Nick looked around the square at the other houses. Which was Alva's? He would simply have to wait and hope that she emerged sooner rather than later.

In the meantime, it was a pleasure to stand here beside the slightly bilious-looking marble monarch who presided over Soho Square and watch all of society scampering past. Horses and carriages, men and women, everyone busy, full of life, chattering to one another like magpies. All the different accents, the cant, the half-loving insults flying from everyone's lips; Nick found himself listening intently to the snatches of conversation that passed him by, his brain spinning with all the old information he had forcefully buried after his jump.

It wasn't that there weren't things to worry about. Kirklaw's insinuations and the marchioness's unhappiness and how to find a way to be with Julia and who was Mr Mibbs and whether to betray the Guild and the looming horror of the Pale – still hundreds of years away but coming closer, according to the Guild, every day. But London was big and brassy and noisome and rude – it was full of suffering and vice and folly – and Nick loved it. This – here and now – this was his city. It was going to be hard to leave and go back to cars and high-rise buildings and underground sewers. He cast an ironic glance at Charles II, who was holding his tummy and sneering down at it all from under his monstrous wig. 'You loved it, too,' Nick told the statue, 'Mr Twelve Illegitimate Children.'

Here was a sight. Walking towards him along Frith Street, a countrified maiden in an old-fashioned homespun skirt and stiff bodice was carrying a huge basket over her arm. It was bulging with beets. She switched between bending uncomfortably forward to carry it and listing comically off to the right or the left. Beside her, an enormous mongrel dog the size of a Dartmoor pony kept pace with her quick, short steps, but it was whining and hopping along on three feet. As they turned the corner onto the square, Nick could see that the dog was harnessed to a cart; clearly this was the intended beet hauler, but the dog had sustained an injury somewhere along the way. The girl was chattering angrily at it, and it hung its heavy, jowly head in sorrow. Together, girl and dog looked like something out of a fairy tale. Nick was about to step forward and offer his help when she looked up, and he saw that she was Alva. He half raised his hand, but she shook her head ever so slightly. He carried his hand on up to his hair and tried to look as if it were the most natural thing in the world to stand in the street scratching one's head.

Alva and her dog continued on their mutually uncomfortable journey round the square, eventually coming to a stop on the corner of Carlisle Street, outside a dapper yellow house with white pilasters. Alva shook her finger at the dog and it dropped onto its belly and put its head down on its paws. She put the basket of beets into the cart, then went up the steps. The door was opened, before she reached the top, by an old woman dressed in black, and Nick watched in some amusement as Alva harangued her with the tale of the dog's failings. Every time she pointed down the steps at the dog it lifted its head, only to drop it again as she continued her tirade. Finally, Alva went in and the old woman came creakily down the steps. She hoisted the basket of beets and led the dog and cart around into Carlisle Street, and presumably thence into the mews.

Nick stood considering the yellow house for a few minutes. Did Alva want him to go away and come back later? Go away and never come back? Or maybe she did not wish to be accosted by a fine gentleman while she was playing at being a beet-toting rustic. He was about to take himself to a coffee shop to consider the problem in more comfort when he saw a window on the third floor of the yellow house raise, and a white arm emerge and beckon him. He set out across the square to his first assignation with his Guild-prescribed mistress.

Alva received him in a green and silver salon on the ground floor of the house. He had no idea how she had managed to change so quickly from her strange street clothes into a fashionable pale pink muslin dress. The Norwich shawl draped over her elbows must have cost a fortune. Her hair was dressed elegantly but without flair; she looked like someone's respectable wife or sister. The dog was with her but clearly still in disgrace, for it sat like a statue gazing at her, and she was refusing to meet its eye. It was a bitch, part mastiff and part Cerberus.

After initial greetings were over, Nick petitioned on behalf of the animal. 'She can't help being in pain,' he said. 'Did she pick up a splinter on your walk?'

Alva put her nose in the air and glanced sidelong at her pet. The animal caught the glance and perked her ears, but Alva withdrew her attention immediately. 'She's a big baby,' she said. 'We bought her on the promise that she would make a good watchdog, but she befriends everyone. Then I decided she could at least help me carry things home from the market, and instead she goes lame. I never liked dogs. She eats us out of house and home, she is ugly, she smells horrible . . .'

'Does she have a name?'

'Solvig. It means "Strong House".'

'Here, Solvig.' Nick snapped his fingers, and the dog limped to him. Nick knelt down and stroked her silky ears and rubbed her between her eyes until he felt that they were good friends. 'I'm going to help you, Solvig,' he said, 'but it

won't be comfortable. Are you ready? Give me your paw.'
She gave him her good paw. It filled his whole hand. 'Not
that one. Paw.'

Solvig whimpered and tremblingly gave Nick her bad paw.
'Good girl.' He pulled on her ear. 'You are an ugly beast,
aren't you?' he said gently as he felt the tender pads. Solvig
whined and made to pull away, but Nick held the paw firm.
'Yes. Good girl.' He looked up at Alva, who was watching
with a half smile on her face. 'She has a stone lodged between
her pads. I think . . .' He focused on what he was doing for a
moment, and Solvig's whine grew sharper. 'Yes . . . oh, shit.
Excuse my French.'

Blood spilled from the dog's paw onto his white cuff. But
he brought away a small, sharp flint. Solvig immediately set
to licking her paw.

'Let her lick it for a while,' Nick said. 'Then she'll need a
bandage.'

'Yes, Doctor.' Alva sat down lightly in a little silver chair.
'You will find a washstand behind the screen over there.'

As he passed it, Nick noticed that the embroidered screen
depicted a mildly lascivious scene of ladies with their bos-
oms spilling out of their clothes, and gentlemen looking
slightly startled; this was the only sign that the house was
something other than a genteel home and, really, it was such
a ridiculous image that it hardly served to stir the senses.

Nick scrubbed his hands clean of the dog's blood. He
didn't even attempt to wash his cuff; it was clearly ruined.
Then he dried his hands, taking his time. He had every intention of betraying someone, and it wasn't going to be Julia. It
was going to be Mother Guild. He pulled his ring up to his
knuckle to dry his finger. Life had certainly taken an interesting turn. He draped the towel over the edge of the washstand,
twisted his ring into place and stepped back round the screen.

Alva gestured for him to take a delicate chair that was the twin of her own. 'Sit down, Nick. Thank you for helping poor Solvig. Look at her. She's in love with you now. I might as well not exist.'

Indeed, devotion shone from the dog's eyes. She lay on the floor, licking her huge paw and staring at Nick in a delirium of adoration. 'Oh dear,' he said, disposing himself in the stiff chair. 'I'm sorry.'

'No. It's wonderful. You will take her home with you and I will be free of the smell, the expense, the feeling that I am constantly being watched.'

'I'm not taking your dog. Besides, who will pull your beet cart for you?'

Alva seemed to consider the problem. 'Perhaps I will buy a donkey.'

'I would like to see that. You in that ludicrous outfit, leading a donkey through the streets of London. But a donkey cannot guard a house. You said you needed a guard dog.'

'Yes, I do, and Solvig is useless.'

'You're just a big cream puff, aren't you?' Nick asked the dog.

Solvig lumbered to her feet and came over to Nick, leaving bloody paw prints on the parquet. Alva groaned and rang for a servant as Nick stroked Solvig's powerful shoulders and murmured endearments into her ears: 'Ugly baby. Smelly puppy.' Solvig blinked her red-rimmed eyes and panted hot breath happily in his face. 'Turnip face.'

Solvig responded to this last sally with a soft woof.

'Do you approve of the nickname,' Nick asked her, 'or disapprove? Shall we try again? Turnip face.' The dog blinked at him and curled her black lips back in a broad grin.

An elderly footman answered the bell. Alva told him to take the dog to the kitchens, bandage its foot and have it ready to leave with Lord Blackdown.

'I am not taking your dog.'

'Oh, but I insist. Solvig is clearly your soulmate.' Alva turned to the servant and spoke quickly in what Nick assumed was Swedish.

Nick was transfixed by the vision of the old man wrestling the enormous dog from the room, managing to bow and close the door without losing control of the animal. Nick heard deep barks of protest descending into the basement.

'Well.' He stretched his legs out and put his arms behind his head. 'I came to set up a mistress, and I leave with one of the hounds of hell. Does the servant come with the dog? Because I'm sure I don't know who in my household will be willing to deal with her.'

'You didn't come to set up a mistress,' Alva said. 'You came to learn about the Ofan.'

Nick stayed in his relaxed position, but every sense was on the alert. And so it was beginning.

Alva folded her hands in her lap. 'What do you want to know?'

'You admit it, straight out? Don't you understand that I am a member of the Guild? That they are out to uproot and perhaps even kill you?'

'I understand that very well, Nick. But do you understand it? Are you working for the Guild and against me?'

He didn't know what to say to that, so he straightened his cuffs. The gesture lost some of its brio when his fingers encountered the still-damp dog blood. 'Damn.'

Alva took a handkerchief from her bodice and handed it to him. 'This is all so hard to talk about,' she said as he wiped his fingers. 'And I can't even properly see your face. Do you mind if I put on my glasses? Since we're discussing realities and not playing games?'

'Be my guest.'

Alva reached into her bosom again and extracted a pair of red plastic cat's-eye glasses, wiped them unceremoniously with a fold of dress fabric and propped them on her nose. She blinked at him a couple of times and then sighed. 'That's so much better.'

He had to laugh. 'You are a woman of contradictions, Alva.'

'How?'

'Oh, I don't know. The medieval peasant costume, the ridiculous dog, the beets, the quick change into demure fashion, the 1960s spectacles stored in your bodice . . . add to that your profession, your modern slang, and the mystery of your Ofanicness . . .'

The violet eyes blinked. 'I am not a contradiction to myself, Nick.'

'Why are you a courtesan?'

Alva's smile turned upside down. It was not an unhappy or an offended frown, but it was thoughtful. 'Why are you a womanizer?'

'I'm not a womanizer.'

'All right,' she said. 'What do you call it?'

'Call what?'

'Your many lovers, Nick. Your trail of broken hearts.'

She wasn't merely contradictory and remarkable – she was disconcerting in the extreme.

'I haven't broken any hearts,' Nick said, sullen.

'Aren't you a Casanova? A rake? A rogue? Come on, Nick. Please. Can we not just speak candidly with each other?'

'Oh, for the love of God. First the Guild and now you. Why do you all seem to know everything about my sex life?'

Alva peeked at him over her glasses. She looked more like a librarian by the second. 'The Guild knows about you because they researched you. You probably have quite the fat file in the archives in Milton Keynes. They needed to know you would be interested in an assignment with a sexual element. Namely, their cockamamie plan whereby you would become my lover in order to gain entrée into the Ofan.'

'Not so cockamamie . . . you seemed to be agreeable at their ball.'

'Well, yes. But as we both know, you have refused to fall into my willing, or at least purchasable, arms.' She tilted her head. 'Which is curious.'

'I didn't intend to offend you,' Nick said. 'It isn't that you aren't desirable . . .'

'I'm not offended.' She righted her head, then tipped it to the other side. 'You have made things easier. Now I can go ahead and tell you everything without the added step of taking you to bed.'

Nick laughed. 'And that's it? You're just going to spill. Upon no knowledge of me whatsoever.'

'But of course! Why else do you suppose I showed up at that ridiculous party?' She held out her hand to him. 'Come. Wouldn't you like to see my catacombs?'

32

Alva led the way down to the cellars. An open door revealed the kitchens, where Solvig, her foot bandaged, lay sleeping, a sonorous snore rattling the pots and pans that hung in gleaming copper glory from the thick, smoke-blackened beams. Alva stooped, lifted a small stone slab from the floor and extracted an ancient-looking key and a blue plastic torch from the hole beneath it. She replaced the stone, fitted the key into the lock of a smaller door opposite the kitchens and pushed it open on creaking hinges into a black hole from which cool, clean-smelling air wafted. She ducked her head to enter. 'The catacombs,' she said, motioning for Nick to follow. 'Please close the door behind you and lock it.' She handed him the key.

She held the light as he turned the key in the lock. 'Don't lose that,' she said. 'We'll need it to get back.'

Nick tucked the key into his pocket to make friends with the acorn and followed her. 'Where are we going?'

'Under Soho Square,' she said. 'You'll see.' She turned and shone her light on what looked like pantry shelves. 'My pickling,' she said of the rows of jars. Then she set off, and quickly enough the shelves of pickles petered out. The white beam picked out rough, arched stone walls and a flagstone floor.

'Who built this?'

'Romans. Extended at various points across the Middle Ages. It is perfectly safe. Look here.' Alva lifted her beam up high and Nick saw that a stone shelf running all along the corridor up near the ceiling was lined with carefully stacked bones, each topped with a skull that grinned down at them. 'We took these catacombs over in 1320, but we didn't feel that we could remove the bodies, so the silent majority are tucked away everywhere.'

'Creepy.'

'Some of them are Ofan, actually. People who wanted to stay here. Personally, I want a glass coffin like Sleeping Beauty.'

'That's even creepier.'

'Different strokes for different folks!' Alva lowered the torch and trotted on.

After a few yards, wooden built-in bookshelves began appearing along the lower walls, crammed with leather-bound books and rolled-up scrolls, most of them looking much the worse for wear. 'Skulls and books,' Nick said. 'Nice.'

'Clear eyes, full hearts.'

'You're sick.'

'Probably.' Alva stopped and shone her light on another door. It was massive and perfectly round. It looked as if it were a cross-section of a single, enormous tree, and indeed, now Nick could see the hundreds of diminishing rings. In the very centre was a big door knocker, its black patina rubbed to shiny brass where generations of hands had grasped it.

Alva banged the knocker against the wood three times, but nothing happened.

'Damn it.' She banged it again, more loudly. Nothing.

'Peter is supposed to be on duty,' she said. 'But I'm sure she's off somewhere, bumming cigarettes or boring someone with her latest obsession.'

'Peter is a woman?'

'Hopefully someday,' Alva said. 'She's fifteen, going on nine.' She lifted the knocker a third time and set up a con-tinuous banging for at least thirty seconds.

Finally, they heard the sound of a heavy piece of wood being lifted away from the door on the other side, and a series of muffled curses, then the door began to swing inward silently.

An older, South Asian woman in jeans and a ratty Aran sweater stood there, one fist firmly planted on a hip, the other lifting a hurricane lamp.

'Hello, Archana,' Alva said. 'Sorry to trouble you. It's just me.'

Archana turned without a word and marched away, her light disappearing as she turned left.

'She's mad at Peter, not at us,' Alva said blithely. 'Will you help me get this thing closed again?'

Nick lifted the heavy wooden board and slotted it into place. 'Not very advanced technology,' he said, remembering the gleaming metal door of Bertrand Penture's inner sanctum. 'The Guild has a much fancier system for keeping out intruders.'

'Yes, well, they like to feel important. Now then. Follow me.'

The corridor now ran at a slant, deeper under the earth, and it was fully lined with shelves to about chest level, and then with glass-fronted cabinets, topped with the ubiquitous bones. The shelves and cabinets bulged with books and papers, interspersed with musical instruments, rusty clockworks, toys, piles of empty picture frames, dusty bottles, swords, a kettle, and here and there a misplaced femur. A corridor branched off to the left, which Alva ignored, then quickly another went to the right. She flicked a switch and, down the length of the corridor, eight or ten dim electric light bulbs flickered to life.

'Electricity? How is that possible?'

'Generator,' Alva said, switching off her torch. 'It's only strong enough to light a few bulbs at a time, so hopefully no one will turn a switch on elsewhere.' This corridor was like the others, arched, with messy shelves and cabinets, but these were interspersed with low wooden doorways, five on each side. 'These are our offices,' Alva said. 'Everyone who is located primarily in this time gets one. Mine is the third on the right. But I barely use it. In fact, it's full of Peter's spill-over right now and I might just let her keep it.'

'There are only ten of you?'

'Yes, give or take. Others travel through. We can't really support more than ten right now in this location. But we're hoping to expand. We have our eyes on a couple of proper-ties . . .' She reached to turn the light off, but they went out with a pop before her fingers touched the switch. 'Crap.' She turned her torch back on. 'I'm not even in favour of the generator. It's Archana's pet project. But it's funny how you'll use things if they're there.'

Nick's head was reeling. 'What is this place? What are you all doing here?'

Alva held the torch under her chin, turning her face into a ghoulish parody of her beautiful features. 'Destroying the future,' she said in sepulchral tones. 'Ruining it for everyone!'

'Yeah,' Nick said. 'So they told me.'

'I bet they did. Come along.' Alva sped away like the White Rabbit, trotting past the endless shelving. 'These all lead into libraries,' she said, flinging a hand towards a series of low, wooden doors on the right.

'Libraries? So what are all the books along the corridors?'

'Overflow. None of it's really well organized, to be honest – even in the libraries. We haven't had an archivist in a generation or two. Ah.' She pointed to a door with a thread of electric light spilling out from underneath. 'That's Archana's lab,' she said. 'If she was in a better mood I'd introduce you, but I don't think it's a good idea just now.'

'How can she bear to work in a hole in the ground?'

'Don't assume that because this is a hole, it is damp and cold like a grave! Archana's lab is warm and full of light.'

'Okay, but . . . this *is* a graveyard. I'm just saying.'

'Technicalities!'

They passed by.

'All right, here we are. The transporter.' Alva touched the handle of a square door. 'Someone dubbed it the transporter because this is where we enter and leave from other times. It's like in *Star Wars*, you know. "Beam me up, Scotty."'

'That's *Star Trek*, not *Star Wars*.'

'Oh, they're different? Someone watched a lot of TV in Chile.'

'It was practically all they had us do.'

Alva sighed. 'Lucky. I adore TV. But I jumped to 1790. I was illiterate, I only spoke Swedish, and all I knew how to do was tote water and grow beets and pray. The Guild locked me up in the most dreary castle in Scotland with a red-headed stepchild from Azerbaijan and a sex fiend from Alsace-Lorraine. I learned to read with the *New England Primer*, which is enough to drive anyone mad, and then advanced to an endless course of David Hume . . . But. Enough of that.' She threw open the door to the transporter. 'Nice, isn't it?'

Nick stepped inside. 'But it's a pub!' And it was. At first glance it was like the perfect country inn from his own time. Beautifully cosy, with low-beamed ceilings, fires crackling in the fireplaces and big, comfortable chairs set by the hearths. There were solid oak tables laid for eating, and candles flickering here and there in wall sconces. But on second glance, there was a pinball machine in a corner, a dartboard on one wall and a mantelpiece piled high with paperback novels, a skull teetering on top. In another corner a wind-up Victrola opened its enormous red mouth into the room, and against a wall by the bar there stood a yellow upright piano

384

with an intricate symbol painted above the keys: a many-spoked wheel, surrounded by eyes. A tuba and a trombone were crammed on top of the piano, and a banjo lay on its bench. A dusty disco ball hung off to the right.

Nick turned around, taking it all in. 'What's the idea?'

Alva leaned in the doorway, her arms crossed. 'This is where we gather most nights. The Ofan who are visiting and those of us who are making our homes here. We hang out, drink, talk, make music, dance – fight, laugh, fall in love, break up – we argue about who the Ofan were and who we are and what we should aim to become. It's a place of community, I suppose. It's been here for ever, and it's got such a strong feeling to it, such a powerful sense of place and belonging and purpose, such a constant flow of feeling outwards in every direction, that it's very easy to jump to. People come and go from here as easily as hopping on and off a bar stool. And for those of us who gather here of an evening – well, we know we're feeding the atmosphere, keeping it going.' She smiled at him. 'Make sense?'

Nick nodded. 'It does. I can almost feel it.'

Alva put her hand on his arm. 'Don't. Not yet. But . . .' She stepped into the room. 'Would you like a beer? I know it's early . . .'

Another morning beer with another powerful time-travelling woman who was about to blow his mind. Nick opened his hands. 'How could I possibly refuse?'

Alva went behind the bar and pulled them each a silver tankard of beer. Nick hooked his leg over a bar stool and watched. 'Where does the smoke from the fireplaces go? I don't remember chimneys sticking up out of Soho Square.'

She pushed his tapered mug across to him. 'We're not under the square any more. Our catacombs extend under the surrounding streets. These chimneys are connected to a house up top.' Alva sipped her beer. Behind the bar, with her glasses perched on her nose and her careful coif beginning to slip, she looked, Nick thought, less and less real and more and more like a creature from a dream. She ought to have cat's whiskers, or wings.

'What is the Guild?' She asked it as if she didn't know, as if she were the most innocent of children.

'Is that a rhetorical question?' He curved his hand around the tankard. It wasn't silver, he realized. It was pewter. Nick hoped it was twenty-first-century pewter and that the Ofan knew about lead poisoning. He lifted it and drank, and enjoyed how gentle the alloy felt against the teeth, how the beer flowing from it tasted smoother. Another set of sensations he'd forgotten.

Alva propped her elbows on the bar, made a cradle of her interlaced fingers and rested her chin in it. 'I'm waiting for your answer.'

'The Guild is an organization,' Nick said. 'A corporation. A government.'

'Yes . . . it's all of those things. But what else?'

'Alice Gacoki – she is the Alderwoman in the early twenty-first century –'

'I know who she is.'

'She said the Guild is gearing up to be at war with the Ofan. So I suppose the Guild is also an army.'

'War . . .' Alva sighed, and all the magic went out of her face. She looked like what she really was – a woman with cares and frustrations. 'She used the word "war", did she?'

'Yes.'

'Alice can be so blind!'

'She says the same about you, you know. And the rest of them seemed to agree about the coming war. Penture and Ahn and Arkady and the cheese inspector –'

'The what?'

Nick held up a hand. 'You don't want to know.'

'From the look on your face I'm fairly sure I do want to know!'

'Her name is Marjory Northway.'

Alva made a sour-milk expression. 'She's a real . . . well. Let's just say she isn't nearly warm enough to be the thing I was about to call her.'

Nick raised his eyebrows. 'Wow. You really don't like her.'

'That's an understatement. I'm surprised you do.'

'I don't.'

'But you slept with her.'

'Oh, my God.' Nick scraped his bar stool back and stood. 'You know that, too?'

Alva laughed and clapped her hands. 'I didn't! I guessed! And you fell into my trap!'

'You are all crazy. All of you. Guild, Ofan . . . total nutters.' He drank.

'Yes, probably. But we are crazy in different ways. Shall we sit?' She pushed her glasses up the bridge of her nose, picked up her tankard, came round to his side of the bar and pulled out a chair at a small table.

Nick took a seat across from her. The tabletop was quarter-sawn oak, and the tiger stripes of the grain shimmered in the firelight. The warmth from the crackling flames enveloped Nick. He could feel the currents and eddies of time all around him, gentle, inviting. 'I like it here,' he said, stretching his legs under the table. 'If this is insanity, it feels good.'

'Yes, and we want it to last. It used to last. Before everything changed.' She propped her elbows on the table and leaned towards him. 'Have they told you?'

'About the Pale?'

'Yes. About the Pale, and the Talisman, and all of it.'

Nick laced his hands behind his head and leaned back. 'I doubt they've told me all of it, Alva. The Guild is stingy with its information. But yes. When you say "Pale" and "Talisman" I understand you. I'm supposed to get you to tell me what the Talisman is and where it is. Perhaps you keep it in your bodice with your glasses.'

She gave his sally a perfunctory smile, but it died immediately. 'I do not hold out much hope that a magical object will save us from the Pale. But we get ahead of ourselves. You were answering my question. The Guild is a corporation, a government, I think you said? And according to Alice et al. it is now also an army preparing for war.'

'The Guild hasn't gone to war before? There's never been a grand Guild–Ofan confrontation?'

Alva shook her head. 'No, never. We haven't been enemies, exactly. More like rivals. Sometimes even friendly rivals.'

'Friendly rivals? But Arkady hates you. And when I say he hates you, I mean he hates your guts. Says the Ofan killed his daughter.'

Alva winced. 'Oh, Nick,' she said. 'You don't understand because you have joined us . . . after. After Eréndira died. After the future turned on itself and the Pale began moving towards us.' She pinched the bridge of her nose under her glasses and closed her eyes. 'Everything is different now. Before, the Guild was the Guild and the Ofan were the Ofan. We were experimenting with the talent, they were insisting that we already knew enough. We stood for knowledge, they stood for stability. We were little, they were big. We were hip, they were stodgy. Blah blah blah. We disliked each other cordially, but we coexisted. Now . . .' She dropped her hand and her glasses readjusted themselves. Her eyes were wet. She looked at Nick and for just a moment she looked helpless and lost, this woman who lived her life on the edge of time.

'Just tell me,' Nick said gently. 'Now . . . ?'

'It's hard to say what "now" is, when the Pale is coming closer and closer. I suppose I mean that now the battle lines are being drawn, all up and down the river. The rumours are flying – the Pale is the fault of the Ofan, there is a talisman that could save us, the Ofan are hiding it . . . Everyone is desperate, and desperation is dangerous. The Guild is arming itself against us – as if we are to blame for what's coming. Fools! Fighting us won't stop the Pale.' She pressed her lips together, struggling with some strong emotion.

'How do you know the Ofan are not to blame?'

'Nobody knows who is to blame! Perhaps we are. Perhaps our experiments disrupted something. I doubt it, but I can't say for sure. But that isn't even the point. If we caused the Pale we don't know how we did it, or when. It will be no good killing us all. The Pale will still come.'

'But Eréndira –'

'Died after the Pale began. She was trying to pierce it. Trying to learn about it. The Pale isn't Eréndira's fault.' Alva bit her lip and the tears spilled over her cheeks. 'It was her killer. And now the Guild will go to war against us – they say it is to save the world, but Arkady's grief is behind it. It is revenge.'

'Surely not,' Nick said. 'War . . . it is not a game.'

'No, but it is a business. The Guild has always thrived on war.' Alva's voice was bitter. 'Now they are simply doing the work themselves.'

'I'm completely lost, Alva. The Guild *thrives* on war?'

'Of course! The Guild exists because of the wars Naturals fight. Wars of conquest. The Guild funds war, and it harvests war. Indeed, who can say which came first? Armies or the Guild?'

'What the hell are you talking about?'

She let out a long breath. In the firelight, her magnified

eyes glowed with luminous intensity. 'All right. I'm sorry. Let's back up.' She opened her hands. 'We endlessly say that time is a river. We describe it that way so often that we tend to forget it's just a figure of speech. But what else besides a river is described as having *flow*?'

'Hair?'

The violet eyes blinked, once.

And Nick knew. It was that feeling, when understanding begins to trickle in, when you know that soon it will burst the dam and that in a moment or two more you will see the world entirely differently from the way you do now. 'Money,' he said slowly. 'Money flows.'

Alva nodded.

'The Guild is . . . a bank?'

'Yes. It trades in futures. Actually, the plural is wrong. It trades in future. In *the* future. In one, singular, unalterable future.'

'Okay,' Nick said, excitement taking hold. 'I get it! So the Guild speculates on the uncertainty of future markets. Hedge funds. Hedging your bets.'

'Yes.'

'But the Guild doesn't have to speculate, does it? It doesn't have to hedge its bets because it *knows* the future.'

'Right.'

'And that's why the past *must* stay the same. So that the future stays the same. I thought they were rich because they knew the past. But it's because they know the future. They know every single thing that's going to happen, right up until the end of the world!'

'But now the end of the world has changed,' Alva said, her voice very soft. 'Do you see, Nick, why they are desperate? Why we are desperate? The end has turned around and is racing back towards the beginning.'

Nick looked at Alva and she looked back at him. Her face was as placid as if they were discussing the weather. For the first time Nick let himself really think about the Pale and what it meant. He gripped the table half a second before he felt panic blow through him full force, panic in the form of the river, cold and deep, and it was filling his lungs, his eyes . . .

'Nick!'

Someone was shouting his name.

'Nick!'

He felt a tickle on his face, like the wing of a butterfly. And then a sharp pain, like a wasp sting.

He slapped his hand to his cheek and heard a chuckle. He opened his eyes. He was on the floor of the pub, and Alva was bending over him. 'What happened?'

'I had to slap you, like I had to slap Henry,' she said, smiling.

Nick clambered to his feet and slumped into his chair. He put his head in his hands. 'It's getting worse,' he said. 'The more I am aware of the river, the more it seems to drag at me. Thinking about the Pale just now . . .'

Alva put her hand on his shoulder. 'It is because you aren't trained,' she said. 'They sent you back with no training and expected you to be safe. It's as if a pilot had taken you up in an aeroplane and then handed you the controls and said, "Land it."'

Nick groaned. 'Then train me, for the love of God. I'm fit, I'm halfway intelligent, I'm a soldier – train me!'

'Training takes months, Nick. To learn to jump, and to learn to do it safely –'

'Yes, yes, I know. They told me. It takes too long. But there must be something I can do to keep from being swept away every time I think about the river.'

Alva sat down opposite him again. 'When it happens, what does it feel like?'

'Like all of time is stampeding through me – like a wind or a . . . well, like a river. And I am like a little boat, or a leaf – clinging to my mooring by the most fragile of threads . . .' Nick found that his hand was in his pocket. He drew out the acorn.

'What is that?'

Nick closed his fingers. He didn't want her to see it.

'An acorn.' She answered her own question. 'The fruit of unenclosed land.'

'Pardon?'

'That's what *acorn* means. "The fruit of unenclosed land."' She smiled at him.

He clenched the acorn tightly in his fist and drew a deep breath. 'I am in love,' he said.

Her eyes opened wide, but she said nothing.

'And this acorn . . . it is . . . it reminds me of that love.' He found that confessing it felt good. 'I don't know why, but it is.' Nick felt calmer now. The rushing in his ears receded. He smiled at Alva. 'There. That's my secret. You have the Pale and the Talisman and time travel and these catacombs. I have an acorn.'

Alva nodded. 'I understand.' She sipped her beer and he sipped his. The moment felt . . . brotherly.

'May I ask you,' Alva said after a moment, 'is that acorn from here? I mean, is it from 1815? Not the twenty-first century?'

'Yes. It is from now.'

Alva sucked in her cheeks. 'I wonder . . .' She tapped the tabletop with one finger. 'I think your acorn might be your salvation. I can't train you to jump in one day, but I might be able to help you anchor yourself firmly to this time. Do you trust me?'

'Of course.'

She smiled. 'You say that quickly, you who are meant to betray me.'

'I think you know that I –' He stopped.

'That you are Ofan?'

Nick frowned. He didn't know if that was what he had been about to say.

Alva shook her head. 'No, never mind. I do not need you to swear allegiance.' She stood. 'Come. Get up. I'd like to try something.'

Nick got to his feet.

Alva took his hands.

'Are we going to jump? This is what Arkady did when –'

'Don't worry. You are in the transporter. At the very worst you'll jump to some Ofan bar brawl in the fifteenth century and they'll just bring you back to me here. But I think this will work. I'm going to begin to jump with you, but I will let go of you just as we enter the river. When that happens, I want you to think about that acorn. Use it to stay here. To resist the river. I don't want you to touch it, for this exercise is about your mind, Nick, not about the acorn itself.' She squeezed his fingers. 'Are you ready?'

'No! What are you doing?'

But she was already doing it. Jumping with Alva was not like jumping with Arkady. With Arkady the feeling had been located in the gut, but with Alva it was in the head. Vertigo . . . he was tumbling, his thoughts were flying away . . . and then Alva let go of his hands and he was lost, tumbling away down a long, dark tunnel . . .

The acorn. She had said to think of the acorn . . . don't reach for it. Do it with your mind. Do it with your mind. He pictured the acorn, its shiny pale brown flanks, its nubbly cap . . . Julia. Julia's dark eyes. Julia's soft hand cupping his cheek, her kisses, sweet and urgent . . .

He opened his eyes. He was in the pub, and he felt strong and alive and firmly planted. Alva was smiling at him. Nothing had changed.

'There,' she said. 'The acorn will keep you here. That's all you have to do next time.'

'Do *you* think it is possible to stop the Pale?' Nick was standing behind the bar, washing up their tankards in a bucket of soapy water. Alva sat across from him, eating a packet of lamb-and-mint-flavoured crisps she'd pulled out of a drawer. She had described them as 'the really evil ones, from the 1980s'.

'No,' she said. 'I don't think it. I believe it. But belief is more fragile than thought. I believe that the Pale can be turned back. But I might be wrong.'

'You can't be wrong,' Nick said, his voice hoarse. 'Surely there's hope.' He set the two tankards upside down on a folded linen towel and planted his hands on the bar, his arms braced.

'I hope so. But all I base my belief on is human nature.'

'Then we're doomed.' Nick plucked a crisp from her packet and popped it in his mouth. 'Humans are the scum of the earth.'

Alva put her head on one side. 'Maybe,' she said. 'But we exist, and therefore we have to try to do good rather than bad.' She ripped the silvery bag along its seam and opened it out to make eating the crisps easier. 'We have talents – ranging from perfect pitch to towering artistic or scientific genius. We usually celebrate these things as gifts from God. So by what right does the Guild say that your ability to manipulate time, which you share with a small fraction of your kind, is too dangerous for you to handle? Surely this talent – this gift – wouldn't exist if we weren't supposed to use it.'

'Maybe it's a curse. Some people are driven to do unspeakable things and they do them well. We don't encourage it.'

Alva rolled her eyes and ate a crisp. 'Please. You know that having our talent isn't the same as being a psychopath. If there is anything that unites the Ofan, that defines us, it is that we want to learn more about our gift. Now that the Pale is coming, we think we might be able to use it to help. But the Guild, with its vaunted tale of protecting the river, is slowly destroying our chance. Going to war against us – for God's sake, it would be like going to war against the Island of Misfit Toys.'

Nick laughed. 'The Misfit Toys band together and save Christmas.'

Alva touched her nose with the tip of her finger. 'Bingo!'

'You're mad.'

'I've already admitted that. But just because I'm paranoid doesn't mean they're not out to get me. The Guild's money and their power – no, let me go even one step further – the very *existence* of the Guild depends upon war. Because that is their beginning, they cannot imagine a way out of it also being their end. Their omega must follow from their alpha. Trouble is, their finale is everyone else's too. They don't give us a choice. They don't even let us know about it!'

Nick shook his head and fished a particularly dark, extra-crispy crisp from the diminishing pile. 'You're foaming at the mouth, Alva. How the hell does the Guild's existence depend on war?' He crunched the crisp between his teeth. There is nothing, he thought to himself, like trans fats.

Alva, meanwhile, was staring at him incredulously. 'Surely you've figured that much out. War is the Guild's recruitment machine.'

Nick swallowed and gave her back her look. 'Rubbish. The Guild might be greedy and secretive, but they want to ease the suffering. They pick us up and dust us off and teach us medieval Finnish . . .'

Alva threw up her hands. 'Oh, use your head. You jumped from battle. I, too. I jumped from war – my village was sacked and I . . . well. It doesn't matter.' Alva was quiet for a moment, making a line of crisps across the bar. When she looked up the passion in her eyes was banked and she spoke with quiet certitude. 'What is the Guild without its thousands of workers, Nick? Without the drones who make it all run? Nine out of ten of us jump from war, did you know that?' She picked up a crisp from her line and broke it into pieces between her fingers, letting the crumbs fall. 'War loosens our bonds to our natural time.' She broke another. 'It sets us leaping like fish from the river. And the Guild is waiting for us with its nets. Some of us they keep, some they throw away.'

'What the hell do you mean? They take everyone they can find.'

'Oh, no they most certainly do not!' Alva dusted off her fingers. 'Think back to Chile. Who were your fellow inductees?' She sucked the salt and oil from her thumb. 'Were any of them crazy? Homicidal?' She popped her forefinger in her mouth and gave it the same treatment. 'Disabled? Maimed?'

'No.'

'Exactly. And those are the obvious things they weren't. There are a lot of other filters, too. War traumatizes, and the Guild needs its members to be shocked and scared but not broken. Nor even breakable. Your run-of-the-mill Guild member isn't an artist or a hermit or another lonely visionary type; the Guild wants team players. And they aren't, for the most part, your ministers or your sea captains either; the Guild doesn't want too many inspirational or leader types. They fish the river for hard workers, followers, good-natured burghers. People who want to settle down and remake their lives as best they can.'

'I suppose that describes me.' Nick picked up a cloth and began wiping down the counter. 'But I had two friends there . . . one was a genius. I mean, he had a gift for languages like nothing I've ever seen. And he wasn't a follower. Neither was the other one.'

'Ah. But you see, they bait their hooks for another kind of fish, as well.' She reached across the bar and touched his ring. 'Your kind of fish. Men and women who were powerful in their time. Either because they were born to power, or because they have extravagant beauty or a shining personality or great genius. You were a marquess. A prize indeed. Power. That was what they saw in you when you jumped.'

'Beauty and genius too, surely.'

She inclined her head. 'Of course, my lord.'

'And the ones who don't make the grade? They are Ofan?'

'No. Not necessarily.' Alva twisted her mouth in a regretful smile. 'We are not saviours. We are simply a haven for those who manage to find us. We provide our members with, at the very least, a good pub.'

Nick couldn't laugh at that. What would it be like to jump . . . to nothing? To be deemed too weird or too impassioned for the Guild? And to never find the Ofan?

Alva put her chin in her hands and watched him. 'You're judging us,' she said.

'I'm sorry for the others,' he said.

'It's a cruel world. And the Ofan are selfish. We aren't a secret, but we don't advertise. If you find us you can join us. We will teach anyone who asks – just as I have taught you something today. And we will answer any questions. But you must find us and you must ask.' She shrugged. 'At least we aren't cannibals, feeding off the destruction of the world.'

'And the Guild is?' Nick hung the two dry mugs on their hooks over the bar. 'You've said they use war to recruit. What you call recruitment, surely they see it as saving people like us from the horrors of conflict among Naturals?'

'Yes, that is what they think. And I'm sure they've told you that the Guild is a global organization with a presence in every age. But it isn't true, Nick. The Guild is a bank, you said, and you were right. Have there been banks in every human culture? In every age? No. Follow the money, follow the mercantile economy, follow the flow . . . and you will find the Guild. No money, no market economy? No time travel, no Guild. It's that simple.'

'So?'

Alva banged her hands down on the table and her eyes turned on again like black lights in a disco. 'It's clear as day! What makes markets? Armies! Set armies on the march, and money flows! Set an army moving across the landscape and you have the trickling beginnings of an economy, for they must eat, Nick. They must be paid. Turn your farmers into warriors and then into consumers. Now blow that picture up big. Set the world at war across time and space. Move your armies and your money further and faster and deeper . . . before you know it you have a river. That river doesn't flow with water, Nick, and it doesn't flow with love. It flows with blood and money!'

Nick looked down at the foil crisp bag, then picked it up and scrunched it into a ball. Surely war itself wasn't the Guild's fault. Surely money wasn't the Guild's fault. Take away the Guild, and the milk of human kindness wouldn't just bubble up from the sewers. Take away money, and people wouldn't just turn to one another and start singing 'Kumbaya'. Take away war, and money wouldn't just become scrap paper. He sighed, and looked for a waste-paper basket. When he couldn't find one, he glanced up at Alva. 'What do you do with anachronistic rubbish?'

'Just leave it. Gordon is the bartender. He'll deal with it later.'

Nick opened his hand and the bag uncrumpled with a tinny crackle. He wiped his greasy palm on the linen towel. The silence between them lasted a moment too long, and was suddenly awkward.

'My lover . . .' Alva paused. 'Ignatz Vogelstein, my lover who recently died, used to wind me up just to see me go. I'm sorry I let myself get worked up just now.'

'It's fine,' Nick said.

'No. This was all too much to lay on you.' She looked down at her long, ringless fingers. 'You're writing the Ofan off as crazed conspiracy theorists now. And maybe we are. Who knows? The real point is, whether I'm right or wrong about the Guild's past, we can all agree that the future – the Pale – isn't acceptable.'

'No,' Nick said. 'It isn't. And I'm a grown-up. You don't have to protect me from your version of the truth.'

'It's just that the Guild's plan – of just keeping on doing what they've always done, with the added distraction of killing Ofan – isn't going to save them or us from the Pale. Maybe there is a talisman. Maybe we can find it and use it. I think it's more likely that we will have to follow in Eréndira's footsteps and risk everything to find the change we need . . . and that even then we might fail.'

Nick looked at the beautiful, contradictory woman who stood before him. Whore, philosopher, queen. He had known that she would mess with his head when he accepted her invitation to drink beer together, but he had no idea that his entire world would be shattered into smithereens down here in this weird simulacrum of a pub. 'Jesus H. Christ,' he said.

'Yes. Mr J. H. Christ saw it all for what it is. And he wasn't alone. A lot of people can see the forest for the trees. Natural and Ofan alike.'

'Don't tell me Jesus was Ofan!'

'Don't worry.' Alice slipped off her bar stool. 'He won't be turning up in this pub.'

Nick laughed, a little shakily.

Alva spared Nick a brief smile, but it faded quickly. 'The situation couldn't be more serious,' she said. 'The future has changed, in spite of the Guild's shepherding. They are scared, as well they should be. Their own future, their tame and miserable slave, has turned and is marching toward them. Towards us all.'

'Like a cornered tiger. That's how Ahn described it to me.'

'Ahn should know.'

Alva went to the door and opened it, turning back and raising her eyebrows at Nick, who was still standing behind the bar like a moose in the headlights. 'Are you coming back up to the sunlit lands with me, or do you intend to stay and become our publican?'

Nick stood on the top steps of the house in Soho Square. Solvig was fastened to a leather leash, and he was taking her home with him. In spite of his protests the huge animal was now his, and she seemed to know it. She stood by him, panting happily, her eyes fixed on his face.

As for Alva, the intensity she had succumbed to in the catacombs had lifted like a fog. 'Don't worry about the end of the world,' she said. 'We are time travellers! We will sail our little skiffs up and down the river until we get it right. For now, you and I must play the game of marquess and mistress. When shall we meet again?'

'Must we actually go through with the charade? Surely not.'

'We absolutely must. The Guild has to believe that you are tricking me, and that I am enthralled with you. We are all searching for the Talisman, you see. And if you or I find it? If the Guild believes that you have conquered me, we will have a much better chance of selling them a lie about its whereabouts. So. Tonight? Shall we have dinner in some public place?'

Nick sighed. 'Fine.'

Alva laughed. 'You remind me of Ignatz! He was just as grumpy.'

'The last thing I want to do is remind you of your lover!'

Alva stared at him, shocked, her eyes filling immediately with tears.

Nick could have bitten his tongue out. Why had he said such a cruel thing? 'Oh, my God, I'm so sorry. I only meant . . . I didn't mean –'

'No. Don't. I know what you meant.' She wiped her eyes quietly with her handkerchief. 'And I didn't mean that you remind me of him as a lover. It's just . . .' She put her head on one side. 'I miss him. He was an irascible old man and a terrible rake, but I loved him dearly. He was a scholar, a teacher, a great Ofan . . .'

'He was Ofan? The Guild thinks your lover was a Natural. Some rich old Englishman.'

'They are idiots.' She smiled. 'And in their idiocy lies our greatest chance of success. Now, before you go, I must tell you the only thing I know about the Talisman. The only thing the Guild does not know.' She looked straight into his eyes. 'I decided to trust you long ago, Nick. And I have not asked you for promises. But what I am about to tell you . . . you must not tell the Guild.'

Nick looked up over her head and into the square. Could she trust him? He put his hand on Solvig's broad head, felt the confident, innocent warmth of the animal. Solvig had chosen him in spite of the fact that he didn't need her. Didn't particularly want her. And the Ofan seemed to have chosen him as well, for equally obscure reasons. He looked back into Alva's eyes. 'I promise,' he said.

She spoke easily, without whispering, without drama. 'When the future changed, and we became aware of the Pale, Ignatz and those of us who were close to him dedicated ourselves to study. Thirteen of us. We set up the Ofan research station near Cachoeira, in Brazil, and we started trying to learn about the Pale. Then Eréndira disappeared over the Pale and we could not find her. Ignatz came back to England and the late eighteenth century a broken man. Eréndira reappeared, only to die. Ignatz called Arkady and he arrived in time to hold her as she slipped away. Ignatz was inconsolable. He left London and the Ofan community here. He spent the last twenty years of his life in near solitude, buried in the country. He came to London only rarely, and only to see me. The Ofan almost forgot about him, and the Guild lost track of him altogether; they thought he was dead. Then, just a month or so ago, I received a letter from him. The letter was cryptic in the extreme; he explained that he was dying, of a fast-moving disease, but he said that he knew for a fact that the Talisman was more than a rumour. It was too dangerous to spell out the details in a letter. But he said that I must race to find it before the Guild. That was all the letter said. He signed it without love, without a personal greeting. Another letter followed a day later, addressed in Ignatz's hand but delivered by a special courier. I tore it open, thinking that this would be his farewell to me. But the page was empty except for a symbol. I have only ever seen that symbol in one other place.'

'Where?'

'In the design of Eréndira's ring.'

'Then that ring is the Talisman! Surely that's the obvious inference. What does the ring look like?'

'It is small, but intricate. Passed down through her family for many generations. The symbol is abstract; you wouldn't recognize it unless it was pointed out to you. It is an eye in a circle.'

'Was it buried with her? Did she leave it to anyone?'

'When I last saw Eréndira – when she was dying the ring, which she wore every day, was gone.'

'Then Arkady has it. He must.'

'Ah. But he doesn't, for he asked for it after her death and was enraged when it couldn't be found. The story goes that one of Eréndira's great grandfathers was a coppersmith, murdered in the Spanish conquest and plundering of the P'urhépechas. This one ring was saved by a daughter, who passed it to her daughter, who passed it to Eréndira's mother. Eréndira's mother was misguided enough to fall in love with Arkady Altukhov, have Eréndira, and pass the ring on to her. But the ring was gone by the time Arkady got to Eréndira's bedside.'

'So we have to find a small copper ring. We have no idea where it is. I am somehow integral to this search, and yet I have never met any of the characters involved.' Nick laughed. 'Where the hell am I even supposed to start? For that matter, why me at all? Why am I not still driving around in my pickup in Vermont?' Solvig whuffed at the anger she could hear in Nick's voice, and he pulled on one of her ears as he glared at Alva.

Alva just smiled. 'Poor Nick. None of it is really about you. It's about your land and your position. Arkady brought you back for two reasons, reasons he does not know are connected. First, he wanted you to help him get close to Castle Dar, where

403

he knows something strange has been going on. What better way than to tie himself to the neighbouring Blackdown estate? Second, he had this wild idea that a virile young marquess could winkle my secrets out of me. It was a wild idea that I encouraged, because I, too, need your help. You see, Nick, I want to get to Castle Dar myself, to search for the Talisman. The reason Castle Dar thrums with time play is that my lover, the great Ofan teacher and scholar, was your neighbour. To the Ofan and the Guild, he was Ignatz Vogelstein. But you knew him as Ignatius Percy, the late Earl of Darchester.'

33

'He's brought home a dog!' Bella came into the drawing room and startled Clare and Julia, who were on the settee, bent over the cushion cover Clare was embroidering, trying to count stitches.

'I cannot understand how I went wrong,' Clare said, glancing up at her sister and then back at her work. 'Look, though.' She held up her frame for Julia to see. 'Apollo's hand is all skewed.'

'Oh, who cares!' Bella snatched the frame away from her sister and tossed it, thread flying, onto an empty chair. 'Did you hear me? Nick has brought home a dog. Move over.' Bella squeezed her small form in between Clare and Julia, and put her arms around their shoulders. 'Is it not lovely all being together?'

'Except that it's like you're eleven years old again.' Clare crossed her arms, refusing to be comfortable.

'Her name is Solvig,' Bella said, ignoring her sister. 'She is enormous. I shall be able to go anywhere with her by my side. Wait until you meet her.' Bella popped up as precipitously as she had wedged herself between them and left the room again, calling Nick's name.

Julia's hand shook as she got up and fetched Clare's embroidery. He was home.

'Are you well?'

'Yes.' Julia clutched the embroidery frame. Only a few days ago she had been able to stand up to Eamon's depravity, even turn back time to keep him from killing her. Now, surrounded by friends and in the lap of luxury, she was entirely off balance, vacillating between fear and joy and absurdly missish confusion.

'Come, sit.'

Julia sat and Clare took the embroidery frame from her. She stroked Julia's hand as she did so. 'Everything is going to be fine,' she said, as if she could read Julia's mind.

Julia said nothing, only watched as Clare untangled her threads.

'I am a spinster, an ape leader,' Clare said after a moment. 'Do you know what that means?'

'That you are unmarried.'

'Yes, but *ape leader*. What does that delightful term mean?'

'Oh, Clare.'

'No, Julia. Say it.' She looked up from her embroidery. 'Say it to my face.'

'Because you have failed to marry and have children, your damnation is to lead the apes in hell.'

'Right.' Clare sat back against the cushions. 'Do you know, it's rather shocking to hear it spoken straight out like that.'

'You made me!'

'Yes, I did. Do you really think that will happen to me?'

'No, of course not. Of course not, Clare, you mooncalf.'

Clare straightened her cap on her head. 'I know I'm neither going to hell nor organizing monkey parades while I'm there. I don't even believe in hell.'

'You don't?'

'No. Do you?'

'I . . . I . . .' Julia realized she had never thought about it. 'Yes, I think I do.'

'Oh,' said Clare. 'How strange. I always felt, you know, that hell was a story made up to frighten us into doing what they want us to do.'

'You sound like my grandfather.'

'I shall take that as a compliment, I suppose. But my point, Julia, is this. They hold whips over our heads to make us be good and do what they want. Many of the whips are imaginary. Or at least I believe them to be so. Hell, for instance, and apes. Other whips are very real. Poverty. Hatred. Loneliness.' Clare smoothed her hand over her deformed Apollo. 'I am lucky. I have an income, friends and family, and a roof over my head. Do you know what that means to me?'

'Happiness?'

Clare looked at Julia, and it wasn't happiness Julia saw in her face. But Clare smiled and said, 'Yes, exactly. Happiness. And just an inch of freedom. But you are an orphan, Julia. And you do not come into your inheritance for three years.'

Julia blinked. Recently other problems had overwhelmed these everyday sorrows. But her old troubles remained, waiting for her, as a cough outlasts a fever.

'I want you to know you may live with us for as long as you like,' Clare said, arranging herself to sew again. 'Do not rush into a marriage simply to be rid of us, or to rid us of you.'

'Thank you,' Julia managed to say.

Clare touched her cheek with a thimbled finger. 'To be honest, Julia, I am not especially fearful for you. You have always had a good head on your shoulders.'

Julia laughed. 'Thank you! I have not had much occasion to use it, locked up at Castle Dar.'

'No, no,' Clare said. 'In my opinion, anyone who manages to survive beyond the age of eighteen with their character intact should be hailed as a hero. Such a person must have the courage of Jason and the strength of Hercules! Most of us do not make it, you know. We emerge on the other side of childhood as spectres, not as real people.' She turned and looked at the enormous portrait of the Falcott family that dominated one wall of the room.

Julia contemplated the painting, too. She usually avoided looking at it, for she did not like what the artist had done with any of the subjects. Bella and Clare were all hair and flowers and the seventh marquess looked like a kindly, if dreary, vicar, when in fact the man had been a self-congratulatory bore who never took notice of anyone but himself. The dowager marchioness was painted to look like a long-suffering angel, which must have flattered her opinion of herself. But the worst part of the painting was the youthful Nicholas, who, as the new marquess, was the centre around which all the movement of the painting swirled. The artist had made him far shinier – hair golden, eyes blue – than he really was, but it wasn't that which repelled her. It was the way the painted youth leaned forward, grasping at attention, his too-pink lip curled in smug self-congratulation. That was not, had never been, Blackdown. Or perhaps it was Blackdown, but it had never been Nick.

Julia glanced at Clare and saw that she, too, was unimpressed. 'My mother loves this painting,' she said.

'I was just thinking that it must be a comfort to her,' Julia said.

Clare rolled her eyes. 'Please. Be honest. It represents the family she wishes were her own. Her dead husband appears to worship her, her daughters are beautiful ninnies, and her son is a smug Adonis. Not a single one of us looks like ourselves, nor appears to have any character at all. Each of those painted people looks tedious to me. And while you may say any number of unpleasant things about the Falcotts, I do not think we are tedious.'

'Meeting men in the kitchens in the middle of night, plotting revolution . . . I'm sorry, Clare. You are a tiresome girl. So dull.'

Clare smiled, but then her eyes grew intent. 'Tell me truly, Julia. Do you think Nick has come back changed?'

Julia blinked and let her eyes stray back to the painting. 'I don't know,' she said.

Clare studied her for a moment, then sat back in her seat with a sigh. 'I am sorry,' she said. 'You do not have to engage me on the topic if you prefer not to.'

Julia frowned. 'I think he has changed beyond recognition. There. Does that satisfy you?'

Clare laughed. 'Prickly! But yes, it does. I think so, too. I am simply at a loss to quite explain what the difference is. That painting, of course, gets him entirely wrong, so it is no use searching there for a clue. See how haughty he looks. In fact, he was overwhelmed. Suddenly, without warning, he was Marquess of Blackdown. My mother became . . . no. My mother *chose* to become impossible. She demanded everything of him, and nothing was good enough.' Clare laid her embroidery aside and contemplated her brother's painted face. 'He disappeared. Long before he disappeared in Spain, he had disappeared into himself. Then he was swallowed by university, and London, and finally war.' She turned to Julia. 'He is a rich and powerful man. Many women would choose him for his money or his position.'

Julia said nothing, and the silence stretched. Clare might goad her to talk about Nick once, but Julia wasn't going to rise to this bait.

Finally, Clare looked down at her hands. 'Well,' she said. 'I only hope that he is eventually chosen by a woman who . . .' She looked back at the painting. 'Who sees him. I suppose that is what I am trying to say. A woman who can really see him.'

'What I don't understand is how you won that animal's undying love in a single morning,' Bella said to the marquess as the three Falcott siblings, plus Julia and Solvig, set out half an hour later for a walk in the park. Blackdown had entered the drawing room with his enormous, ugly dog and he seemed to bring the brightness of the spring day inside with him. Something good has happened to him, Julia thought as he stood smiling down at her and inviting her – and his two sisters, of course – on a walk. Something that has given him purpose.

Hyde Park at midday was sparkling green and fresh after yesterday's rain, the sun was bright, and Julia was arm in arm with Blackdown. His sisters were joking with him about his ridiculous dog, which had an enormous bandage on one paw. For just this hour or two, all was right with the world. The count was off in Devon with Eamon – the fiend fly away with both of them. May they fall into a pit together.

Solvig dragged Bella a few steps ahead, and Clare went with them.

'Penny for your thoughts.' Blackdown's voice was intimate, for her ears only.

'My thoughts are bloodthirsty, I warn you.'

'Tell me now.' He pinched her elbow tightly against his side. 'I want to know your darkest desires.'

'I was imagining Eamon and your count falling together into a fiery pit.'

'Hm.' He seemed to treat it as a scholarly question. 'The fiery pit of hell, or a fiery pit somewhere in Devon? Is this punishment unto death, or punishment after death? For which crimes are the two gentlemen being punished? Eamon I can well understand. I would like to pitchfork him into the pit for you, if you will give me the honour. But why Arkady? Has he been unkind to you?'

Julia could have bitten her own tongue. Of course, Blackdown didn't know she knew about the count and his power.

'I just don't like him,' she said. 'I cannot help but feel that he disapproves of me.'

He took a few steps in silence. 'It does not matter what he thinks of you, Julia. Eamon deserves the pit you have reserved for him. But Arkady is nobody. Forget about him.'

'He is not nobody to you.'

Blackdown stopped and turned to her. 'Arkady *is* nobody to me, do you understand?'

'I think so.' But Julia knew better.

'You don't look as if you understand. You look troubled.'

'You told me . . . that day . . . that you aren't free.'

'That day. When I first kissed your sweet mouth. Is that what you are remembering?' He looked around. The others had drawn ahead, and no one else was near. 'I want nothing more in this world than to kiss you again, right here.'

'It would ruin me,' she laughed. 'Ruin the two of us.'

'It would be a beautiful ruination.'

She shocked them both by dropping his arm and going up on tiptoe to kiss his mouth, quickly. 'There. You are not the only one who dares.'

'Julia!'

She raised her eyebrows at him. 'It pleases you to think you are the only one with courage.'

'Oh, I do not think that.' His smile was gone. 'Your courage encourages me. In fact, I think we ought to walk again, quickly.' He held his arm out.

She took it. They set out walking. Clare and Bella and Solvig were well ahead of them now, and just ahead the path dipped into some trees.

'Did you read the poem?' he asked in a dry tone of voice, as if he were a schoolmaster.

Her blood was singing in her ears. She could barely recall the poem now. She had just kissed him right out under the sun and clouds. And he had liked it. Julia felt a smile spread across her face. 'Oh,' she said nonchalantly. 'It was good enough.'

'Good enough. You minx!' They passed under the trees, and they might have been all alone in a green world. 'So it was all old hat to you, was it?' he asked softly. 'One of the most erotic poems in the English language?'

She shrugged. 'Maybe.'

With a quick motion he grabbed her waist and pulled her close against him; she laughed, but his face was very serious. 'Really, Julia? I would very much like to test your comprehension.'

She pushed her hands against his chest. 'Let me go, you provoking man. I *understood* it very well.'

He released her and took her arm again. 'All right, then,' he said as they resumed walking, 'answer me this. What does John Donne say about freedom?'

Julia blinked. 'Freedom? *Freedom* was not what I was paying attention to in that poem.'

'And you claim to have read it carefully? Tut, tut, Miss Percy. I am disappointed in you.'

'Oh.' She sketched him a low curtsey. 'Mr Schoolmaster Lord Blackdown, sir. I am sorry to have fallen in your regard.' She held out her hand, palm up. 'I am ready for the ruler.'

'No, listen, Julia.' He caught the hand she held out and kissed the palm, then held it firmly as they continued walking. 'The poem isn't simply about . . .' She felt him searching for a word and was glad when he chose the plainest one. 'It isn't simply about sex. Listen.' He quoted: '"How am I blest in thus discovering thee! To enter in these bonds, is to be free."'

They walked hand in hand for a moment, Julia's playful courage dissipating. 'I don't understand what you are saying, my lord.'

'You have called me Nicholas before. Please dispense with this "my lord"-ing.'

'I cannot call you Nicholas in public. You are Blackdown.'

'I am not Blackdown.' His voice was harsh, and his fingers tightened painfully around hers.

'Are you not?' She looked up at his angry face. 'Is that not the most signal thing about you?'

His hand relaxed. 'I'm sorry.' He managed a small smile. 'I know it makes no sense. It's just that I spent years liberated of that man, and I didn't miss him at all. Now I'm back and I find it hard to make peace with him.'

'You had amnesia.'

'Yes,' he said slowly. 'Across those years that I had forgotten myself, I became a different man. A man named Nick Davenant. Now that I am returned, I find that I don't care very much for this great marquess, this Lord Blackdown.'

She said nothing but held his hand tightly. Nick Davenant.

Meanwhile Nick – she could never think of him as Blackdown again – dropped his gaze to their clasped hands. 'When we last spoke about such grandiose topics as freedom, after that kiss, at the edge of the woods . . .'

'You told me you were not free.'

'I was not speaking of another woman, Julia.'

'I know. You were talking of the count.'

He stared. 'How do you know that?'

The truth wanted to burst from her. No . . . it wanted to rise from her like a feather on a breath of wind. But instead she dropped her gaze from his and walked more quickly, pulling on his hand. Who, then, was this Nick Davenant, this new man? She could not quite bring herself to trust him . . . or to break faith with Grandfather.

They emerged from the trees into the sunlight and Nick took her arm decorously again, but she could feel the tension

413

in him. When he spoke, his voice was low and urgent. 'What do you know about Count Lebedev? What do you know about me? What do you know . . . about your grandfather?'

'My grandfather?' Julia's heart lurched. This was cutting to the heart of the matter. Soon enough he would be asking her about time! 'Nothing,' she said emphatically, her memory flashing to Grandfather on his deathbed, begging her to pretend. Her thoughts toppled into panic. 'Oh, God!'

Nick grabbed her hand and held it again, clearly not caring who might see. 'Look at me!'

She met his gaze with caution.

'What do you know about your grandfather?'

She pulled back. 'Let me go!'

He dropped her hand, but his voice gained in urgency. 'You can trust me, Julia. I won't betray you. I am . . . oh, bloody hell, just give me your hand again! I need to touch you.'

She held it out, feeling somewhat unreal, and he took and placed her palm firmly against his chest. 'I consider myself bound to you. And I *am* also free. Do you understand? I told you I was not free, that day in the rain. But I rescind those words. Remember the poem, Julia. "To enter in these bonds, is to be free." Do you understand?'

'I think so.' She could feel his heart beating, and her panic sank again. 'I . . . I don't know why you would ask me about Grandfather.'

Nick searched her face. 'You really don't know? You don't know anything?'

'I don't know what I know. He told me nothing!' She shook her head, to dispel the rushing of blood in her head, the terrible loneliness and fear. 'I know nothing!'

'We must talk,' he said, letting her hand go. 'Privately. And soon.'

She whispered, 'I can't tell you anything.'

Nick frowned, his eyes bleak. Then he glanced up. His sisters were looking back at them. 'We must keep walking.'

He took her arm once more and they walked in tense silence, her elbow tucked so tightly against his side that she could feel the way his body moved beneath his coat.

'What is Count Lebedev to you?' she asked, once Bella and Clare seemed distracted again by Solvig's antics.

Nick puffed up his cheeks and blew the air out slowly as he searched for words. 'In a way, Arkady is a fellow soldier. But I don't know if we are comrades in arms or enemies. It is very hard – impossible – to explain.'

'Count Lebedev has power over you,' she said slowly. 'But not, perhaps, as much as he thinks? Is that it?'

Nick nodded. 'In a way, I am bound to him. *He* doesn't think I am free. He thinks me his lackey. For the time being I must pretend. I must seem to do as he says. But I am determined to be free, Julia, and I would never betray you to him. Do you understand me now?'

So they were both pretending. 'Yes,' Julia said with more certainty. 'You are not free, but you want to be. Arkady is your friend, but he is also your enemy. You are searching for a pathway through, a pathway that will lead you to . . .' She paused, letting herself really look at him, not as Lord Blackdown but as Nick Davenant, a man who had forgotten all his ancient prejudices and manners, and discovered now that he was happy to have lost them. 'A pathway that will lead you to yourself,' she said.

His serious expression didn't change. 'Not just to myself. To you, too.'

In the time it took for her to take a step, she knew that she loved him. 'Yes,' she agreed. 'To me, too.'

Clare, Bella and the dog had stopped up ahead and were playing with a stick. Nothing could have been more prosaic.

Three siblings and their friend walk in the park, not even at the fashionable hour. But Julia felt changed, through and through. The air filling her lungs felt different. And every time she chanced to look up at Nick, he was looking down at her.

'How do you do that?' he asked.

'Do what?'

'Every time I try to steal a look at you, you catch me at it. You are a witch.'

'Perhaps you are able to tell when *I* am stealing a look at *you.*'

She recognized that look – it made her skin tingle. But Solvig, in spite of her bandaged paw, had loped up and was gambolling in a heavy circle around her idol and therefore also around Julia. Solvig's face was upturned, love radiating from her goggling eyes. Julia gestured at the dog. 'There's a lady who wants nothing more in the world than to look at you.'

'Heel, Solvig.' Nick brought the dog to his other side. 'Now, Julia. You will have to compete for my attentions.'

Julia disengaged her arm. 'Oh, no. I yield.' In spite of Nick's protests, she walked ahead to join Bella, and Clare fell back to walk with Nick.

34

Three days later, and no sharing of secrets had occurred. Julia had only seen Nick twice, both times at breakfast, in the company of servants and the dowager marchioness. Each day Bella bragged about how late her brother had been out the night before and speculated on how much fun he was having in what she relished calling 'the fleshpots of London'.

'Enough,' Clare finally snapped as the three young women were walking to Hatchards, Solvig ahead of them on a leather lead, two footmen trailing behind. 'Nick is not a libertine, Bella. We must all be eternally grateful that you are not a man, for you would clearly rake the coals of hell and fan the flames of vice from one end of the year to the other.'

'Indeed I would.' Bella stroked the dog's head. 'Solvig could be my devilish hound, couldn't you?'

The enormous creature looked up at the sound of her name. As the days had passed, Solvig had revealed herself to be entirely craven, going so far as to run from a mouse in the kitchen and try to hide under the cook's skirts, a misadventure that had resulted in her permanent banishment from below stairs.

'Besides,' Bella said, 'I learned all about Nick's recent activities when Mother and I were at Almack's last night. He has been cutting quite the swathe through the town, if the gossips are to be believed. Julia, it is so unfortunate that you cannot come to balls when you are in mourning. You are missing all the diversion.'

Julia indulged herself in a moment of self-pity. It was true.

Clare stayed home with her most evenings, but Bella and her mother were out at balls and routs and masquerades night after night. Bella always came home bursting with some thrilling tale of intrigue or some hint of scandal that she'd heard from the gossips. For the last few days these had mostly involved Nick, blast him. 'Maybe next year,' Julia said.

'Yes. As I have not met a single gentleman I can imagine marrying, I shall have to come back next year, too. It will be delightful.' Bella linked her arm with Julia's.

'What did you learn about Nick last night?' Julia tried to sound nonchalant, but Bella laughed.

'Good show, Julia. But you can't hide from us. We know you are breaking your heart over him, don't we, Clare?'

'Arabella!' Clare spoke sharply.

'Oh. It is serious.' Bella waggled her eyebrows at Julia. 'Is Nick the apple?'

'Please,' Julia said. 'Just hold your tongue.'

'Even though I heard the most delicious gossip about him last night? May I tell, if we all agree not to believe it?'

Clare rolled her eyes. 'You will tell us with or without our permission, Bella, so get on with it.'

'Well.' She took Clare's and Julia's arms and pulled them close on either side. 'Let us take up the entire pavement and I shall tell you.' She led her sister and her friend by the elbows. 'Apparently Nick has been seen everywhere in the company of the most ravishing cyprian. Rumour has it that he has been publicly lavishing attention on her in all the gaming halls. She is elegantly tall, and blonde, with eyes the most magical shade of violet, and it is said he has given her an amethyst necklace that exactly matches them . . .'

Clare frowned. 'We shall stop discussing this foolishness this minute. Not another word. We are at Hatchards.' She handed Solvig's lead to a footman and swept into the bookseller's.

Bella followed her sister, but not before winking broadly at Julia.

And so one of the moments Julia had looked forward to her entire life was destroyed. She had always thought of Hatchards with reverent delight and looked forward to the day that she would be able to peruse its shelves and choose her own reading materials. And now, instead of revelling in the scent of leather and paper and ink, she felt like wringing Bella's neck with one hand and Nick's with the other. She was the Talisman. She could manipulate time. Count Lebedev was out to kill her. But instead of making any headway on these very real problems, she was standing in a bookshop, teetering on the verge of tears, thinking about her swain kissing another shepherdess. A blonde shepherdess dripping with amethysts.

Bella pulled on her sleeve. She looked contrite, to the extent that a pitchfork-wielding devil can look contrite. 'You are scowling,' she said. 'I'm terribly sorry if I caused you distress.'

Julia thinned her lips and said nothing. Instead she stared at the rows of books and the men and women who stood about, looking into them, not talking to each other. Two dozen people in two dozen different worlds. Worlds of knowledge, beauty, romance, discovery.

'Let me take you to visit my friend, the one I told you about when we were having ices,' Bella said. 'We can leave the footmen and take Solvig. No one will trouble us when we have a dog as big as a pony. Clare will be happy here for a couple of hours until we return.'

Julia turned her head and looked out of the window at the bright spring day. Another two dozen people out in the sunshine, dashing here and there, on their way through their different lives. Happy lives, sad lives – who could tell?

Julia had gone twice in the past two days – humiliating fact – to the cupola. Each time she told herself she was going to practise. And she had, to good effect. She had managed to turn the seconds briefly backwards and to freeze time for as long as forty minutes. It was an exhilarating and terrifying power, this control she had. Terrifying and lonely.

She had hoped that Nick would come and find her practising. That he would find her out. That her secret would be revealed, shared, understood, without her having to decide to tell him. He would sense her shifting time and come up to the cupola to find her there in a bubble of timelessness. He would step into the bubble . . .

Well. The cupola and the fantasy were both castles in the air.

She wheeled and faced Bella. 'Yes,' she said. 'Let's go.'

It was a considerable walk from genteel Hatchards to Soho Square, which sat at the edge of a great slum. Julia was pleased to see that although Bella was adventurous, she wasn't a complete fool; she led them all the way north past the construction that was busily transforming old Swallow Street into the much-vaunted, grandiose New Street. They then turned right along busy Oxford Street, rather than cut through the noisome, dark streets of Soho. Solvig began to get excited and pulled on the lead. Julia was surprised to find that she, too, felt a rising thrill, as though she were coming home.

'Here we are, and Solvig seems to know it!' Bella pointed to a pretty yellow house that faced on the square from the south corner of Carlisle Street. Julia looked up at the fanciful façade. Of course, she had never been here before, and yet something seemed to sizzle in the air, some familiar happiness just out of reach. As they mounted the stairs, Julia found herself grasping the iron rail and fighting back tears; this was how Castle Dar had felt, before Grandfather died and Eamon arrived.

Bella's knock was answered by a diminutive elderly man in black, who, when he saw the dog, drew back in horror. But Solvig seemed delighted to see him and surged forward in spite of Bella's hauling back on her lead. 'No. No dog.' The old man's English was not very good. 'You must keep dog.'

'We aren't offering you the dog,' Bella said. 'Down, Solvig.' The beast had her huge paws up on the man's shoulders and was licking his face. 'Down!' With a yank on the lead, Bella managed to pull Solvig away without, herself, tumbling back down the steps and into the street. 'We are here to see Miss Blomgren.'

'Ja, ja . . .' The old man eyed them up and down as he brushed dog hair from his jacket.

'I met Miss Blomgren in the square last week . . .'

'What she offer you?'

'Offer me? Why, nothing. We talked about women's education . . .'

The old man opened his hands and looked to heaven. 'Education! Why you not say? Miss Blomgren help you. But not dog.'

Bella drew herself up. 'We are not here for Miss Blomgren's help. We are visiting. I am Lady Arabella Falcott and this is Miss Percy. Now announce us to her. With dog.'

The old man led them into the house. 'Miss Blomgren is in kitchen. You follow me. Announce yourselves.' He opened a door. 'Down there.' He pointed. 'Take dog.' And he was gone.

Julia and Bella peered down a stairway into darkness. A bright smell, half sweet, half sour, rose to meet their nostrils. It wasn't like anything Julia had smelled before. There was some spice in it that she didn't recognize, and a powerful odour of dill. In fact, the smell was so strong that it was almost unpleasant, with a tang that brought tears to her eyes.

They descended the steps. At the bottom there was a

doorway to the right and a smaller, older-looking doorway to the left. The smell was overwhelming. 'Hello?' Julia called.

Then they heard the sound of coughing, and the door to the right was flung open. Vinegary steam poured out. Solvig gave one deep, joyful bark and launched herself into the room.

'Solvig!' A woman's surprised voice floated out to them through the mist, followed by more coughing. 'What are you doing here?' The steam was dissipating, revealing a tall woman in a homespun dress, her hair tucked up under a starched white cap, except for one white-blonde strand that had escaped and was curling down her neck. Her hands were stained bright pink halfway up to the elbows. 'Oh, hello! I'm sorry about the smell. I put the vinegar in when the pan was too hot.' She spoke with a light accent.

'Hello, Miss Blomgren,' Bella said, holding her hand out. 'We met in the square a week and more ago. Do you remember me? I am Bella.'

Julia thought she saw a flash of annoyance cross Miss Blomgren's face, but it was quickly hidden behind a lovely smile. 'Bella, of course! Isn't this a surprise. And you have Solvig with you . . . How did you come to have her?'

'You know Solvig? My brother brought her home with him earlier this week.'

'Your brother? Ah, and so you are a lady, Bella. I did not know.'

'Yes, I should have told you, I suppose, when we met, but I found our conversation so interesting, and then we said goodbye so precipitously when we reached your house . . .' Bella looked up at the older woman with the light of hero worship in her eyes. But if Miss Blomgren noticed, or felt that it was irregular to be accosted in her basement kitchen by a young lady she had met accidentally, she did not say so. Instead she turned to Julia. 'And what is your name?'

Julia found herself looking into the largest, most beautiful pair of violet eyes she had ever seen. The fine eyebrows slowly rose as Julia stared. She said her name stammeringly, like a ninny.

'What a pretty name. We have it in Sweden, also, but we pronounce it differently: Yulia, so. It means "youth", did you know that?' Miss Blomgren reached out and touched Julia's cheek with her scarlet finger. 'You are young and lovely. Such beautiful brown eyes. Oh dear. I have stained your cheek. These beets. I am pickling them. I thought to make enough for everyone. What a fool I am. It has consumed my life.' Then, just like a mother, she spat on a corner of her apron and used it to scrub at Julia's cheek. 'There. It is gone, as if it had never been.' Her smile deepened and became real. 'Those eyes. They remind me of someone else's brown eyes, someone I loved very much.' She gazed into Julia's face, her own dreamy and sad. Then she shook her head. 'It is good to be young, Julia. Enjoy it. I am forty-three. You look surprised. I know. I am lucky.' She waved her hand as if her looks were nothing. 'The beauty of youth is a gift, but it will go. The memories, though, they pile up, and they never go. Or at least, they do not go for a long, long time.' She sighed and seemed to collect herself. 'Well.' She turned to Bella. 'I am in the midst of my pickling and I cannot leave it. But you may sit and take tea here in the kitchen while I work. Would you like some lemon cake? It is very good.'

'I don't know if we should . . .' Julia looked hopelessly at Bella, but Bella was smiling as if nothing were wrong. Did she not realize that this Miss Blomgren must be Nick's mistress? The woman knew him. She even knew the dreadful dog. 'I . . . I need to go home.'

'Why?' Bella looked at her in all innocence. 'Do you not want lemon cake? You love cake.'

Miss Blomgren began untying her apron. 'Just tea and a small slice of cake, and then I'll have Edvard drive you home in the carriage.' She hung her apron on a hook by the kitchen door, then reached up and pulled her starched cap off her head. Her glorious white-blonde hair tumbled like water, falling all the way down her back. Julia gasped. Miss Blomgren looked at her. 'Yes, my hair. It's pretty, isn't it?'

Julia was able to recognize, dimly, that under normal circumstances she would probably have liked this no-nonsense woman very much. Instead, she was shrivelling with every new proof of Miss Blomgren's perfections. It felt like she was being eaten from the inside out by a gnawing animal. Probably a rat. So this was jealousy. 'It is very beautiful,' she said, and her voice sounded strange to her own ears.

Miss Blomgren looked at her in surprise. 'You look so tragic, my dear. Are you feeling ill? Is it the smell of the beets? I assure you, cake and tea is what you need to set you up again.' She turned to Bella. 'Now, Lady Falcott. I am going to feed you tea and cake and then I am going to send you and your friend home. And you must never visit me again. Whatever were you doing, the sister of a marquess, alone in Soho Square? Exchanging tittle-tattle with strange women and not telling them your title? I never would have encouraged your conversation had I known your identity. Do you not realize that to be seen with me would destroy your reputation? Do you not realize that I am a courtesan?'

'You are?' Bella looked at her heroine with alarm, but the expression quickly transformed into glee. 'But that is marvellous!' She whirled to face Julia. 'I told you she was marvellous.' She looked more closely at Julia. 'Whatever is the matter with you? You look like a goose walked over your grave. Are you upset because Miss Blomgren is a courtesan?' She turned to Miss Blomgren. 'I apologize for my friend. She was raised in the country and now she is in love. She cannot be held responsible for her reactions. But I assure you that neither of us sits in judgement upon you –'

Miss Blomgren interrupted Bella. 'Are you in love, Julia? It's a wonderful feeling, isn't it? But also terrible.'

'Apparently she is in love with my brother, Nick,' Bella said. 'And she's just learned that he has a mistress. Some beautiful creature he's squiring around town and showering with jewels.'

Julia closed her eyes. This was clearly the worst day of her entire life. Perhaps if she just kept her eyes closed, the day would end, and she could begin again.

Cool fingertips touched the back of her hand, and she opened her eyes again. Something like hysteria welled up inside her, and she looked up to meet Miss Blomgren's eyes.

They were sparkling with sympathy. 'Yes,' she said. 'I see.' She raised Julia's hands in her own, smearing them with beet juice, and she kissed Julia soundly on both cheeks. 'How delightful. You are perfect for one another.'

'Do you know Nick?' Bella turned to Miss Blomgren. 'Why didn't you say? Oh! You gave him the dog. That's why Solvig knows you. Of course.'

'My dear, stupid girl.' Miss Blomgren shook her head at Bella, keeping a tight hold on Julia's hands. 'Don't you realize why your friend is so unhappy? She knew it from the first. I am Nick's mistress.'

35

Bella looked like a rabbit held up by its ears. For her part, Julia was ready to either throw herself into Miss Blomgren's arms and weep, or plunge out of the house and into the squalid streets of Soho in a righteous fury. But then everything changed.

There was another person in the very midst of them. A thin black man . . . no, a youth, still really a boy . . . with hair that was short and black on the sides but that stood up in a green ridge down the centre of his skull. A bright green feather dangled from a hoop that pierced his left ear. He was dressed all in black, like Julia, but there any resemblance between them came to a crashing halt. He wore what looked like tight leggings and a short doublet, except that the leggings clung perfectly to his thin calves and thighs and sparkled with thousands of tiny gold flashes and the doublet was not a doublet at all but a thick leather belt wrapped around his hips; it extended neither above his waist nor beyond his upper thigh. His tall boots were laced all the way up with thick golden cords that were then tied in two flourishing bows just under his sparkling knees. He wore a short black leather jacket that seemed to fasten by means of a metal ribbon with serrated edges that ran down the front opening. It was open most of the way down, revealing a leather waistcoat, and beneath that, a shirt of black lace that was somehow wrapped so tightly around that it clung. Julia could see his skin showing through it. Around his neck was a golden chain with what looked like five flat pieces of broken pottery attached. By the time Julia's eyes found their way back to his face, he was smiling, and one hand was thrust forward. 'Sorry to butt in – hello,' he said in friendly tones, but with a very strange accent; it sounded like a Spanish guitar, played flat. He shook Julia's hand, then Bella's. 'Are you guys new Ofan, or what?'

'For God's sake!' Miss Blomgren grabbed his arm and dragged him a few steps away, into the brighter light.

Then she froze time.

Julia felt it coming. She locked her knees and forced herself to keep her expression bland and her limbs perfectly still. Thank God they were in a dark kitchen down in a basement. Thank God Miss Blomgren was more concerned with this intruder than with Julia and Bella.

'Peter, what the hell are you doing?' Miss Blomgren grabbed the young man's shoulders and shook him. 'Can't you tell they're Naturals? You can't wear untimely dress outside of the catacombs. Or jump straight to the kitchens. The transporter – use the transporter!'

Peter shrugged Miss Blomgren's hands away. 'Chill out. I have some really exciting news.'

But Miss Blomgren was not to be calmed. 'How dare you ask them, to their faces, if they are Ofan? Those poor girls, drowning in this ice-cold era. And I must watch them gasp for breath. While you! With your great gift that lifts you above the dreary flow of time – you flaunt it in front of them? If they were Ofan, Peter, would I have them in here, in the kitchen? No. I would be educating them as I educated you, in the transporter. I would be instructing them in the dangers of being Ofan. In the necessity of being very careful about how and when you reveal yourself.'

Julia curled her toes in her slippers. Miss Blomgren and this young man were Ofan! These were the Russian's enemy.

427

She willed them not to look her way; she was sure she was trembling.

Peter held up his hands, laughing. 'I'm sorry, okay? And I have some news. You may have noticed that my hair is much longer?' He stroked his green ridge.

Miss Blomgren put her hands on her hips. 'That's your news.'

'No. My point is, I've been away for three months, not three days.'

'Okay, so? Archana will have your hide either way. You abandoned your post.'

'Archana will forgive me. She always does.' He reached behind his neck and unhooked his chain. 'See these?' He laid the necklace with its broken pieces of pottery on the kitchen table, among Alva's open jars of pickles. 'And these.' He fished in his pockets and brought out two wooden sticks, a ragged-looking piece of green paper and a brightly coloured bracelet that looked as if it were woven from embroidery thread. He tossed them on the table beside his necklace. '*Voilà!*'

Miss Blomgren was unimpressed. 'You've already filled my office with your detritus of the ages, Peter. I'm in the middle of pickling and I have two Naturals to deal with. This is not the moment.'

'It's to do with the Talisman.'

Julia stopped breathing, and Miss Blomgren seemed to, as well. She went very still and half raised a hand as if to touch Peter. 'That's nothing to joke about,' she said quietly.

'No, but really. I've learned something about it. Something that might help us figure out what it is.'

Pretend, Julia screamed to herself inside her own head. Pretend to be a statue.

'All right, then. I'm listening. But tell me quickly, so that I can get rid of these two girls.'

428

Something in the way Peter turned his face, and in the way he held his hand as he reached to touch the embroidery-thread bracelet, made Julia realize: Peter was a girl. Younger than Julia. Maybe sixteen years old.

The girl named Peter held the bracelet out for Miss Blomgren's inspection. 'Do you recognize this? It's a friendship bracelet. Piper Connelly gave it to me in, like, seventh grade. Piper had the most friendship bracelets so she had the most power.'

'Like pickled limes,' Miss Blomgren said, holding the colourful thing up and smiling at it.

Peter cocked her head. 'No . . . it's nothing like pickles. God, Alva, you're obsessed. You know no one is going to actually eat your beets, right? Just like no one eats your green beans or your pickled pumpkin.'

Miss Blomgren pointed at Peter's nose. 'Quickly. What does your friendship bracelet have to do with the Talisman?'

Peter picked up the necklace she had been wearing. 'These are like a friendship bracelet,' she said, fingering one of the broken pieces of pottery. 'This is a symbolon. It's half of a clay disc. You break it when you swear friendship to someone. I have five of them. That's what I've been doing for the past three months.'

'You just left in the middle of guard duty to go make some friends and break clay discs with them.'

'Well . . .' Peter kicked a table leg with her boot. 'To be honest, it wasn't my idea. It was Melitta's. In 1000 BC.'

Julia's ears and eyes felt like they were on stalks, she was straining so hard to see and hear everything. But surely she hadn't heard correctly; it seemed that Peter had just said she had a friend in 1000 BC.

Alva was shocked, too. 'You were able to go to 1000 BC? How?'

'I can't. But that's just the point: Why can't we, Alva? I mean, the Pale is in the future, but we all have a sort of a Pale in the past, too. We can't jump back more than a thousand years, right?'

Julia couldn't help it. She twitched her head to look more directly at them. She saw that Miss Blomgren was unfazed by the suggestion that it was possible to go back a thousand years into the past.

'I thought we could learn about the Pale if we learn about that other barrier in the past,' Peter was saying when Julia found it possible to comprehend human speech again. 'But what I figured out doesn't have to do with the Pale. It has to do with the Talisman.'

'Yes, so you've said.'

'So I've been making friends back upriver to see how far back we go. That's what these symbolon . . . well, it's what they symbolize. Friendship. They're from ancient Greece. I'm friends with this guy named Kaveh from the year 28. He can go back to, like, 1000 BC. Back there he's friends with Melitta, and she sends messages to me through him. She's the one who came up with the idea of all of us wearing the symbolon . . .'

'That's cute,' Miss Blomgren said. 'Like pen pals.'

'It's more than cute. Melitta's made friends even further upriver, and I have their symbolon, too. I have friends going back to 3000 BC and you act like it's the Babysitters Club.' Peter scowled. 'Pen pals. You can be such a jerk, Alva.'

Miss Blomgren leaned into Peter's face and spoke severely. 'I have told you that I want you to make this short.'

'Fine.' Peter started talking very quickly. 'Symbolon. It's one of the ways money developed. You move from these symbols of friendship, where you break these discs in half to show that you are two parts of this emotional whole, to breaking them in half to symbolize debt! Like you owe the person something. You see? Friendship is totally, like, perverted into debt.' Peter was waving her hands now, her words coming out faster and faster. 'Feelings and money are totally connected. We use feelings to travel, but we can only travel to places where there's certain kinds of economies, right? Where there's colonial conquest and debt and that kind of crap. All those other people living in other kinds of cultures are just hanging out in their time without jumping. Which is so weird! Why is that? I mean, the Guild thrives where there's money, and the Ofan always exist in the neighbourhood of the Guild, like suckerfish on a whale. Why, why, why?'

'War,' Miss Blomgren said. 'I've explained it to you many times.'

'That's *your* argument, Alva, and it's totally right, but there's more. You're always like, the river is made out of money and blood. And the Guild is all about how money and war are normal human things and the river is just made out of feelings and we don't travel to certain kinds of cultures because we simply don't have the same feelings. Well, I think you're both right. The river connects different cultures throughout history where feelings have been translated into debt and then into money! Some places in human history haven't sutured their feelings to money – that's why we can't get to them or them to us. Wars of conquest are a big way that that transformation happens because you have to have an economy to feed an army on the march, but even war is a symptom, Alva, not the disease itself!'

Peter paused as if this was a revelation, but Miss Blomgren said nothing – only stared at the girl.

Peter sighed when it was clear that Miss Blomgren was not going to respond, and carried on. 'Don't you see? This means that the Ofan are totally in this with the Guild. There's no structural reason why we're the good guys and they're the bad guys. We both travel the river for the same reason.' Peter rubbed her hands together, almost as if she were cold. 'I know you were all hopped up on the Guild being warmongers who are single-handedly destroying humanity and the Ofan being all rainbows and unicorns and peace symbols. But instead we're both just totally complicit in this shitty system and there's nothing we can do about it.' She smiled, her pleasure in her own brilliance shining from her. 'Isn't that awesome?'

After a long silence, Miss Blomgren spoke quietly. 'That's very impressive, actually.'

Peter opened her hands as if she were releasing a bird. 'I know! I know, I know!'

Miss Blomgren laughed and held out her arms, and Peter jumped into them and was hugged.

Julia bit her lip, forgetting for a moment that Miss Blomgren was Nick's lover. What would it feel like to have a mother who loved you? Who hugged you when you were clever?

When Miss Blomgren pulled away from hugging Peter there was a smile in her voice. 'You are an amazing creature, my dear. You and your friends down through time. Do they all dress like you?'

Peter bristled. 'Of course they don't dress like me, God, Alva. They're from different eras. When are you going to get it through your head that I look normal in my own time?'

'You forget that I have been to the 1980s and I know you lie. Plus, I am driven by forces beyond my control to tease you about it. You bring out the auntie in me.'

Peter clearly liked this scolding. 'It's okay.' She scuffed a heel back and forth.

Miss Blomgren stepped away. 'Good. Now let's try to

figure out a story to tell these two young ladies about you when I start time up again.'

'Wait!' The girl grabbed up the two flat wooden sticks and held them up to show that they were, in fact, one stick that had been snapped down the middle. 'Just one more thing. This,' she said, her voice taking on a pedantic edge, 'is a tally stick. This one's from England, but they were a really big deal in China, too. You notch it to show how much is owed, then you break it in half, and the borrower keeps one half and the lender keeps the other. It's just like a symbolon, but it's never about friendship – it's all about debt. And guess what? It's the precursor of paper money.' She grabbed up the slip of green paper and shook it at Alva. 'Benjamins! Which in turn symbolize real gold, which is valuable because everyone agrees it is. Or rather, they do until 1971, when they get rid of the gold standard, and the whole thing just becomes fantasy! Get it?'

'No.' Miss Blomgren glanced at Bella and Julia; she was clearly worried about how long she could keep time frozen and continue to concentrate on what Peter was saying. 'You're back in Never-Never Land, Peter.'

'But it's back to emotions,' Peter said. 'Don't you see? Gold had this collectively agreed-upon value, so people with lots of money were like, "My paper symbolizes that gold and that symbolic relationship between my paper and that gold makes me feel rich." After 1971, when Richard Nixon is, like, "Let's just all admit money is a fantasy," people had to be like, "Dude, I just feel rich because I feel rich!"' Peter's words tumbled from her mouth. 'See? There's no middleman for them to rest their fantasy on! Nixon was just, like, "Oh my God, I can make everybody's feelings do the work, instead of gold! Everyone will just pretend!"'

Pretend. That word. Julia was lost in Peter's story, drowning in it – but she grabbed on to that word.

433

Miss Blomgren sighed. 'This is crazy, Peter. And what in the name of all that's holy does it have to do –'

'Nineteen seventy-one!' Peter shouted. 'It's after that, Alva! After that it starts getting hard to jump forward! By the twenty-first century it's actively difficult and from there on out you have to be really talented to get anywhere. But it starts in 1971. That's when the future starts turning into a big ugly scar!' She stopped talking and stood with her arms crossed, grinning at Alva.

'Are you done?'

'Yes, I'm done.'

Alva shook her head. 'You had me up until Nixon and the gold standard, Peter. I know you know everything about the late twentieth century, but you need to learn about 1815. There's no gold standard right now, you ignoramus. When they aren't arguing about the Corn Laws, the politicians are fighting over money, and how to make it have any meaning. There won't be a secure gold standard for a few more decades.' Miss Blomgren crossed her arms and smiled triumphantly at the girl. 'This, Peter, is why I think you should go back to America, go back to 1987, finish high school and go to college. Double major in economics and history. *Then* you can join the Ofan. For God's sake, you could leave today, spend six years getting an education, and come back here tomorrow, grown up and with some real scholarship to back up your brilliance. You would be of much more use to us!'

The girl's face fell. 'I'm not going to do that Alva, and you know why! My mother –'

Miss Blomgren held up a hand, and Peter closed her mouth. 'I don't want to go there, Peter. Not again. And what about the Talisman? You got me to listen to this diatribe by saying that your little wooden stick there had something to do with the Talisman.'

'Yeah?'

'Well, what about it?'

'You mean I didn't say?' Peter laughed. 'Oh my God. That's the whole point. It's the tally stick. Tally, talisman – it's the same word, at root!'

'That's it. That's your revelation. *Tally* sounds like *talisman*.'

'Yes.'

Miss Blomgren exploded. 'That's all? Do you understand that the Pale is going to destroy us? Do you understand that if the Talisman exists, it might be the only thing that can stop it, or even help us discover what it is? Your semantics, your three months making friends with teenagers from ye olde days? How the hell is that supposed to help us in the future?'

Peter went very still in the face of Miss Blomgren's anger. Then, when it was over, she took a deep breath and her voice took on an adult gravity. 'Please think about it, Alva. A talisman is just like a tally stick, or a symbolon. Except that it isn't about a debt of money or goods. A talisman is a symbol of the relationship between humans and the supernatural. The relationship of interdependence, of mutual debt, between human beings and the unknown. Gods, or ancestors, or even the future. So, like, yin-yang is that kind of talisman. Or like when a fairy gives you a magical jewel in exchange for your baby.'

Miss Blomgren shook her head slowly. 'Do not go all fairies and warlocks on me, Peter. I can't take it.'

'No.' The girl put up a hand. 'Stop treating me like a child and listen. A tally is a calculation of *human* debt. A talisman is one half of a *magical* deal between humans and otherness. The talisman that we see and can hold might be a word or a symbol or a stone or something. The other half is usually your soul or your firstborn child or something really horrifying like that.'

435

Julia swallowed; her throat was so dry it was painful. A talisman. A magical character. A mark, a stamp, a representation. A symbol. But . . . she was just a young woman from Devon. She wasn't one half of a deal with the devil.

For her part, Miss Blomgren shook her head. 'I need to wake these two girls up and get on with my day, Peter. We're done here.'

Peter grabbed Miss Blomgren's hand as she moved away. 'When we're looking for the Talisman, we're looking for *half* of something. At least get that through your head. Something that's been torn or broken. Some sort of relic of a really intense debt that was never paid, and so now the Pale is coming to kill us all. Who knows what the hell this Talisman is – but I bet you when we find it, it has a jagged edge.'

Julia would have reversed time as she had when Eamon tried to kill her and started it again a few seconds before Peter had appeared in the room. But for some reason Miss Blomgren and Peter didn't think to do that. They got back into the positions they had been in when Miss Blomgren first froze time, and then Miss Blomgren started it up again. Julia did her best to come to life as if in mid gesture, but she felt very awkward. Luckily she had been feeling very awkward before, when all she knew about Miss Blomgren was that she was Nick's lover. Now she knew much, much more, and was even less confident about what steps she should take. Meanwhile, Miss Blomgren explained to Julia and Bella that "Petra" was a servant who had thought it would be a good joke to dress up and surprise her mistress; she had sneaked in the door. Hadn't the girls heard her enter? No? Well, Petra was a tricky one.

Peter, much less gracefully, played the part of the contrite subordinate and left as quickly as she had arrived, but using her feet and the door this time.

When Peter was gone, Miss Blomgren didn't mention tea and lemon cake again, nor did she try to hide that she was suddenly in a bad mood. 'Time for you to go,' she said, and made short work of bustling Julia and Bella out of her house. Bella protested – it wasn't fair that she should be shut away from friendships because of inane social conventions, she didn't mind that Miss Blomgren was Nick's mistress, in fact, Alva could marry Nick, and become respectable!

Miss Blomgren became quite short with Bella then, and scolded her. 'You are hurting Julia's feelings, Lady Arabella. You have said that she is in love with your brother. Not only that, but you are being rude to me.'

'Rude? How?' Bella protested as she and Julia and Solvig were propelled up the basement stairs.

'I have made it clear that I cannot be your friend, my lady, and you persist in pursuing an unwanted connection.' Miss Blomgren got them down the hallway and out of the front door. 'Go and do not come back.' She stood with her hands on her hips.

Bella lifted a tragic face to her idol. 'I am sorry,' she said. 'I enjoyed talking to you so much that day when we met. You told me you believed in education and equality. And I wanted . . .' She stopped, unable to continue.

At that Miss Blomgren's face softened. 'I know, my dear,' she said gently. 'But dreams and reality are at odds in this case. You are a lady and I am the opposite. It is the way of the Natural world. I wish you all the very best, and I hope that you find what you crave. Now goodbye.' She turned and disappeared inside her house, the door snapping shut behind her.

Bella turned to Julia, her face red. 'I am mortified,' she said. 'I had no idea. And I liked her so much. It is unfair!'

Julia put her arm round her shoulder. 'Hush,' she said.

'She was right, you know, to turn us out. But I am glad you brought me to meet her.'

'Even though she is Nick's mistress? You seemed horrified.'

'It is the way of the Natural world.' Julia smiled at her friend.

'You would just accept that? A man with a mistress?'

'That is not what I said.' Julia squeezed Bella's shoulders and grieved for the look of confusion in her friend's eyes. The gulf between them was widening. Poor, hungry Bella had been entirely unaware of the feast that Julia had just attended; Julia had learned more from Alva and Peter in fifteen minutes than she had in an entire lifetime. And Bella, who craved nothing more than knowledge and freedom, had been frozen stiff.

Naturals, Guild, Ofans. It was beginning to make a crazy sort of sense. Ofans could travel in time. Members of the Guild probably could, too. Julia felt the thrill down her limbs, the rushing in her head; so could she. She knew it. She could feel that she could, if only she knew how.

As for Nick, what was he? He was partly Guild, for he was bound in some relationship to Lebedev. But Alva was Ofan, and she knew Nick. She was his lover, by her own admission. Perhaps Nick was Ofan as well. Or perhaps he was a spy. But for which side?

Julia frowned.

She turned to Bella. 'I am going home,' she said. 'Alone. You go along to Hatchards and collect Clare without me.'

36

Julia handed her cloak to the butler. 'Is my Lord Blackdown in, Smedley?'

Smedley flared his nostrils. The Falcotts' London butler was famously priggish. 'He is,' he said repressively.

'Please ask him to attend me in the drawing room at his earliest convenience.'

'The other ladies are out, Miss Percy.'

'I am not inquiring about the other ladies. I am asking about his lordship.'

'You wish to see him alone.' It wasn't a question, it was an accusation.

'Yes. I wish to see him alone.' Julia met the butler's gaze squarely.

Just under his left eye, his cheek was twitching. But after the hall clock had ticked past an echoing seven seconds, he broke and bowed. 'As you wish, Miss Percy.' He walked slowly away towards the study door.

Julia took off her bonnet and set it on the footman's chair. She checked her hair in the hall mirror. It was still brown, as were her eyes. She wasn't very tall, and her face was not a perfect oval. She didn't have any experience. She had no possessions of her own, and she was reliant for her lodging, her clothing and her very life upon the dubious kindness of friends and relations.

But that was no reason for her not to have self-possession. Miss Blomgren had it. So could she. Julia pinched her cheeks, hoping for a little colour, then went into the drawing room to await Blackdown.

He was with her quickly. 'Hello.' He smiled, closed the door behind him and came over to her, holding out his hands. She gave him one of hers but withdrew it quickly. He looked at her quizzically. 'Are you quite well?'

'Yes, thank you. Shall we sit?'

'Certainly.' He waited for her to arrange herself on the settee, then sat down beside her, his long legs stretching out, his highly polished black-top boots reflecting the afternoon sun that was pouring in through the tall front windows. He took her hand again and audaciously stroked her fingers, sending a silvery shiver up her arm. 'What is this mark?' He traced the red stain on the back of her hand.

She watched him, as if from a distance. 'Beet juice,' she said.

He looked at her, his eyes questioning. 'You are in a strange mood. Have you just come home? I thought you had gone to Hatchards, but instead you've been messing about with beets. Where have you been?'

'As Satan says to *another* lord, I've been "going to and fro in the earth, and walking up and down in it".'

Nick laughed uncomfortably. 'Are you Satan in this scene?'

Julia studied his face. It was weathered by his years in Spain, almost harsh in its angles. It had creased where he used it to smile or frown. His changeable eyes were restful on the surface, stormy in their depths. She supposed his face was like Devon. Rich in places, bleak in others, and always there was the grey-blue moody sky. Again she had that feeling that she did not know him, that he was a stranger. And yet he was hers. She felt it fiercely.

'I want you,' she heard herself say. 'I want to lie with you. Like in the poem.'

It seemed to her for a moment that time stopped. It wasn't anything she was doing – time was, in fact, trotting along at its usual pace. Yet the way he sat there perfectly still, his eyes intent upon her . . . the moment might simply go on and on. But then he stood, in one fluid movement. He squeezed her shoulder almost carelessly and went to the door. Was he going to walk out on her? Leave her, pretend she'd said nothing?

He opened the door to the hallway and called the butler. 'When are my mother and sisters expected home?'

'I am not sure, my lord. Your sisters went to Hatchards with Miss Percy.' Smedley looked past Nick at Julia, and for just one moment allowed obvious disapproval to show on his face. 'Perhaps Miss Percy will be better informed than I as to when they will return, and from where.'

'Thank you,' Nick said reprovingly. 'And my mother?'

'Lady Blackdown is visiting Mrs Beauchamp. I cannot say when she may return.'

Nick turned to Julia and said in bright tones, 'We may as well take our walk, then, Miss Percy. There's no telling when they will come home, and it's no good waiting for them. Are you ready?'

Julia heard the light words, but his eyes, bent upon hers with searing intensity, were very serious. He was giving her an order.

She stood and pulled on her gloves. 'Of course, my lord.' In the hallway she pinned her hat on her head again and glanced once more at her face. Did she look different, now that she had dashed to pieces every rule of good behaviour? No. Her hair was dark. Her cheeks were pale. Her eyes were brown. She was the same.

He waited by the door, his own hat already on his head. 'Shall we?'

She sketched him a miniature curtsey and they left the

house. The butler closed the door behind them with evident disdain. Not five minutes had passed since she had made her outrageous request, and she was now standing in the street outside his house – in disgrace?

Blackdown took her arm and they walked down the marble steps together, turned right, then immediately right again onto Davies Street.

'Where are we going?'

Nick said nothing, merely steered her right once again into the mews behind the row of town houses. He led her to the stable door, opened it, and they walked in. The big travelling carriage and three smaller equipages confronted them. The tack room was to the left, and to the right, the row of stalls. The warm, comforting smell of hay and horses enveloped Julia. Down the dim row of stalls she heard horses shifting and one soft, questioning whicker. But Nick was already pulling her forward between the carriages, looking to left and right as he did so. 'If we see a stable hand we will have to pretend we are visiting Marigold and Boatswain,' he whispered. 'But with any luck we won't.'

At the back of the stables was a small, plain wooden door. Nick opened it and pulled Julia inside, then shut it. They were in profound darkness. Julia felt her heart in her throat. 'Where are we?'

'We are back inside. These are the cellars beneath the kitchens.'

'Why?'

'Shh.' He pulled her by the hand, and she followed. 'There should be a stair somewhere here . . .' Julia heard a dull thump. 'Blast! Here it is.' Nick turned and took her elbow. 'Watch your step. I'll follow you up, but walk softly. We shouldn't meet anyone, but if we do we must say that we are . . . exploring.'

'Exploring?' Julia stifled a laugh. 'That sounds convincing.'

'Well then, don't meet anyone.' They began to climb. The stair took a turn, and the darkness eased; after the second turn a skinny window shed dirty light on what was revealed to be a narrow wooden staircase enclosed on both sides, with a door opening onto each floor.

Julia looked back over her shoulder at Nick, climbing behind her. He caught her glance and grinned. Like an idiot she beamed back at him. She wiped the smile away, turned her face resolutely forward, and kept climbing. These were clearly the stairs that led to the cupola. He was taking her there, having told the butler they were going on a walk. No one would know they were at home, up in that forgotten eyrie. Her step faltered.

Nick came up behind her and put his arm round her waist. Standing below her on the steps, his mouth was just at her ear. 'Cold feet?' he whispered. His breath in her hair and on her neck sent shivers down her spine.

'Perhaps.'

'Poor feet. Allow me to relieve them.' Without a word of warning, he scooped her into his arms.

She stifled a shriek. 'Set me down!'

'Hush.' He was laughing silently; she could feel his stomach quivering against her hip. 'Put your arm round my neck. Do you want to send us tumbling back down the stairs? Like Jack and Jill?'

'It would serve you right to break your crown,' Julia said, but she put her arm round his neck as he asked. It sent her breast pressing into his shoulder, and her face was very close to his. This was not at all what she had imagined when she posed her question downstairs. A scramble through secret passageways, ending with a half-hilarious, half-awkward ride in his arms. She felt her cold reserve melting away like one of

Gunter's ices on her tongue. She had asked him to be her lover, and he was going to oblige her.

Nick began climbing.

'You are absurd,' Julia said conversationally.

'You are delicious.' He squeezed her against his chest and buried his nose in her hair. 'Mmm. You smell like plum pudding.'

'Is that a good thing? I thought a girl was supposed to smell of lavender or roses.'

'Let me see.' He bit her earlobe. 'Definitely plum pudding. Stop wriggling.'

'Then stop biting me.'

'Never.'

Julia arrived in the cupola with neither dignity nor poise. Her hair was in disarray and she had a laugh on her lips. It wasn't what she had imagined – she had planned on being aloof and superior. But she didn't care any more.

He set her down and she reached up her arms to draw his smiling face down to hers for a kiss. He was happy to consent, kissing her as he took his hat from his head and sent it flying into a corner, and kissing her again as he untied her bonnet and sent it flying after his hat. He kissed her as he peeled the gloves from her hands, and then from his own, crumpled them together into a ball and threw them over his shoulder. Then he kissed her as he sat down and pulled her into his lap. He looked at her then, his right arm encircling her hips and his left arm around her back, and opened his lips to speak, but she shook her head. 'No words.'

'I must speak, Julia.'

She pressed her lips to his.

But he turned his face and pulled away an inch. 'Talking,

my turtle dove. We must exchange some words, you and I. Now.'

Julia drew her finger down his cheek and found the edge of his cravat. She began to untie it.

'You little vixen.'

'I thought I was a turtle dove. How do you untie these things?'

'It is an art.' He unceremoniously tilted his thighs and tumbled her sideways from his lap onto the cushions. 'Julia.' His voice was firm. 'You must listen to me. Just now, down-stairs –'

'Yes.' She rearranged herself into a sitting position and smoothed her skirts. 'I asked you to take me to bed, Nick.'

'Why?'

She looked up at him in surprise. 'Because . . .' She contemplated her interlaced fingers.

'Because?'

'I desire you?' She frowned at her fingers.

He reached out and touched her cheek. 'My darling, you are talking like a courtesan and pouting like a girl.'

'Very well.' She raised her chin but looked past his shoulder at the treetops. 'I *do* desire you. I am twenty-two and a virgin. I wish to learn . . .' She stopped, and he waited. She was afraid she sounded entirely foolish, but she soldiered on. 'You gave me a poem in which a gentleman offers to teach a lady. What did you expect? That I would simply faint away in shock? That my eyes would shrivel in my head? I think that gentleman is much like you, and I am much like his mistress. I would like you to teach me.' She looked down again at her hands. 'Now, are you going to oblige me, or shall we dismiss the notion? I will not beg you.'

'You have no idea how very much I wish to oblige you. But . . .' She looked up and his eyes seemed to cloud over. 'I have been away for so long, and living such a different life. Among different women.'

'In Spain.'

He was silent for a long time before he answered, and she could see that he was aching to tell her something. But when he spoke he simply repeated her words. 'In Spain,' he said.

As he said it, she realized what he was suppressing: he could travel in time. He had not been lost for three years in Spain. He had been lost in time. And for quite a bit longer than three years. That was why he looked older than he should. She looked at him with new knowledge. How old *was* he? Thirty? Thirty-five?

'Are women so very different from me . . . in Spain?'

Humour and regret combined in his expression. 'It is a foreign country,' he said. 'They do things differently there. I do things differently there.' He pressed his lips tightly together, opened them to speak, then closed them again. She was glad he didn't tell her the truth; she wanted this moment to be uncomplicated by revelation. Instead he clasped her fingers, pressing her hand to his cheek. 'But now I am back. I am confronted with a beautiful woman whom I hold in the very highest esteem. She wishes to become my lover. And you should be impressed with my self-control,' he said, his voice getting a little rough.

'Self-control is the last thing I desire from you.' She put her other hand on his chest. 'Shall I be plainer in my speech? If I do not have reservations, why should you?' She let her hand drift down until it rested on his stomach. '"There is no penance due to innocence."'

He released her hand and stroked her hair. She felt his stomach flex with every movement of his arm. 'Far back in my memory,' he said, 'almost as if it were a dream, I seem to recall something. Some rule of chivalry. Ah, yes. A gentleman must never take a young lady's virtue.'

Julia leaned forward until she could whisper in his ear. 'And that is all it was.' She pulled back and gazed into his eyes. 'Just a dream.'

His eyes glinted. He pulled her face recklessly to his and kissed her mouth.

He toppled back against the cushions, dragging her with him, and she was tossed like a boat on a stormy sea, her hands thrusting into his hair as he kissed her. He pushed her sleeves from her shoulders and kissed her collarbone, and then his hands slid firmly down her back until they met the flare of her hips. 'Glory,' he murmured in her ear, his touch growing lighter as he fanned his hands across her bottom. 'Such loveliness . . .' He let his hands roam. She arched her back, gasping, and found that she was pressing her belly against the long muscle that was straining between his legs. He smiled dreamily into her face, his calm expression at odds with the urgency of his caresses. She could feel the muslin of her dress tickling up her calves; he was stroking it higher as his hands moved.

'Nicholas . . .' She heard herself breathe his name as her hem skimmed above her knees.

'Yes, my lovely girl . . .' He bit her shoulder gently.

'Do you remember how the poem ends?'

'Shhh . . .' He kissed her, pulling her dress higher still. 'Let's make our own poetry . . .'

She couldn't help it; she laughed.

His eyes widened. 'You scoff at me in the middle of your maiden voyage?'

'Yes, but that was just such a ridiculous thing to say, Nick.' She felt his cock leap against her belly; he liked her teasing. 'Do you not remember how the poem ends?'

'I am hardly in a position to recall rhyming couplets.'

She propped herself up on her hands, looking down at

him. 'He spends the whole poem begging her to undress, and then finally he says, "To teach thee, I am naked first."'

That made him unfurl a smile like a banner. 'What are you suggesting?' He took his arms from around her and laced his hands behind his head.

She lay against his chest and played again with his cravat. 'I think that to teach me, you ought to be naked first.'

'You are a literalist.' His smile faded. 'And I'm not a pretty sight. I'm slightly the worse for wear under these fine clothes.'

'I don't mind.' She kissed his suddenly sad mouth. 'I want to see you.'

'Very well. But first you must climb off me.'

Julia slipped from him, smoothed her dress down and sat on the cushions with her knees tucked up under her chin and her arms wrapped round her legs.

Nick sat up and began untying his cravat. He glanced sideways at her. 'You look like a little gargoyle,' he said.

Julia just blinked and watched. It was fascinating, observing how his fingers flew without the use of a mirror. He must have tied his cravat every morning and untied it every night, and yet she found it the most exotic thing. He finished, pulled the long cloth free and tossed it aside. The sight of his strong, bare neck, framed by the starched collar of his shirt, sent a thrill through her.

'Now boots,' he said, yanking awkwardly on one and then the other of his tall, black Hessians. 'It's rather undignified, this undressing part.' He tossed boots and stockings to one side.

Barefoot, he stood up. Julia hugged her knees more tightly to her chest. He looked ridiculous, in unmentionables that stopped at his bare calves, and a shirt and jacket but no cravat. She laughed.

'Yes, you see? He gestured at his own body with a theatrical hand. 'The rest of this absurd rig is still to come off. A jacket so tight I can't get into or out of it on my own, a shirt that doesn't even button all the way down, and trousers with two different fastening devices. While for your part, you can dress in what is basically a sheet. It's unfair, I tell you. Now, will you help me out of this wretched jacket?'

Julia got to her feet and helped him by pushing the jacket up and away from his broad shoulders. She could feel the muscles of his chest stretching as he shrugged off the blue superfine. She laid it carefully aside and looked at Nick in his linen shirt and red braces – the only splash of colour in his sober clothing, colour that no one ever saw. Except that now she was seeing it. As she watched, he pulled the braces from his shoulders with his thumbs and began to unbutton his shirt. But she found herself gently pushing his hands away. 'I want to,' she said.

He let his hands fall to his sides. She reached up and slipped the first button through its hole, her fingers unsteady. A pulse was beating there among the sinews of his throat, and she could feel his chest rising and falling beneath her wrists. She continued, unbuttoning the second button, and then the third and last. The linen fell open to reveal golden skin, dusted with darker, bronze hair. She put a finger to the hollow of his throat and traced downwards to where the buttons stopped. His skin was warm to the touch, and his breath quickened as she touched him. She slowly pulled the shirt from his trousers, and he sucked in his breath. She pushed the linen up, past his ribs, her hands skimming over smooth skin. Then he took over and pulled the shirt quickly over his head.

Her first impression was that he was beautiful. His chest tapered to his hips. His stomach was bisected by a wavering line of hair that plunged down to his navel, then disappeared mysteriously into his trousers. In spite of his obvious arousal

449

he stood at ease, his weight on one leg, watching her look at him. She reached a hand out, stroking over his ribs, passing up and over his flat nipple. She heard and felt his breath quicken.

Then she saw the scar.

He had been shot through the shoulder. It had not been a clean wound. The scar was ragged. His skin was a paler gold than his hair, but the scar was a shiny, sickly white. She passed her hand across it and back, and felt its contours beneath her fingers.

'You are brave,' he said, and she could feel his voice in his chest.

'For touching your scar?' She laid her hand fully over it. 'I am not brave. You are. It must have hurt dreadfully.'

'Yes,' he said simply. 'But I am in no mood to discuss my scars. Especially since you are about to meet another one. If, that is, you wish to continue this lesson?'

'I do.'

He unbuttoned the fall of his trousers. Then he unbuttoned the waistband and looked up at Julia. 'Do you know what my great-grandfather's family motto is?'

'No, of course not.' She smiled at his stalling technique.

His answering smile was slightly lopsided. '*Fear garbh ar mait.*' He began to push the tight breeches down his hips. 'It is Irish. It means "Here is a good, blunt man".'

'Oh, no.' Julia laughed and covered her eyes. When she peeked out from between her fingers, he was stepping out of his breeches and kicking them to one side.

'There.' He straightened, his hands open at his sides. '"To teach thee, I am naked first."' He stood amid the debris of his previously immaculate attire, gloriously naked.

His cock stood up, very proud. It was more . . . forthright than she had thought it would be. Best not to think about it yet. She let her eyes move to the scar that ran down his thigh. It was puckered and cruel, but it was part of him, and so she could not mind it. She let her eyes drift down his legs. She even thought his feet were handsome.

'Your turn, Julia.'

Her eyes flew up the length of his body to his face. He was not smiling. He stepped forward and quickly untied the ribbon at her waist, turned her round and undid the buttons down her back. His breath sent a delicious shiver all down the length of her neck and spine; then he pushed the dress off her shoulders and it simply fell from her like snow. She stood in her shift and turned to face him again. She raised her arms, and with a tickling thrill he whisked the fine linen up and over her head. Her slippers, stockings, and drawers followed, awkwardly and with a few laughs, but then she was in his arms. Never, in her entire life, had she felt anything so incredible as being one of two, standing naked together, wrapped up in each other's arms. She closed her eyes, spreading her hands across the wings of his shoulder blades.

'Julia?' His voice seemed to come from inside her own head.

She opened her eyes. 'Yes.'

He drew her back and down to the cushions. He stretched alongside her, one arm supporting her head, the other pulling her to him. She turned to face him, her hand on his chest. She could feel his cock pressing against her hip. She seemed more aware of it than he did, for he was looking at her almost sternly, though there was a twinkle right at the back of his eyes.

'You were mistaken about the last line of the poem, I fear,' he said in the schoolmasterish voice with which he'd teased her on their Hyde Park walk.

'Oh, really?'

'Yes. It was a grave error.'

A few of the glinting golden hairs that dusted his chest curled over her fingers. She spoke in playful tones. 'Then you must correct me, sir.'

With one quick twist Nick shifted both their bodies so that she lay underneath him, breathless. He had captured her wrists and was pressing them into the cushions above her head. '"To teach thee, I am naked first,"' he said. 'That's the *second*-to-last line. The last line is, "What needst thou have more covering than a man?"'

Julia laughed, but Nick didn't. His expression was intent, and his hands slid up her wrists to grasp her hands, his fingers interlacing with hers. It was both caressing and possessive, the way he had her pinned beneath him, her arms above her head. She could feel how her breasts rose, only to be pressed against his chest. His eyes were almost cold with some emotion she couldn't recognize. 'What needst thou have more covering than *this* man?'

Julia held back on her breath. 'What are you asking me?' she whispered, gripping his hands tightly.

Nick watched her mouth as she answered. His own response was broken. 'I am about to make you mine. I want to promise you . . . but I cannot, in good conscience . . . not until . . .'

It seemed a hundred years ago that she had stormed home in anger, intent upon seducing Nick just to show that she could. Now that she had him here, poised above her, she didn't want to hear empty protestations or promises or excuses. 'Do you know the motto of the earls of Darchester, Nick?' she asked.

'No.'

'*Facta, non verba.*'

'Deeds, not words,' he translated.

Julia nodded. 'Please,' she whispered.

Another heartbeat as his eyes searched hers. Then his hands released her and slid softly down her arms. She reached and drew his face down to her, kissing him. He stroked a hand over her breast, past her waist, and feathered his fingers across her thigh, then brushed his hand lightly across the place between her legs.

He whispered endearments that she couldn't quite hear. It felt luscious and wicked – she bit her lip and closed her eyes; she was poised, sweetly, between the quick, light action of his thumb and the firm, slow movement of his fingers. She gasped with each breath, his murmuring voice keeping her from spinning away. Then his whispers broke into a groan, and his hand thrust and she tightened – and burst exquisitely, like a summer berry. Was that her voice crying out? She shuddered, pressing up against him.

He was positioning himself between her legs. Again he touched her with his thumb, and she thrummed with pleasure even as she felt herself stretch to allow him in. Caught there between bliss and pain, she watched his face. His eyes were closed in concentration as slowly, slowly, he entered her. It felt impossible and it felt wonderful, and edged with alarm. Then, just when she thought she couldn't take any more, he stopped pressing forward, and his serious, passion-dark eyes opened. 'I love you,' he said.

With quick intent, he pushed forward past a barrier she hadn't known was there – and she cried out even as the sharpness gave way to a honey-sweet ache. He kissed her, spoke softly in her ear, stroked her hair, and held very still. Then he began to pull away, and she cried out 'No', wanting him back again. He eased himself into her once more, smiling down at her. She clung to him as he moved within her. She was flying up and up with him in widening circles, gripped by an exquisite vertigo that sang along every nerve; he clasped her to him and she felt him shudder and thrust in more deeply than before; she toppled off some high, wind-blown ledge of pleasure into a deep, endless sea that was all the shifting colours of his eyes.

The bayonet was his own hand and his nails were ripping, catching . . . and now he was flying away, backwards, into a tunnel of smoke at hideous speed, and at the distant end of the tunnel the splash of red and the young man's black eyes fixing in death . . .

There was something pulling him back, something holding him. Instead of the Frenchman's face at the end of the tunnel he saw a pair of dark eyes. Julia was speaking his name, quietly, and he realized he could hear it – 'Nicholas . . .' – piercing the horrible silence of the dream. The power that was drawing him backwards into an unknown future died, as abruptly as a wind can die. Nick awoke, fully. Julia was lying half on top of him, stroking his hair, one leg tossed over his thighs, her breasts resting on his chest. Behind her tousled head and through the glass panes of the cupola he could see the late-afternoon sky, a few clouds drifting across it.

'Hello, Sleeping Beauty.' Julia brushed her knuckles down his cheek. 'You were dreaming. A bad one?'

Nick breathed in deeply, through his nose. He exhaled slowly, letting the air hiss between his teeth.

'Was it Badajoz?'

Her face was alive with that just-loved look and flushed with health. 'I don't want to talk about it.'

Julia reached down and traced the puckered scar on his thigh. 'You don't have to,' she said.

He didn't have much feeling there, but still, her touch tickled the edges of the old wound. The feeling shocked him into sudden realization. He was lying, naked and entwined, with an unmarried woman of gentle birth he had just deflowered. 'Julia.'

'Yes.'

'I . . .' He moved his hand to the back of her head and drew her face down to his for a long kiss. His cock stirred beneath her hip.

She drew back and brushed the tip of her nose against his. 'Mmm,' she said. 'Do you think it's very late? Is there time to . . .' She grinned. 'You know . . .'

He opened his eyes wide. 'I have no idea to what you're referring, Miss Percy.'

She wiggled herself to the right until she was firmly on top of him. His cock strained against her belly. 'You have no idea?' she whispered. 'Are you certain?'

He shook his head and stroked his hands all down her spine. The small of her back was somehow a revelation. 'Julia . . .'

'Yes . . .' She breathed the word.

Half a honeyed hour later, their positions were reversed, with Nick half across Julia, their eyes closing again in drowsy contentment. But this time Nick fought it. 'We must get up and return to the real world.'

'Mmm.' She traced his eyebrow with kisses. 'I don't want to.'

'But we must.'

She pouted, and he had to kiss her mouth. But as he pulled away, he stood up. He looked down at her. She lay at her ease across the cushions, late-afternoon sunlight burnishing her skin and casting half her body in warm shadow. She was perfect, from her ten orderly toes to the curls that decorated her sex to her dream-soft face. He had said he loved her and it was true. He did.

'I love you,' he said again. 'I didn't know it. But I now do. I think I always did.'

Her smile seemed to die, although it stayed in place. Or perhaps it was a trick of the light, for she spoke immediately. 'And I love you,' she said, quite flatly for all that the words were sure and strong. She let it be at that.

It wasn't a moment of jubilation, somehow. But it was enough. He reached for her.

She held up a hand, stopping him. She looked resolved. It was strange. 'You were right,' she said. 'We must descend.'

'We must also talk, Julia. Make plans. I must tell you –'

'I know,' she interrupted him. 'I know you have things to tell me.' She glanced down at her hands and his eyes followed hers. Her fingers were tightly, tensely entwined. 'But not now. Let now be . . . now.'

'I don't want there to be secrets between us,' he said. She was as lovely as a woodland dryad. But she was harbouring some care. He could sense it.

She shook her head matter-of-factly, then sat up and began repinning her hair. 'No,' she said. 'Tomorrow.' She moved with calm purpose, as if she weren't naked at all. He decided he loved the way she sat. He loved the way she was just this second unconsciously scratching her knee as she looked at him. He loved the way she . . .

'Are you daydreaming?'

He came back to earth. 'Yes. About you.'

Now she smiled, and her strange mood seemed to vanish. 'Foolish man. Shall we meet here again tomorrow? After breakfast? And tell one another our secrets?'

'Breakfast? That's tomorrow.' He frowned.

'Yes. I just said so.'

'I can't wait that long.' He reached for her, pulling her to her feet and against him. 'You are too delicious, Julia. I must have you again today. Tonight at the latest. Come to my rooms after everyone is asleep.'

She pushed her hands against his chest. 'You stayed away effortlessly before. For days.'

Nick nipped her back in against him, stroking his hands down and up again. 'That was before. When I still had a fragment of self-control and sanity. Although I did come up here several times looking for you.'

She snuggled close. 'You did? So did I.' She reached up on tiptoes for a kiss.

But when they pulled apart this time, Julia was all business. 'I shall not come to you tonight, Nick,' she said, stepping out of his embrace. 'It's too great a risk. Shall we meet here tomorrow? To talk.'

'Oh yes, to talk.'

'Good.' She looked about her at the clothes that were strewn across the floor. 'Will you hand me my shift, over there? To teach thee, I will dress first.'

37

Nick found he couldn't bear the thought of making polite and proper conversation over dinner with the woman who had just turned his life inside out. Instead he left via the kitchens, grabbing a wedge of game pie for himself and a bone for the dog. Then he struck out with Solvig, who had chewed off her bandage and seemed as good as new, for a long evening's walk north, up through Camden Town and then over the fields to Highgate Hill. He leaned against a stile, ate his pie and considered the story of Dick Whittington. It was here that young Dick, discouraged and leaving the big city behind, had heard the Bow Bells ring out his fate: 'Turn again, Whittington, thrice Lord Mayor of London.' The young man had gone back down the long hill to find that his cat had made him a fortune. Whittington married, and led the city into the future.

The sun was thinking about setting now, and the city below – so small by twenty-first-century standards – was beginning to glow in the lengthening light, the river uncurling through it like a silver chain. The great, soot-stained dome of St Paul's Cathedral looked like the round breast of a contented grey goose, the other, smaller steeples like her goslings, beaks pointing upwards. Nick scratched Solvig's broad forehead. She sighed.

Dick Whittington, Nick Davenant . . . could he, Nick, be called back again to the London he loved, this London? Bells were ringing, tolling across the city, their discordant conversation carried to him on the breeze. Could they tell him the future? He listened for a moment. But they were just bells. He supposed the bells didn't need to talk to him, for he knew the future of London town.

Down there in the Houses of Parliament the lords were probably still giving their speeches. The Marquess of Blackdown was not among them. And those venerable medieval buildings gleaming now in the long light – they would go up in flames soon enough. Nick couldn't remember now why Parliament would burn, but he could see Turner's painting of the conflagration in his mind's eye – a terrible inferno. '"Then the fire of the Lord fell,"' Nick said to the city, '"and consumed the burnt sacrifice, and the wood, and the stones, and the dust."' Nick thought about the Blitz, and that three-dimensional image of St Paul's dome that Ahn had shown him. The dome, blasted half away. And then . . . the Pale.

Swallows were swooping back and forth across the sky. It was a five-mile walk back to Berkeley Square. 'Come on, Solvig,' Nick said. The huge dog got to her feet, the bone he'd brought for her clamped fast in her jaws. She clearly intended to carry it all the way home. Nick let his hand find the acorn. The bells were still ringing.

Julia wanted no dinner, and she didn't want to talk to anyone. She certainly didn't want to see Nick tonight. She needed to think.

She informed Bella that her head ached and asked her to please make her excuses. Then Julia kept to her room. It was a glorious evening, and if she were in the country she would have struck out on a walk, or saddled Marigold and gone for a good, long gallop through the golden light and unfurling shadows.

Instead she curled up in the armchair by her window, looking out into the branches of the plane trees. Birds were settling in for the evening. Julia realized that the trees were populated, just as a city is, by different characters. Pert sparrows, cocky magpies, elegant turtle doves. She watched them for a while as they flitted up and down, strutted along branches, argued over matters that were clearly of enormous importance but were comprehensible only, she supposed, to birds.

She snuggled down into her chair, tired, as if she had actually walked a long way. She'd had no idea that loving was so completely physical. Somehow she had imagined it being contained, confined to the nether regions, as writing is confined to the hand. She had thought that the rest of the body and perhaps even the mind simply went to sleep until the event was over. How wrong she had been. He had kissed the backs of her knees. She had explored him with hands and kisses. She had gripped his shoulders, his behind, his strong arms, and clung to him for dear life, crying his name as she shattered.

She closed her eyes. Her body was tired. But if there was a change, it felt more emotional than physical. She was calm, in soul as well as in body.

That calmness could not last. He'd said he loved her and she believed him. She had answered him with the truth. She loved him, too. They loved one another. But he was still keeping confidences from her, and she from him. Indeed, betwixt the two of them, they had licked the platter of secrets clean. He was a time traveller caught between an Ofan mistress and a Guild master. Both mistress and master were seeking the Talisman. As for Julia, his supposedly Natural love? Julia smiled to herself, too content to not see the humour in the situation – she was the Talisman they sought, and Nick didn't know it.

Julia curled still more comfortably in her chair. It was a conundrum. One she couldn't solve tonight. She felt herself drifting into sleep, the happy satisfaction of her body and soul winning over the confusion of her mind.

Some time later – the room was duskier – she opened her eyes from a dream. She and Nick had been in the tack room in the stables at Falcott House, and he was searching for a favourite curry comb. She asked him why he didn't just leave brushing the horses to the groom, and he said that in his new life, he had become used to doing everything for himself. He was desperate as he searched, tossing the tackle here and there in his single-minded desire to find what he was looking for. Then, when he finally found the palm-sized tool, he turned triumphantly to show it to her. But it wasn't a comb at all. It was a small hedgehog, curled up in his palm. She stepped forward to see the animal, and it uncurled to reveal its pointed little nose and beady eyes. It looked straight at her and said, in Grandfather's voice: 'Then you shall be orphaned after all.'

She stretched, remembering the dream. Grandfather *was* such a hedgehog. And Julia was an orphan. She had been since she was three months old. Her mother and father were dead. So why had Grandfather said 'after all'? Julia mused on it, almost tumbling again into sleep . . . then suddenly she sat bolt upright. Grandfather had said exactly those words, just a few moments before he died. You shall be orphaned after all . . . you shall be orphaned after all . . . what if instead he had been saying that she would be *Ofan* after all? Grandfather could play with time. Had he known these people, these Ofans? Had Grandfather been Ofan himself?

Julia got to her feet and stared blindly out of her bedroom window. Pretend, Grandfather had said. Pretend, and trust the angels to watch over you. You shall be Ofan after all. Was it a message? Pretend to be something other than you are.

461

Do not reveal that you are the Talisman. Find the Ofan and trust them to watch over you.

Miss Blomgren was Ofan.

The sky had darkened yet another few shades. The birds in the trees were quieter. All across the city, the bells were tolling seven o'clock. Julia adored bells, the way each one had its own distinct voice. 'My America, my Newfoundland.'

Several new worlds had risen up on her horizon today.

The bells rang on.

Julia stayed up late, thinking about her mother, whom she very rarely considered; thinking about Miss Blomgren; and thinking about the Ofan . . . but most of all, she was thinking about Nick Davenant. She drifted off sometime after her bedside candle guttered and went out . . . and now it must have been very late in the morning indeed, for the maid had been in to build up the fire, and the logs were fallen to embers. Julia remembered that she had made a plan to meet Nick after breakfast in order to tell all. Instead she had slept the morning away.

She swung her legs out of bed and saw that there was a note slipped under her door, the paper folded in half. Julia swooped on it, knowing it would be from Nick. It was.

He had received word that the lords were finally voting on the Corn Bill today, and he was desolate to postpone his appointment with Julia – but he had to go and vote against it. She would of course rejoice with him that he need not wear his robes in order to make this hopeless stand against the inevitable; he would be allowed to raise his futile protest dressed like a rational man. If she would please fold along the dotted lines and follow the agreed-upon procedure he would sign himself sick with longing for the way the curtain of her hair fell around his face when she kissed him: Nick.

But, if she felt she could not follow those instructions, then he must sign himself regretfully – and then an absurdly flourishing signature: Blackdown.

There were tiny dots in pale, watery ink beneath his black script, showing her how to fold the sheet of paper into a glider. She considered what to do. This was her first love letter, but only if she burned it. If she didn't burn it, it wasn't a love letter.

She shook her head and started folding.

The day passed slowly. Clare fretted about the possibility of a riot but wouldn't say that out loud in the presence of the dowager marchioness or Bella, both of whom she considered too volatile to handle the greater knowledge she had of what might occur. Bella could tell Clare was withholding something, and that talk of the riot annoyed her sister, so she mentioned it at every turn. The servants were also worried. They clattered the china and dropped the silverware, thus sending the dowager marchioness into a pet. Wasn't it always the way that on a clear, lovely day one's griefs and trials seemed too much to bear? The marchioness took to her bed.

It was, indeed, a lovely day, but no one suggested going out, and no one came to call. Berkeley Square itself was strangely deserted. Gunter's was shut up tight; no ices today. No carriages dashed by, no ladies from either half of the world paraded their fashions beneath the trees.

At around four in the afternoon, Clare and Julia stood by a drawing-room window and watched as the butler of a house across the square from them slipped out and carefully removed the knocker from the door. 'Cowards,' Clare muttered. 'They are not leaving town. I know for a fact that they are holding a ball in four days' time.' She turned on her heel.

'It would serve us right if we were all burned to cinders tonight.' At that moment Bella burst into the room, announcing that it was teatime, and that if Clare was going to insist on pretending that no riot was looming, then she must carry the pretence to its logical conclusion and have tea, as usual. Clare folded her lips tightly on her feelings.

After dinner Julia escaped to the upstairs drawing room, where she spent a half-hour writing to Pringle. It was a jolly letter about London fashions as observed by a young lady in deep mourning who rarely left the house, but Julia knew that poor Pringle was starving for details. As she finished the last sentences, she became aware that the quiet square outside her window was not so quiet any more. She could hear voices. She got to her feet and crossed to the window.

Berkeley Square was filling up with people. Men and women were streaming in from the north and the east. They talked quietly, but their faces were intent, serious, like the faces of people who watch a fire consume a building. They passed the Falcott mansion, pressing towards some destination on the other side of Berkeley Square. Julia watched them from above, her brow to the glass; she could not cast more than a glance upon each impassioned visage. Still it seemed that she could frequently read, even in that brief interval, the history of long years in the passing faces.

She heard the door open and she turned. It was Bella and Clare. They greeted Julia quietly, but they were there to look out of the windows, which had the best view down onto the square. Clare and Julia stood at one casement, Bella at the other. 'Soho is flowing into Mayfair,' Clare said. 'They are getting ready.' Apparently she and Bella were on speaking terms again.

'What will they do?' Bella did not turn from the window to ask her question.

'I do not know. Make their displeasure known. Attack the homes of politicians known to have supported the Corn Bill.'

'This house?'

'I do not know.' Clare glanced at Julia. 'Do you know how Nick was planning to vote?'

'Yes,' Julia said, amazed at the power of sisterly discernment; apparently they simply understood that Julia knew the secrets of Nick's soul. 'He stands against the bill.'

'Thank God! I knew he could not be so blind.' Clare grasped Julia's hand and held it tightly.

'I wonder whose house it is that they are all pressing towards,' Bella said.

At that moment, Julia sensed it. A rushing of blood at the back of her head. A shuddering in the air around her.

Someone in the house was shifting time.

Someone was slowing time down, freezing it.

Whoever it was, they were coming closer. She could feel time coming to a standstill not so very far away. She could feel it like an aching in her bones.

She had successfully feigned immobility yesterday. But that had been in Miss Blomgren's dark basement kitchen, when Miss Blomgren was distracted by Peter – and when the last thing Miss Blomgren would have expected would be to find that Bella's lovelorn little friend could control time. That trick wouldn't work up here in the bedroom, which was aglow with evening light. If whoever it was were to enter this room, he would see two women turned apparently to stone, and one who was only holding very still, her breast rising and falling as she breathed. He would see her fingers twitch in

Clare's stiff grasp. Then he would know about her. He would know she was the Talisman.

The aura reached them. Julia glanced at Bella. Her eyes were fixed.

Julia span away from the gruesome vision and ran to the door. She wrenched it open and looked into the hall. It was empty, but she could hear footsteps coming up from the floor below.

The door at the hallway's end, the one that opened onto the back staircase! She raced to it, glancing once over her shoulder, then opened it as quickly and quietly as she could and slipped inside, closing it behind her. She whirled around, then crouched, eye to the keyhole.

It was the Russian, back from Devon. He was searching for her. He must already know that she was the Talisman. He was coming for her.

He was trying doors. They were locked – but in a second he would see that the drawing-room door was open and that the Falcott sisters stood like waxworks at the windows, Clare's fingers curled to grasp a hand that was no longer there.

And there was no key in the lock to the staircase door.

Julia stood up, took a deep breath and began descending the stairs as quickly and silently as possible. She had no coat, no hat, no money – but she knew she must flee this house. Disappear. Her heart was pounding in her throat and she felt as if she might be sick. Pretend. You shall be Ofan after all. Pretend.

Reaching the floor below, she allowed herself to speed up, and by the time she reached the basement she was flying down the stairs. She wrenched open the door to the stables and saw four horses still hitched to a mud-spattered carriage. The horses were steaming, their mouths frothy, their backs

466

black with sweat. The Russian must have driven them to within an inch of their lives. Julia squeezed past the horses and the shocked grooms. 'Please. Don't tell him you saw me!' She darted out of the stable door, down the mews and towards the river of men and women streaming into the square. She ducked into the crowd and let it carry her along.

38

The crowd was waiting for the lords outside the Houses of Parliament. Nick, who was in the centre of the pack of blustering aristocrats, watched as those who went before him were accosted. 'How did you vote, milord?' Refusal to answer or the wrong answer was met with boos and hisses, but the lords were allowed to pass through the gauntlet of disapproval unharmed. Then the Duke of Kirklaw made the mistake of answering angrily: 'I voted for the Corn Laws and you are a pack of savages!' The crowd simply picked the duke up and passed him hand to hand over the mob. In his black and grey and white clothing, with his outraged mouth open and shouting, the duke looked like nothing so much as a mackerel, flip-flopping on the top of a heaving pile of fish. He was dumped in a mound of horseshit in the street and had to pick himself up. There was a moment of silence, and then there sailed over the heads of the multitude a great, broad laugh, issuing from the mouth of an enormous innkeeper who towered above everyone, his apron stretched across his chest like a flag. Other laughs made a chord with his and the contagion was spreading among the crowd; then, all at once, it seized upon Nick, and he sent forth a shout of laughter that echoed through the street. He looked around him and saw that the lords themselves were having difficulty repressing their mirth, and even the moon, rising in the still-light evening sky, was tilted at a jocular angle.

When it was Nick's turn to answer for himself, he said, 'I voted against the bill.' His answer was met with a cheer and he was passed through the press of bodies as quickly and as lightly as a hot potato. When he tumbled out on the other side, his clothes dishevelled and his hat missing, he cut left off Whitehall into smaller streets and made his way up toward Pall Mall. There were chalk drawings of Castlereagh and Robinson hung in effigy all over the blank walls, and pictures of Robinson's head on a platter; he recalled that Robinson, the man who had introduced the Corn Bill into Parliament, lived in Berkeley Square, and he stepped out more quickly. But he found another arm of the crowd again in Pall Mall. These men and women weren't happy; they were streaming away from Mayfair, their faces grey.

'What happened?' Nick asked an old man.

'Two dead in Berkeley Square,' he said, eyeing Nick's rumpled but fine attire. 'You a nob?'

'Yes, but I voted against the bill. Who is dead? Please, tell me what happened.'

'A young man and a widow woman. Shot by those damned tin soldiers from John Robinson's parlour windows.'

'A woman?'

The man stared at him, the crowd pouring past them. 'You voted against the bill, you say? And I suppose you think that makes you a hero. Well, answer me this: What if you knew her, and found her dead on the ground?' He turned and began to walk away.

'Wait!' Nick grabbed his arm. 'I –'

The man jerked his hand away. 'Oh, no, my fine lord. There is nothing you can say. Two lie dead in Berkeley Square, and the only good that can come of it is that the tide will turn now against you and your kind. Now scuttle off home to your wife and children. They are probably cowering like frightened mice under your mahogany dining table.'

Nick pushed, in an agony of fear, against the tide of

humanity. When Berkeley Square finally came into view he could see that his house was untouched. The square was almost entirely empty now. The iron paling around Robinson's house was bent and broken, and pales were scattered across his steps. The door hung open on its hinges and there was broken furniture in the street. A clutch of people stood beneath the parlour window, bending over two poor, huddled forms; Nick could see a woman's arm extending from beneath the greatcoat that had been tossed over her.

Nick bowed his head. But the gesture of respect was empty; all he could think was, Thank God Julia is safe at home.

Smedley was waiting to receive his lordship's hat and coat, but there was no hat, which elicited concern; had the rabble been violent? Smedley was relieved to hear it; his lordship had perhaps divined that Berkeley Square had not been so lucky? The revolting peasants had ignored the house, but there was some unpleasantness. Happily Miss Percy was already abed by the time the shootings occurred, and by the grace of God their ladyships had not been able to see the violence; the young plane trees might have been planted by good angels to preserve the women from having a clear view. Their ladyships were exhausted from the evening's excitements and had followed Miss Percy's lead; all the females of the house were abed. But his lordship will wish to know: Count Lebedev returned in the midst of the troubles and awaits his lordship in the library.

Nick escaped the butler and opened the library door to a cloud of smoke. The Russian was sitting in one of the chairs by the fire, a black cigarette with a gold filter dangling from his lips. He didn't stand, and he neither looked at Nick nor answered his greeting. He merely raised a languid hand and let it fall again. Nick shrugged and headed to the sideboard for a brandy.

Solvig ambled into the library and sniffed the smoky air, her eyebrows twitching. Then she lumbered past Arkady without a glance and collapsed in front of the fire.

After a long moment, Arkady mumbled around his cigarette. 'That's a large dog. Yours?'

'Mm.' Nick poured a splash of golden brandy into a balloon. 'I acquired her recently. Don't ask how.'

'We had such dogs in Russia.' Arkady drew on his cigarette. 'For fighting the bears. Their strength is something incredible. Their endurance and loyalty . . . once I knew one in Turkey; he tracked down and killed a wolf that had been devouring the sheep.' Arkady subsided into smoky silence.

Nick leaned against the sideboard, enjoying the smell of brandy and cigarettes. It reminded him . . . of what? The past or the future? He sniffed again. Something about it wasn't right. Arkady's cigarette – it didn't smell quite . . . clean. Black with a gold filter. 'That kind of cigarette has definitely not been invented yet, Arkady,' Nick said. 'Just in case you hadn't realized it.'

Arkady held the cigarette aloft and eyed it like it was a precious jewel. 'This is a Sobranie Black Russian. I smoke them when I am angry. They are perfect in any century. Do you want one?' From his pocket he produced the box and gestured at Nick with it, though he still didn't meet Nick's eyes.

'No thanks. I don't want to know what your anger tastes like.'

Arkady kept staring at the fire. He twirled the cigarette between thumb and forefinger and seemed to disappear into his thoughts.

For his part, Nick swirled the brandy in his glass. He wasn't happy to see Arkady again so soon. He'd hoped to have more time to learn from Alva before having to deal with the Guild again. He and Alva had spent the last several nights publicly establishing their so-called relationship, going to parties, being seen all over town. The one hour they had had to talk had been spent by Nick telling Alva his story. She had been especially interested in Mr Mibbs, just as the Guild had been. Nick had told her more, including what Mibbs had said to Leo, and how Leo had warned Nick away. Alva was fascinated. Had Mibbs really pressed into Nick's emotions? Had he really used despair? Why did Nick think he had asked Leo about stolen children? Alva had even wondered if there was a connection between those questions posed in Chile and the incident outside the Foundling Hospital. Nick had shrugged, and said that he thought the Ofan and the Guild should know more about Mibbs and his obsessions than Nick himself did. After all, Mibbs clearly had the talent in spades, while Nick only knew how to hold on to his present moment by thinking about an acorn.

And now Arkady was back, and Nick hadn't learned anything more. Did Arkady know, somehow, that Nick had turned firmly against the Guild?

Arkady smoked. Nick might as well not have been in the room.

Nick took a sip.

Arkady exhaled, slowly, a series of smoke rings.

Nick took another sip.

Arkady drew again on his cigarette.

Nick sighed. So he was going to have to push the issue. Fine. 'Are you going to tell me why you're angry?'

The Russian said nothing at first, and Nick noticed that his white hair was lank, his clothing less than crisp. Then he turned, and Nick saw that his eyes were bloodshot. 'Give,' he said, and

472

reached out a hand imperiously for Nick's glass. Nick handed it over. The Russian tipped his head back and drank the brandy down in one gulp. 'I have learned a great deal in Devon,' he said. 'A very great deal. About your little mouse, Julia Percy. About her cousin, the imbecile earl. And about her grandfather. Her precious grandfather, Ignatius Percy, who is so recently and conveniently deceased.' Arkady hurled the brandy balloon into the fire and watched impassively as it shattered.

Nick stiffened, shocked by Arkady's dramatics. He didn't like this new, splintering mood of the Russian's. 'What did you learn?'

'The question is more material than that, my priest. What did I *find*?'

Nick shrugged, impatient. 'I have no idea.'

'Look.' Arkady pointed to Nick's desk. 'I've left them there for you to see.'

Nick walked over to his desk. There, cluttered together, were some papers he had been working through, a photograph, a quill and inkwell, a Rubik's Cube ... it took a moment for his time-addled eyes to be shocked by the mix of old and new. 'What the hell?' He picked up the photo. It was a somewhat battered snapshot of a beautiful young woman's laughing face. Her blue eyes were Arkady's. 'Is this . . . ?' He turned to look at the Russian, to find him sitting with his eyes closed. 'Is this Eréndira?'

The clock on the mantel ticked. Finally, Arkady opened his eyes and slowly focused on Nick. 'Is that my daughter? No. My Eréndira was a living human being, a brilliant and passionate woman. That slip of paper you hold there? That is a photograph. A trick of the light. It pretends to capture a moment in time.'

Nick looked at the photo. So this was Arkady's daughter, Arkady's lost, dead child. 'Where did you find this?'

Instead of answering the question, Arkady flung his hand toward the Rubik's Cube on the desk. 'Have you ever played with one of those?'

'Not recently.'

'Try. You'll find you can solve it in under a minute.'

'Yes. I remember doing it once or twice before, in the future.' Nick picked it up. He had not touched anything plastic in many days. Its particular slickness, its strange lightness, set his teeth on edge. Nick put it down beside the photo. 'You found these things in Devon? In 1815? What do they have to do with each other? What do they have to do with Castle Dar?'

'Ignatz Vogelstein.' There was pungent loathing in Arkady's voice.

Nick took a shallow breath. So Arkady now knew that old Lord Percy had been that famous Ofan.

'I went to Castle Dar,' Arkady said, 'expecting to find a crazy Ofan. This Eamon, this new earl – he is crazy, yes. As crazy as that water bird, you know, the one that laughs.'

'A loon.'

'Yes. He is crazy like that. But he is not the Ofan I thought I was going to find. Instead I found another Ofan. Very powerful. But . . . dead. Ignatz Vogelstein. The leader of the Ofan investigations in Brazil. The killer of my daughter. The man I have waited so many years to strangle with these, my bare hands!' Arkady held up his long white fingers, his cigarette clamped between his teeth. 'Always I have hoped to find him, so I could kill him. But he is dead. He has escaped me.'

'Darchester killed your daughter? I don't believe it. I knew the old earl my whole life. He was a harmless old windbag.'

'Oh, you think so?' Arkady pointed his cigarette at Nick. 'Before he went into hiding after the death of my daughter, your harmless old windbag was a man of middle age. A

474

powerful man. A leader of men, a teacher, a prophet. She was young, and brilliant, and he? He seduced her. Not as a lover, no. But he seduced her as a teacher. He had in Brazil an Ofan think tank to try to pierce the Pale and learn its secrets. He stole the very best young minds from the Guild and Ofan alike. They experimented with the power. And my daughter, she was the strongest. One day she crossed the Pale. They were all working together, but Eréndira, she was the one, she went across. Vogelstein was holding her hand, and he let go. How could he let go? My daughter was lost . . .' Arkady stopped. He could not go on.

'She died,' Nick said gently.

'Yes,' Arkady whispered. 'She reappeared across the world and in another century. In her fear and pain she found Vogelstein, not me!' Arkady flicked his cigarette into the fire and pressed his palms to his eyes. 'But he had this much of the humanity. He told me where to find her. She spent her final moments in my arms.' Tears seeped out from under Arkady's hands. 'She could not even speak! When she was dead I went to find him, to kill him. But he was gone. Never to be seen or heard from again.' Arkady lowered his hands and his tear-washed eyes shone electric blue. 'The coward disappeared, my priest, poof! Like a puff of smoke.'

'And he came to Devon.'

'Yes. Now I know that he came to Devon. All along he had been this Georgian earl, this Lord Ignatius Percy. Ignatz Vogelstein, that was his Ofan name. After he fled Brazil he stepped back into his aristocratic life. He grew old in hiding, as the earl. Then he died.'

'Why is that important now?'

'Because Ignatz, of course, he didn't just go to ground. All those years he continued with his research. He knew there was a talisman, and he searched for it. Perhaps he even found it. The crazy Eamon, even he knew there was such a thing. He thought it was that stupid cube! But Ignatz *was* up to something in Castle Dar, and he was not alone.'

'What do you mean?'

'What do you think?' The Russian stood, unfolding up out of his chair until he loomed over Nick. 'Where do you suppose your little Julia Percy is this evening, Nick?'

'In her room. She went early to bed,' Nick said.

'No, no.' The Russian smiled down at him. 'She is not in her room. This is why I am so glad you have the other woman. You will not be too heartbroken when I tell you.'

Nick found himself on his feet. 'Arkady . . . do not play with me.'

'Your old girlfriend.' Arkady spread his hands. 'The little pretty Julia. The poor little orphan. She is gone.'

Nick felt the air leave his lungs. His world contracted to a tiny point.

'What time is it?' Arkady looked at the clock on the mantel. 'Nine o'clock? She ran away into the crowd at seven. I am just back from looking for her myself . . .' He opened his box and extracted another cigarette, then waved it, unlit, between his fingers: 'But – poof! Like her grandfather before her, she runs.'

'Arkady, there is a riot out there! A woman lies dead in the square! It could be Julia!'

'It is not. I checked. That dead woman, she has the red hair.'

'Why did she run?' Nick heard his voice as if from a great distance, his body taut and still.

'Because,' Arkady said, fishing a Zippo lighter out of his pocket. 'She is Ofan. I was coming to find her. She fled.' With one smooth gesture he flipped the Zippo's lid and made the tall flame leap up. He lit his gilded cigarette and leaned back in his chair.

476

Nick watched Arkady's display of self-indulgence, willing himself to stay still and calm. He felt himself shift into battle-field mode, his intention focused narrowly on the problems at hand. The first problem was Arkady and how to play him for information. 'Oh,' he said, his tone sarcastic. 'So Miss Percy is Ofan now? First the crazy earl and now that charming girl?'

Arkady pointed his cigarette at Nick. 'She is *his* grand-daughter. And the talent is sometimes inherited. My daughter had it, and so does your Julia. We were watched, that day we all went to Castle Dar, Nick. It was not that ridiculous earl who duelled with me. It was someone else. Someone very powerful but untrained. I found a secret closet. I saw the candles, the holes drilled through the wall. The air reeked of time play, I tell you. Who was it who hid there? I tested the servants and it could not have been any of them. Which means it was either Julia Percy or your spinster sister.'

'You're mad.'

Arkady shook his head. 'Oh, no. That earl is mad, but I? I am only very angry. When I arrive tonight in London I seek them. I stop time as I go. If I find her breathing, blinking, *living* in a moment that I have stopped . . . then I know.' Arkady put the cigarette to his lips and drew, hard. Nick watched the glowing tip flare hot and bright.

'What happened?'

Arkady blew the smoke out slowly and tapped ash onto the Axminster carpet. He shrugged. 'I was a fool. The other night at dinner, I might have begun to suspect, but she charmed me. Those dark eyes . . . almost they made me cry! And today, again, I did not think. If she is Ofan, she can feel me coming. So she escapes. I find a room with your sisters, frozen. But no Julia. She felt me coming and she ran down a back stairway out through the stables. She is gone into the night. I start up time again. I tell your sisters that the little

477

Julia, she went to bed. I go out to find her. But the crowd is huge, and there is the shooting . . .' He shrugged.

Nick swallowed his fear. Just as he'd learned to do it in Spain, during raids. Put the fear aside. Then three deep breaths to come up with a plan. Three calm breaths, and then action. At the end of the first breath he knew he had to trick Arkady into believing he was on his side. At the end of the second breath, he knew that he had to somehow get to Alva and enlist her help without Arkady's knowing. And at the end of the third breath . . .

Nick held that third breath and felt his heart beating. He held it until he wanted to gasp. Nothing came to him. He let the breath out in a long, silent sigh. He took a fourth breath. This wasn't Spain. Julia was alone in an angry crowd, in London in 1815, without a weapon, perhaps without money . . . he thought, for some reason, of her thin slippers.

Arkady eyed him. 'I see you struggling with your feelings, Nick. You can't hide them from me. This is because you still love the girl?'

'I don't love her,' Nick lied. 'I am concerned for her, and for the Guild. And I'm thinking, damn it, so shut up.' Nick ground out the words to keep from shouting them. 'We need to get her back. For the Guild.'

'Indeed we do.' Arkady put his cigarette to his lips, then lowered it without taking a drag. 'And when you say the Guild, Nick, I hope that is what you mean. I hope your new girlfriend the lovely golden lioness and your old girlfriend the little brown mouse have not conspired together to make an Ofan out of you.'

'Just shut up and let me think.'

Arkady bowed. 'Please, my lord. Think.'

Nick turned his back to Arkady and stared at the fire. Think. He concentrated on the leaping flames. Julia could manipulate time? Could this be true? And if it were true, would that keep her safe? But how could she have that power? Nick breathed through the fear and thought about his lover. She must have run from Arkady because she believed it was the safer course, and if she was Ofan then she had some defences. Nick had to trust her choices and come up with a plan that left Arkady behind.

At his feet, Solvig snorted in her sleep. The huge dog lay on her side, her nose and paws twitching. She was hunting something in her dreams. Hunting . . . hunting! Solvig was a terrible guard dog . . . but perhaps she could hunt.

'Solvig,' he said out loud. She woke and her droopy eyes found his. She lumbered to her feet and pressed her nose into his hand. Nick turned to Arkady. 'The dog,' he said. 'She will find Julia.'

Arkady crossed his arms. 'It is possible. We must give her something of the girl's for scent. It could work. Let us go immediately.'

'Not you. You can't come with me. For God's sake, man, she's terrified of you. She trusts me. I must go alone.'

Arkady scowled. 'She trusts you, does she? But do I? How do I know you will bring her to me?'

'The girl's life is in danger. Our first priority must be to find her. Then, I promise I will bring her to you. You can perform your Ofan tests on her. I think you'll find that she is just a nice young lady from Devonshire, much like any other.'

'No. She is Ofan. Or worse. What she did to me at the dinner table . . . the way she made me trust her? It was like nothing I have ever experienced. It is true, I am susceptible to beautiful women. But this Julia Percy, I am not attracted to her. She is too young, too innocent – not like your lovely sister –'

'Oh, for fuck's sake!' Nick snapped his fingers for Solvig.

'Enough! Go to the Guild's house in Fleet Street and wait. Once I find Julia I shall meet you there.'

'With the girl?'

Nick put his hand on Solvig's head. 'I'll see you later, in Fleet Street.'

39

'My dear.'

Julia looked up, startled. It seemed like hours since she'd seen those two people shot dead at close range, since she'd lost Jem Jemison in the crowds in Berkeley Square, since she had run blindly into the tangled web of Soho streets, hoping to find Soho Square on her own. At first she had moved with the crowds pouring back into Soho, but they had quickly dispersed to their homes, leaving the streets empty. Now the kindly looking old man she had been following in hopes that he would lead her somewhere safe had turned and was facing her.

'Sir?' She drew herself up, trying to look self-assured.

He was small and thin and much older than she had thought, his skin wrinkled and his eyes sunken. 'Why are you following me? I have walked the same circle through the streets twice, testing you. Do you plan to rob me? I assure you I have no money.' He smiled gently at her.

'Oh, no, sir. I am sorry. I am lost, you see. I was trying to appear confident, so I followed you, thinking no one would trouble me if I looked like I was with you.'

The old man tipped his head back and laughed, a young laugh, at odds with his fragile frame. 'That's rich. As if I could protect a flea. Well, my dear. Where is a well-dressed young lady like you trying to go this late at night? I shall do my best to help you.'

'Soho . . . Soho Square,' Julia stammered.

He regarded her soberly. 'Indeed? Well, I shall guide you there. Come, take my arm.'

So they set off through the streets together. As they walked, the old man told her of how the neighbourhood had declined across his lifetime. His name was Roland LeCrue, he explained, and yes, his name gave him away – he was of French descent. A century and more ago his Huguenot grandfather had fled Catholic France and come to Protestant England, where he had bought a fine house in Soho, which was a French neighbourhood in those days. Monsieur LeCrue could remember when French was the language most spoken in these streets, can you imagine? Now he was the only Frenchman left. The aristocrats who had lived on Soho Square in his childhood had all sold their grand houses and moved elsewhere, and now the neighbourhood was squalid, filthy. He poked at a pile of rags with his stick and shook his head. 'Times are hard. Now a young girl like you must fear for her life as she walks these streets. Everything changes,' he said, and fell silent.

Julia squeezed his arm. 'I never feared for my life,' she assured him. 'And you helped me. You are a true Cavalier. I thank you, *monsieur. Merci.*'

'*Plus ça change, plus c'est la même chose.*' He patted Julia's cheek. 'May young ladies like yourself always find the help and respect that they desire. And look. Here we are. Soho Square.' He spread his thin arms. '*Voilà!*'

Julia turned and held out her hand. 'I thank you from the bottom of my heart.'

Monsieur LeCrue took her hand, his eyes quizzical. 'Ah, but you do not want me to show you to the door, do you? You do not want me to see which house you enter?' He nodded. 'Never mind, my dear. I understand. I do not judge you. God bless you.' He sketched a funny little antique bow, and she turned away.

Julia faced the square. Which house had it been? She looked along the row of mismatched mansions and saw the yellow façade. Yes. There was a big, old-fashioned travelling coach and steaming team of horses stopped in front. Those horses must have made a long, arduous journey. But now they had arrived, and were finally able to rest. She hoped her story had a similarly happy ending.

Julia took a deep breath and prepared to beg her lover's lover for shelter.

Nick and Solvig were deep in Soho, and Solvig was dragging him down every tiny street. The dog was on the trail of something, but Nick was beginning to despair of its actually leading to Julia. She could be anywhere. The city, which had looked so small and quaint from Highgate Hill last night, now felt like an endless rabbit warren. Julia could be in any room in any house, down any noisome street. She could be alive, dead, dying – she could be in pain, frightened . . .

Nick shoved the thoughts away and concentrated on Solvig. Her nose was pushing through the filth, and she was grunting softly, giving herself encouragement. Every once in a while she turned a confident, grinning face back at Nick, then resumed her quest. And yet hadn't they passed this intersection once already?

'My lord.' A hand touched his shoulder and Nick wheeled around, pulling Solvig to a reluctant stop.

'Jemison!'

The man looked haggard. 'You are seeking Miss Percy,' he said.

'However do you know that?'

Jemison eyed Nick up and down. 'How did you vote, my lord?'

'Against.'

'Ah.' He frowned, nodding. 'Your sister will be pleased.'

Nick grabbed his arm. 'If you bear me any love as a fellow soldier, please – what do you know of Julia?'

'I saw her. In Berkeley Square. She was out in the crowd, in nothing but a flimsy black gown. She told me a tarradiddle about needing to run away. I told her to stay by me and I would help her, but just then the shooting started –'

'Yes, the two dead.'

'Shot dead by men in scarlet,' Jemison said. 'After the first shot I stepped in front of Miss Percy and shouted for her to hang on to my belt; the crowd was turning and pushing back against us. Then another shot was fired and I felt the crowd pull us apart. I turned, and I saw that she was running – she could not help but run – pushed away on the breast of the crowd. I tried to follow, but she disappeared out of the square, heading in the direction of Soho. I have been searching for her since the crowd dispersed.'

Nick couldn't help it. He grabbed Jemison's hand and shook it. 'Thank you!'

Jemison pulled away and stepped back. 'I do not do it for you. And now that you are here to look for her, it is best we part. I can go back to others who need me more.' He turned away.

'No, Jemison!' Nick's words came without thought. 'The two in Berkeley Square are dead. I . . . Julia needs you more.'

For a long moment it seemed that Jemison would simply stand there, his back to Nick. But then he turned. 'I wonder if you know what else died tonight in your gracious square, with those two.'

Nick stepped forward. He was taller than Jemison, and broader, but he knew that the man had a will as strong and as supple as a whip, and a fierce, unflinching ability to do what must be done. 'I need you, Jemison,' Nick said. 'We must find

Julia. Not only because she is in danger . . .' How to explain? Nick stared at the man who had seen him disappear from under the dragoon's sword. 'Jemison,' he said. 'I want –' He stopped.

Jemison said nothing, and his eyes glittered in the darkness.

'I want to tell you what happened to me at Salamanca,' Nick said, pushing on, 'and I need you to believe me.'

'I am a rational man. I do not believe in demons.'

'When the dragoon reared above me, I jumped forward in time,' Nick said, his voice a whisper. 'Two hundred years. A group of . . .' Nick paused, searching for words. 'A group of aristocrats from throughout history control the flow of time just as if it were money. They control who can travel, who can even know that time is malleable. Are you following me?'

Jemison blinked. His expression had not changed even one iota since Nick began his incredible confession.

'History itself is now threatened by an unknown power emanating from the future. And Julia . . .' Here Nick ground to a halt.

Jemison let his gaze soar up, above the rooftops, to where the moon rode silver in the sky. 'Julia,' he said. 'Julia is what?' The black eyes met his again, and Nick could read nothing in them.

'Julia is also able to manipulate time,' Nick said. 'But she is alone; she does not even know that I have the gift, or that I know she has the gift. Now she is running from a man who hopes to find her and perhaps kill her. That is why she could not go home again. And why it was the hand of God that swept her from you tonight, and kept you from dragging her back to my house, where that man was waiting for her. Perhaps that is a sign that she is lucky. Perhaps she has come to no harm.'

Jemison was silent, his hands thrust deep into the pockets

of his jacket. His face was expressionless, neither friendly nor hostile.

Solvig snorted, eager to continue her search.

Nick sighed. 'You do not believe me,' he said. 'You think me war-addled.'

Jemison smiled as calmly as if Nick had been describing the theory of gravity. 'On the contrary, my lord. I believe you completely.'

40

'I tell you, Nick, she is not here.'

'Your godforsaken dog thinks she's here.' Nick yanked at Solvig's lead; the dog was pulling away from him, straining down the front steps of Alva's house. She was fascinated by some spot in the street.

Solvig turned resentful eyes on Nick and barked, then with one strong yank of her lead she broke free and bounded down the stairs, to stand over that spot on the pavement, her nose pushing back and forth in the dirt.

Alva was wearing a silver wrap over not very much, and her hair was piled on top of her head in a complicated confection of loops and curls. Now she watched her former pet, a furrow between her brows. 'Perhaps she didn't follow the trail at all. Perhaps she just led you home to me.'

'She was following some sort of scent,' Nick said. 'She dragged us up and down every street in Soho, her nose down and her tail up like a flag.'

Alva pursed her lips, then turned to Jemison. 'Who is your friend, Nick? Are you going to introduce us?'

'Miss Blomgren, Mr Jemison,' Nick said, gesturing impatiently from one to the other. 'I've told him about the Ofan and the Guild, Alva, so you've no need to be secretive.'

'Oh, have you?' Alva tipped her head on one side and gave her full attention to Jemison. 'And you believe his lordship, Mr Jemison?'

Jemison bowed. 'I have reason to trust what he says.'

Alva nodded once. 'That is high praise indeed.' She turned

back to Nick, who was almost quivering with impatience. 'That was a remarkable decision you made, Nick, to tell a Natural about the River of Time. You must trust Mr Jemison, in return.'

'Obviously.' Nick punched his fist into his open palm. 'Now can we stop caring and sharing and get on with finding a young woman who might well be in mortal danger? Why, for instance, would Julia come here, of all places?'

Alva glanced down and fingered the fine texture of her garment. 'I'm not sure.'

'That is not the truth,' Jemison said.

Alva's gaze flew up and Nick watched as the courtesan and the ex-soldier locked eyes.

'You are an observant man,' Alva said.

Jemison bowed his head.

'Your friend is correct.' Alva turned to Nick with a half smile. 'Or at least, he is not wrong. I don't know why Julia would come to me. But she was here yesterday. She came with your sister.'

'They visited you? A prostitute?'

Alva put her hand on Nick's arm. 'Please do not play the marquess with me, Nick. I met your sister on a harmless walk a week or so ago. She did not inform me of her rank, and we chatted quite naturally. Then she and Julia turned up yesterday hoping to extend the friendship. When I learned who they were, I sent them on their way with a flea in their ear.'

'I find that not at all comforting.'

'The young lady is missing,' Jemison said. 'And the dog led us to you, Miss Blomgren. You know her, Nick knows you. There must be some reason she came here.'

'The only reason I can think of is no reason at all,' Alva said in answer. 'The poor child thinks I am Nick's mistress.'

'And how,' Nick said with contempt, 'did she come to think that?'

Alva's eyes warmed. 'The icy resolve of a man in love,' she said. 'How lovely for Julia. But I'm afraid you can't blame me. She arrived fully aware that you had a mistress and what she looked like. When she saw me, she put two and two together.'

'This was yesterday? Yesterday morning?'

'Yes.'

The icy resolve melted like a snowflake. Nick sat down on the step, not caring if it cost him his dignity. So Julia had come directly from Alva's house, called for him, and then she had simply . . . made him her lover. What must she have thought when he told her he loved her? No wonder that strange expression had flitted across her face. No wonder her reply had been so flat.

Alva stepped out of her doorway and sat down next to him, her garment shimmering in the light of the flambeaux that flanked her steps. 'I felt I couldn't explain,' she said gently. 'Given everything.'

'No, you couldn't.' Nick propped his elbows on his knees and pushed his fingers into his hair. 'But it seems so unlikely that she would run to you, knowing what she thinks she knows.'

'Especially since I stood on this very step and told them in no uncertain terms that they were never welcome here again.' Alva shook her head. 'It was hard. Your sister feels trapped by her sex and her class, she is hungry for knowledge, and she wasn't wrong to think that I have found a way to be free. But it is not a way that she can emulate.' She stretched her arms down between her knees and clasped her hands. 'I had to freeze them while they were here. I hate doing that – it is such a violation of human dignity. But Peter came back. You remember, the girl who wasn't on duty? She jumped right into the midst of us without warning and I had to freeze your sister and Julia in order to deal with Peter. She was full

489

of some crazy theory about the Talisman. She . . . Why are you looking at me like that?'

Nick held up a hand, his thoughts tumbling over one another. 'Wait . . . I'm thinking.' He counted to three in his head, and when he was done, he knew. 'She heard everything you said.'

'What?'

'Julia is one of us, Alva!' Nick felt something like hope unfurl in his chest. 'I've only just learned it, from Arkady of all people.'

'Arkady! How does he know?'

'Oh, God, he's figured everything out, Alva. He even knows about Ignatz.'

Alva raised her eyebrows. 'He does?'

'Yes. And he's convinced that Julia is Ofan, or at least that she has the talent. It must be true, because the only reason she would know to come to you is if she knew you were Ofan as well. She wasn't frozen at all while you were talking to Peter – she was pretending. Thank God, because it means she knows you can help her, knows that you are safe.'

'Except,' Alva said gently, 'that she is not here.'

At that moment Solvig's bark broke the night's stillness like cannon fire. Nick shot to his feet and went down to her. She was scrabbling in the dust at the edge of the road, trying to pick something up in her teeth. Nick dragged her away by the collar and bent to pick it up himself. It was dirty and it was wet with Solvig's slobber, but he could see the badly stitched J.P. even in the flickering light.

It was Julia's hussif.

He charged back up the stairs. Jemison and Alva bent over the sorry little bag. 'Is it hers?' Alva asked.

'Yes. I saw her with it just the other day. It was in the gutter . . . why?'

'Did she know you had seen it?' Jemison plucked it from

Nick's fingers and looked at it closely. 'Might she have dropped it as a sign to you?' He untied the ribbon that secured the square pouch and unfolded it.

'That's exactly what she must have done,' Alva said. 'A way of saying "I was here!"'

Jemison pulled out the tangle of red thread that Julia had been working on that glorious morning of the paper aeroplanes. Then he came up with a small ring stuck on the end of his forefinger like a crown. 'Look at this twisty piece of trash. I wonder why she carries it.'

Alva reached out slowly, as if she were pushing her hand through sand. 'Please,' she breathed. 'Oh, please!' She plucked it from Jemison's finger and fumbled in her bosom for her glasses. She popped them on her nose and examined the ring as tears slipped unnoticed down her cheeks, like raindrops on a window.

'What is it?' Nick tried to keep the desperation from his voice.

She held the ring out on her open palm, for Nick to see. 'Eréndira,' she said. 'It is her ring.'

'The Talisman!' Nick snatched it up for a closer look. At first glance it appeared cheap, for it was only copper. But the craftsmanship was flawless. The ring looked as if it were made of several intricately intertwining cords. The motif of the eye within the circle was so abstract as to be almost illegible; if Alva hadn't described it to him in the transporter, he never would have seen it as representational at all. 'This looks . . . either very old or very modern,' he said.

'Why is it important?' Jemison reached out for the ring, and Nick handed it over.

'It is a talisman,' Nick said. 'Something both the Ofan and the Guild are seeking. We hope it has the power to change the future.'

Jemison frowned and turned the ring over in his hand, then gave it back to Alva. 'Are you saying it is magical?' Jemison cast a doubting glance at Nick. 'This little thing?'

Alva folded her fingers over the ring. 'I don't know,' she said. 'I have never believed in magic; to my mind the things we do with time aren't supernatural. They don't rely on incantations or spells or potions; we simply have a talent. But . . .' She looked up at Jemison. 'Ignatz Vogelstein, our great teacher and visionary, sent me a letter, Mr Jemison, with a hint enclosed about the Talisman. The hint was the symbol that is worked into this little ring.' Alva looked from Jemison to Nick, her eyes alight. 'Tell me now, Nick. How is Julia connected to Ignatz Vogelstein?'

'She is his granddaughter.'

Alva stared at him. 'Oh,' she whispered. 'Of course! Why didn't I realize it when I saw her yesterday? Her eyes reminded me of his; I even told her so. And yet I didn't put two and two together. Even though she was there with your sister . . . he never let me meet the child, you know –'

Jemison interrupted. 'So either the ring is the Talisman, or her grandfather gave her the ring as a sign for her to show others that she can be trusted. She holds the secret.'

Nick shook his head. Something was tickling his memory. 'I don't think she does know,' he said. 'I don't think she has any idea that this ring is important at all. There was something she said . . .' He gestured towards Jemison. 'May I have that hussif?'

Jemison handed the pouch over and Nick held it in his hand, remembering Julia talking to him about it. She'd said she didn't keep sewing notions in it, but rather some keepsakes . . . He opened it again and found a fossil trilobite. 'This is a memento of her grandfather,' he said. 'And that . . .' He pointed to the ring in Alva's hand. 'She thinks that is a trinket, the only memento she has of her mother, who died when she was three months old. She called it a "fairing".'

Alva reached for the trilobite and held it in her palm beside the ring. 'Ignatz,' she whispered. She sighed. 'When I saw Julia's gestures, and when I saw those dark eyes . . . Ignatz used his hands in just that way when he talked, and he had dark eyes too. Like good, strong Assam tea. A redder brown than Julia's. I almost wept right there in my kitchen, surrounded by half-pickled beets . . .'

'Alva.' Nick touched her shoulder. 'Julia is lost. We need to stay focused.'

But Alva held the ring up and contemplated it with that same misty expression. 'It is beautiful, isn't it,' she mused. 'Crafted before the fall of Mesoamerica by a P'urhépecha metallurgist – did you know that their work was even finer than the Mexicas? It is priceless.'

Nick pushed his fingers into his hair and sighed. 'I beg of you, Alva –'

'No – follow me, Nick. Something doesn't make sense here. The ring is a treasure in two ways. The Spanish melted down every piece of metal they could lay their hands on, so almost no pre-Conquest jewellery remains, and yet here is this ring. Second, this ring was Eréndira's inheritance from her mother, but Arkady doesn't have it – Julia does. And Julia thinks it is a trinket of no value except as a sentimental connection to her own dead mother. Why?'

'It must have been Ignatz's way of making the ring significant to her,' Nick said. 'He passed the ring off as her dead mother's so that she would carry it around with her all the time. But why would he make her the keeper of the Talisman, and yet not tell her what it was? We're back where we started.'

Alva shook her head. 'No, we're not back where we started.

It's clear! The ring itself isn't the Talisman, it marks the Talisman. It is a sign.' She turned those eyes, glowing like a bluebell wood at dusk, on Jemison and then on Nick. 'Ignatz told Julia the ring was her mother's so that she would always have it near her, but he didn't want Julia to protect the ring. He wanted the ring to reveal the truth about Julia. Julia Percy is the Talisman.'

'That's mad,' Nick whispered.

'Why else would she carry that ring of Eréndira's close to her all the time and yet not know what it is?'

'From what I'm beginning to understand about your boyfriend,' Nick said, 'he kept Julia in the dark about everything. His lies don't prove anything about either the ring or Julia. They only prove that he was a pig-headed old man –'

But Alva wasn't listening. She was staring at the ring, and she looked as if she might faint.

'What? What is it?'

'Oh, dear God,' Alva said, and raised her still, shocked face to Nick's.

'Tell me!'

'It was not Ignatz Vogelstein's eyes I recognized in Julia's,' Alva said, her voice a trembling thread. 'I was led astray by the brown colour of them and the familiarity of her gestures. The ring *did* belong to her mother, Nick. Julia is not Ignatz's granddaughter. She is Arkady's.'

The marquess rose up like a wall of fire at Alva's words, enraged by the suggestion that the woman he intended to marry was not legitimate, was not English. But Nick met that rage with his own, and he simply reached inside and pinched the marquess out like a puny candle flame.

He knew in his bones that it was true. Julia was Eréndira's daughter.

It made Julia's isolation, her danger and his own fear for her more tangible. She was alone, and she had no idea who she was. The man she had loved as a grandfather had tried to protect her by wrapping her up in a tissue of lies, and her blood grandfather, Arkady, was hell-bent on . . . Nick swallowed. He was hell-bent on harming her, perhaps even killing her.

'All right then,' Nick said, taking a deep breath. 'Julia is Eréndira's daughter. She is the Talisman. Can that new information shed any light on what might have happened to her?'

But Alva was frantically trying to make sense of the new revelation. 'Eréndira had no children when I knew her,' Alva said. 'She was young. She took on lovers like she took on ideas: fully, passionately – and then she moved on. But when she returned to us, dying of wounds I could not see? She had aged in her time across the Pale. She must have had a child and given it to Ignatz. And he must have hidden it. An hour after her death Ignatz disappeared to Devon, only to return to London now and then, and only as the Earl of Darchester. It wasn't long after he left that we heard he was raising an orphaned granddaughter.'

'But how does it follow that Julia is a human talisman? What does that even mean?'

'It means Peter was right.' Alva scowled. 'Which she usually is, damn it. She told me that the Talisman would have a jagged edge, that it was broken. That it was one half of a desperate promise with the unknown.'

'There is nothing broken about Miss Percy,' Jemison said.

'Her terrible birth – that's what I'm thinking of,' Alva said. 'What if she was born across the Pale? Or born in her mother's violent transition back? She was torn into this world, don't you see? Torn from another world. An orphan, a foundling . . . her very brilliance a threat to her life.'

Jemison shrugged. 'Sounds like the human condition.'

'If you're right,' Nick said, 'Julia was conceived, or carried, or born in a world where time is moving backwards. Perhaps she has some hidden knowledge about the Pale, hidden even from herself? Or some power? Something so powerful that Ignatz decided to bury it away and hope it never surfaced?'

'Yes,' Alva said musingly. 'Eréndira brought her back here, back to this forward-moving time – a talismanic connection to that other world, torn from one time and given to another. Eréndira died of the effort it took to return, or of complications from childbirth – and she put little Julia into the arms of her teacher, not her father. Ignatz went to great lengths to hide Julia from Arkady. Which must mean that Eréndira and Ignatz both feared what the Guild would make of Julia.'

'But the Guild wants to turn the Pale back too,' Nick said. 'For all that you hate them, they are more misguided than evil. And how different was Julia's life with Ignatz from life in the Guild? The Guild relies on ignorance to keep their power. They lie to us and keep us happy with money. Well, isn't that what Ignatz did to Julia? Raised her as an earl's granddaughter and told her nothing at all? He might have been a great Ofan teacher, but he used Guild methods to control her. I think . . .' Nick took the copper ring from Alva's fingers and turned it so that he could see the motif of the eye in the circle. 'I think there must be something bigger, something more at stake than just the old feud between the Guild and the Ofan.'

All three were silent then, under the weight of this revelation and the possibility that they might never find Julia.

Nick closed his eyes. He had no idea where to even start. She was lost. Lost, perhaps, because Ignatz had lied to her. Julia was truly orphaned – orphaned even from herself – and

Nick was powerless to help. He felt despair well up in him, deep and cold.

Despair . . . a spider held over a flame . . . the Foundling Hospital! 'Orphans,' he said, his voice rough. 'Stolen children!'

'Yes?' Alva's voice was threaded with confusion.

Nick turned to her, but it wasn't her eyes he saw. Flat, blue eyes. Despair. The terrible nothingness sucking at his soul . . .

'Nick? Nick!'

He looked at his palm and found that he was holding the acorn, in addition to the copper ring. 'Mibbs,' he said, and closed his fingers around them. 'He is here, in London. A man accosted my mother the other day about a baby . . . it must have been him.'

'A baby?' Alva frowned. 'The Foundling Hospital   ' Her eyes flew to Nick's. 'Oh God, and what he said to Leo!'

'Exactly.' Nick got to his feet. 'Everywhere Mibbs has been, and every question he has asked, begins to make sense. He is looking for Julia. He was looking for her in America, among indigenous people, because he must know about her mother's connection to the P'urhépecha. But now he is also looking for her in Europe. He has been looking up and down the River of Time, always searching for an infant.'

'Yes,' Alva said. 'Babies. It is always babies. He's not thinking that she might be grown!'

'That must be it. And thank God she is grown, in this time, for it might keep her from him. But Mibbs is getting close. He knows now that Julia is connected to Arkady, because he asked for Arkady the other day.'

'What if he is now looking for her as a grown woman?' Alva whispered. 'Perhaps he followed her from Berkeley Square today.'

'If that is the case,' Nick said, 'then we have lost —'

The sound of running feet and a shout interrupted him. A little old man came careening around the corner of Carlisle Street, a Bow Street Runner in tow.

'It was right here,' he said breathlessly, pointing with his stick. 'Right where that great dog is now. It was a grand old travelling coach, sir. As the girl walked past it, a big, pale man got out brandishing a club. She seemed to know him, for she laughed at first and said something. But the man had hit her over the head, tossed her into the carriage, and then the coachman whipped up the horses and drove away. I saw the coat of arms on the coach door then, sir. Very simple, sir, a red field with a silver shield, and three weasels on it. I called and tried to run after them but . . .' He broke down in frustrated tears. 'Please believe me. A young lady is in grave danger.'

The little old man, the runner, and Solvig now stood together, looking at the blank cobblestones of the street. Nick felt a laugh of relief bubbling up in his throat, and Alva clearly understood, too, for her eyes were sparkling.

Mibbs didn't have Julia. Eamon did.

'Why can't you just go back in time and catch Miss Percy as she leaves your house? Why do we have to go chasing after the coach? For that matter, why can't you go back before Vogelstein's death and ask him about Julia?'

Alva pressed her seal into the hot wax on the last of three notes she had written. 'Because we can't,' she said simply.

A servant had been dispatched to Berkeley Square and to Jemison's house in Camden Town for their things, including pistols and horses. Jemison had been peppering them with questions as they waited. Nick was jumping out of his skin with impatience, now that there was something he could actually do. He paced up and down in front of the fire like a caged animal, listening to the conversation with one ear and to the pounding of his heart with the other.

'But why?'

Alva answered patiently. 'Because we move back and forth in time on streams of human emotion, Mr Jemison. Big streams. We have the ability to use those streams of feeling, but we ourselves – we are just bit players, and our own feelings, our own life stories, they plod forwards day to day. So if I'm here today and in 2029 tomorrow and in 1580 the next day, I will still tell the story of my life as a story that proceeds forwards in time.'

'Your life moves forwards day to day, even if those days don't follow each other on the calendar.'

'Exactly. Which means that I cannot know what is coming for me, and I cannot go back to a day I have already lived through.'

'"Solomon Grundy,"' Nick said, without turning from the window. '"Born on a Monday, Christened on Tuesday, Married on Wednesday" . . . Where the bloody hell are the horses?'

'But other time travellers must know your future. They should be able to tell you when you die, for instance!'

Alva caught Nick's eye. 'You see what happens when you invite Naturals into your world? They invariably start criticizing.' She turned back to Jemison. 'Our talent is queer,' she said. 'Why do our stories proceed unmolested even as we jump about in the river? If we time travellers know the big shapes of human history, the movements of markets and epochs, you would think we could know what is destined in our own piddling lives. And yet . . . we cannot.'

'That makes no sense,' Jemison said. 'Naturals are condemned to a preordained story, we are bound to live lives that you, the time travellers, can know – but that we cannot. While you, the time travellers, don't know your own futures,

499

even though you can travel forwards in time. You have possibility, movement, hope, and from what you have just told me, I can only assume that we Naturals are doomed.'

'Oh, no,' Alva said. 'You misunderstand me. You are not doomed, Mr Jemison, any more than I am. I mean, you shall die one day and so shall I, but how you arrive at that final chapter is up to you. You have choices to make. It is only the big picture that continues always to look the same, no matter what we small actors do – and by we I mean all of us, Natural, Ofan, Guild. We run about like busy ants, but the wars do not change. They never change. And that is exactly what we Ofan hope to learn how to alter. What we *must* learn how to alter, else one day the Pale will wash across us and we will vanish like a dream.'

Jemison's dark eyes were intent. 'So the future of mankind is set in stone, and while individual lives may sparkle and shine, we are little more than spirits, melting into air. You seem to be basing your hopes in fairy dust, Miss Blomgren.' He sounded doubtful in the extreme, almost condescending.

Alva shrugged. 'But surely that is what hope is! "The tune without the words." Maybe not knowing the words means that we can make them up as we go along. And more importantly, it means that we can go back and change them. We can already change the river in tiny ways, you know. Nick did today when he told you about us. But it is only play, the level at which we dabble now. A dip in the river, a splash, a brief obstruction of the flow, and then our individual revels end. But I believe that if we can learn to channel our dreaming, then we can make the fact that we don't know the little things alter the things we know too well . . .'

Nick was ready to tear his hair out. 'Oh my God, Alva, Arkady told me you Ofan were all a bunch of dangerous dreamers. How can you be wittering on like this when Julia is lost? If you don't shut up I'm going to kill you. There. How's that for a hopeless ending to your story?'

'I would simply jump away from you, Nick. You know that.' Alva smiled a little sadly at Jemison. 'We are cowards, really, we time travellers. We cheat death over and over. Jumping away from one story and into another. Always pursuing the hope of another day.'

Jemison curled a lip. 'That's a fancy way of saying you are seeking immortality, Miss Blomgren. All dressed up as charity to a benighted humanity.'

Alva's eyes widened; she was startled by the scorn in his voice. 'No . . . not individual immortality. I'm talking about group action. The fact that we don't know what happens to us individually – that's what gives me hope for humans collectively. It must be possible to change the big story.'

'I am just a poor Natural,' Jemison said. 'But would that not be to grasp too much power, Miss Blomgren? You have read your Milton, I assume. God will punish you if you claim too much knowledge . . .'

'He's right, Alva,' Nick said peevishly. 'And what you're describing sounds quite a lot like fascism. Or corporate personhood.'

Alva snorted. 'Says Mr Aristo. What is your title but a kind of immortality?'

Nick pointed at her. 'I didn't ask for it.'

'And yet you wear it so well.'

Nick stared at her. If the horses didn't arrive in the next minute . . .

But then the sound of hooves rang in the street. They all rushed to the window.

It was the servants, with their mounts.

'Thank God!' Nick tossed his own note to Arkady on Alva's pile of letters on his way out of the door. He had told the Russian that Julia remained unfound but that he was following leads. Hopefully that would keep Arkady at bay, but Nick and Alva were sure that Arkady would come immediately to check if Alva had gone with Nick. It was therefore vital that she remain at home in Soho Square to try to put him off. But she was sending several Ofan after Nick and Jemison, so that they would have some backup in Devon.

'I wish I had had time to teach you more,' Alva said as she stood beside the two men and their horses a few minutes later. 'I can't believe I'm sending you off like this, and with no one but a Natural for protection.'

'Thanks a lot.' Nick checked and tightened Boatswain's girth.

'Yes,' Jemison said. 'Thank you for the kind words of support.'

'I'm being realistic,' Alva said.

'Look.' Nick turned to her. 'The fact is, I'm finally doing something I know I how to do, and I am with a companion in whom I am completely confident.' He swung up and into the saddle, Boatswain shifting under him. 'Tracking down Julia and thrashing Eamon is, in fact, an easy proposition for two Peninsular soldiers. So although we thank you for your concern, we are quite capable.'

'Yes, I see. I'm sorry.' Alva looked up at him, her hand on his knee. Nick was sure they made a touching picture – a beautiful woman bidding her menfolk farewell. But what she said next hardly matched the tableau. 'The Guild and Mr Mibbs – they want Julia because they think she is the Talisman,' she said. 'I wonder if there is a way to convince them that she is not? When you find her and free her from Eamon, work out how much she knows and how well she is trained.

Surely Ignatz at least taught her how to use her talent, even if he didn't tell her of her own importance.'

Nick shrugged. 'Arkady thinks she is untrained, and when I pressed her for information about her grandfather, she almost wept with confusion.'

Alva shook her head over this. 'Ignatz! I'd kill him now if he weren't already dead. You have the ring, yes? Give it to Julia and tell her as much as you can. Hopefully a few Ofan will reach you soon, and together you can come up with a plan that will protect Julia for the long term.' In the flickering light Alva looked like the angel from whom the Ofan took their name. The face she tipped up towards Nick was radiant with purpose, the two iron flambeaux holders rising behind her like a brace of wings. 'Make it seem as if she is entirely innocent of what's going on. That way, we can save her for the Ofan.'

'I'm guessing she will make her own choice about the Ofan and the Guild,' Nick said. 'I'm hoping to save her for herself.'

'That is disgustingly romantic,' Alva said, and stepped away from the horses. 'Now go!'

Nick tipped his beaver hat and let Boatswain dance in a circle. Then he and Jemison galloped away over the cobblestones, heading for Oxford Street.

41

It felt as if her skull were broken and as if her body were being shaken to pieces. Her ears were filled with a crashing, rattling sound. Julia lifted a hand to touch her head. Just that movement alone set her retching.

An arm lifted her, and there was a sharp rapping sound. Then the rattling slowly subsided, and the terrible swaying and bumping ceased. Julia opened her eyes to almost complete darkness, but even that was enough to sting. She closed her eyes. Something smelled rank and close and mildewy. She retched again.

A door was opened and she was lifted outside. Chilly air made her head hurt sharply for a moment, then soothed it. She took a breath of the clean air, tried to open her eyes again, then leaned forward and threw up. Her face was wiped roughly, and then a flask was held to her lips.

'Drink.'

Eamon. That was Eamon's voice. Julia struggled to remember, even as she drank the nasty warm brandy that was being forced on her. Why was she with Eamon? She had been walking somewhere, running from someone . . . who was it? Eamon? She didn't think so . . . Someone was chasing her, someone scary . . . Her head was spinning now, and she was swirling down into a whirlpool of darkness . . . swirling . . . but at the centre of the whirlpool there was a little pointy-nosed face, surrounded by quills . . . a hedgehog. It opened its mouth and it said, in Grandfather's voice: 'Pretend.'

*

Boatswain was not a young horse, and Nick was not as fit as he had been in Spain, the last time life's rich pageant had called for him to ride for hours across open countryside. As for Jemison, his piebald horse could not be kept to the gallop for more than a few minutes at a time. So here they were, three hours later, posting decorously along instead of galloping *ventre à terre* to the rescue. But Eamon was driving a blown team – Monsieur LeCrue had said that they were already covered in sweat when they set out, and Eamon would find it hard to change horses in the middle of the night. That blown team was hauling an old carriage, one coachman, one young lady, and one big, heavy, crazed earl.

Ah. Nick and Jemison reined in. Just ahead, a coach was pulled over to the side of the otherwise deserted road. Nick couldn't see the team, but there seemed to be two people standing outside the equipage . . . he watched, narrowing his eyes. It was a wretched dark night, and in spite of the moon he couldn't make out very much.

The bigger figure was lifting the smaller figure back into the coach. That had to be them. Nick smiled. The little one had been on her feet, so she was alive. But then the big one had lifted her. Perhaps Eamon had drugged her, the scoundrel. It would be hard to ride off with a drugged woman over his saddle. After a moment's whispered conversation, Nick and Jemison decided that if the team wasn't completely blown, they could dump Eamon by the roadside and steal the whole rig.

They checked their pistols as they let the coach lumber back into the road. Then they watched.

The coach set out at a good clip, so Eamon must have managed to find a new team somewhere.

'We'll steal it, then,' Nick said. 'You ride ahead and hold them up; I'll follow behind and get Eamon out.'

Jemison was standing in the stirrups, stretching out his

legs. 'Bloody hell, my arse hurts! How did we ride back and forth across Spain so easily?'

Nick grinned. 'Are your pistols ready?'

'Yes.' Jemison settled again in the saddle and chirruped to his horse. It was a flashy animal, with big black handprints on a white ground; hardly a highwayman's horse. But . . . they had to make do with what they had. He watched as the animal walked over to the grassy edge of the road, then trotted along silently, slowly gaining ground on the lumbering coach.

When Jemison drew level with their quarry, Nick set out after him. He saw Jemison rein his horse, saw him raise the pistol; he didn't shout to make the team stop, but the team did stop, and Nick spurred up to the door. He knocked loudly on it. 'Eamon! Show yourself!'

Eamon stuck his head out of the window, his mouth gaping open.

'Beautiful night,' Nick said. 'Now get out of the coach and leave Julia behind.'

Eamon's eyes protruded eggily from his head. 'The devil I will!' He ducked back inside, shouting, 'Drive on!'

But the coachman did not drive on. Nick glanced up ahead and saw that Jemison still had his pistol trained on the unfortunate man. He knocked again on the door. 'Eamon! Come out now. We are two armed men . . .'

The door burst open, sending Boatswain rearing. Nick held to the reins with one hand and grabbed for a pistol with the other. Eamon was scrambling out of the coach, a pair of pistols waving wildly in his fists. 'Leave me!' he screamed. 'Leave me or by God I'll kill you!'

Boatswain dropped back down onto all four hooves and capered, Nick holding him tightly and cocking the gun. He watched in disbelief as Eamon raised a pistol and aimed it directly at Nick's head.

'Leave me!'

Nick kicked Boatswain; the horse leapt forward as Eamon's pistol exploded. Nick heard the bullet whizz past his ear; he turned in the saddle, cocking his pistol and aiming at Eamon, just as Eamon raised his other pistol.

The guns fired simultaneously, the sparks flying. Boatswain squealed and Nick felt the horse's panic, but he pulled him in a tight circle and rode back to the coach; Eamon was lying on the ground, shot through the chest.

Nick swung down from Boatswain and stood by him as he calmed, then looped the horse's reins over the handle of the coach door. Only then did he look at Eamon.

There he lay, dying, his hand fluttering like a butterfly over his chest, his eyes glimmering in the scanty moonlight.

Nick stepped over him and into the coach. Julia was there on the seat, unconscious, looking small and broken. But she was breathing. Nick searched in her hair for the place where Eamon had coshed her. There. An alarming swelling.

He cradled her head for a moment, hating the way it lolled, feeling for a pulse in her throat. It was strong and steady. For just a moment, he buried his head in her hair and breathed in her scent. She was going to be all right.

He arranged her more comfortably on the seat, then climbed down from the coach.

Eamon lay silently, staring up past Nick at the dark sky. Blood was pumping from between his fingers. Jemison, the coachman and the team were silent, too; the only sound came from Boatswain, munching loudly on the long, sweet grass that grew by the side of the road.

'I'm for it,' Eamon whispered after a moment.

'Yes,' Nick said brusquely. 'It looks that way.'

'Now I will never know the secret. She knew what it was. She knew . . .'

507

'The Talisman is not for you, Eamon. You could never have used it.'

'That Russian came, and then he left,' Eamon said, his voice gaining a little strength. 'I followed – I knew he was going for Julia, and she is mine. I went to the house of the old man's mistress to find your direction. There was Julia, walking along. I am going to marry her, and she will tell –' He collapsed back, gasping and looking with incomprehension at the blood that flowed beneath his fingers.

'You are dying,' Nick reminded him more gently. 'You must tell me if there is anything you wish done, any final messages you need me to deliver.'

But Eamon was choking, the blood oozing sluggishly from his wound. Nick stood aside and bowed his head; he did not want Eamon's last sight to be the face of his killer.

After Eamon's final stuttering breath, Nick walked toward the team; Jemison still had his pistol held on the coachman. 'He is dead,' Nick called. 'It's over.'

But Jemison didn't move. The team was as still as if they were carved from stone.

The hair on Nick's neck rose, and he raised his eyes slowly to the coachbox.

The coachman was facing forward, but as Nick watched, he turned his head and shoulders, and that broad, white face hove into view like the sails of a ghost ship.

It was Mr Mibbs.

Nick raised his other pistol and fired, but the lead ball stopped six inches from Mibbs's nose. It hung there for a moment, suspended in front of his expressionless face. Then he lifted a thick hand and plucked it from the air. He examined it, bit it and tossed it back to Nick.

Nick reached up and caught the bullet in his hand. It was

half the size of the acorn and much heavier. He let it fall to the ground and stood weaponless and strangely calm as Mibbs climbed down from the coachbox.

Mibbs was wearing a ridiculously overblown many-caped coachman's cloak and a too-small, too-tall top hat. The colour of the hat and cloak was hard to discern in the moonlight, but Nick thought it was probably a bright orange-yellow. The buttons were the size of saucers.

'May I ask you,' Nick said, 'for the direction of your tailor? You are invariably dressed in the most interesting of fashions.'

Mibbs walked forwards, staring at Nick. And Nick felt it again, the despair . . . he clung to the thought of Julia in the carriage, to the thought of the acorn in his pocket, but he could feel the power of Mibbs's will like an undertow.

'I am looking for a baby,' Mibbs said. He had a generic American accent, smooth and confident – almost friendly. Yet those eyes were pressing Nick back, and down . . . Nick lost his concentration, blinked, and Mibbs drew close; he lifted a hand to touch Nick . . .

With a huge effort, Nick launched himself forward and tackled Mibbs, knocking him off his feet. They crashed to the ground, and the breath left Mibbs's body with a harsh gasp; Nick felt that hot breath wash his face as he heard the carriage horses spring to life and Jemison shout, 'Your money or your life!'

Beneath him, Mibbs was writhing like a serpent, his face mottled. Nick put his hands to the man's fleshy throat and shouted to Jemison. 'You were frozen in time! Secure the team and whatever you do don't look in this man's eyes!' As soon as he saw Jemison leap from his horse, he turned his attention back to Mibbs.

He lay still now beneath Nick's choking hands, not fighting for breath. He seemed more like an apparitional snake than a man; even as Nick choked the life from the limp body, those flat eyes glared up at Nick with the same expressionless despair that Nick had seen each time Mibbs had crossed his path.

Nick opened his hands and drew in a gasping breath, as if he were the one who had been strangled.

'Where is the baby?' Mibbs said it again, without struggling to rise, without any change in demeanour – as if nothing had happened, as if Nick hadn't just been crushing his windpipe.

'There is no baby,' Nick said, a hand going to his own throat.

Mibbs reached up and touched Nick's face in a fatherly gesture. 'Who is the Talisman, buddy? Is it the girl in the coach? She is unconscious. I could not reach her emotions.'

'There is no such thing as the Talisman,' Nick whispered. But he felt a bursting urge to tell. Nick knew, somewhere back in the heart of him, that he was feeling Mibbs's feelings. That his own emotions would have sent his fist smashing into Mibbs's face. Instead, he was enthralled to hideous rites, unable to remember anything except the truth: Julia is the Talisman.

'Tell me, buddy,' Mibbs said, and Nick opened his mouth to say he knew not what.

But it was Jemison's voice he heard, speaking from just behind him. 'I am the Talisman. I am the child, now grown.'

42

Someone was stroking her hair, carefully avoiding that throbbing spot, the spot that felt like a crack in her skull. She seemed to be curled up against him, and her ear seemed to be pressed against his chest. His voice was rumbling in the most comforting way as he murmured words she couldn't quite make out . . .

Julia's eyes fluttered open. She was in a coach – in Grandfather's coach. But it wasn't moving. Why was she in Grandfather's coach? This wasn't Grandfather who was holding her so gently in his arms. Grandfather was dead. She knew that. This was a younger man. He was leaning his head back against the cushions, his eyes closed, and he was simply stroking her hair and murmuring to himself. He should shave, Julia thought. But if he started shaving, then he would stop talking and his voice would stop rumbling so deliciously in her ear. His stubble was darker than his hair. Quite dark. Like his eyebrows. She liked his eyebrows. They were strongly drawn. Somehow she knew the shifting colours of his eyes. And he smelled good. He smelled familiar. Who was he? She searched her memory. Somebody nice. He was somebody very nice.

Pale dawn light filtering in, and she could see trees outside the coach, and a hint of pearly sky . . . why weren't they moving? Julia let her eyes close again, and she drifted away to the sound of that rumbly, murmuring voice . . .

Nick opened his eyes. He could hear hoofbeats growing louder beneath the nonsense he was murmuring to stay awake.

He gently disentangled himself from Julia. She moaned but subsided again into sleep. He kissed her forehead, then picked up a cleaned and reloaded pistol. Not that he could stand a chance against anyone who could stop time. He glanced again at Julia, then opened the coach door and climbed down to defend his little fiefdom: one carriage, six horses, a drugged woman, and a dead man.

He stood blinking in the dawn light. There was a horseman approaching, and well behind him on the road, another. Nick's six equine charges whinnied their welcome, and the horseman's mount – a flashy white beast with a pink nose – raised its head and neighed.

Well, shit.

It was that iceberg of an Alderman, Bertrand Penture, sitting astride the white horse like a prince. So it was to be the Guild who found him waiting here by the side of the road, not the Ofan.

Nick thrust his hand into his pocket, searching for the acorn. He might as well throw it away. But instead his fingers closed around it. He would have to play along, invite them to join him at Blackdown, and then hope and pray the Ofan got there quickly enough to help him get Julia away. To another time, probably. A hiding place somewhere up- or downriver. They wouldn't need much. A hut somewhere, a cow, a nice straw mattress . . .

Penture urged his horse to a trot. As he rode up Nick could see that the animal had, of all the outlandish and affected characteristics, one blue eye and one brown.

Penture looked at the coach, the six horses, and then at the bloodstain on the gravel. 'A mishap?'

'Julia's cousin,' Nick said. 'He's reposing behind the hedgerow.' He jerked his thumb behind him to the coach. 'Julia's in there. Safe. But unconscious.'

'Ah, yes, Julia. How fortunate. But where is your companion – Mr Jemison, isn't it? And you appear to have misplaced the coachman.'

At that moment the other rider pulled up next to Penture. He was a tall, dark-skinned man, his face shadowed by his hat. He sat his sluggish horse uncomfortably; clearly, he had only just learned to ride.

Then Nick saw him grin, and his world reeled. It was Leo Quonquont.

'Hi, Nick,' Leo said, as if not a day had passed since they last saw one another, in Chile, in 2003. 'How are you?'

'You are acquainted?' Penture looked from one to the other. 'How?'

'Oh, we were at school together,' Leo said. He doffed his hat – tall, like a beaver, but made of wool – and the three long braids of his scalplock came tumbling down like a banner. It made Nick happy to see them; whatever had happened to Leo, he hadn't cut his hair. Nick opened his mouth to say something, but it was as if his voice had died in his throat. So he put his hand up, and Leo reached down from the saddle. Nick had to swallow hard when he felt that strong grip.

'Good to see you, Nick,' Leo said.

Nick found his voice. 'You too.' He looked up into his friend's eyes – how was it possible that he was here, now, at this terrible moment, an agent of the Guild?

Leo grinned. 'Wondering how to get Julia away from us, Nick?' he asked. 'Or have you figured it out? We're not the Guild. We're Alva's Ofan band.'

Penture dismounted. 'What happened here?'

'Why the hell should I trust you even one inch? You shot me, you bastard! And the whole time it turns out you're a double agent?'

Penture's nostrils flared. 'I told you why I was shooting you, before I pulled the trigger. I wanted you to make up your mind about which side to join.'

'Yes, the side of the Guild. But all the while you were Ofan.'

'I staged that little drama so that you would finally see the Guild for what it is,' Penture said. 'I told you to choose sides and you chose the one I wished you to, and in the way that I wished you to choose it. You chose the Ofan, but you decided to pretend that you chose the Guild. That was exactly what I wanted.'

'Oh! Bravo!' Nick clapped.

Penture gave him a cold, green, stare then went to the coach door and opened it. Nick had to force himself to stand still as Penture leaned in and touched Julia's head. 'She is unconscious?' He turned, his eyebrows raised.

'Eamon knocked her out, but I think she's okay.'

'Good.' He came back to them. 'Her injury is real, Davenant. I believe if you examine the thing that is paining you, you will discover that it is only your pride.'

Nick didn't realize that his fists were up until Leo put a hand on his shoulder. 'Chill out, Nick. Bertrand is the cagiest, most cold-hearted and mysterious dude it's ever been my pleasure to meet. But he's Ofan through and through.'

'I am not cold-hearted,' Penture said. 'But neither am I sentimental. Now, Davenant, explain yourself immediately.'

Leo grinned. 'See what I mean? We find you here, guarding Julia like a hero of old, clearly having vanquished the enemy, and he treats you like a criminal. He's a dickhead, but we need him.'

'You trust him?'

'I do,' Leo said. 'And since I know you're dying to ask, I can assure you that the irony of a Pocumtuk adjudicating between a Frenchman and an Englishman over the respective qualities of their honour is not lost on me.'

Nick surprised himself by chuckling. 'You haven't changed,' he said.

'No,' Leo agreed. 'Have you?'

Nick glanced at the carriage, its door still open. He could see one of Julia's hands, and the shadowy shape of her curled form. He took a deep breath and looked down the road as far as he could, to where it bent in the undergrowth. 'I don't know,' he said.

Penture sighed. 'Have we finished with this therapy session? Will you tell us now why we find you alone with too many horses? And why a bloody corpse has been dragged from here . . .' he pointed at the bloody patch on the road, 'and away behind that hedgerow?'

So Nick told them how he had killed Eamon, only to be surprised by Mibbs. How Mibbs had overpowered him, and about how Jemison had then sacrificed himself. He described, in a few terse words, how Mibbs had thrown Nick from him with a roar and scrambled to his feet reaching for Jemison, who had his gun raised, and how in the moment of the gun's explosion the two of them had disappeared into nothingness, the bullet singing off into the trees. How Nick had dragged Eamon's corpse off the road and how then, unable to both drive the coach and watch over Julia, he had settled down to wait for the Ofan, or for the Guild, or for Mibbs to return.

'And you are sure it was Mibbs?' Penture asked.

'Absolutely.' Nick cocked his head at Leo. 'Ask him if he believes me. He's met him.'

'Yep,' Leo said. 'That sounds like the guy who tried to suck my soul out of my eyeballs in Chile.'

'You met him in Chile, too?' Penture bent a frown on

Nick. 'You didn't tell us that when you were telling us about Mibbs.'

'No,' Nick said. 'Why should I? You were the Alderman of the Guild and Leo was a renegade. Did you think I wanted you on his trail?' Nick fought the urge to look at Leo, to see how he took the news that Nick had protected him.

Penture's frown deepened. 'And you're sure Jemison is a Natural?'

'I'm fairly certain. He didn't know about time travel until I told him.' Nick held up a hand. 'And before you say anything about that, Penture, I told him because I needed his help to find Julia. And because I'm not abiding by Guild rules any more.'

'Your choice to tell Jemison was your own, and I'm sure you had good reason. I don't care about that. I care about Mibbs, and how it came to be that he could drag a Natural away with him into the River of Time. That should be entirely impossible.'

'He can do things we can't,' Nick said. 'Like I told you. Pushing his feelings into other people's heads. Controlling despair somehow.'

Penture nodded, his green eyes narrowing. 'Interesting. Although perhaps Jemison was tricking you. Perhaps he does have the talent.'

'Tricking me like you tricked me, you mean? Pretending to be one thing when you're another? Manipulating my ignorance and my pride? Maybe,' Nick said. 'But I doubt it. I know Jemison well. He is enigmatic, to be sure, but . . .' he let his eyes travel up and down Penture's body. 'He isn't a liar.'

The Frenchman's green eyes flickered. 'And neither am I, Nick Davenant. You must lay down this petty dislike of me if we are to work together.'

'Oh, for Pete's sake,' Leo said. 'Calm down, both of you. Mibbs stole a Natural. Mibbs can invade people's feelings. He's probably from over the Pale, and he wants Julia so badly that he's been trailing her all over the world and all up and down the river. That is all extremely scary, in case you hadn't quite let it sink in. Now what the fuck, I politely ask, are we going to do about it?'

Penture stared at Leo for a moment, and then that gorgeous grin broke across his face. 'We are going to run,' he said, 'and we are going to hide.'

'Thank God,' Leo said. 'Let's get on with it.'

Penture laughed, and turned to Nick. 'Come now, Davenant. Forgive me. Trust me. Take my hand.' He held his right hand out and Nick had to revise his casting yet again. Not Cary Grant; George Clooney.

Nick sighed. 'Fine.' He shook the Frenchman's hand with distaste. 'But before we beat our craven retreat, what should we do with Eamon?'

Together they traipsed behind the hedgerow and stood over Eamon's corpse.

'He's ugly,' Leo said.

'Well, he is dead,' Nick said. 'It tends to mar the looks.'

Leo laughed, but Penture held up a hand for silence. His eyes were closed. 'The fifteenth century . . . 1428,' he said, opening his eyes.

'Right,' Leo said. 'You bring us there. I'll take the shoulders, you take the feet.'

Penture bent and lifted Eamon by the ankles.

Leo heaved Eamon up under the shoulders, the head lolling, the ghastly face smudged with blood and dirt. 'Hang tight. Back in two seconds.' And before Nick could blink the two men and the corpse had disappeared. More than two seconds passed before they returned, but in well under a minute they were back again, and Leo was holding a whole roast goose: 'Breakfast!'

Julia opened her eyes. She lay in blessed shadow. It was spattered with points of light. Out beyond the shadow was a terrible brightness. Julia closed her eyes again quickly. The air smelled of hay and grain and faintly, underneath it all, she could detect the slightly sour, slightly feathery scent of chickens. In fact, she could hear chickens gossiping not far away. Was she in a barn? She opened her eyes a crack and let them adjust. She was in a barn – but what a barn. It was vast, like a cathedral. Built of massive stones, with chinks like arrow slits here and there in the walls, through which the sun was filtering in, casting rectangles of light on the floor and the opposite wall. The roof was wooden and constructed of massive, ancient beams. The barn must be hundreds of years old. She lay on a pile of hay towards the back of the huge space. Before her, the darkness dissolved into the bright light, as if an entire wall were missing. A few chickens were scratching there in the brightness.

Three figures appeared in the light, sending the chickens squawking away into the shadows. Three men, silhouetted for an instant at the boundary between dark and light. They walked into the shadowy part of the barn, gaining dimension as they came. Should she be afraid? Somehow she wasn't.

Two of the men stopped a few feet away, but one of them came forward, and when he was close she could see that he was the nice man from the coach. He knelt down next to her. He smiled, and she felt herself smiling back. She loved him. She reached out a hand to touch his cheek, but he grabbed her hand before she could. 'Thank God you're all right.'

It was Nick. Nick Davenant. It all came flooding back in

an instant. He was Nick. She let her memories settle like dust. She loved him. He had a mistress. He could manipulate time. So could she. But he didn't know she could. She had run, and been bashed on the head by Eamon the Horrible, but now here she was in a barn with Nick again, and some strangers. And some chickens.

'Are you all right?' He was peering at her closely and holding her hand so tightly it almost hurt.

She blinked and pulled back her hand. He released it, but she didn't want that and reached for him again. 'Just not so hard,' she said, and her voice was a scratchy remnant of itself. 'Oh. I'm thirsty.'

'Water.' Nick spoke urgently, over his shoulder, and one of the men set off at a trot. Nick turned back to her. 'Does it hurt? Your head?'

Julia considered the question. Did her head hurt? Yes, she decided. Yes, this feeling that her world might crack into a thousand pieces at any moment was pain. She nodded slowly, and Nick stroked her hand.

'Poor darling,' he said.

The man came back with a ladleful of water from somewhere and held it to Julia's lips. She looked at him as she drank. He was the most handsome man she had ever seen. 'You're the most handsome man I've ever seen,' she said when she had drained the ladle.

He smiled and became even more handsome. 'Thank you,' he said in a slight French accent. Julia looked to Nick to ask him if he thought the Frenchman was handsome, but Nick was scowling. Julia began to chuckle, then winced as her head seemed to explode with pain. 'You're jealous,' she whispered. 'And I'm sleepy. Are you going to sleep with me?'

She took a scientific interest in watching him blush. Had she ever seen a grown man blush before? It spread up his neck like a rash, then out under his stubble, which was heavier than last time she had seen it, back in the coach. 'If you are going to sleep with me, Nick, you should shave first.' She closed her eyes, and let sleep come and waft her away.

Nick and Leo were out walking across a field towards a line of trees, looking for firewood.

Nick had no idea what to say.

Leo had been alive all these years. An Ofan. But he had never once contacted Nick, never even shot him an e-mail. And now it had been ten hours since that goose breakfast, and Nick and Leo hadn't spoken again. Nick had stayed in the coach with the sleeping Julia, with Leo driving. Penture had ridden alongside, keeping an eye on the two horses now tied behind the coach. It had been more than enough time for Nick to remember that maybe Leo didn't consider Nick his friend. More than enough time for Nick to remember that he had taken Guild money for nine long years while Leo had managed on his own, making his own way.

As dusk began to fall, Penture, who seemed to know the country like the back of his hand, had led the strange entourage off along a narrow track between several long meadows to an enormous, half-ruined medieval barn. They had lit a fire with the few logs they had found in the barn and settled Julia in a pile of hay. But then Leo had turned and said to Nick, 'Come on. Let's go scare up some more wood.' And now they were marching silently off into the gloaming.

'How is Meg?'

Leo glanced at him. 'She's okay. She's seventy-five now. She worked with us in Brazil for about seven years, but then she retired. Lives in an apartment in Salvador. She has a Natural lover, Tabitha, and the two of them are making hay while the sun shines.'

'Is she fat yet?'

Leo grinned. 'No. She says she must have hollow legs, because she eats all the time and she's still just as skinny as the day she first jumped.'

They kept walking. The meadow grasses were lush, and the ground was wet. Their tall boots made squelching sounds as they walked. 'It's funny to see you all dressed up like this,' Nick said. 'In this kind of gear.'

'You, too.' Leo looked Nick up and down. 'I mean, I know it's your natural habitat and everything, but when I think of you it's in that pair of faded jeans you wore practically every day.'

'I can't tell you how much I miss those jeans. Actually, jeans were the first things I loved about the future.'

'Not me. I hated them. Still do. But then, I had been wrenched away from the most beautiful couture in the world.'

Nick glanced at his friend. 'I'm glad to see you kept your scalplock.'

Leo reached back and threaded the three long braids through his fingers. 'Yes, well. Some things never change.'

'Everything changes. Or everything could change. I thought that's what Ofan believe. Or want to believe.'

Leo shrugged. 'I guess you saw the "end of the world" pictures. And heard about the Pale.'

'Yes.'

They reached the trees and began gathering whatever wood they could find, wandering away from one another. When they both had an armful they caught each other's eye and started back again. They could see the path they had made as they came, the grass silvery where they had stepped. Without discussing it, they started a new path and walked back towards the magnificent barn looming up in the middle distance. It was dark against the clear sky, which glowed with that blue-green evening light so specific to an English spring-time.

'Why did you leave?'

Leo didn't answer for a minute. Nick stared ahead at the barn, hearing the silence, which was in fact alive with the evening chatter of birds and insects. 'We had to,' Leo finally said. 'We had realized. We didn't *know* anything, of course. About the Guild and its money and its policing of the past and the future. But we realized that we just couldn't stay and be in the Guild. I was convinced there had to be other communities of time travellers. People who were doing it differently from the Guild. It was easy enough to leave the compound. Anyone could just walk away down the road, which is what we did. Early that morning.'

'But why didn't you tell me?'

'You weren't ready.'

It was Nick's turn to say nothing. Leo was right. He hadn't been ready. In fact, he'd been perfect material for the Guild. Rich all his life. Too accustomed to security and too easily distracted by the material pleasures of life. The comfort of jeans. An old house in the Vermont woods. If he hadn't been called by the Guild to play a minor role in their drama, he would have remained happily drowned, full fathom five, in the twenty-first century.

Meg and Leo had been right to abandon him.

'Sorry,' Leo said. Nick could tell he was. Sorry that Nick hadn't been ready, that he and Meg had had no option but to leave him behind. Sorry, in other words, but not regretful.

'So did you go to Brazil?' Nick kept his voice light. 'Alice and Arkady said you must have, when I asked why they'd killed you. That's what I thought. That they had killed you. And yes. Before you say anything, I went ahead and took their money anyway.'

Leo stopped walking, and Nick stopped too. The birds and insects were loud all around them, and the sky seemed to be lighter than a minute ago, and darker at the same time. 'We went to Brazil,' Leo said. 'We found the Ofan in Cachoeira, but they were in disarray. Eréndira Altukhov had disappeared in the effort to cross the Pale, and Ignatz Vogelstein had gone off somewhere – to raise Eréndira's daughter, I just learned from Alva.'

'Yes.' Nick nodded towards the barn. 'Julia.'

'The Talisman.' Leo sounded doubtful.

'You don't believe Julia is the Talisman?'

'I don't know,' Leo said slowly. 'Alva told us all about Peter's theories, and about the P'urhépecha ring. Peter is a brilliant kid, and I'd never discount anything she had to say. And Alva's insights are always really interesting. So I'm not saying Julia isn't important. I just don't know what it means to say that she is the Talisman.'

'Me neither,' Nick said. 'But I'm only the brawn. You're the brains.'

Leo smiled. 'I've got brawn too, *kemosabe*. So if you're applying for the role of sidekick, I don't need one.'

'I wasn't,' Nick said. 'But you can let me know if the position opens up.'

They set out walking again. 'I've been studying the talent for ten years now,' Leo said, turning the topic. 'Looking into the group control of time. The gift changes, you see. It gets weirder, and more powerful, if we work in groups of three or five or more – instead of individually. I don't think one person, one special magical saviour, is going to save us from the Pale. It's going to take collective effort.'

'I've been wondering – maybe the Pale is a good thing,' Nick said. 'A kind of cleansing. Washing over time and space. A new beginning. Ahn says no, but . . .'

'Like the Ghost Dance? Everything will be good again? Jesus coming as a cloud to cleanse the land?' Leo frowned. 'You know the funny thing about the end of the world, my old friend? We always talk about it as if it hasn't happened already. Because of course the world has ended many times. And when it ends for some people, other people report it in the papers or on TV as a new beginning.' He kicked along for a moment. Then he stopped walking and turned, tapping Nick on the chest with a finger. 'But maybe not for you, Nick. You know. "Though worlds may change and go awry, while there is still one voice to cry, there'll always be an England!"'

'That's not fair,' Nick said.

'You're right,' Leo murmured. 'It's not.'

They stood for a moment, their arms full of dry wood, looking up at the glorious twilight sky.

'I'm sorry,' Nick said after a brief pause.

Leo said nothing for a moment, then gestured upwards with his chin. 'There's your Mars and your Venus.'

Nick looked up above the apex of the barn at the bright planet and the brooding one. 'I'm going to have to go after him,' he said, and whether he was making his promise to Jemison, to Leo or to the emerging stars, he didn't know.

43

'Julia is not an experiment. She is a human being.'

Had Nick said her name? Julia blinked her eyes open. It was dark, and there were flames crackling somewhere to her left. She was still on the pile of hay . . . still in the barn. Someone had lit a fire, right in the middle of the floor. There must be a hole in the roof for the smoke, Julia thought dreamily. There was a breeze, but she was perfectly snug. Her head still felt heavy, and it ached, but much less than before.

Nick and his friends were sitting around the fire, talking. Julia could see Nick's face clearly. He had shaved and looked like himself again, though his hair was rumpled and his shirt was open at the throat. His handsome friend was next to him, and the third man had his back to her, silhouetted in front of the flames. It looked cosy, and Julia thought about getting up and joining them. But when she lifted her head it throbbed. She laid it down again gingerly.

'Of course she's not an experiment.' The Frenchman's face was strangely aloof and devoid of expression. But he spoke with frustration, as if he had explained this already. 'At least, we don't think she should be treated as an experiment. We think she should be educated, just as we think you and everyone else should be educated.'

'I've heard nothing else for weeks except about how I *should* be educated,' Nick said. 'But when am I actually going to start learning?'

'Alva is your tutor, Nick. You were supposed to learn from her.' The man named Bertrand turned his gaze on Nick.

'Is that what you meant when you told me to take her as a mistress? You meant I should ask her to be my tutor? Excuse me for misunderstanding. In my world there's a difference between whores and schoolteachers.'

Julia opened her eyes wide in the darkness. Nick was very angry. He had been told to take Miss Blomgren as his mistress? By this cold, beautiful Frenchman? It made no sense.

'The sex was just a front, Davenant, to fool Arkady and the rest of them. You could sleep with Alva or not, depending on how the two of you felt about each other. Don't you understand that we were orchestrating a double bluff back in Fleet Street? You were to seem to be spying for the Guild, when in fact you were to visit Alva for instruction in time play.' Impatience flickered across his face and was repressed. 'But your pride, Nick, is not my concern. I am interested in a far more important problem. That problem is named Julia Percy, and she lies over there, mercifully alive. If you are desperate to begin your education, just think what it must be like for Julia. You *know* you want to learn more. But she doesn't even know that her so-called grandfather was duping her all those years. Ever since she was tiny he was watching her, trying to figure out how she did what she did – a mere child, and so gifted. But as for inducting her into the mysteries of her incredible talent – well.' The Frenchman stared into the fire. 'He kept her entirely ignorant, inert, like a stone. I will always respect Ignatius Percy. He was a great Ofan, a great teacher. But still. It is unforgivable.'

Julia listened, her heart pounding. Her so-called grandfather? Had duped her? He knew all along that she had the talent, knew that she could manipulate time? But she couldn't play with time until after he'd died. She had never done it herself until that time she stopped Eamon from cutting her throat. It had always been Grandfather. It had *always* been him. And anyway, what was so special about her talent? Everyone in this barn seemed to be members of this group called the Ofan. They seemed to have the talent, too. What was so different about her?

In the firelight Nick's face looked careworn. 'If I'd known all of this about Julia, I would have told her,' he said. 'The moment I first saw her again, I would have told her. I'd have given her every scrap of information at my disposal, though believe me, there weren't many scraps.' He looked at his friends. 'I understand that you are all concerned for Julia too. You are concerned because you think she is the Talisman. But I know her. What I feel for Julia is . . .' He stopped, and stared at his hands.

The others sat still, waiting for him to continue, but he didn't.

In the silence, Julia felt something heavy lift from her. Something she hadn't even realized she was carrying until it was gone. It wasn't because of Nick. It was because they all *knew*, all three of them. They knew she was the Talisman, they knew she was in danger, they were her friends. She could stop pretending.

The man who had been quiet until now spoke. His accent was staccato and yet melodious. 'With the right training she should be able to hide that talent with skill rather than ignorance. So we're going to tell her the truth about herself, and the extent of the danger from both the Guild and Mr Mibbs. We're going to learn about her talents from her own mouth. Then we're going to teach her to act as if it isn't true. In a way, we are going to continue Ignatz's policy of total camouflage. But with one essential difference. Julia will know she's hiding something. She will know what she's hiding, and why, and she will know how to hide it.'

'Alva said something like that, as I was leaving London last night,' Nick said. 'Something about finding a way for her to pretend.'

'Yes, it was Alva's idea.'

But Julia wasn't listening any more. She watched the smoke rise from the fire and let her gaze travel all the way up to the darkness behind the firelit rafters. She was among friends. The secrecy was at an end. But Grandfather . . . she closed her eyes and confronted the darkness inside. There was no more hiding from the truth. Grandfather *had* kept her from knowing about herself. He had lied to her. For her entire life. She had been able to manipulate time all along. Since she was a child. She knew the men sitting around the fire were right; she could feel it in her fingertips, all up her spine, even at the roots of her hair. The knowledge was there, so quick and ready and bright that it must have been with her all along. She was like these men, but she was more powerful, more gifted somehow. She was the Talisman not because she made Grandfather stronger, but because she was so strong herself. And Grandfather had walled her up.

She had frozen time before he died. She had. She knew it now, and it was as if she had always known it, but the knowledge had stayed just beyond her reach, like a dream only just forgotten. It had been when she was in a temper or seized by fear. When her emotions got the best of her. She had been the one to freeze Eamon and his team of horses all those years ago when she was four. She had frozen him again, those times they dressed him up and made fun of him. She remembered now, the way he had teased her into a rage, and her sights would narrow on him. Her blood would sing in her ears, and he had seemed to fix in her gaze. He had been locked in a moment of time. But Grandfather had always been there, ready to pretend that it was he who had frozen Eamon, just for fun.

And then . . . in those last moments of his life. Grandfather had sped time up so that he could die before Eamon arrived. But he hadn't actually been the one to do it. He was too weak. He was dying. He had incited her to do it. She remembered how he had focused her attention on the dust, how she had felt his power as the dust flew. Except that it hadn't been his power she had felt. It had been her own. Her power, speeding his death. Hot tears welled up behind her eyelids and oozed out over her cheeks. His very last act had been to use her and then hide the truth from her. He tricked her into killing him. Or used her to kill himself. What was the difference? There was none.

Grandfather. Julia felt herself tumbling down, down, into a deep well of cold rage, a well encrusted with an icy rime of grief.

It was unforgivable, like Bertrand said.

Yet as the tears tracked down her cheeks, their salt, their warmth, restored her to what was real. The flesh and its failures, love and its limits. The ancient barn surrounded her, the huge, rough stones catching the flickering firelight. Julia breathed in the scent of smoke, hay and chickens, the scent of now. Beneath the present moment she could sense the deep movements of time, the seasons that had been laid away in this barn, year after year. The harvests stretching back and back . . . She sighed, and floated back up to the present. She was in an ancient barn, with Ofan men. In those last moments Grandfather had given her the clues she needed. He had told her to pretend. And he had told her that she would be Ofan after all.

Maybe he had given her just enough knowledge to protect her, and ultimately to save herself. Maybe trust and clues were more powerful than instructions. He hadn't told her who she was, he hadn't provided for her. It was a betrayal.

And it was a gift. He hadn't *told* her who she was; he hadn't dictated the terms and limits of her life. He'd left her to do that for herself.

Julia opened her eyes. Her head felt clearer. The pain was gone.

'You're the Alderman, in this era, anyway,' Nick was saying. 'Why can't you just call off the dogs? Tell Arkady and the rest of them to leave Julia alone?'

'I could do that, and I will,' Bertrand said, 'but Julia has to agree, at least in the beginning, to pretend to be nobody. We must train her to be able to withstand the tests. Arkady is on the scent, and Mr Mibbs could return at any moment, having discovered that Jemison is nothing but a very courageous Natural. For all our sakes Julia must learn to pretend.'

'Poor Julia,' Nick said. 'To be finally told the truth and then immediately told to hide it.'

Silence fell around the fire. A log settled, and sparks flew. Outside, an owl called.

Julia spoke. 'I am awake,' she said.

And awake she stayed, all night, long after the others had fallen asleep. As the dawn broke, revealing that the roof of the great barn not only had a hole but was half missing, the massive rafters holding up nothing but the pinkening sky, she lay curled in blankets on a bed of straw. The four travellers were arranged around the fire in a circle, and Nick was sleeping at Julia's feet. Sometime in the night she had felt Nick's hand creep under her blankets and find her bare foot. He'd slept holding it. He held it now. It was as if she were a kite, and he was holding the string, so that she wouldn't fly up and up until she disappeared.

She looked at her hands, and at the copper ring she now wore on the little finger of her left hand. Her mother's ring . . .

but not the mother she had thought she had. A mother and no known father, and a new grandfather . . . a terrifying Russian grandfather whom she hated. A grandfather who wanted to kill her. She twisted the ring so that the eye in the circle could be seen. Another ancestor she had never imagined, a long-ago grandfather, had made this ring, across the seas, before Europeans had even known that the world was round or that half the world still lay over the western horizon.

Half the world.

Julia closed her eyes. That long-ago grandfather had been P'urhé . . . she couldn't even recall the name of the country in which he had lived. But it meant that Julia wasn't legitimate, or the descendant of earls. Indeed, she didn't even belong in the nineteenth century. Her mother had been a woman whom Bertrand had described as possessed of a flaming courage and an astonishing intelligence: the very woman she had seen in the strange painting that Eamon had shown her, the woman he had called a mulatto. It meant that Julia had been born in the future, born in a terrible future, and that her mother had probably died to save her from it. Her mother had put her in the hands of a beloved and brilliant teacher, Ignatz Vogelstein, né the Earl of Darchester . . . Grandfather. Julia clenched her fists against that word, *Grandfather*. How much had Ignatz Vogelstein known? How much had he hidden from her?

The four of them had stayed up talking, putting more logs on the fire. Julia had spent those hours propped between Nick's legs, his arms around her, her head leaning back against his chest. The things she learned had been terrible, but they had also relieved her. It had been wonderful, simply to ask questions and to have them answered.

She had learned about the Guild and the River of Time. That it was possible to jump forwards and backwards along the stream. She learned about what the Guild did and what the Ofan hoped to achieve. She had been told about Mr Mibbs and Jem Jemison, and Nick had talked about how he must learn to jump and go after his comrade-in-arms. Bertrand had said that was ridiculous, and Nick had said it wasn't up for discussion.

For a long time they had talked about her childhood, and the four of them had pieced together how Grandfather must have kept her talent from her. She had told them about what she could do without ever having jumped. They had been very excited. She was more special than they'd even guessed. Apparently they thought it was impossible to turn time itself backwards or forwards, and yet she had done both, untrained and without having first jumped.

They made her describe it several times. How at the dinner table she had reversed time and Eamon had melted back to his seat. How at Grandfather's deathbed he had sped time up . . . no, *she* had sped time up, and the dust had blown in the light, and Grandfather's death had come just in time to save him from Eamon's taunts. She offered to show the Ofan then and there, but when she started to push time back her head began to hurt. So instead they had talked about the plan, about how to make it seem as if she were nobody at all, certainly not the Talisman and not even an Ofan. Just an ordinary young woman – a Natural. Bertrand had looked at her with that green, commanding gaze and said that she must prepare herself to learn a great deal, and quickly. They would use the next few days, as they rode across country to Blackdown, to develop a plan and teach her what she needed to know.

Finally, Bertrand said he thought they should stop talking about serious things – they should be celebrating. He believed he might have a bottle of wine in his saddlebags. There was cheering, and then there was drinking, the bottle passed from hand to hand. Nick and Leo relived some adventures they'd had when they were in school together in South America, including a triumph at something called an 'eighties talent show'. Apparently their victory had involved singing a song entitled 'Islands in the Stream'. Julia insisted on hearing the song, and it didn't take much encouragement to get Nick and Leo on their feet. She expected it to be bawdy, but it turned out to be very pretty, with clever harmonies. Julia liked the pace and rhythm, but Bertrand almost drowned out the singers with his groans and laughter. Perhaps it was the way they performed it; for some reason each man held a fist up in front of his mouth, and leaned into it, staring into the other's eyes as he warbled. When they were done they demanded a song of her, and before she knew it Julia found herself deep into an off-key rendition of 'Gude Wallace'. At first her audience listened politely enough, but really, Julia could not carry a tune, and before long Nick and Leo had their hands over their ears. After three verses Bertrand took pity and joined her. His voice was as rich and as strong as chestnut honey, and with someone to follow she was able to do better. When the last notes had faded, Julia replaced herself in the circle of Nick's arms, and they all sat again around the fire, staring into its glowing heart and thinking their own thoughts.

'Does Mr Mibbs want to take me back across the Pale?' Julia sent her question out into the crackling silence. She felt a wave of some complicated emotion travel around the pool of light. Fear, sadness, hope, and anger.

'We don't know,' Leo said after a moment.

'You really don't know, or is that your way of saying "don't borrow trouble from tomorrow"?'

'"Don't borrow trouble from tomorrow,"' Bertrand murmured. 'Ignatz said that almost every day.'

'Yes, every day,' Julia agreed, and heard the bitterness in her voice.

'You have every right to hate him for what he hid from you,' Bertrand said. 'It enrages me, too. But still, he was a great man. He saved my life and taught me how to live it once he'd saved it.'

'Tell me about him.' Julia leaned in. 'About Ignatz, not Ignatius.'

Bertrand leaned in, too, so that Julia felt it was just the two of them, their faces red in the light of the dying fire. 'You have a great deal of Ignatz in you, Julia Percy, for all that you are not related to him by blood. He gave you many gifts.'

'I have his temper,' Julia said.

Bertrand smiled. 'That is a gift and curse.'

'I know.'

Bertrand poked the fire. 'Ignatius Percy was the second son of the Earl of Darchester. He jumped when he was nineteen years old, in the aftermath of the Massacre of Devil's Hole. Something to do with Seneca warriors behind him and Niagara Falls in front of him. Very dramatic.'

Leo snorted. 'It wasn't a massacre,' he said. 'It was a battle. And the battleground is at least three miles from the falls.'

Bertrand inclined his head in Leo's direction. 'Battle,' he said, then turned back to Julia with a smile. 'Whatever the truth of his story, Ignatius jumped, and he found himself in the state of New York of the 1930s. The Guild never detected him. Soon enough he connected with the Ofan and learned how to return to his era. His elder brother died and he became the earl. He lived his life half in his own natural time and half in late-twentieth-century Brazil, working with the Ofan host there. But he travelled all up and down the river. I first met him in England in the late 1530s, when he was around twenty-eight years old. I later got to know him better in Brazil, when he was in his forties. For me, it had only been a difference of two years.'

'Is that when you're from? The sixteenth century?' Leo sounded eager for the answer, but Bertrand merely glanced across at him before returning his focus to Julia.

'As I was saying, I spent time with him in Brazil in the twenty-first century. But the twenty-first century is a bad time for Ofan activity. The Guild is very strong in the computer era, and it is difficult to hide. And once Eréndira – your mother – disappeared over the Pale, Ignatz fell apart. He was a passionate man. Swayed by his desires, his loves, his griefs. He lost control.'

'I cherished that in him!' Julia felt the fire hot on her face and realized she was leaning ever closer to Bertrand. 'Do not say that his passion was a weakness.'

'I do not say it.' The Frenchman's green gaze cooled her, and she leaned back. 'It takes all kinds, Julia. All kinds. Do you think that because I am one kind of man, I judge other kinds?'

'I don't know. I don't know you.'

'No one really knows Bertrand Penture,' Leo said. 'Ofan or Guild? Friend or foe? Man or machine? When is he from? What does he believe?'

Bertrand's eyes never wavered from Julia's. He had said that Ignatz taught him to live. Grandfather had taught her to be blind to life. They had learned very different lessons from the same man. They both loved him, and they both felt the enormity of his betrayal. But for all that they shared so much, and for all that she had seen him laugh and even sung with him, there was nothing in Bertrand's beautiful face that suggested that he could be a friend. Julia was grateful for the warmth of Nick's arms around her, his legs on either side of hers. Grateful for the way his breath matched hers.

Bertrand continued. 'Ignatz's vision was a beautiful one. A community of Ofan working together to learn about the talent, to pierce the Pale and learn its secrets. But he could not keep it going. Alva and I are working to establish a similar community here, in England, in 1815. Alva's catacombs beneath Soho Square are known as a safe space all up and down the river, but because they are known by Guild and Ofan alike, we cannot build on them. I am the Guild Alderman and therefore I will be able to obfuscate our activities. But to expand, we need property.' His eyes caught the light and flashed. 'A very specific property.'

For a moment there was silence, except for the faint crystalline music of the dying fire.

Property. Julia thought about Castle Dar. The home she had loved . . . the place where she had been made a fool. She thought of Grandfather's stone that had caught and preserved the impression of a bird. Her life had been nothing more than an impression at Castle Dar. A hollowed-out trace. Now she was flown.

Here in the open, around a fire, in a barn with a broken roof — here was where she had woken up. Here and in this place and in this moment she knew what she could do, who she was. 'Is Castle Dar mine?' Julia asked after a moment. 'Now that Eamon is dead? Or did Grandfather neglect to adopt me?'

Bertrand smiled. 'You are very intelligent, Julia. Like your mother. Ignatius spent a great deal of energy trying to disinherit Eamon so that he could establish Castle Dar as an Ofan stronghold. But he never managed to destroy Eamon's claim. Which means that with Eamon's death the property does, indeed, descend to you, his granddaughter. He had no need to adopt you, because from the very beginning he made sure you were his real granddaughter in the eyes of the law. He forged papers proving that his son had married a Scottish woman. You will find that your father's wedding and your legitimate birth is on record in a little church in Prestonpans. For all intents and purposes, you are Lord Percy's lawful descendant.'

'And Castle Dar is mine.'

Bertrand nodded.

'Then you may buy it from me.' As she said the words she felt a final weight lift from her shoulders. 'I don't want it.'

Bertrand smiled at her. 'Thank you, Julia,' he said. 'But it is not Castle Dar we need.' She watched as his eyes lifted from hers to Nick's. 'We need Falcott House.'

Julia felt Nick's body, wrapped so comfortingly around hers, tense. 'Pardon me?' he said softly. 'I think I just heard you demand my home of me.'

'Indeed,' the Frenchman said. 'Falcott House is perfect for our needs.'

'Julia has just offered you Castle Dar. It is twice the size of Falcott House.'

'Nevertheless. Yours is the house we need. And no other.'

'Why?'

Bertrand looked at Nick in some annoyance. 'That is none of your concern. Give me the Blackdown estate, Davenant.'

Nick's body relaxed, but not back into inattention. 'I recommend to you a certain document, Penture,' he said, a laugh in his voice. 'It is called the Magna Carta. It was designed expressly to keep upstart kings from demanding property of their lords.'

'But I am not a king,' Bertrand said silkily. 'And in the eyes of the Ofan, you are not a lord.'

The laugh broke through. 'Ah, but there's the rub,' Nick said. 'If I am not a lord, then Blackdown is not mine to give. It is entailed to the Blackdown marquessate. And if I am a lord, then I cannot give you Blackdown, for exactly the same reason. I am only the brief tenant of the title, which must descend from me to my eldest son, should such an unfortunate child ever be born. And if Lord Blackdown dies without an heir, the lands descend to my sister Clare. Believe you me, I know her plans for the estate, and they do not involve the Ofan.' Nick put his hands out, palms up, on either side of Julia's body. 'And so you see I have nothing, Alderman. I am a man of means by no means.'

The Frenchman stared across the fire at Nick. Julia watched him closely – something was boiling up in him. Was it rage that made his mouth twitch, or was it . . .

Bertrand's stern face broke into a ruffian grin, and he put his head back and laughed to shake the rafters. 'You are cleverer than you look, Nick Davenant!' He smiled at Julia. 'I accept your offer, Julia Percy,' he said. 'I will settle for second-best and buy Castle Dar for . . . shall we say fifteen thousand pounds?'

'I prefer twenty-five,' Julia said.

'Done.'

Julia felt herself hugged fiercely by Nick. She turned to smile at him and was kissed on the mouth.

Bertrand leaned back out of the firelight and shook his head. '"In love the heavens themselves do guide the state,"' he said, speaking up and into the darkness. '"Money buys lands, and wives are sold by fate."'

'For God's sake, Bertrand,' Leo said. 'Do you have to drop ice cubes down the back of every human feeling?'

44

Julia sat, her expression bland. Bertrand leaned against the mantel and Nick stood with his arms folded in front of him. Leo was nowhere to be seen. The Russian – her grandfather, though she couldn't admit that truth to herself for more than a second at a time – was eyeing her with distaste. 'I suppose I am convinced that she is innocent,' he said. 'But someone was at Castle Dar that day, Nick. An Ofan.'

'I assure you, Arkady,' Bertrand said smoothly, 'we will continue the investigation. You may return home to Alice and leave it in our hands.'

Arkady glowered. Julia could feel his frustration, but she didn't glance up. The past hour had been an ordeal to say the least. Pretending. So this was what it felt like, to really hide the truth, a truth you actually knew. She was breathless and tense, because she understood what she was hiding. She knew the stakes.

The Russian had questioned and cross-questioned her ruthlessly, and she had given him answers that made her seem like a sheltered young woman, confused by the attention. She had run away from him that day in the London house because she was afraid of ghosts. She didn't know anything about priests' holes. Was it a kind of biscuit? The biscuit comment had made the Russian bark with derisive laughter, and for just a second, Julia thought she would get off easily.

But then the Russian had performed the ultimate test. He had frozen time, and Julia had to freeze with it.

She had practised this trick with the Ofan during the three days' ride from the medieval barn where they had spent that first night. They had left the carriage in the barn, sold the extra horses, and ridden west, sleeping in the open like brigands. At every stop they would practise. One or another of them would freeze time, and her task was to let herself freeze, too. It was a terrifying thing to do; simply allowing time to end felt like dying. She finally managed it late on the second afternoon, somewhere near Sherborne. She had come back to consciousness to the sight of Leo and Bertrand congratulating each other, while Nick stared at her, as white as a sheet. He caught her up in a hug the minute he saw her blink, and kissed her. Then he set her away from him, straightened his cuffs and congratulated her on her achievement in a stilted, formal voice.

The Ofan assured her it was a sign of her great talent, that she could let herself into and out of the river in whatever way she chose. They had her practise again and again, until it felt like second nature.

So when she felt the Russian slow time to a halt, she let herself go with it, felt her consciousness fade and wink out into nothingness.

When she blinked back, the Russian was pulling on his gloves. Nick surreptitiously held up three fingers – she had been out for half an hour while they discussed her. But she had passed the test; Count Lebedev believed her to be nothing more than a silly young lady from Devon, where it rains six days out of seven.

She tamped down the urge to dance around the room and instead sat still, her insipid smile pasted on her face. She had tricked him. She was almost free.

'Miss Percy.'

She looked up and met Lebedev's blue eyes. They were

melting with tears. The force of his emotion – grief – hit her like a blast of wind.

'Did your grandfather ever . . .' His tears spilled over. 'Did he ever talk to you of another child, a brilliant child? A child of incredible gifts? Once he was her teacher, far away. She was unlike you, this girl. She was . . .'

Before Julia knew it, his grief for her mother had pulled her to her feet and he was hugging her close and sobbing into her hair. His pain flooded her. His tears were wet on her forehead and temple and tears were streaming down her own cheeks. She was becoming this Russian, this man named Arkady, her mother's father . . . this man who had lost his daughter and would never be whole again. When he finally stumbled away from her, apologizing and drying his eyes, she gathered herself just enough to flee the room, throwing open the double doors into the hallway and shutting them with a bang behind her. She leaned back against the doors, gasping for breath. She could still feel him in the room behind her, dragging at her soul.

Someone grabbed her hand. It was Leo, who had clearly been listening through the door. 'Hold on to me,' he whispered fiercely. 'Hold on!'

Julia stared blindly at him, and clutched first at his hand and then at his shoulders. Now she could feel Leo! Sense the terrible pain that lay at *his* core. She shrank, terrified.

'No!' He gathered her up into his arms. 'Stop it, Julia. Don't reach out to me. Reach in. Find your mooring. Reach in.'

She closed her eyes and breathed. She turned her attention to herself. Leo's arms around her, which had at first felt as if they were grabbing at her very soul, were now stabilizing her like a scaffold. She felt her heartbeat. Slowing. Her breath. Slowing. She felt the pull from the other room weaken. Then, like water falling away as the swimmer climbs up from the river, it left her altogether.

She raised her face to Leo's, and he stepped away from the embrace, smiling at her. He held a finger to his lips. 'Shh,' he whispered. 'You're all right now. You're fine.'

'Yes.' Julia was whispering too. 'I was in his feelings!'

Leo shook his head. 'And I felt you entering mine.'

'Is that part of the talent?' she asked.

'No. It isn't part of the talent.'

'But . . . I can put my feelings into people. I've done it once to Count Lebedev and once to Jemison. I can make them feel what I feel. You can't do that?'

'No.' Leo frowned. 'No one can. Except . . .' He stopped, his lips folded.

'Except who? You must tell me.'

'Mr Mibbs.'

'But . . .' Julia whispered. 'What does that mean?'

Leo looked at the ground, then up again at Julia. He took her hand and squeezed it. 'That is what we will have to find out.'

It was raining. Leo and Bertrand were playing hazard and Bertrand was winning. Leo was talking, a steady stream of nonsense. Hazard was such an interesting game. So complex . . . and yet it could be more complex, didn't Bertrand think so? It rather reminded Leo of a Pocumtuk gambling game that took a lifetime to master. Perhaps Bertrand would like to learn? It was played with painted stones instead of dice, but if you just imagined that that you had a stone in your hand . . .

Bertrand told him in a dry tone to shut up.

Julia sat staring out of the window, her spirits low. It had been a full day since Arkady had left, and Nick and Julia hadn't had a moment alone together. And now it was raining.

But then Nick was standing up, stretching, and announcing he was going to walk over to Castle Dar, the rain be damned, and would anyone like to join him? He looked directly at Julia.

'I will,' Leo said from the card table. 'I'm losing anyway.'

'You will not.' Bertrand handed him the dice. 'You will continue to gamble away your fortune.'

'But I want to get out of the house.'

'Roll the dice.'

Leo glanced at Nick and then at Julia. 'Oh,' he said. 'I see. Yes. All right then. I'll raise you ten, you evil Frenchman.' He rolled the dice with a practised flick of the wrist.

45

They had walked up to this spot together without exchanging a word. Now they stood in the cold rain, at the edge of the woods, at the exact spot where they had met on the day of the seventh marquess's funeral. Where they had met again not so long ago. And then a third time, for that searing kiss up against a tree . . . Nick felt for the acorn in his pocket. He turned to look at Julia, and she was smiling at him. She reached up, put her hands behind his neck and drew him down for a kiss. Her lips were wet again with rain, cool and perfect. He put his arms around her waist and drew her to him, slowly, feeling the way her body fitted against his so exactly, even through their rain-soaked clothes. He ran his hand up her back until he cradled her head, and then he broke the kiss and stared down into her smiling, dark eyes.

'You know now that have no mistress,' he said.

'Yes.'

'And when I said I loved you, that day in the cupola, I meant it.'

'I think I always knew that,' she said.

'But in the cupola, you lay with me – and all the while you thought that Alva was my lover.' He searched her face. It was serious and yet there was a laugh lurking there, too, as if she found him comical, somehow.

'Hush.' She put a finger up to his mouth, then dropped her hand to his chest.

She was right. Words were pointless. He lifted her towards him, helping her reach his kisses.

When they eased out of the embrace, Nick took both of Julia's hands in his, and her fingers closed around the object he'd been holding. 'What is this? I've seen you with it before.'

'It's an acorn.' He glanced up at the trees. 'From one of these oaks. I picked it up that day, after we first kissed. I've carried it with me ever since.' He handed it to her.

She rolled it between her fingers. Her eyes were deep and dark, like the woods behind her. He couldn't tell what she was thinking. 'May I have it?'

'Yes.' He spoke without thinking, but then, when he saw her toss it from her, out into the open field, he gasped. 'Wait!'

'No.' She held his hand and kept him from going after it. 'I want you to do this with me.'

'What?'

'Do you trust me?'

'Of course.'

'Good.' She smiled. 'Because I want my first time to be with you.' She kissed him quickly and gripped his hand. Then, without another word of warning, she jumped, and dragged him along with her.

It was nothing like the time he jumped from the battlefield, or the time he jumped with Arkady. This felt like falling into a feather bed, or rather, falling out into an ocean of feathers, falling forwards and up into a glowing softness.

Then the world resolved itself again around them, and they stood together in bright evening light, on the same hillside, under the spreading limbs of a magnificent oak tree. The forest that had been at their back was gone, and the single tree dominated the hill, a glorious monument to time itself. Nick dropped Julia's hand and turned in a slow circle. Down across the fields was Falcott House, and away in the other direction he could see Castle Dar. Castle Dar, which hadn't been there in the future he had known, when he had driven across Devon with Arkady. In its place he had seen the enormous shed of combine harvesters. Now, sprawling and ancient, there it stood. Castle Dar.

Were they in the past? But no. This was the future. In the distance he could see the lazily spinning turbines of a wind farm. Their blades glowed pink in the evening light.

Nick took Julia's hand again. She was staring around her, a little afraid, a little proud. 'Is this what the future looks like?'

'No,' he said softly. 'Or at least, not the future I knew.'

'The oak tree wasn't here in that future,' she said, her dark eyes shining.

'No.' Nick clasped her fingers. 'No, my love, it wasn't.'

Acknowledgements

To Tina Bennett; thank you for quietly enabling yet another happy chapter in my life. To Alexandra Machinist, thank you for grabbing the future by the collar; you are the best agent in this universe and any other. To Alex Clarke across the pond but still somehow in my backyard – thank you. To Trevor Horwood, the king of copy-editors, thank you. And to Denise Roy, for elbow grease, kindness, and X-ray vision – you are a genius and I'm so grateful.

To Holly Kosisky, who read and reread the ever-changing manuscript; thank you for being my Bip.

To family, friends, and mentors without whose contributions, large or small, this stone soup would never have been boiled – thank you. Pinckney Benedict, Duncan Black, Suzanne Brennan, Megan Brown, Eiren Caffall, Kim Cassidy, Margaret Clardy, Lindsay Feldman, George the Germ, Peter Gervickas, Laura Hawley, Gail Hemmeter, Tom Hemmeter, Jen Hill, Jeremy Hornik, Sarah Kavanagh, Deanna Kreisel, Joan Logan, Antonia Losano, Imke Meyer, Michael Moon, Margaret Robison, Jen Roder, Jordana Rosenberg, Mark Rounds, Heidi Schlipphacke, Laurel Schneider, Pat Schneider, Paul Schneider, Peter Schneider, Rebecca Schneider, Rosi Song, Georg Steinmeyer, Ellen Summers, Elizabeth Thomas, Michael Thomas, Sharon Ullman, Lelah Ridgway Vought, Matt Wright, David Young and Sandy Zagarell.

To my students, who are ferocious and stubborn and

brilliant and the best readers I know – thank you for loving books and for keeping me nimble.

And to Katie, whose insights and ideas are scattered throughout this novel like acorns.